Gay Pride & Prejudice

by Jane Austen

& Kate Christie

SECOND GROWTH

Second Growth Books
Seattle, WA

Printed in the United States of America on acid-free paper
First published 2012

Cover Design: Kate Christie

ISBN 13: 978-09853677-0-1

DEDICATION

To Anne Lister, Harriet Freke, and all the nameless
men and women, real and imaginary, who
came before. It truly *has* gotten better.

CHAPTER ONE

I t is a truth universally acknowledged, that a single man in possession of a good fortune, must be in want of a wife—even if he does not particularly desire female companionship.

However little known the feelings or views of such a man may be on his first entering a neighbourhood, this truth is so well fixed in the minds of the surrounding families, that he is considered the rightful property of some one or other of their daughters.

"My dear Mr. Bennet," said his lady to him one day, "have you heard that Netherfield Park is let at last?"

Mr. Bennet replied that he had not.

"But it is," returned she; "for Mrs. Long has just been here, and she told me all about it."

Mr. Bennet made no answer. The odds that the addition to the neighborhood would include a man of the right age and comportment were not strong, as he well knew.

"Do you not want to know who has taken it?" cried his wife impatiently.

"*You* want to tell me, and I have no objection to hearing it."

This was invitation enough.

"Why, my dear, you must know, Mrs. Long says that Netherfield is taken a young man of large fortune from the north of England; that he came down on Monday in a chaise and four to see the place, and was so much delighted with it, that he agreed with Mr. Morris immediately; that he is to take possession before Michaelmas, and some of his servants are to be in the house by the end of next week."

"What is his name?"

"Bingley."

"Married or single?"

"Oh! Single, my dear, to be sure! A single man of large fortune; four or five thousand a year. What a fine thing for our girls!"

"How so? How can it affect them?"

"My dear Mr. Bennet," replied his wife, "how can you be so tiresome! You must know that I am thinking of his marrying one of them."

"Is that his design in settling here?"

"Design! Nonsense, how can you talk so! But it is very likely that he *may* fall in love with one of them, and therefore you must visit him as soon as he comes."

"I see no occasion for that. You and the girls may go, or you may send them by themselves, which perhaps will be still better, for as you are as handsome as any of them, Mr. Bingley may like you the best of the party."

"My dear, you flatter me. I certainly have had my share of beauty, but I do not pretend to be anything extraordinary now. When a woman has five grown-up daughters, she ought to give over thinking of her own beauty."

"In such cases, a woman has not often much beauty to think of."

"But, my dear, you must indeed go and see Mr. Bingley when he comes into the neighbourhood."

Mr. Bennet spoke with assumed diffidence: "It is more than I engage for, I assure you."

"But consider your daughters. Only think what an establishment it would be for one of them. Sir William and Lady Lucas are determined to go, merely on that account, for in general, you know, they visit no newcomers. Indeed you must go, for it will be impossible for us to visit him if you do not."

"You are over-scrupulous, surely. I dare say Mr. Bingley will be very glad to see you; and I will send a few lines by you to assure him of my hearty consent to his marrying whichever he chooses of the girls; though I would expect the obvious choice to be my little Lizzy."

"Lizzy is not a bit better than the others; and I am sure she is not half so handsome as Jane, nor half so good-humoured as Lydia. But you are always giving *her* the preference."

"They have none of them much to recommend them," replied he; "they are all silly and ignorant like other girls; but Lizzy has something more of quickness than her sisters."

In addition to other amiable qualities, his favourite daughter had lately appeared to be quite happily attached to her friend, Charlotte Lucas. No delicate way for a father to inquire after such matters, but if the friendship were indeed become romantic, as he suspected, he wished to see Elizabeth established in a manner that would allow her to pursue her material desires under the semblance of propriety. He had been fortunate enough to find a tolerable situation himself, and could not help but wish the same for the most capable of his daughters.

"Mr. Bennet, how *can* you abuse your own children in such a way? You take delight in vexing me. You have no compassion for my poor nerves."

"You mistake me, my dear. I have a high respect for your nerves. They are my old friends. I have heard you mention them with consideration these last twenty years at least."

"Ah, you do not know what I suffer."

"But I hope you will get over it, and live to see many young men of four thousand a year come into the neighbourhood."

"It will be no use to us, if twenty such should come, since you will not visit them."

"Depend upon it, my dear, that when there are twenty, I will visit them all."

Mr. Bennet was so odd a mixture of quick parts, sarcastic humour, reserve, and caprice, that the experience of three-and-twenty years had been insufficient to make his wife understand his character. This, of course, was his intent, as his situation would have quickly turned intolerable had his wife discovered his preference for the company of other men. *Her* mind was less difficult to develop. She was a woman of mean understanding, scant information, uncertain temper, and little regard for the material duties of marriage—the ideal wife for someone such as himself. When she was discontented, she fancied herself nervous. The business of her life was to get her daughters married; its solace was visiting and news.

The business of her husband's life, on the other hand, had been to evade discovery in his often successful pursuit of pleasure; its solace was his daughters, whom, despite his distaste for the method of their conception, he loved sincerely and delighted in almost daily. Except, perhaps, Mary, who had neither Jane's beauty, nor Lizzy's liveliness.

If this Bingley fellow proved to be unavoidably daft, perhaps he might be persuaded to agree to a match with Mary.

CHAPTER TWO

M r. Bennet was among the earliest of those who waited on Mr. Bingley, and found their new neighbour to be an accommodating sort, handsome and with an appealing freshness to his countenance. When asked why he had left his original domicile, however, the young man coloured, and admitted only to being predisposed to a new beginning.

To the last, Mr. Bennet was always assuring his wife that he should not go; and till the evening after the visit was paid, she had no knowledge of it. It was then disclosed in the following manner. Observing his second daughter employed in trimming a hat, he suddenly addressed her: "I hope Mr. Bingley will like it, Lizzy."

"We are not in a way to know *what* Mr. Bingley likes," said Mrs. Bennet resentfully, "since we are not to visit."

"But you forget, Mamma," said Elizabeth, "that we shall meet him at the assemblies, and that Mrs. Long promised to introduce him."

"I do not believe Mrs. Long will do any such thing. She has two nieces of her own. She is a selfish, hypocritical woman, and I have no opinion of her."

"No more have I," said Mr. Bennet; "and I am glad to find that you do not depend on her serving you."

Mrs. Bennet deigned not to make any reply, but, unable to contain herself, began scolding one of her daughters.

"Don't keep coughing so, Kitty, for Heaven's sake! Have a little compassion on my nerves. You tear them to pieces."

"Kitty has no discretion in her coughs," said her father; "she times them ill."

"I do not cough for my own amusement," replied Kitty fretfully. "When is your next ball to be, Lizzy?"

"Tomorrow fortnight."

"Aye, so it is," cried her mother, "and Mrs. Long does not come back till the day before; so it will be impossible for her to introduce him, for she will not know him herself."

"Then, my dear," said Mr. Bennet, "you may have the advantage of your friend, and introduce Mr. Bingley to *her*."

"Impossible, Mr. Bennet, impossible, when I am not acquainted with him myself; how can you be so teasing?"

"I honour your circumspection. A fortnight's acquaintance is certainly very little. One cannot know what a man really is by the end of a fortnight." In the metaphysical sense, this was certainly true; but in the material sense, it often took only a minute to ascertain what a man truly was. Though not, perhaps, in Bingley's case.

"But if *we* do not venture," added Mr. Bennet, "somebody else will; and after all, Mrs. Long and her daughters must stand their chance; and, therefore, as she will think it an act of kindness, if you decline the office, I will take it on myself."

The girls stared at their father. Mrs. Bennet said only, "Nonsense, nonsense!"

"What can be the meaning of that emphatic exclamation?" said he. "Do you consider the forms of introduction, and the stress that is laid on them, as nonsense? I cannot quite agree with you *there*. What say you, Mary? For you are a young lady of deep reflection, I know, and read great books and make extracts."

Mary wished to say something sensible, but knew not how.

"While Mary is adjusting her ideas," he continued, "let us return to Mr. Bingley."

"I am sick of Mr. Bingley," said his wife.

"I am sorry to hear *that*; but why did not you tell me before? If I had known as much this morning I certainly would not have called on him. It is very unlucky; but as I have actually paid the visit, we cannot escape the acquaintance now."

The astonishment of the ladies was just what he wished; that of Mrs. Bennet perhaps surpassing the rest; though, when the first tumult of joy was over, she began to declare that it was what she had expected all the while.

"How good it was of you, my dear Mr. Bennet! But I knew I should persuade you at last. I was sure you loved your girls too well to neglect such an acquaintance. Well, how pleased I am! And it is such a good joke, too, that you should have gone this morning and never said a word about it till now."

"Now, Kitty, you may cough as much as you choose," said Mr. Bennet; and, as he spoke, he left the room, fatigued with the raptures of his wife but pleased with the events of the day. Though Bingley's partiality toward one sex or the other might not be obvious upon first meeting, Mr. Bennet looked forward to forging a closer connection with their new neighbour.

"What an excellent father you have, girls!" said his wife, when the door was shut. "I do not know how you will ever make him amends for his kindness; or me, either, for that matter. At our time of life it is not so pleasant, I can tell you, to be making new acquaintances every day; but for your sakes, we would do anything. Lydia, my love, though you *are* the youngest, I dare say Mr. Bingley will dance with you at the next ball."

"Oh!" said Lydia stoutly, "I am not afraid; for though I am the youngest, I'm also the tallest."

The rest of the evening was spent in conjecturing how soon he would return Mr. Bennet's visit, and determining when they should ask him to dinner. Even Elizabeth, whose interest in eligible young gentlemen did not approach that of her sisters, or even that of her mother, found herself drawn into the lively discussion.

CHAPTER THREE

Not all that Mrs. Bennet, however, with the assistance of her five daughters, could ask on the subject, was sufficient to draw from her husband any satisfactory description of Mr. Bingley. They attacked him in various ways—with barefaced questions, ingenious suppositions, and distant surmises; but he eluded the skill of them all, and they were at last obliged to accept the second-hand intelligence of their neighbour, Lady Lucas. Her report was highly favourable. Sir William had been delighted with him. He was quite young, wonderfully handsome, extremely agreeable, and, to crown the whole, he meant to be at the next assembly with a large party. Nothing could be more delightful! To be fond of dancing was a certain step towards falling in love; and very lively hopes of Mr. Bingley's heart were entertained.

"If I can but see one of my daughters happily settled at Netherfield," said Mrs. Bennet to her husband, "and all the others equally well married, I shall have nothing to wish for."

In a few days Mr. Bingley returned Mr. Bennet's visit, and sat about ten minutes with him in his library. He had entertained hopes of being admitted to a sight of the young ladies, of whose beauty he had heard much; but he saw only the father. The ladies were somewhat more fortunate, for they had the advantage of ascertaining from an upper window that he wore a blue coat, and rode a black horse.

An invitation to dinner was soon afterwards dispatched; and already had Mrs. Bennet planned the courses that were to do credit to her housekeeping, when an answer arrived which deferred it all. Mr. Bingley was obliged to be in town the following day, and, consequently, unable to accept the honour of their invitation, etc. Mrs. Bennet was quite disconcerted. She could not imagine what business he could have in town so soon after his arrival in Hertfordshire; and she began to fear that he might be always flying about from one place to another, and never settled at Netherfield as he ought to be. Lady Lucas quieted her fears a little by starting the idea of his being gone to London only to get a large party for the ball; and a report soon followed that Mr. Bingley was to bring twelve ladies and seven gentlemen with him to the assembly. The girls grieved over such a number of ladies, but were comforted the day before the ball by hearing, that instead of twelve he brought only six with him from London—his five sisters and a cousin. And when the party entered the assembly room it consisted of only five altogether— Mr. Bingley, his two sisters, the husband of the eldest, and another young man.

Mr. Bingley was good-looking and gentlemanlike; he had a pleasant countenance, and easy, unaffected manners. His sisters were fine women, with an air of decided fashion. Miss Bingley, the younger of the two, was tall for a woman, but striking in a gown of the latest style. Her brother-in-law, Mr. Hurst, merely looked the gentleman; but her brother's friend Mr. Darcy soon drew the attention of the room by his fine, tall person, handsome features, noble mien, and the report which was in general circulation within five minutes after his entrance, of his having ten thousand a year. The gentlemen pronounced him to be a fine figure of a man, the ladies declared he was much handsomer than Mr. Bingley, and he was looked at with great admiration for about half the evening, till his manners gave a disgust which turned the tide of his popularity; for he was discovered to be proud; to be above his company and above being pleased; and not all his large estate in Derbyshire could then save him from having a most forbidding, disagreeable countenance, and being unworthy to be compared with his friend.

Mr. Bingley had soon made himself acquainted with all the principal people in the room; he was lively and unreserved, danced every dance, was angry that the ball closed so early, and talked of giving one himself at Netherfield. Such amiable qualities must speak for themselves. What a contrast between him and his friend! Mr. Darcy danced only once with Mrs. Hurst and once with Miss Bingley, declined being introduced to any other lady, and spent the rest of the evening in walking about the room, speaking occasionally to one of his own party. His character was decided. He was the proudest, most disagreeable man in the world, and everybody hoped that he would never come there again.

Amongst the most violent against him was Mrs. Bennet, whose dislike of his general behaviour was sharpened into particular resentment by his having slighted one of her daughters.

Elizabeth had been obliged, by the scarcity of gentlemen, to sit down for two dances; and during part of that time, Mr. Darcy and Miss Bingley had been standing near enough for her to hear a conversation between them and Mr. Bingley, who came from the dance for a few minutes to press his friend and younger sister to join it.

"Come, Caroline and Darcy," said he, "I must have you dance. I hate to see you standing about in this manner. You had much better dance."

"I certainly shall not," Mr. Darcy returned. "Your sister is in need of rest, and there is not another woman in the room whom it would not be a punishment to me to stand up with. You know how I detest it, unless I am particularly acquainted with my partner. At such an assembly as this it would be insupportable."

"I would not be so fastidious as you are," said Mr. Bingley, "for a kingdom! Upon my honour, I never met with so many pleasant girls in my life as I have this evening; and there are several of them you see uncommonly pretty."

"Dear brother," said Miss Bingley, "your admiration of the fairer sex is unaccountably obliging."

"You, sir, are dancing with the only handsome girl in the room," added Mr. Darcy, looking at the eldest Miss Bennet.

"Oh! She is the most beautiful creature I ever beheld! But there is one of her sisters sitting down just behind you, who is very pretty, and I dare say very agreeable. Do let me ask my partner to introduce you."

"Which do you mean?" Darcy asked.

Miss Bingley looked round for a moment at Elizabeth, till catching her eye, she withdrew her own and said, "She is tolerable, but hardly the sort to tempt Mr. Darcy, I dare say."

"Indeed," said Darcy. "Besides, I am in no humour at present to give consequence to young ladies who are slighted by other men. You had better return to your partner and enjoy her smiles, for you are wasting your time here."

Mr. Bingley followed his advice. Mr. Darcy and Miss Bingley walked off; and Elizabeth remained with no very cordial feelings toward either. She told the story, however, with great spirit among her friends, for she had a lively, playful disposition that delighted in anything ridiculous. Still, she was careful to mark Mr. Darcy as the villain. Caroline Bingley had behaved if not warmly, then at the least politely to everyone else present; and Elizabeth was reluctant to call attention to the slight for fear it might reflect poorly on the lady's brother.

The evening altogether passed off pleasantly to the whole family. Mrs. Bennet had seen her eldest daughter much admired by the Netherfield party. Mr. Bingley had danced with Jane twice, and she had been distinguished by his sisters. Jane was as much gratified by this as her mother could be, though in a quieter way. Elizabeth felt Jane's pleasure, and had spent an enjoyable amount of time with Charlotte Lucas, her intimate friend, observing their friends and neighbours engaged in revelry. Mary had heard herself mentioned to Miss Bingley as the most accomplished girl in the neighbourhood; and Catherine and Lydia had been fortunate enough never to be without partners, which was all that they had yet learnt to care for at a ball. They returned, therefore, in good spirits to Longbourn, the village where they lived, and of which they were the principal inhabitants. They found Mr. Bennet still up. With a book he was regardless of time; and on the present occasion he had a good deal of curiosity as to the event of an evening which had raised such splendid expectations. He had rather hoped that his wife's views on the stranger would be disappointed; but he soon found out that he had a different story to hear.

"My dear Mr. Bennet," said his wife as she entered the room, "we have had a most delightful evening, a most excellent ball. I wish you had been there. Jane was so admired, nothing could be like it. Everybody said how well she looked; and Mr. Bingley thought her quite beautiful, and danced with her twice! Only think of *that*, my dear; he actually danced with her twice! And she was the only creature in the room that he asked a second time. First of all, he asked Miss Lucas. I was so vexed to see him stand up with her! But, however, he did not admire her at all; and he seemed quite struck with Jane as she was going down the dance. So he inquired who she was, and got introduced, and asked her for the two next. Then the two third he danced with Miss King, and the two fourth with Maria Lucas, and the two fifth with Jane again, and the two sixth with Lizzy, and the *Boulanger*—"

"If he had had any compassion for *me*," said her husband, "he would not have danced half so much. For God's sake, say no more of his partners. Oh, that he had sprained his ankle in the first dance!"

"My dear, I am quite delighted with him. He is so excessively handsome! And his sisters are charming women. I never in my life saw anything more elegant than their dresses. I dare say the lace upon Mrs. Hurst's gown—"

Here she was interrupted again. Mr. Bennet protested against any description of female finery. She was therefore obliged to seek another branch of the subject, and related, with much bitterness of spirit and some exaggeration, the shocking rudeness of Mr. Darcy.

"But I can assure you," she added, "that Lizzy does not lose much by not suiting *his* fancy; for he is a most disagreeable, horrid man, not at all worth pleasing. He walked here, and he walked there, fancying himself so very great! Not handsome enough to dance with! I wish you had been there, my dear, to have given him one of your set-downs. I quite detest the man."

CHAPTER FOUR

When Jane and Elizabeth were alone, the former, who had been cautious in her praise of Mr. Bingley before, expressed to her sister just how very much she admired him.

"He is just what a young man ought to be," said she, "sensible, good-humoured, lively; and I never saw such happy manners—so much ease, with such perfect good breeding!"

"He is also handsome," replied Elizabeth, "which a young man ought likewise to be, if he possibly can. His character is thereby complete."

"I was very much flattered by his asking me to dance a second time. I did not expect such a compliment."

"Did not you? I did for you. But that is one great difference between us. Compliments always take *you* by surprise, and *me* never. What could be more natural than his asking you again? He could not help seeing that you were about five times prettier than every other woman in the room. No thanks to his gallantry for that. Well, he certainly is very agreeable, and I give you leave to like him. You have liked many a stupider person."

"Dear Lizzy!"

"You are a great deal too apt, you know, to like people in general. You never see a fault in anybody. All the world are good and agreeable in your eyes. I never heard you speak ill of a human being in your life."

"I would not wish to be hasty in censuring anyone; but I always speak what I think."

"I know you do; and it is *that* which makes the wonder. With your good sense, to be so honestly blind to the follies and nonsense of others! Affectation of candour is common enough—one meets with it everywhere. But to be candid without ostentation or design—to take the good of everybody's character and make it still better, and say nothing of the bad—belongs to you alone." She paused. "And so you like this man's sisters, too, do you? Their manners are not equal to his." She thought again of Miss Bingley's disparaging eye turned upon her.

"Certainly not—at first. But they are very pleasing women when you converse with them. Miss Bingley is to live with her brother, and keep his house; and I am much mistaken if we shall not find a very charming neighbour in her."

Elizabeth listened in silence, but was not convinced. Miss Bingley was certainly a handsome, distinguished woman, but her behaviour at the assembly had not been calculated to please. Elizabeth, with more quickness of observation and less pliancy of temper than her sister, and with a judgment too unassailed by any attention to herself, was very little disposed to approve either Bingley female. They were in fact very fine ladies; not deficient in good humour when they were pleased, nor in the power of making themselves agreeable when they chose it, but proud and conceited. They had been educated in one of the first private seminaries in England, had a fortune of thirty thousand pounds each, were in the habit of spending more than they ought and of associating with people of rank, and were therefore in every respect entitled to think well of themselves and meanly of others. They were of a respectable family in the north of England—a circumstance seemingly more deeply impressed on their memories than that their brother's fortune and their own had been acquired by trade.

Mr. Bingley had inherited property to the amount of nearly a hundred thousand pounds from his father, who had intended to purchase an estate, but did not live to do so. Mr. Bingley intended it likewise, and sometimes made choice of his county; but as he was now provided with a good house and the liberty of a manor, it was doubtful to many of those who best knew the easiness of his temper, whether he might not spend the remainder of his days at Netherfield, and leave the next generation to purchase.

His family was anxious for his having an estate of his own; but, though he was now only established as a tenant, Mrs. Hurst, who had married a man of more fashion than fortune, was not indisposed to consider his house as her home when it suited her. His younger sister, Miss Bingley, would have preferred to be in town among her particular group of friends for the season; but as this was not currently an option allowed her, thought Netherfield would probably do as well as any other country house that was a favourable distance from their home county. For there, she would not—could not—return at any near point in time. Mr. Bingley, aware of his sister's forced estrangement from the north, had been on the lookout for a residence for them both, when he was tempted by an accidental recommendation to look at Netherfield House. He did look at it, and into it for half-an-hour—was pleased with the situation and the principal rooms, satisfied with what the owner said in its praise, and took it immediately.

Between him and Darcy there was a very steady friendship, in spite of great opposition of character. Bingley was endeared to Darcy by the easiness, openness, and ductility of his temper, though no disposition could offer a greater contrast to his own, and though with his own he never appeared dissatisfied. On the strength of Darcy's regard, Bingley had the firmest reliance, and of his judgment the highest opinion. In understanding, Darcy was the superior. Bingley was by no means deficient, but Darcy was clever. He was at the same time haughty, reserved, and fastidious, and his manners, though well-bred, were not inviting. In that respect his friend had greatly the advantage. Bingley was sure of being liked wherever he appeared, while Darcy was continually giving offense.

The manner in which they spoke of the Meryton assembly was sufficiently characteristic. Bingley had never met with more pleasant people or prettier girls in his life; everybody had been most kind and attentive to him; there had been no formality, no stiffness; he had soon felt acquainted with all the room; and, as to Miss Bennet, he could not conceive an angel more beautiful. Darcy, on the contrary, had seen a collection of people in whom there was little beauty and less fashion, for none of whom he had felt the smallest interest, and from none received either attention or pleasure. Miss Bennet he acknowledged to be pretty, but she smiled too much.

Miss Bingley owned that she seconded most of his opinions, except perhaps with regards to Miss Bennet, whom she had admired and liked; Mrs. Hurst agreed with her, and pronounced Miss Bennet to be a sweet girl, one whom she also would not object to knowing more of. Miss Bennet was therefore established as a sweet girl, and Bingley felt authorized by such commendation to think of her as he chose.

CHAPTER FIVE

Within a short walk of Longbourn lived the Lucases, a family with whom the Bennets were particularly intimate. Sir William Lucas had been formerly in trade in Meryton, where he had made a tolerable fortune, and risen to the honour of knighthood by an address to the king during his mayoralty. The distinction had perhaps been felt too strongly. It had given him a disgust to his business, and to his residence in a small market town; and, in quitting them both, he had removed with his family to a house about a mile from Meryton, denominated from that period Lucas Lodge, where he could think with pleasure of his own importance, and, unshackled by business, occupy himself solely in being civil to all the world. For, though elated by his rank, it did not render him supercilious; on the contrary, he was all attention to everybody. By nature inoffensive, friendly, and obliging, his presentation at St. James's had made him courteous.

Lady Lucas was a very good kind of woman, not too clever to be a valuable neighbour to Mrs. Bennet. They had several children. The eldest of them, Charlotte, a sensible, intelligent young woman of twenty-five, had been Elizabeth's intimate friend for a number of years, and somewhat more these past two; though of late, they had appeared to look for fewer excuses to spend time in one another's company as they had once readily found.

That the Miss Lucases and the Miss Bennets should meet to talk over a ball was absolutely necessary; and the morning after the assembly brought the former to Longbourn to hear and to communicate.

"*You* began the evening well, Charlotte," said Mrs. Bennet with civil self-command to Miss Lucas. "You were Mr. Bingley's first choice."

"Yes; but he seemed to like his second better."

"You mean Jane, I suppose, because he danced with her twice. To be sure that *did* seem as if he admired her—indeed I rather believe he did—I heard something about it—but I hardly know what—something about Mr. Robinson."

"Perhaps you mean what I overheard between him and Mr. Robinson; did not I mention it to you? Mr. Robinson's asking him how he liked our Meryton assemblies, and whether he did not think there were a great many pretty women in the room, and which he thought the prettiest? And his answering immediately to the last question: 'The eldest Miss Bennet, beyond a doubt; there cannot be two opinions on that point.'"

"Upon my word! Well, that is very decided indeed—that does seem as if—but, however, it may all come to nothing, you know."

"My overhearings were more to the purpose than yours, Eliza," said Charlotte. "Mr. Darcy is not so well worth listening to as his friend, is he? Poor Eliza—to be only just *tolerable*."

To Charlotte alone had Elizabeth confessed Miss Bingley's part in the rejection. She gazed upon her friend now, silently entreating her to maintain her vow of secrecy.

"I beg you would not put it into Lizzy's head to be vexed by Mr. Darcy's ill-treatment," Mrs. Bennett said, "for he is such a disagreeable man, that it would be quite a misfortune to be liked by him. Mrs. Long told me last night that he sat close to her for half-an-hour without once opening his lips."

"Are you quite sure, Ma'am? Is not there a little mistake?" said Jane. "I certainly saw Mr. Darcy speaking to her."

"Aye—because she asked him at last how he liked Netherfield, and he could not help answering her; but she said he seemed quite angry at being spoke to."

"Miss Bingley told me," said Jane, "that he never speaks much, unless among his intimate acquaintances. With them he is remarkably agreeable."

Miss Bingley certainly seemed to be among Mr. Darcy's intimate acquaintances, Elizabeth acknowledged. Was there an agreement between them? No such arrangement had been mentioned at the assembly, but that did not preclude the existence of something of an informal nature.

"I do not believe a word of it," her mother said. "If Mr. Darcy had been so very agreeable, he would have talked to Mrs. Long. But I can guess how it was; I dare say he had heard somehow that Mrs. Long does not keep a carriage, and had come to the ball in a hack chaise."

"I do not mind his not talking to Mrs. Long," said Miss Lucas, "but I wish he had danced with Eliza."

"Another time, Lizzy," said her mother. "I would not dance with him, if I were you."

"I believe, Ma'am, I may safely promise you never to dance with him." Nor to seek out Miss Bingley's companionship, either.

"His pride," said Miss Lucas, "does not offend me so much as pride often does, because there is an excuse for it. One cannot wonder that so very fine a young man, with family, fortune, everything in his favour, should think highly of himself. If I may so express it, he has a right to be proud."

"That is very true," replied Elizabeth, considering that these conditions applied equally well to the haughty Miss Bingley, "and I could easily forgive her—that is, *his* pride, if he had not mortified mine."

"Pride," observed Mary, who piqued herself upon the solidity of her reflections, "is a very common failing, I believe. By all that I have ever read, I am convinced that there are very few of us who do not cherish a feeling of self-complacency on the score of some quality or other. Vanity and pride are different things, though the words are often used synonymously. Pride relates more to our opinion of ourselves, vanity to what we would have others think of us."

"If I were as rich as Mr. Darcy," cried a young Lucas, who had come with his sisters, "I should not care how proud I was. I would keep a pack of foxhounds, and drink a bottle of wine a day."

"Then you would drink a great deal more than you ought," said Mrs. Bennet; "and if I were to see you at it, I should take away your bottle directly."

The boy protested that she should not; she continued to declare that she would, and the argument ended only with the visit.

As Charlotte left with barely a glance back, Elizabeth pondered her part in the conversation. It seemed almost as if Charlotte had been pushing her toward Mr. Darcy, a bachelor with a fortune even superior to that of Mr. Bingley's. Elizabeth thought she understood her friend's motivation—a disagreement had risen between them some weeks previous, occasioned by Charlotte insisting that marriage was the only option for women of their class and standing, despite their very real attachment to one another. When Elizabeth had protested that she should never marry a person whom she did not love, and would sooner run away with one she did, Charlotte had only smiled gently and said she did not believe Elizabeth possessed the coldness of heart such a course of action would require. She herself could never consider disappointing her family and friends so, she had declared; and believing her, Elizabeth had become aware of a rising sense of disillusionment. This pronouncement had ended their argument, and their visit, simultaneously; and the two had not found time to be alone together since.

CHAPTER SIX

The ladies of Longbourn soon waited on those of Netherfield, and the visit was returned in due form. On each occasion, Elizabeth sat erect in her seat, hands folded primly, avoiding Miss Bingley's eye and speaking to her only when directly required. Miss Bennet's pleasing manners grew on the goodwill of Mrs. Hurst and Miss Bingley; and though the mother was found to be intolerable, and the three younger sisters not worth speaking to, a wish of being better acquainted with the two eldest was expressed. By Jane, this attention was received with the greatest pleasure, but Elizabeth still saw superciliousness in their treatment of everybody, hardly excepting even her sister, and could not like them; though their kindness to Jane, such as it was, had a value as arising in all probability from the influence of their brother's admiration. It was generally evident whenever they met that he *did* admire her, and to Elizabeth it was equally evident that Jane was yielding to the preference that she had begun to entertain for him from the first, and was in a way to be very much in love; but Elizabeth considered with pleasure that it was not likely to be discovered by the world in general, since Jane united, with great strength of feeling, a composure of temper and a uniform cheerfulness of manner which would guard her from the suspicions of the impertinent. She mentioned this to her friend Miss Lucas the next time they met.

"It may perhaps be pleasant," replied Charlotte, "to be able to impose on the public in such a case; but it is sometimes a disadvantage to be so very guarded. If a woman conceals her affection with the same skill from the object of it, she may lose the opportunity of fixing him; and it will then be but poor consolation to believe the world equally in the dark. There is so much of gratitude or vanity in almost every attachment, that it is not safe to leave any to itself. We can all *begin* freely—a slight preference is natural enough; but there are very few of us who have heart enough to be really in love without encouragement. In nine cases out of ten a woman had better show more affection than she feels. Bingley likes your sister undoubtedly; but he may never do more than like her, if she does not help him on."

"But she does help him on, as much as her nature will allow. If I can perceive her regard for him, he must be a simpleton, indeed, not to discover it, too."

"Remember, Eliza, that he does not know Jane's disposition as you do."

"But if a woman is partial to someone, and does not endeavour to conceal it, the other must find it out. You, after all, found out my feelings easily enough," added she, smiling as she recalled the day in the park two summers past when Charlotte had kissed her as she had sought vainly for words with which to describe her recently discovered love for her friend.

Charlotte allowed a small smile, but did not meet her eyes. "Perhaps, if they see each other enough. But, though Bingley and Jane meet tolerably often, it is never for many hours together; and, as they always see each other in large mixed parties, it is impossible that every moment should be employed in conversing together. Jane should therefore make the most of every half-hour in which she can command his attention. When she is secure of him, there will be more leisure for falling in love as much as she chooses."

"Your plan is a good one," replied Elizabeth, "where nothing is in question but the desire of being well married, and if I were determined to get a rich husband, or any husband, I dare say I should adopt it. But these are not Jane's feelings; she is not acting by design. As yet, she cannot even be certain of the degree of her own regard nor of its reasonableness. She has known him only a fortnight. She danced four dances with him at Meryton; she saw him one morning at his own house, and has since dined with him in company four times. This is not quite enough to make her understand his character."

"Not as you represent it. Had she merely dined with him, she might only have discovered whether he had a good appetite; but you must remember that four evenings have also been spent together—and four evenings may do a great deal."

"Yes; these four evenings have enabled them to ascertain that they both like Blackjack better than the game of Commerce; but with respect to any other leading characteristic, I do not imagine that much has been unfolded."

"Well," said Charlotte, "I wish Jane success with all my heart; and if she were married to him tomorrow, I should think she had as good a chance of happiness as if she were to be studying his character for a twelvemonth. Happiness in marriage is entirely a matter of chance. If the dispositions of the parties are ever so well known to each other or ever so similar beforehand, it does not advance their felicity in the least. They always continue to grow sufficiently unlike afterwards to have their share of vexation; and it is better to know as little as possible of the defects of the person with whom you are to pass your life."

"You make me laugh, Charlotte; but it is not sound. You know it is not sound, and that you would never act in this way yourself."

Charlotte did not reply to this charge, and the conversation soon turned to another topic. Neither was anxious to revisit contested territory, as any talk of marriage would surely occasion.

Occupied in observing Mr. Bingley's attentions to Jane, Elizabeth was far from suspecting that she was herself becoming an object of some interest in the eyes of the gentleman's younger sister. Caroline Bingley had at first scarcely allowed the second eldest Miss Bennet to be pretty; she had looked at her without admiration at the ball; and when they next met, looked at her only to criticize. But no sooner had she made it clear to herself that the younger Miss Bennet had hardly a good feature in her face, than she began to find it was rendered uncommonly intelligent by the beautiful expression of her dark eyes. To this discovery succeeded some others equally mortifying. Though she had detected with a critical eye more than one failure of perfect symmetry in Elizabeth's form, Caroline was forced to acknowledge her figure to be light and pleasing; and in spite of her asserting that Miss Bennet's manners were not those of the fashionable world, she was caught by their easy playfulness. Of this Elizabeth was perfectly unaware; to her Miss Bingley was only the relation of her own sister's object of affection, and the woman who had thought her not handsome enough for Mr. Darcy to dance with.

Caroline began to wish to know more of Elizabeth, and as a step towards conversing with her, attended to her conversation with others.

This practice drew Elizabeth's notice. It was at Sir Willia
where a large party was assembled.

"What did Miss Bingley mean," said she to Charlotte, "by
to my conversation with Colonel Forster?"

"That is a question which only Miss Bingley can answer."

"But if she does it any more I shall certainly let her know that I see
what she is about. She has a very satirical eye, and if I do not begin by
being impertinent myself, I shall soon grow afraid of her."

On Miss Bingley's approaching them soon afterwards, Miss Lucas
defied her friend to mention such a subject to her; which immediately
provoking Elizabeth to do it, she turned to the newly arrived Miss
Bingley and said: "Did you not think that I expressed myself
uncommonly well just now, when I was teasing Colonel Forster to give
us a ball at Meryton?"

"With great energy; but it is always a subject which makes one
energetic."

"You are severe on us."

"It will be your turn soon to be teased, Eliza," said Charlotte. "I am
going to open the instrument, and you know what follows."

"You are a very strange creature by way of a friend—always wanting
me to play and sing before anybody and everybody! If my vanity had
taken a musical turn, you would have been invaluable; but as it is, I
would really rather not sit down before those who must be in the habit
of hearing the very best performers." On Miss Lucas's persevering,
however, she added, "Very well, if it must be so, it must." And glancing
at Miss Bingley, "There is a fine old saying, which everybody here is of
course familiar with: 'Keep your breath to cool your porridge'; and I
shall keep mine to swell my song."

Her performance was pleasing, though by no means capital. After a
song or two, and before she could reply to the entreaties of several that
she would sing again, she was eagerly succeeded at the instrument by her
sister Mary, who having, in consequence of being the only plain one in
the family, worked hard for knowledge and accomplishments, was always
impatient for display.

Mary had neither genius nor taste; and though vanity had given her
application, it had given her likewise a pedantic air and conceited
manner, which would have injured a higher degree of excellence than she

had reached. Elizabeth, easy and unaffected, had been listened to with much more pleasure, though not playing half so well; and Mary, at the end of a long concerto, was glad to purchase praise and gratitude by Scotch and Irish airs, at the request of her younger sisters, who, with some of the Lucases, and two or three officers, joined eagerly in dancing at one end of the room.

Mr. Darcy stood near them in morose contemplation of how he would have preferred to pass the evening. His thoughts were so engaged by a subject close to his heart but far from his person that he failed to perceive Sir William Lucas was his neighbour, till Sir William thus began: "What a charming amusement for young people this is, Mr. Darcy! There is nothing like dancing after all. I consider it as one of the first refinements of polished society."

"Certainly, sir; and it has the advantage also of being in vogue amongst the less polished societies of the world. Every savage can dance."

Sir William only smiled. "Your friend performs delightfully," he continued after a pause, on seeing Bingley join the group; "and I doubt not that you are an adept in the science yourself, Mr. Darcy. Do you often dance at St. James's?"

"Never, sir."

"Do you not think it would be a proper compliment to the place?"

"It is a compliment which I never pay to any place if I can avoid it."

At that instant Sir William spotted Elizabeth moving towards them, and was struck with the action of doing a very gallant thing. He called out to her: "My dear Miss Eliza, why are you not dancing? Mr. Darcy, you must allow me to present this young lady to you as a very desirable partner."

And, taking her hand, he would have given it to Mr. Darcy who, though surprised, was not altogether unwilling to receive it, when she instantly drew back, and said with some discomposure to Sir William: "Indeed, sir, I have not the least intention of dancing. I entreat you not to suppose that I moved this way in order to beg a partner."

"You excel so much in the dance, Miss Eliza," said Sir William, "that it is cruel to deny me the happiness of seeing you; and though this gentleman dislikes the amusement in general, he can have no objection, I am sure, to oblige us for one half-hour."

"Mr. Darcy is all politeness," said Elizabeth.

"He is, indeed; but, considering the inducement, my dear Miss Eliza, we cannot wonder at his complaisance—for who would object to such a partner?"

Elizabeth chose to excuse herself without answering Sir William's question, but had only gone a few paces when Caroline Bingley intercepted her.

"Miss Bennet," Caroline said, inclining her head. She was dressed, as ever, in a gown of the latest fashion, trimmed with blue fabric that highlighted the corresponding colour of her eyes.

"Miss Bingley," Elizabeth said.

"I wished to compliment you on your performance. You play quite well—not that I am surprised by your accomplishment."

"Why, because you are of the belief that we country girls have nothing else to do but work on our pianoforte-playing?"

"To the contrary. I only meant that it seems natural to me that someone as handsome as you would play well."

"And here I believed I was only barely *tolerable* in your estimation." Glancing around, she spotted Charlotte on the other side of the room. "Good evening, Miss Bingley."

As Caroline watched Elizabeth's retreating form, a slight frown marring her countenance, Mr. Darcy approached and said, "I believe I can guess the subject of your reverie."

"I would be surprised if you could."

"You are considering how insupportable it would be to pass many evenings in this manner; and indeed I am quite of your opinion. The nothingness, and yet the self-importance of these people, is altogether distasteful."

"Your conjecture is totally wrong, I assure you," said Caroline. "I have been meditating on the very great pleasure which a pair of fine eyes in the face of a handsome woman can bestow."

Mr. Darcy immediately fixed his eyes on her face, and desired she would tell him what lady had the credit of inspiring such reflections.

"Miss Elizabeth Bennet, of course."

"Miss Elizabeth Bennet!" repeated Darcy. "I am all astonishment. How long has she been such a favourite? And pray, when exactly did you become such intimates?"

"That is exactly the question I would expect you to ask," Caroline said. "A man's imagination is very rapid; it jumps from admiration to intimacy in a moment."

"If you are serious about it, I shall consider the matter absolutely settled. Though I myself am immune to the Bennet sisters' appeal, I cannot say I have missed their mother's charm; and, of course, she will always be with her daughters, wherever they go."

Caroline dismissed Darcy's attempt at wit, and gave over to wondering when and how she might convince Elizabeth that her admiration was sincere. Though, if she were wise, she would in fact leave off pondering the younger Miss Bennet's attractions. Darcy's satire was not far off the mark; while the elder Bennet sisters had much to recommend them in temperament, bearing, and intelligence, their connections left rather more to be desired. Besides, on the last occasion Caroline had initiated a friendship with a lady, she had found herself forced to relocate merely to placate the lady's jealous husband. Perhaps the longing to convince Elizabeth Bennet she found her much more than merely tolerable was an urge she had far better ignore.

CHAPTER SEVEN

Mr. Bennet's property consisted almost entirely in an estate of two thousand a year, which, unfortunately for his daughters, was entailed, in default of heirs male, on a distant relation; and their mother's fortune, though ample for her situation in life, could but ill supply the deficiency of his. Her father had been an attorney in Meryton, and had left her four thousand pounds.

She had a sister married to a Mr. Phillips, who had been a clerk to their father and succeeded him in the business, and a brother settled in London in a respectable line of trade.

The village of Longbourn was only one mile from Meryton; a most convenient distance for the young ladies, who were usually tempted thither three or four times a week, to pay their duty to their aunt and to a milliner's shop just over the way. The two youngest of the family, Catherine and Lydia, were particularly frequent in these attentions; their minds were more vacant than their sisters', and when nothing better offered, a walk to Meryton was necessary to amuse their morning hours and furnish conversation for the evening; and however bare of news the country in general might be, they always contrived to learn some from their aunt. At present, indeed, they were well supplied both with news and happiness by the recent arrival of a militia regiment in the neighbourhood; it was to remain the whole winter, and Meryton was the headquarters.

Their visits to Mrs. Phillips were now productive of the most interesting intelligence. Every day added something to their knowledge of the officers' names and connections. Their lodgings were not long a secret, and at length they began to know the officers themselves. Mr. Phillips visited them all, and this opened to his nieces a store of felicity unknown before. They could talk of nothing but officers; and Mr. Bingley's large fortune, the mention of which gave animation to their mother, was worthless in their eyes when opposed to the regimentals of an ensign.

After listening one morning to their effusions on this subject, Mr. Bennet coolly observed: "From all that I can collect by your manner of talking, you must be two of the silliest girls in the country. I have suspected it some time, but I am now convinced."

Catherine was disconcerted, and made no answer; but Lydia, with perfect indifference, continued to express her admiration of Captain Carter, and her hope of seeing him in the course of the day, as he was going the next morning to London.

"I am astonished, my dear," said Mrs. Bennet, "that you should be so ready to think your own children silly. If I wished to think slightingly of anybody's children, it should not be of my own."

"If my children are silly, I must hope to be always sensible of it."

"Yes—but as it happens, they are all of them very clever."

"This is the only point, I flatter myself, on which we do not agree. I had hoped that our sentiments coincided in every particular, but I must so far differ from you as to think our two youngest daughters uncommonly foolish."

"My dear Mr. Bennet, you must not expect such girls to have the sense of their father and mother. When they get to our age, I dare say they will not think about officers any more than we do. I remember the time when I liked a red coat myself very well—and, indeed, so I do still at my heart; and if a smart young colonel, with five or six thousand a year, should want one of my girls I shall not say nay to him; and I thought Colonel Forster looked very becoming the other night at Sir William's in his regimentals."

A few moments' recollection led Mr. Bennet to a certain uniformed gentleman who had once caught his own fancy, decades earlier; but unlike his daughters, he had not ever been free to publish his sentiments abroad. This, he could now admit, was rather a fortunate position in which he had found himself, than unfortunate; for else he might well have fawned and effused in a manner even surpassing that of Lydia, his silliest daughter by far.

"Mamma," cried Lydia, "my aunt says that Colonel Forster and Captain Carter do not go so often to Miss Watson's as they did when they first came; she sees them now very often standing in Clarke's library."

Mrs. Bennet was prevented replying by the entrance of the footman with a note for Miss Bennet; it came from Netherfield, and the servant waited for an answer. Mrs. Bennet's eyes sparkled with pleasure, and she was eagerly calling out while her daughter read, "Well, Jane, who is it from? What is it about? What does he say? Well, Jane, make haste and tell us; make haste, my love."

"It is from Miss Bingley," said Jane, and then read it aloud.

"MY DEAR FRIEND,—

"If you would be so compassionate as to dine today with Louisa and me, I shall be indebted to you, for a whole day's tête-à-tête with just the two of us, alone together, is not likely to end well. Come as soon as you can on receipt of this. My brother and the gentlemen are to dine with the officers.—Yours ever,

"CAROLINE BINGLEY"

"With the officers!" cried Lydia. "I wonder my aunt did not tell us of *that.*"

"Dining out," said Mrs. Bennet, "that is very unlucky."

"Can I have the carriage?" Jane asked.

"No, my dear, you had better go on horseback, because it seems likely to rain; and then you must stay all night."

"That would be a good scheme," said Elizabeth, "if you were sure that they would not offer to send her home."

"The gentlemen will have Mr. Bingley's chaise to go to Meryton, and the Hursts have no horses to theirs."

"I had much rather go in the coach."

"But, my dear, your father cannot spare the horses, I am sure. They are wanted in the farm, Mr. Bennet, are they not?"

"They are wanted in the farm much oftener than I can get them."

"But if you have got them today," said Elizabeth, "my mother's purpose will be answered."

She did at last extort from her father an acknowledgment that the horses were engaged. Jane was therefore obliged to go on horseback, and her mother attended her to the door with many cheerful prognostics of a bad day. Her hopes were answered; Jane had not been gone long before it rained hard. Her sisters were uneasy for her, but her mother was delighted. The rain continued the whole evening without intermission; Jane certainly could not come back.

"This was a lucky idea of mine, indeed!" said Mrs. Bennet more than once, as if the credit of making it rain were all her own. Till the next morning, however, she was not aware of all the felicity of her contrivance. Breakfast was scarcely over when a servant from Netherfield brought the following note for Elizabeth:

"MY DEAREST LIZZY,—

"I find myself very unwell this morning, which, I suppose, is to be imputed to my getting wet through yesterday. My kind friends will not hear of my returning till I am better. They insist also on my seeing Mr. Jones—therefore do not be alarmed if you should hear of his having been to me—and, excepting a sore throat and headache, there is not much the matter with me.—Yours, etc."

"Well, my dear," said Mr. Bennet, when Elizabeth had read the note aloud, "if your daughter should have a dangerous fit of illness—if she should die, it would be a comfort to know that it was all in pursuit of Mr. Bingley, and under your orders."

"I am not afraid of her dying. People do not die of little trifling colds. She will be taken good care of. As long as she stays there, it is all very well. I would go and see her if I could have the carriage."

Elizabeth, feeling really anxious, was determined to go to Jane, though the carriage was not to be had; and as she was no horsewoman, walking was her only alternative. She declared her resolution.

"How can you be so silly," cried her mother, "as to think of such a thing, in all this dirt! You will not be fit to be seen when you get there."

"I shall be very fit to see Jane—which is all I want."

"Is this a hint to me, Lizzy," said her father, "to send for the horses?"

"No, indeed, I do not wish to avoid the walk. The distance is nothing when one has a motive; only three miles. I shall be back by dinner."

"I admire the activity of your benevolence," observed Mary, "but every impulse of feeling should be guided by reason; and, in my opinion, exertion should always be in proportion to what is required."

"We will go as far as Meryton with you," said Catherine and Lydia. Elizabeth accepted their company, and the three young ladies set off together.

"If we make haste," said Lydia, as they walked along, "perhaps we may see something of Captain Carter before he goes."

In Meryton they parted; the two youngest repaired to the lodgings of one of the officers' wives, and Elizabeth continued her walk alone, crossing field after field at a quick pace, jumping over stiles and springing over puddles with impatient activity, and finding herself at last within view of the house, with weary ankles, dirty stockings, and a face glowing with the warmth of exercise.

She was shown into the breakfast-parlour, where all but Jane were assembled, and where her appearance created a great deal of surprise. That she should have walked three miles so early in the day, in such dirty weather, and by herself, was almost incredible to Mrs. Hurst; and Elizabeth was convinced that both sisters held her in contempt for it. Caroline, in fact, was divided between admiration of the brilliancy which exercise had given to her complexion, and doubt as to the occasion's justifying her coming so far on foot. In their brother's manners, however, there was something better than politeness; there was good humour and kindness. Mr. Darcy said very little, and Mr. Hurst nothing at all. The former was thinking of a letter he had received from the continent that morning, and the latter was thinking only of his breakfast.

Her inquiries after her sister were not very favourably answered. Miss Bennet had slept ill, and though up, was very feverish, and not well enough to leave her room. Elizabeth was glad to be taken to her immediately; and Jane, who had only been withheld by the fear of giving alarm or inconvenience from expressing in her note how much she longed for such a visit, was delighted at her entrance. She was not equal, however, to much conversation, and when Miss Bingley left them together, could attempt little besides expressions of gratitude for the extraordinary kindness she was treated with. Elizabeth silently attended her.

When breakfast was over they were joined by the sisters; and Elizabeth began to like them a little better herself, when she saw how much affection and solicitude they showed Jane. Even Miss Bingley seemed to have lost her haughty air, pressing Elizabeth's hand with her own and assuring her they would see Jane well very soon. Elizabeth let her fingers remain within the lady's grasp for the briefest of moments, more from surprise than any other sensation. She had not expected such attention from Miss Bingley.

The apothecary came, and having examined his patient, said, as might be supposed, that she had caught a violent cold, and that they must endeavour to get the better of it; advised her to return to bed, and promised her some draughts. The advice was followed readily, for the feverish symptoms increased, and her head ached acutely. Elizabeth did not quit her room for a moment; nor were the other ladies often absent; the gentlemen being out, they had, in fact, no need to be elsewhere.

Caroline took advantage of the opportunity to watch Elizabeth tend to her sister. The relationship between the two Bennets was clearly devoted, and quite mutual—as far different from her own filial bonds as was possible. Elizabeth sat beside her sister on the bed, rubbing her hands with fine, sensitive fingers and amusing her with stories of their younger sisters' adventures in Meryton among the gathered militia, while Jane smiled up at her in gratitude and what could only be genuine affection.

At length, Louisa, noticing Caroline's close attendance to the Bennets, fixed her with a knowing, ill-humoured look. She, along with Charles and Darcy, was intimately acquainted with the circumstances behind their hasty removal to Netherfield. In fact, Louisa knew better than anyone of Caroline's affection for members of their sex, for they had attended together Mrs. Betwee's School for Young Ladies in Derbyshire, where Caroline had first fallen under the spell of Lady Rosalind Emmett, the unmarried aunt of one of their classmates. Lady Rosalind had introduced Caroline to the pleasures of female companionship, and ever since, she had been in search of a situation that would allow her to be true to her heart without losing the good opinion of her connections. With Darcy, she believed she may have uncovered an ideal plan for achieving future happiness for both; but given his proud, somewhat obstinate nature, the idea would have to be planted and tended to subtly, until he believed it came from his own reasoning, and not another's.

For her part, Elizabeth was aware of Caroline's gaze, but strove to ignore it as she worked to amuse and soothe Jane. Her sister had long been prone to consumptive fits, and she castigated herself for not interfering the day before in her mother's scheme. Really, was securing a husband worth dying for? Not that Jane was dying. Indeed, with Miss Bingley's and Mrs. Hurst's kind attentions, she would likely be well quite soon. *Kind*—Elizabeth had not anticipated invoking the word anywhere near Caroline Bingley.

When the clock struck three, Elizabeth felt that she must go, and very unwillingly said so.

"Of course," said Miss Bingley. "Please, take the carriage."

"I couldn't possibly."

"I insist. We cannot have you falling ill, too."

Elizabeth was about to accept, when Jane spoke hesitantly: "Truly, I would not part from you, Lizzy."

"In that case," said Miss Bingley, "perhaps, Miss Bennet, you ought to consider staying at Netherfield for the present."

Mrs. Hurst cleared her throat, but did not add materially to the discussion, while Elizabeth pictured Charlotte Lucas, and guiltily remembered their shared pleasure at savaging Miss Bingley's character.

"Do stay," said Jane, gazing up at her from the bed.

"I will," promised Elizabeth, holding her sister's hand. "I won't leave you."

"You are both welcome to remain with us for as long as you wish," added Caroline.

"Thank you," said Elizabeth. "Your hospitality is genuinely appreciated."

"You are quite welcome. I am sure you would do as much for Louisa and I, should our positions be reversed."

As a servant was dispatched to Longbourn to acquaint the family with her stay and bring back a supply of clothes, Elizabeth reflected that before today, she might not have done even half as much for Mr. Bingley's sisters.

CHAPTER EIGHT

At five o'clock the two ladies retired to dress, and at half-past six Elizabeth was summoned to dinner. To the civil inquiries which then poured in, and amongst which she had the pleasure of distinguishing the genuine solicitude of Mr. Bingley's, she could not make a very favourable answer. Jane was by no means better. Mrs. Hurst, on hearing this, commented on how much she was grieved, how shocking it was to have a bad cold, and how excessively she disliked being ill herself; and then appeared to think no more of the matter. Miss Bingley did not say much of anything at all, and the sisters' apparent indifference towards Jane when not immediately before them soon restored Elizabeth to the enjoyment of all her former dislike.

The younger brother, indeed, was the only member of the party whom she could regard with any complacency. His anxiety for Jane was evident, his attentions to herself were most kind, and they prevented her feeling herself so much an intruder as she believed she was considered by the others. She had very little notice from any but him. Miss Bingley and Mrs. Hurst appeared engrossed by Mr. Darcy, who was engrossed as ever by himself; and as for Mr. Hurst, by whom Elizabeth sat, he was an indolent man, who lived only to eat, drink, and play at cards; who, when he found her to prefer a plain dish to a ragout, had nothing to say to her.

When dinner was over, Elizabeth returned directly to Jane, and Mrs. Hurst began abusing her as soon as she was out of the room. Her manners were pronounced to be very bad indeed, a mixture of pride and impertinence; she had no conversation, no style, no beauty.

Caroline held her tongue, for she easily recognised the game at which her sister was playing. Louisa suspected her of harboring an "unnatural affection," as her elder sister deemed her sentiments, toward Elizabeth Bennet. This conversational bent was simply a trap intended to lure her out; but if she were to admit to any great interest in Miss Bennet, much less to obviously pursue a friendship, no matter how innocent, Louisa might have her sent away; could perhaps even have her cut off from her inheritance, as she had threatened to do more than once on the long journey south from Cumbria, and numerous times since arriving in Hertfordshire.

"She has nothing, in short," added Louisa, "to recommend her, but being an excellent walker. I shall never forget her appearance this morning. She really looked almost wild."

Caroline drew in a breath, and spoke: "She did, indeed. I could hardly keep my countenance. Why must she be scampering about the country, because her sister had a cold? Her hair, so untidy, so blowsy."

Her sister, confused, merely blinked at her. Then, recovering her composure, she continued in the original vein, "Yes, and her petticoat; I hope you saw her petticoat, six inches deep in mud, I am absolutely certain; and the gown which had been let down to hide it not doing its office."

"Your picture may be very exact," said Bingley; "but this was all lost upon me. I thought Miss Elizabeth Bennet looked remarkably well when she came into the room this morning. Her dirty petticoat quite escaped my notice."

"You observed it, Mr. Darcy, I am sure," said Caroline; "and I am inclined to think that you would not wish to see your own sister make such an exhibition."

"Certainly not."

"To walk three miles, or four miles, or whatever it is, above her ankles in dirt, and quite alone—it seems to me to show an abominable sort of conceited independence, a most country-town indifference to decorum." Parroting this statement afforded Caroline a certain sense of dark satisfaction, for it was just what her sister and their school friends had used to say about her after one of her many solitary gambols about the Derbyshire countryside.

"I think it shows an affection for her sister that is very pleasing," said Bingley, and Caroline could have kissed him for the unswerving goodness that neither she nor her sister had ever been able to afford.

"I am afraid, Miss Bingley," observed Mr. Darcy in a tone only she could hear, "that this adventure has rather affected your admiration of Miss Bennet's fine eyes."

"Not at all," she replied; "they were brightened by the exercise."

Darcy raised an eyebrow at this retort.

Mrs. Hurst began again: "I have an excessive regard for Miss Jane Bennet, she is really a very sweet girl, and I wish with all my heart she were well settled. But with such a father and mother, and such low connections, I am afraid there is no chance of it."

"I think I have heard you say that their uncle is an attorney in Meryton," commented Darcy to Caroline.

"Yes," admitted she, "and they have another who lives somewhere near Cheapside." Beneath the table, she closed her hand in a fist. Louisa often conveniently ignored the fact that their own fortune came not from historically overflowing family coffers but from trade very recently completed, while Darcy rarely overlooked anything having to do with matters of fortune, his having been procured the time-honored way.

"That is capital," said Mrs. Hurst, and she and Darcy both laughed.

"If they had uncles enough to fill *all* Cheapside," cried Bingley, "it would not make them one jot less agreeable."

"But it must very materially lessen their chance of marrying men of any consideration in the world," replied Darcy.

To this speech Bingley made no answer; but his eldest sister gave it her hearty assent, while Caroline forced herself to smile as the others indulged their mirth for some time at the expense of the Miss Bennets' vulgar relations.

With a renewal of an insincere tenderness that irked Caroline, Louisa suggested they return to Jane's room on leaving the dining-parlour, and they sat with her till summoned to coffee. She was still very poorly, and Elizabeth would not quit her at all till late in the evening, when she had the comfort of seeing her sleep, and when it seemed to her rather right than pleasant that she should go downstairs herself. On entering the drawing-room she found the whole party at loo, and was immediately invited to join them; but suspecting them to be playing high she declined it, and making her sister the excuse, said she would amuse herself for the short time she could stay below, with a book.

Mr. Hurst looked at her with astonishment. "Do you prefer reading to cards?" said he. "That is rather singular."

"Miss Bennet," said Miss Bingley, with a sideways glance at her elder sister, "must be a great reader, with pleasure in little else."

"I deserve neither such praise nor such censure," said Elizabeth; "I am not a great reader, and I have pleasure in many things."

"In nursing your sister I am sure you have pleasure," said Bingley; "and I hope it will be soon increased by seeing her quite well."

Elizabeth thanked him from her heart, and then walked towards the table where a few books were lying. He immediately offered to fetch her others—all that his library afforded.

"And I wish my collection were larger for your benefit and my own credit; but I am an idle fellow, and though I have not many, I have more than I ever looked into."

Elizabeth assured him that she could suit herself perfectly with those in the room.

"I am astonished," said Mrs. Hurst, "that my father should have left so small a collection of books. What a delightful library you have at Pemberley, Mr. Darcy."

"It ought to be good," he replied, "as it has been the work of many generations."

"And then you have added so much to it yourself; you are always buying books."

"I cannot comprehend the neglect of a family library in such days as these."

"Neglect!" exclaimed Mrs. Hurst. "I am sure you neglect nothing that can add to the beauties of that noble place. Charles, when you build *your* house, I wish it may be half as delightful as Pemberley."

"I wish it may, too."

"But I would really advise you to make your purchase in that neighbourhood, and take Pemberley for a kind of model. There is not a finer county in England than Derbyshire."

"With all my heart; I will buy Pemberley itself if Darcy will sell it."

"I am talking of possibilities, Charles."

"Upon my word, Louisa, I should think it more possible to get Pemberley by purchase than by imitation."

Elizabeth was so much caught with what passed, as to leave her very little attention for her book; and soon laying it wholly aside, she drew near the card-table, and stationed herself between Mr. Bingley and his eldest sister, to observe the game.

"Is Miss Darcy much grown since the spring?" asked Miss Bingley; "will she be as tall as I am?"

"I think she will," said Mr. Darcy. "She is now about Miss Elizabeth Bennet's height, or rather taller."

"How I long to see her again," said Mrs. Hurst. "I never met with anybody who delighted me so much. And so extremely accomplished for her age! Her performance on the pianoforte is exquisite."

"It is amazing to me," said Bingley, "how young ladies can have the patience to be so very accomplished as they all are."

"All young ladies accomplished!" repeated Mrs. Hurst. "My dear Charles, what do you mean?"

"Yes, all of them, I think. They all paint tables, cover screens, and net purses. I scarcely know anyone who cannot do all this, and I am sure I never heard a young lady spoken of for the first time, without being informed that she was very accomplished."

"Your list of the common extent of accomplishments," said Darcy, "has too much truth. But I am very far from agreeing with your estimation of ladies in general. I am sure that I know not more than half-a-dozen, in the whole range of my acquaintance, who are really accomplished."

"Nor I, I am sure," put in Caroline.

"Then," observed Elizabeth, "you must comprehend a great deal in your idea of an accomplished woman."

"I do comprehend a great deal in it," agreed Caroline. "No one can be esteemed accomplished who does not greatly surpass what is usually met with. A woman must have a thorough knowledge of music, singing, drawing, dancing, and the modern languages; and besides all this, she must possess a certain something in her air and manner of walking, the tone of her voice, her address and expressions, or the word will be considered but half-deserved."

"All this she must possess," added Darcy, "and to all this she must yet add the improvement of her mind, by extensive reading."

"I am no longer surprised at your knowing only six accomplish. women. I rather wonder now at your knowing *any*."

"Are you so severe upon our sex as to doubt the possibility of all this?" challenged Caroline.

"I never saw such a woman. I never saw such capacity, and taste, and application, and elegance, as you describe united."

Mrs. Hurst cried out against the injustice of her implied doubt, and was protesting that she knew many women who answered this description, when Mr. Hurst called them to order, with bitter complaints of their inattention to what was going forward. As all conversation was thereby at an end, Elizabeth soon afterwards left the room.

"Elizabeth Bennet," said Mrs. Hurst, when the door was closed on her, "is one of those young ladies who seek to recommend themselves to the other sex by undervaluing their own; and with many men, I dare say, it succeeds. But, in my opinion, it is a paltry device, a very mean art."

"Undoubtedly," replied Darcy, to whom this remark was chiefly addressed, "there is a meanness in all the arts which ladies sometimes condescend to employ."

Caroline covered her smile, while her sister, who was not entirely satisfied with this reply, failed to continue the subject.

Elizabeth joined them again only to say that her sister was worse, and that she could not leave her. Bingley urged Mr. Jones being sent for immediately; while his sisters, convinced that no country advice could be of any service, recommended an express to town for one of the most eminent physicians. This Elizabeth would not hear of; but she was not so unwilling to comply with their brother's proposal; and it was settled that Mr. Jones should be sent for early in the morning, if Miss Bennet were not decidedly better. Bingley was quite uncomfortable; his sisters declared that they were miserable. In Caroline's case, this was closer to the truth. However, to maintain the appearance of indifference, she sang duets after supper with Louisa, while their brother could find no better relief to his feelings than by giving his housekeeper directions that every attention might be paid to the sick lady and her sister.

CHAPTER NINE

Elizabeth passed the chief of the night in her sister's room, and in the morning had the pleasure of being able to send a tolerable answer to the inquiries which she very early received from Mr. Bingley by a housemaid, and some time afterwards from the two elegant ladies who waited on his sisters. In spite of this amendment, however, she requested to have a note sent to Longbourn, desiring her mother to visit Jane, and form her own judgment of her situation. The note was immediately dispatched, and its contents as quickly complied with. Mrs. Bennet, accompanied by her two youngest girls, reached Netherfield soon after the family breakfast.

Had she found Jane in any apparent danger, Mrs. Bennet would have been very miserable; but being satisfied on seeing her that her illness was not alarming, she had no wish of her recovering immediately, as her restoration to health would probably remove her from Netherfield. She would not listen, therefore, to her daughter's proposal of being carried home; neither did the apothecary, who arrived about the same time, think it at all advisable. After sitting a little while with Jane, on Miss Bingley's appearance and invitation, the mother and three daughters all attended her into the breakfast parlour, where they found Bingley and Mr. Darcy.

Bingley met them with hopes that Mrs. Bennet had not found Miss Bennet worse than she expected.

"Indeed I have, sir," was her answer. "She is a great deal too ill to be moved. Mr. Jones says we must not think of moving her. We must trespass a little longer on your kindness."

"Removed!" cried Bingley. "It must not be thought of. My sisters, I am sure, will not hear of her removal."

"You may depend upon it, Madam," said Miss Bingley, "that Miss Bennet will receive every possible attention while she remains with us."

Mrs. Bennet was profuse in her acknowledgments.

"I am sure," she added, "if it was not for such good friends I do not know what would become of her, for she is very ill indeed, and suffers a vast deal, though with the greatest patience in the world, which is always the way with her, for she has, without exception, the sweetest temper I have ever met with. I often tell my other girls they are nothing to *her*. You have a sweet room here, Mr. Bingley, and a charming prospect over the gravel walk. I do not know a place in the country that is equal to Netherfield. You will not think of quitting it in a hurry, I hope, though you have but a short lease."

"Whatever I do is done in a hurry," replied he; "and therefore if I should resolve to quit Netherfield, I should probably be off in five minutes. At present, however, I consider myself as quite fixed here."

"That is exactly what I should have supposed of you," said Elizabeth.

"You begin to comprehend me, do you?" asked he, turning towards her.

"Oh, yes—I understand you perfectly."

"I wish I might take this for a compliment; but to be so easily seen through I am afraid is pitiful."

"That is as it happens. It does not follow that a deep, intricate character is more or less estimable than such a one as yours."

"Lizzy," cried her mother, "remember where you are, and do not run on in the wild manner that you are suffered to do at home."

"I did not know before," continued Bingley immediately, "that you were a studier of character. It must be an amusing study."

"Yes, but intricate characters are the *most* amusing. They have at least that advantage." Here she couldn't help but glance at Miss Bingley, who had reversed course again and was now the picture of warm sincerity.

"The country," said Darcy, "can in general supply but a few subjects to study, for a country neighbourhood provides a fairly confined and unvarying society."

"But people themselves alter so much," said Caroline, "that there is something new to be observed in them forever."

"Yes, indeed," cried Mrs. Bennet, offended by Darcy's manner of mentioning a country neighbourhood. "I assure you there is quite as much of *that* going on in the country as in town."

Everybody was surprised, and Darcy, after looking at her for a moment, turned silently away. Mrs. Bennet, who fancied she had gained a complete victory over him, continued her triumph.

"I cannot see that London has any great advantage over the country, for my part, except the shops and public places. The country is a vast deal pleasanter, is it not, Mr. Bingley?"

"When I am in the country," he replied, "I never wish to leave it; and when I am in town it is pretty much the same. They have each their advantages, and I can be equally happy in either."

"Aye—that is because you have the right disposition. But that gentleman," looking at Darcy, "seemed to think the country was nothing at all."

"Indeed, Mamma, you are mistaken," said Elizabeth, blushing for her mother. "You quite mistook Mr. Darcy. He only meant that there was not such a variety of people to be met with in the country as in town, which you must acknowledge to be true."

"Certainly, my dear, nobody said there were; but as to not meeting with many people in this neighbourhood, I believe there are few neighbourhoods larger. I know we dine with four-and-twenty families."

Nothing but concern for Elizabeth could enable Caroline to keep her countenance at this comment. She avoided looking at Darcy, who from the corner of her eye she noted was slanting an expressive smile toward her.

Elizabeth, for the sake of saying something that might turn her mother's thoughts, asked her if Charlotte Lucas had been at Longbourn since she and Jane had come away.

"Yes, she called yesterday with her father. What an agreeable man Sir William is, Mr. Bingley, is he not? So much the man of fashion! So genteel and easy! He has always something to say to everybody. *That* is my idea of good breeding; and those persons who fancy themselves very important, and never open their mouths, quite mistake the matter."

"Did Charlotte dine with you?"

"No, she would go home. I fancy she was wanted about the mince-pies. For my part, Mr. Bingley, I always keep servants that can do their own work; *my* daughters are brought up very differently. But everybody is to judge for themselves, and the Lucases are a very good sort of girls, I assure you. It is a pity they are not more handsome! Not that I think Charlotte so very plain—but then she is our Lizzy's particular friend."

Caroline turned her gaze upon Elizabeth, who, she noted, had flushed again at her mother's comments.

"She seems a very pleasant young woman," said Bingley.

"Oh, yes; but you must own she is not terribly handsome. Lady Lucas has often envied me Jane's beauty. I do not like to boast of my own child, but to be sure—one does not often see anybody better looking. It is what everybody says. I do not trust my own partiality. When she was only fifteen, there was a man at my brother Gardiner's in town so much in love with her that my sister-in-law was sure he would make her an offer before we came away. But, however, he did not. Perhaps he thought her too young. However, he wrote some verses on her, and very pretty they were."

"And so ended his affection," said Elizabeth impatiently. "There has been many a one, I fancy, overcome in the same way. I wonder who first discovered the efficacy of poetry in driving away love."

"I have been accustomed to consider poetry as the food of love," commented Caroline.

"Of a fine, stout, healthy love it may," allowed Elizabeth. "Everything nourishes what is strong already. But if it be only a slight, thin sort of inclination, I am convinced that one good sonnet will starve it entirely away."

The general pause which ensued made Elizabeth tremble lest her mother expose herself—or Charlotte—again. She longed to speak, but could think of nothing to say; and after a short silence Mrs. Bennet began repeating her thanks to Mr. Bingley for his kindness to Jane, with an apology for troubling him also with Lizzy. Mr. Bingley was unaffectedly civil in his answer, as was his younger sister, who performed her part with much graciousness. Mrs. Bennet was satisfied, and soon afterwards ordered her carriage. Upon this signal, the youngest of her daughters put herself forward. The two girls had been whispering to each other during the whole visit, and the result of it was, that the youngest should tax Mr. Bingley with having promised on his first coming into the country to give a ball at Netherfield.

Lydia was a stout, well-grown girl of fifteen, with a fine complexion and good-humoured countenance; a favourite with her mother, whose affection had brought her into public at an early age. She had high animal spirits, and a sort of natural self-consequence, which the attention of the officers, to whom her uncle's good dinners and her own easy manners recommended her, had increased into assurance. She was very equal, therefore, to address Mr. Bingley on the subject of the ball, and abruptly reminded him of his promise; adding, that it would be the most shameful thing in the world if he did not keep it.

His answer to this sudden attack was delightful to their mother's ear: "I am perfectly ready, I assure you, to keep my engagement; and when your sister is recovered, you shall, if you please, name the very day of the ball. But you would not wish to be dancing when she is ill."

Lydia declared herself satisfied. "Oh, yes—it would be much better to wait till Jane was well, and by that time most likely Captain Carter will be at Meryton again. And when you have given *your* ball," she added, "I shall insist on their giving one also. I shall tell Colonel Forster it will be quite a shame if he does not."

Mrs. Bennet and her daughters then departed, and Elizabeth returned instantly to Jane, worrying over the remarks Miss Bingley and Mr. Darcy would share regarding her relations' behaviour, for she did not believe that the kind incarnation of the former was the genuine article. Caroline, however, like her brother, could not be prevailed upon to join in any censure of the Bennets, in spite of Mr. Darcy's attempted witticisms on *fine eyes*.

CHAPTER TEN

The day passed much as the day before had done. Mrs. Hurst and Miss Bingley had spent some hours of the morning with the invalid, who continued, though slowly, to mend; and in the evening Elizabeth joined their party in the drawing-room. The loo-table, however, did not reappear. Mr. Darcy was writing, and Miss Bingley, seated near him, was reading a book and attending to the progress of his letter. Mr. Hurst and Mr. Bingley were at piquet, and Mrs. Hurst was observing their game.

Elizabeth took up some needlework, and was sufficiently amused in attending to what passed between Caroline and her companion.

"You write uncommonly fast. You must be writing to a favorite connection."

"You are mistaken, I write rather slowly. And I am writing to Georgiana, as I have already told you."

"Again? This is the third in as many days. What a devoted brother!"

To this he made no answer.

"Pray tell your sister that I long to see her."

"I have already told her so once, by your desire."

"Oh, it is of no consequence. I shall see her in January. But do you always write such charming long letters to her, Mr. Darcy?"

"They are generally long; but whether always charming, it is not for me to determine."

"It is a rule with me, that a person who can write a long letter with ease, cannot write ill."

"That will not do for a compliment to Darcy," said her brother, "because he does not write with ease. He studies too much for words of four syllables. Do not you, Darcy?"

"My style of writing is, admittedly, very different from yours."

"Charles writes in the most careless way imaginable," said Caroline, directing her comments to Elizabeth. "He leaves out half his words, and blots the rest."

"My ideas flow so rapidly that I have not time to express them—by which means my letters sometimes convey no ideas at all to my correspondents."

"Your humility, Mr. Bingley," said Elizabeth, "must disarm reproof."

"Nothing is more deceitful," announced Darcy, "than the appearance of humility. It is often only carelessness of opinion, and sometimes, indeed, an indirect boast."

"And which of the two do you call my little piece of modesty?" asked Bingley.

"An indirect boast," replied his friend promptly; "for you are proud of your defects in writing, because you consider them as proceeding from a rapidity of thought and carelessness of execution, which, if not estimable, you think at least highly interesting. When you told Mrs. Bennet this morning that if you ever resolved upon quitting Netherfield you should be gone in five minutes, you meant it to be a sort of compliment to yourself—and yet what is there so very laudable in a precipitance which can be of no real advantage to yourself or anyone else?"

"Nay," said Bingley, "this is too much, to remember at night all the foolish things that were said in the morning. And yet, upon my honour, I believe what I said of myself to be true, and I believe it at this moment. At least, therefore, I did not assume the character of needless precipitance merely to show off before the ladies."

"I dare say you believed it; but I am by no means convinced that you would be gone with such celerity. Your conduct would be quite as dependent on chance as that of any man I know; and if, as you were mounting your horse, a friend were to say, 'Bingley, you had better stay till next week,' you would probably not go—and at another word, might stay a month."

"You have only proved by this," noted Elizabeth, "that Mr. Bingley did not do justice to his own disposition. You have shown him off now much more than he did himself."

"I am exceedingly gratified," said Bingley, "by your converting what my friend says into a compliment on the sweetness of my temper. But I am afraid you are giving it a turn which that gentleman did by no means intend; for he would certainly think better of me, if under such a circumstance I were to give a flat denial, and ride off as fast as I could."

"Would Mr. Darcy then consider the rashness of your original intentions as atoned for by your obstinacy in adhering to it?"

"Upon my word, I cannot exactly explain the matter; Darcy must speak for himself."

"Allowing the case to stand according to your representation," Darcy said, "you must remember, Miss Bennet, that the friend who is supposed to desire the delay of his plan, has asked it without offering one argument in favour of its propriety."

"To yield readily—easily—to the persuasion of a friend, then, is no merit with you."

"To yield without conviction is no compliment to the understanding of either."

"You appear to me, Mr. Darcy, to allow nothing for the influence of friendship and affection. In general and ordinary cases between friend and friend, where one of them is desired by the other to change a resolution of no very great moment, should you think ill of that person for complying with the desire, without waiting to be argued into it?"

"Shall we, before we proceed any further, arrange with rather more precision the degree of importance which is to appertain to this request, as well as the degree of intimacy subsisting between the parties?"

"By all means," said Caroline, inserting herself into the discussion, "let us hear all the particulars, not forgetting their comparative height and size; for that will have more weight in the argument, Miss Bennet, than you may be aware of. I assure you, that if Darcy were not such a great tall fellow, he should not be paid half so much deference. I declare I do not know a more awful object than Darcy, on particular occasions, and in particular places; at his own house especially, and of a Sunday evening, when he has nothing to do."

Mr. Darcy smiled; but Elizabeth checked her laughter, not wishing to let on how amusing she found Miss Bingley's comments.

"I see your design, Miss Bingley," said Darcy. "You dislike an argument, and want to silence this."

"Perhaps I do," said Caroline. "If you and Miss Bennet will defer yours till I am out of the room, I shall be very thankful; and then you may say whatever you like."

"What you ask," said Elizabeth, "is no sacrifice on my side; and Mr. Darcy had much better finish his letter."

Mr. Darcy took her advice, and did finish his letter.

When that business was over, he applied to Miss Bingley and Elizabeth for an indulgence of some music, and the two women moved together to the pianoforte.

"Please, Miss Bennet," said Caroline, inclining her head to the instrument, "do play for us."

"Not I," said Elizabeth. "I should hate to be compared to the half-dozen accomplished women whom you purport to know."

At this, Miss Bingley, with some reluctance, seated herself and began playing quite skillfully. Mrs. Hurst soon joined her sister in a duet, and while they were thus employed, Elizabeth could not help observing, as she turned over some music-books that lay on the instrument, how frequently Miss Bingley's eyes were fixed on her. She hardly knew how to suppose that she could be an object of admiration to the woman before her; and yet that she should look at her because she disliked her, was still more strange. She could only imagine, however, at last that she drew this notice because there was something more wrong and reprehensible in her, according to Caroline's ideas of right, than in any other person present. The supposition did not pain her. She liked Miss Bingley too little to care for her approbation.

After playing some Italian songs, Miss Bingley varied the charm by a lively Scotch air; and soon afterwards Mr. Darcy, drawing near Elizabeth, said to her: "Do not you feel a great inclination, Miss Bennet, to seize such an opportunity of dancing a reel?"

She smiled, but made no answer. He repeated the question, with some surprise at her silence.

"Oh!" said she; "I heard you before, but I could not immediately determine what to say in reply. You wanted me, I know, to say 'Yes,' that you might have the pleasure of despising my taste; but I always delight in overthrowing those kinds of schemes, and cheating a person of their premeditated contempt. I have, therefore, made up my mind to tell you, that I do not want to dance a reel at all—and now despise me if you dare."

"Indeed, I do not dare."

Elizabeth, having rather expected to affront him, was amazed at his gallantry; but there was a mixture of sweetness and archness in her manner which made it difficult for her to affront anybody; and Darcy was beginning to understand what Caroline saw in her. Were it not for the inferiority of her connections, he might even consider her as an advantageous prospect for himself. After all, some day he would have to attend to his duty to provide an heir for Pemberley. Most women left him cold, but Miss Elizabeth Bennet would keep him sharp, that much was certain. Stimulating company would be better than no company; and given the situation on the continent, his hopes for companionship looked to be on hold for some time.

Still playing and singing, Caroline saw the spark of interest in Darcy's look. He could not possibly be entertaining any idea of a future with Elizabeth, could he? He knew of her feelings for the lady, as well as of Louisa's threat to banish her, should she divine any forbidden sentiments on Caroline's part. And yet, as the evening wore on, Caroline could not convince herself otherwise.

"I hope," said she, as they were walking together in the shrubbery the next day, "you are not honestly considering Miss Elizabeth Bennet as a possible match for yourself."

"Why should I not?" asked Darcy.

"Because she is a sweet, intelligent girl, and does not deserve to be trapped in an unhappy marriage with one such as yourself."

"By which I can only conjecture that you, as a sentimental woman, think the lady deserves a union with someone who could one day truly love her?"

"I would point out that sentimentality is not reserved to my sex alone. You of all people—with your incessant letter-writing—should know this."

"You may have a point. But I confess, I thought you would be pleased by the notion. This way you would have Miss Bennet always close at hand."

"Perhaps; though I doubt Miss Bennet would find as much enjoyment in such a guarantee of our everlasting proximity."

"I am certain she does not dislike you, any more than she does me. You and I can both be quite charming, you know, when we set our minds to it. "

"Unfortunate, then, that we should so rarely choose to do so."

"The dangers of the life we lead. On some days, I almost believe it would be a relief to be married to someone like Elizabeth Bennet, with the immediate respectability such a connection—even to one with her vulgar relations—could not help but convey."

Caroline understood perfectly. But as she could not approve the idea of his pursuing Elizabeth when she was not free to do so, and as Darcy did not like to be told what to do, especially not by one he considered an inferior in fortune, connection, and sex, she said: "In that case, when this desirable event takes place, I hope you will give your mother-in-law Mrs. Bennet a few hints as to the advantage of holding her tongue; and, if you can compass it, do cure the younger girls of running after officers."

"Have you anything else to propose for my domestic felicity?"

"Oh, yes. Do let the portraits of your Uncle and Aunt Phillips be placed in the gallery at Pemberley. Put them next to your great-uncle the judge. They are in the same profession, you know, only in different lines."

"A fine idea. As for Miss Bennet's picture, I would not have it taken at all, for what painter could do justice to those beautiful eyes?"

At that moment they were met from another walk by Mrs. Hurst and Elizabeth herself.

"I did not know that you intended to walk," said Miss Bingley, in some confusion, lest they had been overheard.

"You used us abominably ill," answered Mrs. Hurst, "running away without telling us that you were coming out."

Then taking the disengaged arm of Mr. Darcy, she left Elizabeth to walk by herself. The path just admitted three. Miss Bingley felt her sister's rudeness, and after a hesitation said: "This walk is not wide enough for our party. We had better go into the avenue."

But Elizabeth, who had not the least inclination to remain with them, laughingly answered: "No, no; stay where you are. You are charmingly grouped, and appear to uncommon advantage. The picturesque would be spoilt by admitting a fourth. Good-bye."

She then ran gaily off, rejoicing as she rambled about, in the hope of being at home again in a day or two. Jane was already so much recovered as to intend leaving her room for a couple of hours that evening, which meant that Elizabeth would not again be left alone evading the censorious gaze of Miss Bingley, or struggling to make conversation with Mr. Darcy.

CHAPTER ELEVEN

When the ladies removed after dinner, Elizabeth ran up to her sister, and seeing her well-guarded from cold, attended her into the drawing-room, where she was welcomed by her two friends with many professions of pleasure; and Elizabeth had never seen them so agreeable as they were during the hour which passed before the gentlemen appeared. Their powers of conversation were considerable. They could describe an entertainment with accuracy, relate an anecdote with humour, and laugh at their acquaintance with spirit. Elizabeth found herself pondering Caroline Bingley's behavior once again. On the one hand, she could be determinedly arrogant, even, as it were, outright rude; on the other, nearly as insistently delightful. Truly, at her best, she was one of the most appealing women Elizabeth had ever met. If only she would remain this, her most convivial self.

But when the gentlemen entered, Miss Bingley's eyes instantly turned toward Darcy, and she had something to say to him before he had advanced many steps. He addressed himself to Jane with a polite congratulation; Mr. Hurst also made her a slight bow, and said he was "very glad;" but diffuseness and warmth remained for Bingley's salutation. He was full of joy and attention. The first half-hour was spent in piling up the fire, lest she should suffer from the change of room; and she removed at his desire to the other side of the fireplace, that she might be further from the door. He then sat down by her, and talked scarcely to anyone else. Elizabeth, at work in the opposite corner, saw it all with great delight.

When tea was over, Mr. Hurst reminded his sister-in-law of the card-table—but in vain. She had obtained private intelligence that Mr. Darcy did not wish for cards; and Mr. Hurst soon found even his open petition rejected. She assured him that no one intended to play, and the silence of the whole party on the subject seemed to justify her. Mr. Hurst had therefore nothing to do, but to stretch himself on one of the sofas and go to sleep. Miss Bingley again took up a book; Darcy commenced to his usual writing; and Mrs. Hurst, principally occupied in playing with her bracelets and rings, joined now and then in her brother's conversation with Jane.

Mr. Darcy's attention appeared nearly as much engaged in watching Miss Bingley's progress through her book, as in writing his letter. Several times he made a low-voiced inquiry, to which she replied in a matching tone, and read on. At length, frowning furiously, he gave up attempting to write and took up a book himself. But he did not become invested in the content, and at last threw aside his book, casting his eyes round the room in quest for some distraction.

"I say, Mr. Darcy," said Caroline, setting her own volume aside, "you make it nearly impossible to concentrate. What about your letter? Surely dear Georgiana will be disappointed if you do not finish it?"

The look he leveled at her was noticeably cross, and she recognized immediately that he was in no mood for their usual veiled banter, probably because he had not received nearly as many missives in response lately as he had once been known to do. Hearing her brother mentioning a ball to Miss Bennet, she turned towards him and said: "By the bye, Charles, are you serious in meditating a dance at Netherfield? I would advise you, before you determine on it, to consult the wishes of the present party. I am much mistaken if there are not some among us to whom a ball would be rather a punishment than a pleasure." She found balls, frankly, exhausting, with all of the compulsory dancing with men who bored her combined with the necessity of pretending not to gaze overlong at pretty women dressed in their finest gowns.

"If you mean Darcy," said her brother, "he may go to bed, if he chooses, before it begins—but as for the ball, it is quite a settled thing; and as soon as Nicholls has made white soup enough, I shall send round my cards."

"I should like balls infinitely better," replied she, "if they were carried on in a different manner; but there is something tedious in the usual process of such a meeting. It would surely be much more rational if conversation instead of dancing were made the order of the day."

"Much more rational, my dear Caroline, I dare say; but it would not be near so much like a ball."

Caroline made no answer, and soon afterwards she got up to walk about the room. After a moment, pausing beside Elizabeth, she said: "Miss Bennet, let me persuade you to follow my example, and take a turn about the room. I assure you it is very refreshing after sitting so long in one attitude." Louisa glanced their way suspiciously, but Caroline kept a polite smile fixed to her lips.

Elizabeth was surprised, but agreed to it immediately, as Caroline had remained pleasant to her throughout the day. Darcy looked up, as much awake to attention in that quarter as Elizabeth herself could be. He was directly invited to join their party, but he declined it, observing that he could imagine but two motives for their choosing to walk up and down the room together, with either of which his joining them would interfere.

"Do you understand his meaning?" Elizabeth asked Caroline as they reached the far end of the room.

"Usually only too well," was her answer. "But not this time. Depend upon it, however, he means to be severe on us, and our surest way of disappointing him will be to ask nothing about it."

Despite the rancor in Darcy's tone, she was not concerned that he would expose her. She knew that he was as glad as she was to have discovered a trusted confidante. From the day one of his "sister's" letters had found its way into her stack of correspondence, their friendship had developed a far deeper aspect. Each finally had an intimate friend with whom they could be absolutely honest without fear of recrimination, and even if sometimes one or the other of them took their longstanding game of teasing a bit too far, they would never purposely endanger one another's reputation. Given what they were, a sense of safety was something each prized dearly, and mistrusted greatly.

Elizabeth and Caroline maintained their strategic silence, but Mrs. Hurst insisted on absolute curiosity, and persevered therefore in requiring an explanation of Darcy's two motives.

"I have not the smallest objection to explaining them," said he, smiling archly. "The ladies either choose this method of passing the evening because they are in each other's confidence, and have secret affairs to discuss, or because they are conscious that their figures appear to the greatest advantage in walking; if the first, I would be completely in the way, and if the second, I can admire them much better as I sit by the fire."

Caroline glared at him. *Secret affairs*—the phrase had clearly set Louisa's hackles to rising, she could tell even from across the room.

"Indeed," said Elizabeth, "I never heard anything so calculated. How shall we punish him for such a speech?"

"Nothing very difficult, if you have but the inclination," said Caroline. "Tease him—laugh at him. With four sisters, you must know how that is to be done."

"I wish I could say that I did not, as it would perhaps cast me in a better light, but truly, we are a family that enjoys laughing at one another's expense. Besides, as second eldest, it is beholden upon me to keep my younger sisters in their place. Jane has such a kind disposition that she is quite unable to knowingly inflict damage."

"But you are? Able, as it were?"

"Exceedingly. It would appear I have claws sharp enough for the both of us."

"I must confess, I had noticed."

"Had you?"

"Indeed; I rather enjoy a woman with a few sharp edges in among the softer ones." She glanced sideways, and felt Elizabeth start a little as their eyes met. "In any case," she added, "we may not succeed even if we do set out to vex him. Mr. Darcy may simply refuse to comply."

"Is Mr. Darcy not to be laughed at?" asked Elizabeth, appearing to recover her composure. "That is an uncommon advantage, and uncommon I hope it will continue, for it would be a great loss to me to have many such acquaintances."

"Miss Bingley," said Darcy, overhearing this last bit, "has given me more credit than can be. The wisest and the best of men—nay, the wisest and best of their actions—may be rendered ridiculous by a person whose first object in life is a joke."

"Certainly," replied Elizabeth, "there are such people, but I hope I am not one of them. I hope I never ridicule what is wise and good. Follies and nonsense, whims and inconsistencies, do divert me, I own, and I laugh at them whenever I can. But these, I suppose, are precisely what you are without."

"I doubt that is truly possible for anyone; but it has been a priority of mine to avoid those weaknesses which often expose one to ridicule."

"Such as vanity and pride."

"I dare say, I cannot be expected to comment upon my own vanity. As for the other, where there is a genuine superiority of mind, pride will always be well-regulated."

Elizabeth turned away to hide a smile.

"Your examination of Mr. Darcy is over, I presume," said Caroline, her light tone belying, she hoped, her serious interest; "and pray what is the result?"

"I am perfectly convinced that Mr. Darcy has no defect. He owns it himself without disguise."

"I have forwarded no such pretension," said Darcy. "My temper I dare not vouch for. I cannot forget the follies and vices of others so soon as I ought, nor their offenses against myself. My temper would perhaps be called resentful. My good opinion once lost, is lost forever."

"*That* is a failing indeed," said Elizabeth. "Implacable resentment is a shade in a character. But you have chosen your fault well. I really cannot laugh at it. You are safe from me."

"Yet there is, I believe, in every disposition a natural defect, which not even the best education can overcome."

"Then *your* defect is to hate everybody."

"And yours," he replied with a smile, "is to willfully misunderstand them."

"Do let us have a little music," said Caroline as they neared the pianoforte, eager to interrupt the conversation to which she had become a mere witness. "Louisa, you will not mind my waking Mr. Hurst?"

Her sister had not the smallest objection, and the instrument was opened; and Caroline, after a few moments' singing and playing, was only a little sorry to have lost Elizabeth's nearness. From the pianoforte she could watch the object of her increasing affection all she wanted without Louisa's notice, and watch, too, Darcy's manner toward the younger Miss Bennet. From his attitude, it appeared that she may well have a rival of sorts on her hands. If only there were some way to divine which of them Elizabeth might prefer—but then, that was always the case when it came to finding love, was it not, particularly with a member of one's own sex? Careful maneuvering, unremitting watchfulness, and awareness that all might well—likely would—end in disappointment.

CHAPTER TWELVE

I n consequence of an agreement between the sisters, Elizabeth wrote the next morning to their mother, to beg that the carriage might be sent for them in the course of the day. But Mrs. Bennet, who had calculated on her daughters remaining at Netherfield till the following Tuesday, which would exactly finish Jane's week, could not bring herself to receive them with pleasure before. Her answer, therefore, was not propitious, at least not to Elizabeth's wishes, for she was impatient to get home. Mrs. Bennet sent them word that they could not possibly have the carriage before Tuesday; and in her postscript it was added, that if Mr. Bingley and his sisters pressed them to stay longer, she could spare them very well. Against staying longer, however, Elizabeth was positively resolved—nor did she much expect it would be asked; and fearful, on the contrary, as being considered as intruding themselves needlessly long, she urged Jane to borrow Mr. Bingley's carriage immediately, and at length it was settled that their original design of leaving Netherfield that morning should be mentioned, and the request made.

The communication excited many professions of concern; and enough was said of wishing them to stay at least till the following day to work on Jane; and till the morrow their going was deferred. Miss Bingley was then almost sorry that she had proposed the delay, for her feelings for the younger sister presented a far greater danger than her affection for the eldest. With Louisa's hawkish gaze close upon her, she wisely resolved to be particularly careful that no sign of admiration should escape her, nothing that could alert her sister to the rising tide of her felicity; sensible that her behaviour during the last day must have material weight in confirming or crushing Louisa's suspicions. Steady to her purpose, she scarcely spoke ten words to Elizabeth through the whole of Saturday, and though they were at one time left by themselves for half-an-hour, she adhered most conscientiously to her book, and would not even look at her.

To Mr. Darcy, news of the Bennet sisters' intended leave-taking was welcome intelligence. Elizabeth interested him, but Caroline was clearly drawn to her—another affair doomed from the start, as far as he could tell—and was considerably more mocking than usual to him in Elizabeth's presence. He would be just as glad to see the Bennet sisters leave Netherfield. Only the master of the house heard with real sorrow that they were to go so soon, and repeatedly tried to persuade Miss Bennet that it would not be safe for her—that she was not enough recovered; but Jane was firm where she felt herself to be right.

On Sunday, after morning service, the separation, so agreeable to almost all, took place. Caroline's civility to Elizabeth increased at last very rapidly, as well as her affection for Jane; and when they parted, after assuring the latter of the pleasure it would always give her to see her either at Longbourn or Netherfield, and embracing her most tenderly, she warmly shook hands with the former. Elizabeth took leave of the whole party in the liveliest of spirits, assured that her happiness arose from their imminent homecoming.

The sisters were not welcomed home very cordially by their mother. Mrs. Bennet wondered at their coming, and thought them very wrong to give so much trouble, and was sure Jane would have caught cold again. But their father, though very laconic in his expressions of pleasure, was really glad to see them; he had felt their importance in the family circle. The evening conversation, when they were all assembled, had lost much of its animation and almost all of its sense by the absence of Jane and Elizabeth.

They found Mary, as usual, deep in the study of thorough-bass and human nature; and had some extracts to admire, and some new observations of threadbare morality to listen to. Catherine and Lydia had information for them of a different sort. Much had been done and much had been said in the regiment since the preceding Wednesday; several of the officers had dined lately with their uncle, a private had been flogged, and it had actually been hinted that Colonel Forster was going to be married.

CHAPTER THIRTEEN

I hope, my dear," said Mr. Bennet to his wife, as they were at breakfast the next morning, "that you have ordered a good dinner today, because I have reason to expect an addition to our family party."

"Who do you mean, my dear? I know of nobody that is coming, I am sure, unless Charlotte Lucas should happen to call in—and I hope my dinners are good enough for her. I do not believe she often sees such at home."

Elizabeth touched the locket at her throat, a gift from Charlotte these several years past. She had been privately rehearsing how to describe to Charlotte her visit to Netherfield, and the behavior of Mr. Bingley and his friends. Charlotte was the one person to whom she had always told everything, even the things she could not tell Jane. But since their recent disagreement, she was uncertain their friendship could continue on the same intimate footing. At the same time, how could it not? She had loved Charlotte for so long now that doing so had become a comfortable habit.

"The person of whom I speak is a gentleman," her father said, "and a stranger."

Mrs. Bennet's eyes sparkled. "A gentleman and a stranger! It is Mr. Bingley, I am sure! Well, I shall be extremely glad to see Mr. Bingley. But—good Lord! How unlucky! There is not a bit of fish to be got today. Lydia, my love, ring the bell—I must speak to Hill this moment."

"It is not Mr. Bingley," said her husband; "it is a person whom I never saw in the whole course of my life."

This roused a general astonishment; and he had the pleasure of being eagerly questioned by his wife and his five daughters at once.

After amusing himself some time with their curiosity, he thus explained: "About a month ago I received this letter; and about a fortnight ago I answered it, for I thought it a case of some delicacy, and requiring early attention. It is from my cousin, Mr. Collins, who, when I am dead, may turn you all out of this house as soon as he pleases."

"Oh! My dear," cried his wife, "I cannot bear to hear that mentioned. Pray do not talk of that odious man. I do think it is the hardest thing in the world, that your estate should be entailed away from your own children; and I am sure, if I had been you, I should have tried long ago to do something or other about it."

Jane and Elizabeth tried to explain to her the nature of an entail. They had often attempted to do it before, but it was a subject on which Mrs. Bennet was beyond the reach of reason, and she continued to rail bitterly against the cruelty of settling an estate away from a family of five daughters, in favour of a man whom nobody cared anything about.

"It certainly is a most iniquitous affair," said Mr. Bennet, "and nothing can clear Mr. Collins from the guilt of inheriting Longbourn. But if you will listen to his letter, you may perhaps be a little softened by his manner of expressing himself."

"No, that I am sure I shall not; and I think it very impertinent of him to write to you at all, and very hypocritical. I hate such false friends. Why could he not keep on quarreling with you, as his father did before him?"

"Why, indeed; he does seem to have had some filial scruples on that head, as you will hear."

"Hunsford, near Westerham, Kent, 15th October.

"Dear Sir,—

"The disagreement subsisting between yourself and my late honoured father always gave me much uneasiness, and since I have had the misfortune to lose him, I have frequently wished to heal the breach; but for some time I was kept back by my own doubts, fearing lest it might seem disrespectful to his memory for me to be on good terms with anyone with whom it had always pleased him to be at variance.—'There, Mrs. Bennet.'—My mind, however, is now made up on the subject, for having received ordination at Easter, I have been so fortunate as to be distinguished by the patronage of the Right Honourable Lady Catherine de Bourgh, widow of Sir Lewis de Bourgh, whose bounty and beneficence has preferred me to the valuable rectory of this parish, where it shall be my earnest endeavour to demean myself with grateful respect towards her ladyship, and be ever ready to perform those rites and ceremonies which are instituted by the Church of England. As a clergyman, moreover, I feel it my duty to promote and establish the blessing of peace in all families within the reach of my influence; and on these grounds I flatter myself that my present overtures are highly commendable, and that the circumstance of my being next in the entail of Longbourn estate will be kindly overlooked on your side, and not lead you to reject the offered olive-branch. I cannot be otherwise than concerned at being the means of injuring your amiable daughters, and beg leave to apologise for it, as well as to assure you of my readiness to make them every possible amends—but of this hereafter. If you should have no objection to receive me into your house, I propose myself the satisfaction of waiting on you and your family, Monday, November 18th, by four o'clock, and shall probably trespass on your hospitality till the Saturday se'ennight following, which I can do without any inconvenience, as Lady Catherine is far from objecting to my occasional absence on a Sunday, provided that some other clergyman is engaged to do the duty of the day.—I remain, dear sir, with respectful compliments to your lady and daughters, your well-wisher and friend,

"WILLIAM COLLINS"

"At four o'clock, therefore, we may expect this peace-making gentleman," said Mr. Bennet, as he folded up the letter. "He seems to be a most conscientious and polite young man, upon my word, and I doubt not will prove a valuable acquaintance, especially if Lady Catherine should be so indulgent as to let him come to us again."

"There is some sense in what he says about the girls, however, and if he is disposed to make them any amends, I shall not be the person to discourage him."

"Though it is difficult," said Jane, "to guess in what way he can mean to make us the atonement he thinks our due, the wish is certainly to his credit."

Elizabeth was chiefly struck by his extraordinary deference for Lady Catherine, and his kind intention of christening, marrying, and burying his parishioners whenever it were required.

"He must be an oddity, I think," said she. "I cannot make him out.—There is something very pompous in his style.—And what can he mean by apologising for being next in the entail?—We cannot suppose he would help it if he could.—Could he be a sensible man, sir?"

"No, my dear, I think not. I have great hopes of finding him quite the reverse. There is a mixture of servility and self-importance in his letter, which promises well. I am impatient to see him."

"In point of composition," said Mary, "the letter does not seem defective. The idea of the olive-branch perhaps is not wholly new, yet I think it is well expressed."

To Catherine and Lydia, neither the letter nor its writer was in any degree interesting. It was next to impossible that their cousin should come in a scarlet coat, and it was now some weeks since they had received pleasure from the society of a man in any other colour. As for their mother, Mr. Collins's letter had done away much of her ill-will, and she was preparing to see him with a degree of composure that astonished her husband and daughters.

Mr. Collins was punctual to his time, and was received with great politeness by the whole family. Mr. Bennet indeed said little; but the ladies were ready enough to talk, and Mr. Collins seemed neither in need of encouragement, nor inclined to be silent himself. He was a tall, heavy-looking young man of five-and-twenty. His air was grave and stately, and his manners were very formal. He had not been long seated before he complimented Mrs. Bennet on having so fine a family of daughters; said he had heard much of their beauty, but that in this instance fame had fallen short of the truth; and added, that he did not doubt her seeing them all in due time disposed of in marriage. This gallantry was not much to the taste of some of his hearers; but Mrs. Bennet, who quarreled with no compliments, answered most readily.

"You are very kind, I am sure; and I wish with all my heart it may prove so, for else they will be destitute enough. Things are settled so oddly."

"You allude, perhaps, to the entail of this estate."

"Ah! Sir, I do indeed. It is a grievous affair to my poor girls, you must confess. Not that I mean to find fault with you, for such things I know are all chance in this world. There is no knowing how estates will go when once they come to be entailed."

"I am very sensible, Madam, of the hardship to my fair cousins, and could say much on the subject, but that I am cautious of appearing forward and precipitate. But I can assure the young ladies that I come prepared to admire them. At present I will not say more; but, perhaps, when we are better acquainted—"

He was interrupted by a summons to dinner; and the girls smiled on each other. They were not the only objects of Mr. Collins's admiration. The hall, the dining-room, and all its furniture, were examined and praised; and his commendation of everything would have touched Mrs. Bennet's heart, but for the mortifying supposition of his viewing it all as his own future property. The dinner too in its turn was highly admired; and he begged to know to which of his fair cousins the excellency of its cooking was owing. But he was set right there by Mrs. Bennet, who assured him with some asperity that they were very well able to keep a good cook, and that her daughters had nothing to do in the kitchen. He begged pardon for having displeased her. In a softened tone she declared herself not at all offended; but he continued to apologise for about a quarter of an hour.

CHAPTER FOURTEEN

During dinner, Mr. Bennet scarcely spoke at all; but when the
servants were withdrawn, he thought it time to have some
conversation with his guest, and therefore started a subject in
which he expected him to shine, by observing that he seemed
very fortunate in his patroness. Lady Catherine de Bourgh's attention to
his wishes, and consideration for his comfort, appeared very remarkable.
Mr. Bennet could not have chosen better. Mr. Collins was eloquent in
her praise. The subject elevated him to more than usual solemnity of
manner, and with a most important aspect he protested that "he had
never in his life witnessed such behaviour in a person of rank—such
affability and condescension, as he had himself experienced from Lady
Catherine. She had been graciously pleased to approve of both of the
discourses which he had already had the honour of preaching before her.
She had also asked him twice to dine at Rosings, and had sent for him
only the Saturday before, to make up her pool of quadrille in the
evening. Lady Catherine was reckoned proud by many people he knew,
but he had never seen anything but affability in her. She had always
spoken to him as she would to any other gentleman; she made not the
smallest objection to his joining in the society of the neighbourhood nor
to his leaving the parish occasionally for a week or two, to visit his
relations. She had even condescended to advise him to marry as soon as
he could, provided he chose with discretion; and had once paid him a
visit in his humble parsonage, where she had perfectly approved all the
alterations he had been making, and had even vouchsafed to suggest
some herself—some shelves in the closet upstairs."

"That is all very proper and civil, I am sure," said Mrs. Bennet, "and
I dare say she is a very agreeable woman. It is a pity that great ladies in
general are not more like her. Does she live near you, sir?"

"The garden in which stands my humble abode is separated only by a lane from Rosings Park, her ladyship's residence."

"I think you said she was a widow, sir? Has she any family?"

"She has only one daughter, the heiress of Rosings, and of very extensive property."

"Ah!" said Mrs. Bennet, shaking her head, "then she is better off than many girls. And what sort of young lady is she? Is she handsome?"

"She is a most charming young lady indeed. Lady Catherine herself says that, in point of true beauty, Miss de Bourgh is far superior to the handsomest of her sex, because there is that in her features which marks the young lady of distinguished birth. She is unfortunately of a sickly constitution, which has prevented her from making that progress in many accomplishments which she could not have otherwise failed of, as I am informed by the lady who superintended her education, and who still resides with them. But she is perfectly amiable, and often condescends to drive by my humble abode in her little phaeton and ponies."

"Has she been presented? I do not remember her name among the ladies at court."

"Her indifferent state of health unhappily prevents her being in town; and by that means, as I told Lady Catherine one day, has deprived the British court of its brightest ornaments. Her ladyship seemed pleased with the idea; and you may imagine that I am happy on every occasion to offer those little delicate compliments which are always acceptable to ladies. I have more than once observed to Lady Catherine, that her charming daughter seemed born to be a duchess, and that the most elevated rank, instead of giving her consequence, would be adorned by her. These are the kind of little things which please her ladyship, and it is a sort of attention which I conceive myself peculiarly bound to pay."

"You judge very properly," said Mr. Bennet, "and it is happy for you that you possess the talent of flattering with delicacy. May I ask whether these pleasing attentions proceed from the impulse of the moment, or are the result of previous study?"

"They arise chiefly from what is passing at the time, and though I sometimes amuse myself with suggesting and arranging such little elegant compliments as may be adapted to ordinary occasions, I always wish to give them as unstudied an air as possible."

Mr. Bennet's expectations were fully answered. His cousin was as absurd as he had hoped, and he listened to him with the keenest enjoyment, maintaining at the same time the most resolute composure of countenance, and, except in an occasional glance at Elizabeth, requiring no partner in his pleasure.

By tea-time, however, the dose had been enough, and Mr. Bennet was glad to take his guest into the drawing-room again, and, when tea was over, glad to invite him to read aloud to the ladies. Mr. Collins readily assented, and a book was produced; but, on beholding it (for everything announced it to be from a circulating library), he started back, and begging pardon, protested that he never read novels. Kitty stared at him, and Lydia exclaimed. Other books were produced, and after some deliberation he chose Fordyce's Sermons.

Lydia gaped as he opened the volume, and before he had, with very monotonous solemnity, read three pages, she interrupted him with: "Do you know, Mamma, that my Uncle Phillips talks of turning away Richard; and if he does, Colonel Forster will hire him. My aunt told me so herself on Saturday. I shall walk to Meryton tomorrow to hear more about it, and to ask when Mr. Denny comes back from town."

Lydia was bid by her two eldest sisters to hold her tongue; but Mr. Collins, much offended, laid aside his book, and said: "I have often observed how little young ladies are interested by books of a serious stamp, though written solely for their benefit. It amazes me, I confess; for, certainly, there can be nothing so advantageous to them as instruction. But I will no longer importune my young cousin."

Then turning to Mr. Bennet, he offered himself as his antagonist at backgammon. Mr. Bennet accepted the challenge, observing that he acted very wisely in leaving the girls to their own trifling amusements. Mrs. Bennet and her daughters apologised most civilly for Lydia's interruption, and promised that it should not occur again, if he would resume his book; but Mr. Collins, after assuring them that he bore his young cousin no ill-will, and should never resent her behaviour as any affront, seated himself at another table with Mr. Bennet, and prepared for backgammon.

CHAPTER FIFTEEN

r. Collins was not a sensible man, and the deficiency of nature had been but little assisted by education or society; the greatest part of his life having been spent under the guidance of an illiterate and miserly father; and though he belonged to one of the universities, he had merely kept the necessary terms, without forming at it any useful acquaintance. The subjection in which his father had brought him up had given him originally great humility of manner; but it was now a good deal counteracted by the self-conceit of a weak head, living in retirement, and the consequential feelings of early and unexpected prosperity. A fortunate chance had recommended him to Lady Catherine de Bourgh when the living of Hunsford was vacant; and the respect that he felt for her high rank, and his veneration for her as his patroness, mingling with a very good opinion of himself, of his authority as a clergyman, and his right as a rector, made him altogether a mixture of pride and obsequiousness, self-importance and humility.

Having now a good house and a very sufficient income, he intended to marry; and in seeking a reconciliation with the Longbourn family he had a wife in view, as he meant to choose one of the daughters, if he found them as handsome and amiable as they were represented by common report. This was his plan of amends—of atonement—for inheriting their father's estate; and he thought it an excellent one, full of eligibility and suitableness, and excessively generous and disinterested on his own part.

His plan did not vary on seeing them. Miss Bennet's lovely face confirmed his views, and established all his strictest notions of what was due to seniority; and for the first evening she was his settled choice. The next morning, however, made an alteration; for in a quarter of an hour's tête-à-tête with Mrs. Bennet before breakfast, a conversation beginning with his parsonage-house, and leading naturally to the avowal of his hopes, that a mistress might be found for it at Longbourn, produced from her, amid very complaisant smiles and general encouragement, a caution against the very Jane he had fixed on. "As to her younger daughters, she could not take upon her to say—she could not positively answer—but she did not know of any prepossession; her eldest daughter, she must just mention—she felt it incumbent on her to hint, was likely to be very soon engaged."

Mr. Collins had only to change from Jane to Elizabeth—and it was soon done—done while Mrs. Bennet was stirring the fire. Elizabeth, equally next to Jane in birth and beauty, succeeded her of course.

Mrs. Bennet treasured up the hint, and trusted that she might soon have two daughters married; and the man whom she could not bear to speak of the day before was now high in her good graces.

Lydia's intention of walking to Meryton was not forgotten; every sister except Mary agreed to go with her; and Mr. Collins was to attend them, at the request of Mr. Bennet, who was most anxious to get rid of him, and have his library to himself; for thither Mr. Collins had followed him after breakfast; and there he would continue, nominally engaged with one of the largest folios in the collection, but really talking to Mr. Bennet, with little cessation, of his house and garden at Hunsford. Such doings discomposed Mr. Bennet exceedingly. In his library he had been always sure of leisure and tranquility; and though prepared, as he told Elizabeth, to meet with folly and conceit in every other room of the house, he was used to be free from them there; his civility, therefore, was most prompt in inviting Mr. Collins to join his daughters in their walk; and Mr. Collins, being in fact much better fitted for a walker than a reader, was extremely pleased to close his large book, and go.

In pompous nothings on his side, and civil assents on that of his cousins, their time passed till they entered Meryton. The attention of the younger ones was then no longer to be gained by him. Their eyes were immediately wandering up the street in quest of the officers, and nothing less than a very smart bonnet indeed, or a really new muslin in a shop window, could recall them.

But the attention of the entire party was soon caught by a young man, whom they had never seen before, of most gentlemanlike appearance, walking with another officer on the other side of the way. The officer was the very Mr. Denny concerning whose return from London Lydia came to inquire, and he bowed as they passed. All were struck with the stranger's air, all wondered who he could be; and Kitty and Lydia, determined if possible to find out, led the way across the street, under pretense of wanting something in an opposite shop, and fortunately had just gained the pavement when the two gentlemen, turning back, had reached the same spot. Mr. Denny addressed them directly, and entreated permission to introduce his friend, Mr. Wickham, who had returned with him the day before from town and, he was happy to say, had accepted a commission in their corps. This was exactly as it should be; for the young man wanted only regimentals to make him completely charming. His appearance was greatly in his favour; he had all the best part of beauty, a fine countenance, a good figure, and very pleasing address. The introduction was followed up on his side by a happy readiness of conversation—a readiness at the same time perfectly correct and unassuming; and the whole party were still standing and talking together very agreeably, when the sound of horses drew their notice, and Darcy and Bingley were seen riding down the street. On distinguishing the ladies of the group, the two gentlemen came directly towards them, and began the usual civilities. Bingley was the principal spokesman, and Miss Bennet the principal object. He was then, he said, on his way to Longbourn on purpose to inquire after her. Mr. Darcy corroborated it with a bow, when his gaze was suddenly arrested by the sight of the stranger, and Elizabeth happening to see the countenance of both as they looked at each other, was all astonishment at the effect of the meeting. Both changed colour; one looked white, the other red. Mr. Wickham, after a few moments, touched his hat—a salutation which Mr. Darcy just deigned to return. What could be the meaning of it? It was impossible to imagine; it was impossible not to long to know.

In another minute, Mr. Bingley, but without seeming to have noticed what passed, took leave and rode on with his friend.

Mr. Denny and Mr. Wickham walked with the young ladies to the door of Mr. Phillips's house, and then made their bows, in spite of Miss Lydia's pressing entreaties that they should come in, and even in spite of

Mrs. Phillips's throwing up the parlour window and loudly seconding the invitation.

Mrs. Phillips was always glad to see her nieces; and the two eldest, from their recent absence, were particularly welcome, and she was eagerly expressing her surprise at their sudden return home, which, as their own carriage had not fetched them, she should have known nothing about, if she had not happened to see Mr. Jones's shop-boy in the street, who had told her that they were not to send any more draughts to Netherfield because the Miss Bennets were come away, when her civility was claimed towards Mr. Collins by Jane's introduction of him. She received him with her very best politeness, which he returned with as much more, apologising for his intrusion, without any previous acquaintance with her, which he could not help flattering himself, however, might be justified by his relationship to the young ladies who introduced him to her notice. Mrs. Phillips was quite awed by such an excess of good breeding; but her contemplation of one stranger was soon put to an end by exclamations and inquiries about the other; of whom, however, she could only tell her nieces what they already knew, that Mr. Denny had brought him from London, and that he was to have a lieutenant's commission in the ——shire. She had been watching him the last hour, she said, as he walked up and down the street, and had Mr. Wickham appeared, Kitty and Lydia would certainly have continued the occupation, but unluckily no one passed the windows now except a few of the officers, who, in comparison with the stranger, were become "stupid, disagreeable fellows." Some of them were to dine with the Phillipses the next day, and their aunt promised to make her husband call on Mr. Wickham and give him an invitation also, if the family from Longbourn would come in the evening. This was agreed to, and Mrs. Phillips protested that they would have a nice comfortable noisy game of lottery tickets, and a little bit of hot supper afterwards. The prospect of such delights was very cheering, and they parted in mutual good spirits. Mr. Collins repeated his apologies in quitting the room, and was assured with unwearying civility that they were perfectly needless.

As they walked home, Elizabeth related to Jane what she had seen pass between the two gentlemen; but though Jane would have defended either or both, had they appeared to be in the wrong, she could no more explain such behaviour than her sister.

Mr. Collins on his return highly gratified Mrs. Bennet by admiring Mrs. Phillips's manners and politeness. He protested that, except Lady Catherine and her daughter, he had never seen a more elegant woman; for she had not only received him with the utmost civility, but even pointedly included him in her invitation for the next evening, although utterly unknown to her before. Something, he supposed, might be attributed to his connection with them, but yet he had never met with so much attention in the whole course of his life.

CHAPTER SIXTEEN

As no objection was made to the young people's engagement with their aunt, and all Mr. Collins's scruples of leaving Mr. and Mrs. Bennet for a single evening during his visit were most steadily resisted, the coach conveyed him and his five cousins at a suitable hour to Meryton; and the girls had the pleasure of hearing, as they entered the drawing-room, that Mr. Wickham had accepted their uncle's invitation, and was then in the house.

When this information was given, and they had all taken their seats, Mr. Collins was at leisure to look around him and admire, and he was so much struck with the size and furniture of the apartment, that he declared he might almost have supposed himself in the small summer breakfast parlour at Rosings; a comparison that did not at first convey much gratification; but when Mrs. Phillips understood from him what Rosings was, and who was its proprietor—when she had listened to the description of only one of Lady Catherine's drawing-rooms, and found that the chimney-piece alone had cost eight hundred pounds, she felt all the force of the compliment, and would hardly have resented a comparison with the housekeeper's room.

In describing to her all the grandeur of Lady Catherine and her mansion, with occasional digressions in praise of his own humble abode, and the improvements it was receiving, he was happily employed until the gentlemen joined them; and he found in Mrs. Phillips a very attentive listener, whose opinion of his consequence increased with what she heard, and who was resolving to retail it all among her neighbours as soon as she could. To the girls, who could not listen to their cousin, and who had nothing to do but to wish for an instrument, and examine their own indifferent imitations of china on the mantelpiece, the interval of waiting appeared very long. At last, however, the gentlemen approached.

The officers of the ——shire were in general a very creditable, gentlemanlike set, and the best of them were of the present party; but Mr. Wickham was as far beyond them all in person, countenance, air, and walk, as they were superior to the broad-faced, stuffy Uncle Phillips, breathing port wine, who followed them into the room.

Mr. Wickham was the happy man towards whom almost every female eye was turned, and Elizabeth was the amiable woman by whom he finally seated himself; and the agreeable manner in which he immediately fell into conversation, though it was only on its being a wet night, made her feel that the most threadbare topic might be rendered interesting by the skill of the speaker. Briefly she recollected Caroline Bingley, the night that Jane had rejoined the party after dinner—her surprising good cheer and high spirits, as she and Elizabeth had strolled about the drawing-room teasing the imperious Mr. Darcy. When they wished to, Miss Bingley and Mr. Wickham emanated that same fortunate combination of beauty and charm that attracted members of both sexes, and shone felicitously upon anyone within reach.

With such rivals for the notice of the fair as Mr. Wickham and the officers, Mr. Collins seemed to sink into insignificance; to the young ladies he certainly was nothing; but he had still at intervals a kind listener in Mrs. Phillips, and was by her watchfulness most abundantly supplied with coffee and muffin. When the card-tables were placed, he had the opportunity of obliging her in turn, by sitting down to whist.

"I know little of the game at present," said he, "but I shall be glad to improve myself, for in my situation in life—" Mrs. Phillips was very glad for his compliance, but could not wait for his reason.

Mr. Wickham did not play at whist, and with ready delight was he received at the other table between Elizabeth and Lydia. At first there seemed danger of Lydia's engrossing him entirely, for she was a most determined talker; but being likewise extremely fond of lottery tickets, she soon grew too much interested in the game, too eager in making bets and exclaiming after prizes to have attention for anyone in particular. Allowing for the common demands of the game, Mr. Wickham was therefore at leisure to talk to Elizabeth, and she was very willing to hear him, though what she chiefly wished to hear she could not hope to be told—the history of his unexpected acquaintance with Mr. Darcy. She dared not even mention that gentleman. Her curiosity, however, was unexpectedly relieved when Mr. Wickham began the subject himself. He inquired how far Netherfield was from Meryton; and, after receiving her answer, asked in a hesitating manner how long Mr. Darcy had been staying there.

"About a month," said Elizabeth; and then, unwilling to let the subject drop, added, "He is a man of very large property in Derbyshire, I understand."

"Yes," replied Mr. Wickham; "his estate there is a noble one. A clear ten thousand per annum. You could not have met with a person more capable of giving you certain information on that head than myself, for I have been connected with his family in a particular manner from my infancy."

Elizabeth could not but look surprised.

"You may well be surprised, Miss Bennet, at such an assertion, after seeing, as you probably might, the very cold manner of our meeting yesterday. Are you much acquainted with Mr. Darcy?"

"As much as I ever wish to be," said Elizabeth. "I have spent four days in the same house with him, and I think him very disagreeable."

"I have no right to give my opinion," said Wickham, "as to his being agreeable or otherwise. I have known him too long and too well to be a fair judge. But I believe your opinion of him would in general astonish—and perhaps you would not express it quite so strongly anywhere else. Here you are in your own family."

"Upon my word, I say no more here than I might say in any house in the neighbourhood, except Netherfield. He is not at all liked in Hertfordshire. Everybody is disgusted with his pride. You will not find him more favourably spoken of by anyone."

"I cannot pretend to be sorry," said Wickham, after a short interruption, "that he or that any man should not be estimated beyond their deserts; but with him I believe it does not often happen. The world is blinded by his fortune and consequence, or frightened by his high and imposing manners, and sees him only as he chooses to be seen."

"I should take him, even on my slight acquaintance, to be an ill-tempered man."

Wickham only shook his head.

"I wonder," said he, at the next opportunity of speaking, "whether he is likely to be in this country much longer."

"I do not at all know; but I heard nothing of his going away when I was at Netherfield. I hope your plans in favour of the ——shire will not be affected by his being in the neighbourhood."

"Oh! No—it is not for me to be driven away by Mr. Darcy. If he wishes to avoid seeing me, he must go. We are not on friendly terms, and it always gives me pain to meet him, but I have no reason for avoiding him but what I might proclaim before all the world, a sense of very great ill-usage, and most painful regrets at his being what he is. His father, Miss Bennet, the late Mr. Darcy, was one of the best men that ever breathed, and the truest friend I ever had; and I can never be in company with this Mr. Darcy without being grieved to the soul by a thousand tender recollections. His behaviour to myself has been scandalous; but I verily believe I could forgive him anything and everything, rather than his disappointing the hopes and disgracing the memory of his father."

Elizabeth found the interest of the subject increase, and listened attentively; but the delicacy of it prevented further inquiry.

Mr. Wickham began to speak on more general topics, Meryton, the neighbourhood, the society, appearing highly pleased with all that he had yet seen, and speaking of the latter with gentle but very intelligible gallantry.

"It was the prospect of constant society, and good society," he added, "which was my chief inducement to enter the ——shire. I knew it to be a most respectable, agreeable corps, and my friend Denny tempted me further by his account of their present quarters, and the very great attentions and excellent acquaintances Meryton had procured them. Society, I own, is necessary to me. I have been a disappointed man, and my spirits will not bear solitude. I must have employment and society. A military life is not what I was intended for, but circumstances have now made it eligible. The church ought to have been my profession—I was brought up for the church, and I should at this time have been in possession of a most valuable living, had it pleased the gentleman we were speaking of just now."

"Indeed!"

"Yes—the late Mr. Darcy bequeathed me the next presentation of the best living in his gift. He was my godfather, and excessively attached to me. I cannot do justice to his kindness. He meant to provide for me amply, and thought he had done it; but when the living fell, it was given elsewhere."

"Good heavens!" cried Elizabeth; "but how could that be? How could his will be disregarded? Why did you not seek legal redress?"

"There was just such an informality in the terms of the bequest as to give me no hope from law. A man of honour could not have doubted the intention, but Mr. Darcy chose to doubt it—or to treat it as a merely conditional recommendation, and to assert that I had forfeited all claim to it by extravagance, imprudence—in short anything or nothing. Certain it is, that the living became vacant two years ago, exactly as I was of an age to hold it, and that it was given to another man; and no less certain is it, that I cannot accuse myself of having really done anything to deserve to lose it. I have a warm, unguarded temper, and I may have spoken my opinion of him, and to him, too freely. I can recall nothing worse. But the fact is, that we are very different sort of men, and that he hates me."

"This is quite shocking! He deserves to be publicly disgraced."

"Some time or other he will be—but it shall not be by me. Till I can forget his father, I can never defy or expose him."

Elizabeth honoured him for such feelings. "But what," said she, after a pause, "can have been his motive? What can have induced him to behave so cruelly?"

"A thorough, determined dislike of me—a dislike which I cannot but attribute in some measure to jealousy. Had the late Mr. Darcy liked me less, his son might have borne with me better; but his father's uncommon attachment to me irritated him, I believe, very early in life. He had not a temper to bear the sort of competition in which we stood—the sort of preference which was often given me."

"I had not thought Mr. Darcy so bad as this—though I have never liked him. I had not thought so very ill of him. I had supposed him to be despising his fellow-creatures in general, but did not suspect him of descending to such malicious revenge, such injustice, such inhumanity as this." After a few minutes' reflection, however, she continued, "I do remember his boasting one day, at Netherfield, of the implacability of his resentments, of his having an unforgiving temper. His disposition must be dreadful."

"I will not trust myself on the subject," replied Wickham; "I can hardly be just to him."

Elizabeth was again deep in thought, and after a time said, "To treat in such a manner the godson, the friend, the favourite of his father!" She could have added, "A young man, too, like you, whose very countenance may vouch for your being amiable"—but she contented herself with, "and one, too, who had probably been his companion from childhood, connected together, as I think you said, in the closest manner!"

"We were born in the same parish, within the same park; the greatest part of our youth was passed together; inmates of the same house, sharing the same amusements, objects of the same parental care. My father began life in the profession which your uncle, Mr. Phillips, appears to do so much credit to—but he gave up everything to be of use to the late Mr. Darcy and devoted all his time to the care of the Pemberley property. He was most highly esteemed by Mr. Darcy, a most intimate, confidential friend. Mr. Darcy often acknowledged himself to be under the greatest obligations to my father's active superintendence, and when, immediately before my father's death, Mr. Darcy gave him a voluntary promise of providing for me, I am convinced that he felt it to be as much a debt of gratitude to him, as of his affection to myself."

"How strange," said Elizabeth. "I wonder that the very pride of this Mr. Darcy has not made him just to you. If from no better motive, that he should not have been too proud to be dishonest—for dishonesty I must call it."

"It is wonderful," replied Wickham, "for almost all his actions may be traced to pride; and pride had often been his best friend. It has connected him nearer with virtue than with any other feeling. But we are none of us consistent, and in his behaviour to me there were stronger impulses even than pride."

"Can such abominable pride as his have ever done him good?"

"Yes. It has often led him to be liberal and generous, to give his money freely, to display hospitality, to assist his tenants, and relieve the poor. Family pride, and filial pride—for he is very proud of what his father was—have done this. Not to appear to disgrace his family, to degenerate from the popular qualities, or lose the influence of Pemberley House, is a powerful motive. He has also brotherly pride, which, with some brotherly affection, makes him a very kind and careful guardian of his sister, and you will hear him generally cried up as the most attentive and best of brothers."

"What sort of girl is Miss Darcy?"

He shook his head. "I wish I could call her amiable. It gives me pain to speak ill of a Darcy. But she is too much like her brother—very, very proud. As a child, she was affectionate and pleasing, and extremely fond of me; and I have devoted hours and hours to her amusement. But she is nothing to me now. She is a handsome girl, about fifteen or sixteen, and, I understand, highly accomplished. Since her father's death, her home has been London, where a lady lives with her, and superintends her education."

Elizabeth remembered the warmth with which Mrs. Hurst had described Georgiana Darcy, and wondered now if the latter counted among the half dozen truly accomplished women Miss Bingley had claimed to know. She could not help saying: "I am astonished at Mr. Darcy's intimacy with Mr. Bingley and his family. How can Mr. Bingley, who seems good humour itself and is, I really believe, truly amiable, be in friendship with such a man? Do you know Mr. Bingley?"

"Not at all."

"He is a sweet-tempered, amiable, charming man, with elegant and accomplished sisters. He cannot know what Mr. Darcy is."

"Probably not; but Mr. Darcy can please where he chooses. He does not want abilities. He can be a conversable companion if he thinks it worth his while. Among those who are at all his equals in consequence, he is a very different man from what he is to the less prosperous. His pride never deserts him; but with the rich he is liberal-minded, just, sincere, rational, honourable, and perhaps agreeable—allowing something for fortune and figure."

The whist party soon afterwards breaking up, the players gathered round the other table and Mr. Collins took his station between his cousin Elizabeth and Mrs. Phillips. The usual inquiries as to his success was made by the latter. It had not been very great; he had lost every point; but when Mrs. Phillips began to express her concern thereupon, he assured her with much earnest gravity that it was not of the least importance, that he considered the money as a mere trifle, and begged that she would not make herself uneasy.

"I know very well, Madam," said he, "that when persons sit down to a card-table, they must take their chances of these things, and happily I am not in such circumstances as to make five shillings any object. There are undoubtedly many who could not say the same, but thanks to Lady Catherine de Bourgh, I am removed far beyond the necessity of regarding little matters."

Mr. Wickham's attention was caught; and after observing Mr. Collins for a few moments, he asked Elizabeth in a low voice whether her relation was very intimately acquainted with the family of de Bourgh.

"Lady Catherine de Bourgh," she replied, "has very lately given him a living. I hardly know how Mr. Collins was first introduced to her notice, but he certainly has not known her long."

"You know of course that Lady Catherine de Bourgh and Lady Anne Darcy were sisters; consequently that she is aunt to the present Mr. Darcy."

"No, indeed, I did not. I knew nothing at all of Lady Catherine's connections. I never heard of her existence till the day before yesterday."

"Her daughter, Miss de Bourgh, will have a very large fortune, and it is believed that she and her cousin will unite the two estates."

"Mr. Collins speaks highly both of Lady Catherine and her daughter; but from some particulars that he has related of her ladyship, I suspect his gratitude misleads him, and that in spite of her being his patroness, she is an arrogant, conceited woman."

"I believe her to be both in a great degree," replied Wickham. "I have not seen her for many years, but I very well remember that I never liked her, and that her manners were dictatorial and insolent. She has the reputation of being remarkably sensible and clever; but I rather believe she derives part of her abilities from her rank and fortune, part from her authoritative manner, and the rest from the pride for her nephew, who chooses that everyone connected with him should have an understanding of the first class."

Elizabeth allowed that he had given a very rational account of it, and they continued talking together with mutual satisfaction till supper put an end to cards, and gave the rest of the ladies their share of Mr. Wickham's attentions. There could be no conversation in the noise of Mrs. Phillips's supper party, but his manners recommended him to everybody. Whatever he said, was said well; and whatever he did, done gracefully. Elizabeth went away with her head full of what he had told her; but there was not time on the way home for her even to mention his name as they went, for neither Lydia nor Mr. Collins were once silent. Lydia talked incessantly of lottery tickets, of the fish she had lost and the fish she had won; and Mr. Collins in describing the civility of Mr. and Mrs. Phillips, protesting that he did not in the least regard his losses at whist, enumerating all the dishes at supper, and repeatedly fearing that he crowded his cousins, had more to say than he could well manage before the carriage stopped at Longbourn House.

CHAPTER SEVENTEEN

Elizabeth related to Jane the next day what had passed between Mr. Wickham and herself. Jane listened with astonishment and concern; she knew not how to believe that Mr. Darcy could be so unworthy of Mr. Bingley's regard; and yet, it was not in her nature to question the veracity of a young man of such amiable appearance as Wickham. The possibility of his having endured such unkindness, was enough to interest all her tender feelings; and nothing remained therefore to be done, but to think well of them both, to defend the conduct of each, and throw into the account of accident or mistake whatever could not be otherwise explained.

"They have both," said she, "been deceived, I dare say, in some way or other, of which we can form no idea. Interested people have perhaps misrepresented each to the other. It is, in short, impossible for us to conjecture the causes or circumstances which may have alienated them, without actual blame on either side."

"Very true, indeed; and now, my dear Jane, what have you got to say on behalf of the interested people who have probably been concerned in the business? Do clear them too, or we shall be obliged to think ill of somebody."

"Laugh as much as you choose, but you will not laugh me out of my opinion. My dearest Lizzy, do but consider in what a disgraceful light it places Mr. Darcy, to be treating his father's favourite in such a manner, one whom his father had promised to provide for. It is impossible. No man of common humanity, no man who had any value for his character, could be capable of it. Can his most intimate friends be so excessively deceived in him?"

"I can much more easily believe his friends being imposed on, than that Mr. Wickham should invent such a history of himself as he gave me last night; names, facts, everything mentioned without ceremony. If it be not so, let Mr. Darcy contradict it. Besides, there was truth in his looks."

"It is difficult indeed—it is distressing. One does not know what to think."

"I beg your pardon; one knows exactly what to think."

But Jane could think with certainty on only one point—that Bingley and his sisters, if they had been imposed on, would have much to suffer when the affair became public.

The two young ladies were summoned from the shrubbery, where this conversation passed, by the arrival of the very persons of whom they had been speaking; Mr. Bingley and his sisters had come to give their personal invitation for the long-expected ball at Netherfield, which was fixed for the following Tuesday. The two ladies were delighted to see Jane, their dear friend, again, called it an age since they had met, and repeatedly asked what she had been doing with herself since their separation. To the rest of the family they paid little attention; avoiding Mrs. Bennet as much as possible, saying not much even to Elizabeth, and nothing at all to the others. They were soon gone again, rising from their seats with an activity which took their brother by surprise, and hurrying off as if eager to escape from Mrs. Bennet's civilities. Near the door, while Mrs. Hurst made their apologies, Miss Bingley caught Elizabeth's eye.

"Will you come to Netherfield for the ball, then, Miss Eliza?"

After a moment's surprise at being thus addressed, Elizabeth answered: "Of course. Unlike certain others, I enjoy dancing in equal proportion to rational conversation." She had noted Caroline's dismissive attitude during the visit, and had been in danger of deciding Bingley's younger sister deserved Darcy, when this belated notice of herself was taken.

"I fear I may have misrepresented myself previously," said Caroline; "for I, too, enjoy dancing, given the right partner. Unhappily, I do not often encounter the opportunity to dance with the person I might wish to." Here she held Elizabeth's gaze with seeming intent before adding: "Good day, Miss Eliza." And then, with a slight bow that would have done many a gentleman proud, she preceded her brother and sister from the room.

Only Jane stood close enough to have overheard this exchange. "Are you become intimate friends with Caroline Bingley, then?" she asked as Elizabeth stared in not a little bemusement after the subject of their discussion.

"I would not have thought so."

"She is certainly a handsome woman, and can be nearly as amiable as her brother."

"Not even you, dear sister, could mistake the greater part of what has passed between Miss Bingley and myself for amiability."

"I only mean to say that I find her agreeable, and I dare say she finds you much the same."

"I am sure I would not know," said Elizabeth; and she turned away from the question she pretended not to read in Jane's countenance.

Many times had she wished she were brave enough to inquire after Jane's opinion of her friendship with Charlotte Lucas; but each time she had come close, she had backed away again. Elizabeth could not bear to entertain the idea of losing her sister's good opinion—Jane was all that one could hope for in filial loyalty and sisterly companionship. Indeed, other than Charlotte, Elizabeth had long considered her elder sister her dearest friend. Troubling enough that persons she had never met looked to despise her for whom she loved, or rather for whom she could not; far better to pretend to all the world that she had simply not yet met the right man, even as she acknowledged to herself that no man would ever likely prove right for her. One such as Wickham, with his long eyelashes and the feminine fullness of his lips, might be made to do. But he was still a man, there was no doubt about that; just as she was unarguably a woman who cared not for men in matters of love, despite her every effort to do so. Could Caroline Bingley possibly be, as her manners seemed to hint, a woman such as she?

As the sound of the retreating carriage penetrated the Longbourn drawing room, Elizabeth lifted the novel she had recently begun, but was unable to focus on the words arrayed in orderly lines across the page. Instead she found herself picturing the look in Caroline Bingley's eye as she had bade Elizabeth adieu, her mannish bow at distinct odds with the fashionable cut of her walking dress. Not that the lady's disposition mattered in the least; she was a haughty, conceited woman toward whom Elizabeth could not imagine ever feeling anything excepting a disinterested antipathy. Still, to meet a lady who, like her, preferred the company of their own sex, must elicit curiosity at the least. Elizabeth knew that she and Charlotte and the celebrated Ladies of Llangollen could not be the only specimens like themselves in existence, and yet she had not knowingly encountered another—until, it would seem, now.

She was soon distracted from this line of thought by the chatter that followed Bingley's visit. The prospect of the Netherfield ball was extremely agreeable to every female of the family. Mrs. Bennet chose to consider it as given in compliment to her eldest daughter, and was particularly flattered by receiving the invitation from Mr. Bingley himself, instead of a ceremonious card. Jane pictured to herself a happy evening in the society of her friends, and the attentions of Bingley, while Elizabeth thought of spending time with Charlotte and dancing with Mr. Wickham. The happiness anticipated by Catherine and Lydia depended less on any single event, or any particular person, for though they both meant to dance half the evening with Mr. Wickham, he was by no means the only partner who could satisfy them, and a ball was, at any rate, a ball. Even Mary could assure her family that she had no disinclination for it.

"While I can have my mornings to myself," said she, "it is enough—I think it is no sacrifice to join occasionally in evening engagements. Society has claims on us all; and I profess myself one of those who consider intervals of recreation and amusement as desirable for everybody."

Elizabeth, though she did not often speak unnecessarily to Mr. Collins, asked him whether he intended to accept Mr. Bingley's invitation, and if he did, whether he would think it proper to join in the evening's amusement; and she was rather surprised to find that he entertained no scruple whatever on that head, and was very far from dreading a rebuke either from the Archbishop, or Lady Catherine de Bourgh, by venturing to dance.

"I am by no means of the opinion, I assure you," said he, "that a ball of this kind, given by a young man of character, to respectable people, can have any evil tendency; and I am so far from objecting to dancing myself, that I shall hope to be honoured with the hands of all my fair cousins in the course of the evening; and I take this opportunity of soliciting yours, Miss Elizabeth, for the two first dances especially, a preference which I trust my cousin Jane will attribute to the right cause, and not to any disrespect for her."

Elizabeth felt herself taken in. She had fully proposed being engaged by someone far more personable—Mr. Wickham, perhaps, or almost anyone else, really—for those very dances. There was no help for it, however; Mr. Collins's proposal was accepted with as good a grace as she could manage. She was not the better pleased with his gallantry from the idea it suggested of something more. It now first struck her, that she was perhaps selected from among her sisters as worthy of being mistress of Hunsford Parsonage, and of assisting to form a quadrille table at Rosings, in the absence of more eligible visitors. The idea soon reached to conviction, as she observed his increasing civilities toward herself, and heard his frequent attempt at a compliment on her wit and vivacity; and though more astonished than gratified herself by this effect of her charms, it was not long before her mother gave her to understand that the probability of their marriage was extremely agreeable to her. Elizabeth, however, did not choose to take the hint, being well aware that a serious dispute must be the consequence of any reply. Mr. Collins might never make the offer, and till he did, it was useless to quarrel about him.

If there had not been a Netherfield ball to prepare for and talk of, the younger Miss Bennets would have been in a very pitiable state at this time, for from the day of the invitation, to the day of the ball, there was such a succession of rain as prevented their walking to Meryton once. No aunt, no officers, no news could be sought after—the very shoe-roses for Netherfield were got by proxy. Even Elizabeth found some trial of her patience in weather which confined her to Longbourn where she had not a chance of seeing anyone outside of family; and nothing less than a dance on Tuesday could have made such a Friday, Saturday, Sunday, and Monday endurable to Kitty and Lydia.

CHAPTER EIGHTEEN

The evening of the ball, Elizabeth dressed with care, and prepared in the highest spirits for the night ahead. When she entered the drawing-room at Netherfield, she looked for Charlotte among the brood of well-dressed women there assembled, but in vain. Next she looked for Mr. Wickham, only to discover that he was not to be found, either, among the cluster of red coats gathered at the opposite end of the room. A doubt of his being present had never occurred to her, but in an instant arose the suspicion of his being purposely omitted for Mr. Darcy's pleasure in the Bingleys' invitation to the officers; and though this was not exactly the case, the absolute fact of his absence was pronounced by his friend Denny, to whom Lydia eagerly applied, and who told them that Wickham had been obliged to go to town on business the day before, and was not yet returned; adding, with a significant smile, "I do not imagine his business would have called him away just now, if he had not wanted to avoid a certain gentleman here."

This part of his intelligence, though unheard by Lydia, was caught by Elizabeth, and, as it assured her that Darcy was not less answerable for Wickham's absence than if her first surmise had been just, her feelings of displeasure against the former were so sharpened that she could hardly reply with tolerable civility to the polite inquiries which he directly afterwards approached to make. She was resolved against any sort of conversation with him, and turned away with a degree of ill-humour which she only partially surmounted in ascertaining the proximity of Caroline Bingley. As she watched, Caroline paused to talk to a group of fashionable ladies whom Elizabeth did not recognise, likely visitors in from town for the occasion. One of the ladies, a small, fair woman whose neckline seemed a bit more generous than was really necessary, placed her hand on Caroline's arm and leaned in to speak privately to her. At that moment, Caroline looked up, her gaze finding Elizabeth's among those of the gaily decorated guests.

Elizabeth looked away, but not before she had seen what she needed. The woman with the bountiful bust was an intimate of Caroline's of a nature that Elizabeth was certain she recognised from her own limited experience, which meant that Caroline Bingley was indeed a woman such as she; and, like her, also settled already in an attachment.

Soon after this realization, Elizabeth observed Caroline detach herself from her companions and approach the spot where she stood with Jane.

"Good evening," said Caroline, inclining her head to Jane. "I am so happy to see you both."

"Good evening, Caroline," said Jane. "What a lovely ball! Thank you again for inviting us."

"Of course. Without the two of you, there would not be nearly so much beauty in the room." Her gaze rested with the weight of a touch on Elizabeth before returning to Jane. "You are looking well, my dear friend! Are all your disagreements well and truly behind you?"

"I believe they are. How kind of you to inquire." She glanced over Caroline's shoulder and waved vaguely. "Why, look, there is my mother's sister! I believe I will say hello, if you both will excuse me?" And she moved away, casting back a smile that seemed to Elizabeth to suggest that her elder sister comprehended her disposition, and loved her not any the least for it.

She swallowed against a sudden, uncharacteristic shyness threatening to overtake her upon being left alone with Caroline Bingley. They stood silently for a moment, both surveying the crowd. Finally Elizabeth spoke: "I have never seen Netherfield looking quite so lively, Miss Bingley."

Caroline smiled. "Please, you must call me Caroline. And there is nothing like a ball to raise the spirits."

"Do call me Eliza. But is that not a far cry from what you said when your brother proposed the event?"

"Unfortunately, I am not always at liberty to say what is truly in my heart."

Elizabeth could not help asking, "Why ever not?"

"Having done so in the past with the wrong party has landed me in a world of difficulty, more than once. Have you never found the same?"

"While I am not one to hold back my opinion, in most situations," said Elizabeth, choosing her words carefully, "it is true that I have on occasion found that I could not vent my true feelings upon the world. It is most vexing, to be unable to allow one's cherished sentiments to be found out."

"Far better, then, would you say, to sublimate those feelings into a more acceptable vein?"

"Perhaps. But is that always possible? For wouldn't one still feel one's sentiments, suppressed or not?"

"I would argue just so. However, I have yet to find a situation where sentiments that challenge the accepted order are not cruelly received, even by those closest to us."

Elizabeth pictured Mrs. Hurst, seeming to watch Caroline all the time with something akin to disgust in her countenance. Even now, Caroline's elder sister was half-turned from her companions, another group of fine ladies in from town, to observe their exchange. In contrast was Jane, who stood with Mrs. Philips occasionally sneaking curious glances at the two of them.

"I must admit," said Elizabeth, "I have found the opposite to be true. Sometimes the bosom of one's family is the only place one can safely confess one's differences and find a reception free of prejudice."

Caroline followed her gaze to where Jane conversed with their aunt. "In that case, you are truly fortunate, Eliza."

"To be sure."

"Still, I would own that we women have it easier than men, in many ways. We can spend the majority of our days at home with family and friends, unseen and unknown to the outer world, while most men do not have the same luxury of retirement, not until they reach a certain age." She was watching Darcy as she said this, and Elizabeth was struck by a thought that had not reached full maturity when Caroline laughed lightly and spoke again: "But what a serious conversation, given our surroundings! Perhaps I should engage you on a topic far less commodious, such as the line of your gown or the dismal nature of the weather with which we have been accosted of late."

"Indeed. And I might talk about my dance card, or the number of couples present."

"Perhaps by and by I may observe that private balls are much pleasanter than public ones."

"Are they? I do not have significant experience with the latter." Elizabeth stopped, realizing that she had just called attention to the social division between them, a line that had seemed important to her companion on previous encounters.

"Truly, you have not missed much. Although I do enjoy a good masquerade, with everyone in costume and the expected state of affairs credibly disrupted for the whole of an evening," said Caroline, smiling at her with such warmth that Elizabeth could not help but smile back, missing as she did so the approach of Charlotte Lucas.

"Eliza," said Charlotte, touching her elbow.

"Charlotte! How are you?" The question was genuine. Despite exchanging regular letters, Elizabeth had not seen her dear friend for an entire week. "Miss Bingley, do you know Miss Lucas?"

"We have met," said Caroline, inclining her head regally.

Charlotte nodded back, her usually open face veiled. "Miss Bingley. Thank you so much for the invitation."

"You are quite welcome. Please excuse me—the music is about to begin, and I promised Mr. Darcy the first two dances." She bowed slightly, again opting for a masculine gesture of leave-taking, and swept away in her London gown while Elizabeth and Charlotte stood awkwardly together, done up in their Meryton finest.

"I did not know the two of you were on such familiar terms," said Charlotte at last, her voice stilted.

"We are not. Or perhaps we are, but only because of Jane. Look, there is Mr. Collins. Is he not just as I described in my letters? I believe he might actually have it in his designs to try to make a wife of me. Can you imagine me, the wife of a rector?"

"And why not? Are you somehow above assuming the duties of mistress of a parsonage, owing perhaps to the quality of your new connections?"

"Charly," Elizabeth said, her hand on her friend's bare arm, the skin of which only a matter of weeks before she had caressed pleasurably as they enjoyed a few rare stolen hours together at Lucas Lodge. "Do not be cross with me. I am sorry I have not been to see you. The weather was abysmal, you know it was."

"A bit of rain does not seem to have prevented you from forming a friendship with a woman you previously assured me you despised. But perhaps I am no longer privy to the inner workings of your mind, Lizzy, and for that, I am sorry indeed." Abruptly she turned away, her cheeks bright spots of red in her otherwise uniformly pale countenance.

Elizabeth made to go after her, but then glanced around, aware of their surroundings. It would be a serious mistake to allow herself to be observed running after Charlotte, in what must look to all the world like nothing more than a lover's spat. Instead, she approached Jane and their mother's sister and forced herself to engage spiritedly in what suddenly felt like odious small talk.

But Elizabeth was not formed for ill-humour; and though most of her prospects for gentle amusement seemed to have been destroyed for the evening, this loss could not dwell long on her spirits. The first two dances, however, brought a return of distress; they were dances of mortification. Mr. Collins, awkward and solemn, apologising instead of attending, and often moving wrong without being aware of it, gave her all the shame and misery which a disagreeable partner for a couple of dances can give, while Darcy and Miss Bingley moved elegantly about the floor, looking as if they were made for one another. Each time the dance pattern brought her near Caroline, Elizabeth was careful to avert her eyes. The notion that Charlotte had any need to be suspicious of their interaction was ridiculous, of course—Caroline would never allow herself to care for one such as her, while Elizabeth could not imagine overlooking Caroline's arrogance, no matter if they happened or not to share a preference in the type of companionship they sought.

After Mr. Collins, Elizabeth danced with an officer, and had the refreshment of hearing from him that Wickham, their mutual friend, was universally liked. When those dances were over, she returned to Charlotte to make amends. Her friend, not being prone to the enjoyment of rancor, received her courteously and soon engaged her in a discussion of all that had passed during their week apart. They were deep in conversation, when Elizabeth found herself suddenly addressed by Mr. Darcy, who took her so much by surprise in his application for her hand that, without knowing what she did, she accepted him. He walked away again immediately, and she was left to fret over her own want of presence of mind.

Charlotte tried to console her: "I dare say you will find him very agreeable."

"Heaven forbid! Do not wish on me such an evil."

When the dancing recommenced, however, and Darcy approached to claim her hand, Charlotte could not help cautioning her in a whisper, not to appear unpleasant in the eyes of a man of Darcy's consequence. Elizabeth made no answer to this incitement, and took her place in the set, amazed at the dignity to which she was arrived in being allowed to stand opposite Mr. Darcy, and reading in her neighbours' looks their equal amazement in beholding it. They stood for some time without speaking a word; and she began to imagine that their silence was to last through the two dances, and at first was resolved not to break it; till suddenly fancying that it would be the greater punishment to her partner to oblige him to talk, she made some slight observation on the dance. He replied, and was again silent.

Recalling her earlier conversation with Miss Bingley, she said: "It is your turn to say something now, Mr. Darcy. I talked about the dance, and you ought to make some sort of remark on the size of the room, or on the quality of the musicians."

"Do you talk by rule, then, while you are dancing?"

"Sometimes. One must speak a little, you know. It would look odd to be entirely silent for half an hour together; and yet for the advantage of some, conversation ought to be so arranged, as that they may have the trouble of saying as little as possible."

"Are you consulting your own feelings in the present case, or do you imagine that you are gratifying mine?"

"Both," replied Elizabeth archly; "for I have always seen a great similarity in the turn of our minds. We are each of an unsocial, taciturn disposition, unwilling to speak, unless we expect to say something that will amaze the whole room, and be handed down to posterity with all the éclat of a proverb."

"That is hardly a very striking resemblance of your own character," said he. "How near it may be to mine, I cannot pretend to say. You believe it a faithful portrait, undoubtedly."

"I must not decide on my own performance."

He made no answer, and they were again silent till they had gone down the dance, when he asked her if she and her sisters did not very often walk to Meryton. She answered in the affirmative, and, unable to resist the temptation, added, "When you met us there the other day, we had just been forming a new acquaintance."

The effect was immediate. A deeper shade of hauteur overspread his features, but he said not a word, and Elizabeth, though blaming herself for her own weakness, could not go on. At length Darcy spoke, and in a constrained manner said, "Mr. Wickham is blessed with such happy manners as may ensure his making friends—whether he may be equally capable of retaining them, is less certain."

"He has been so unlucky as to lose your friendship," replied Elizabeth, "and in a manner which he is likely to suffer from all his life."

At that moment, Sir William Lucas appeared close to them, meaning to pass through the set to the other side of the room; but on perceiving Mr. Darcy, he stopped with a bow to compliment him on his dancing and his partner.

"Such very superior dancing is not often seen, my dear sir. It is evident that you belong to the first circles. Allow me to say, however, that your fair partner does not disgrace you, and that I must hope to have this pleasure often repeated, especially when a certain desirable event, my dear Eliza"—glancing at Jane and Bingley, who were dancing together—"shall take place. What congratulations will then flow in! But let me not interrupt you, Mr. Darcy. You will not thank me for detaining you from the bewitching converse of that young lady, whose bright eyes are also upbraiding me."

The latter part of this address was scarcely heard by Darcy; but Sir William's allusion to his friend seemed to strike him forcibly, and his eyes were directed with a very serious expression towards Bingley and Jane. Recovering himself, however, shortly, he turned to his partner, and said, "Sir William's interruption has made me forget what we were talking of."

"I do not think we were speaking at all. Sir William could not have interrupted two people in the room who had less to say for themselves. We have tried two or three subjects already without success, and what we are to talk of next I cannot imagine."

"What think you of books?" said he, smiling.

"I cannot talk of books in a ball-room; my head is always full of something else."

"The present always occupies you in such scenes—does it?" said he, with a look of doubt.

"Yes, always," she replied, without knowing what she said, for her thoughts had wandered far from the subject, as soon afterwards appeared by her suddenly exclaiming, "I remember hearing you once say, Mr. Darcy, that you hardly ever forgave, that your resentment once created was unappeasable. You are very cautious, I suppose, as to its being created."

"I am," said he, with a firm voice.

"And never allow yourself to be blinded by prejudice?"

"I hope not. May I ask to what these questions tend?"

"Merely to the illustration of your character," said she. "I hear such different accounts of you as puzzle me exceedingly."

"I can readily believe," answered he, "that reports may vary greatly with respect to me; and I could wish, Miss Bennet, that you were not to sketch my character at the present moment, as there is reason to fear that the performance would reflect no credit on either."

"But if I do not take your likeness now, I may never have another opportunity."

"Then I would by no means suspend any pleasure of yours," he replied.

She said no more, and they went down the other dance and parted in silence; and on each side dissatisfied, though not to an equal degree, for in Darcy's breast there was a powerful feeling which directed all his anger toward another.

They had not long separated, when Miss Bingley came towards her again, her expression far more serious than before.

"I hear you have found a friend in George Wickham. Is that true?"

Elizabeth frowned. "He is a new, not unpleasant acquaintance, that much is accurate. Why do you ask?"

"Your younger sisters have been talking to me about him, and Darcy told me of your conversation."

"Already? We only finished our dance a moment ago. If I may ask, what is the nature of the disagreement between him and Wickham?"

Caroline paused, her glance seeking out Darcy where he stood beside her brother half a room away, surveying the dance scene. "I am not at liberty to tell you everything, but let me recommend you, as a friend, not to give implicit confidence to all Wickham's assertions. As to Darcy's using him ill, it is perfectly false. On the contrary, Darcy has always been remarkably kind to him, though Wickham has treated him in a most infamous manner. I imagine he failed to inform you that he is the son of the late Mr. Darcy's steward, a longtime servant at Pemberley. "

Her voice had taken on shades of the haughty tone Elizabeth had learned to detest during their earliest meetings, and she could not help but take exception. "Their enmity appears to me to be entirely mutual, Miss Bingley. And so far I have heard you accuse Wickham of nothing worse than being the son of Mr. Darcy's steward, a fact of which, I can assure you, he did inform me himself."

"I beg your pardon," replied Caroline, after a moment. "Excuse my interference, Miss Bennet—it was kindly meant." She turned away without another word, her previous warmth replaced by cool indifference.

Elizabeth watched her go, with warring emotions. Perhaps Caroline truly had been trying to help, and her own presumptions of the lady's prejudice against Wickham's low beginnings were erroneous. And yet, Caroline had demonstrated more than once an offensive air of superiority in matters of rank and fortune; surely it was only natural that Elizabeth would treat her comments regarding Wickham with circumspection.

Seeking comfort as well as information, she approached her eldest sister, who had undertaken to make inquiries of Bingley on the same subject. Jane met her with a smile of such sweet complacency, a glow of such happy expression, as sufficiently marked how well she was satisfied with the occurrences of the evening. Elizabeth instantly read her feelings, and at that moment her irritation with Miss Bingley, and everything else, gave way before the hope of Jane's being in the fairest way for happiness.

"I wanted to know," said she, with a countenance nearly as smiling as her sister's, "what you have learnt about Wickham and Darcy. But perhaps you have been too pleasantly engaged to think of any third person?"

"No," replied Jane, "I have not forgotten; but I have nothing satisfactory to tell you. Mr. Bingley does not know the whole of the history between them, and is quite ignorant of the circumstances which have principally offended Mr. Darcy; but he will vouch for the good conduct, the probity, and honour of his friend, and is perfectly convinced that Mr. Wickham has deserved much less attention from Mr. Darcy than he has received; and I am sorry to say by his account as well as his sister's, Mr. Wickham is by no means a respectable young man. I am afraid he has been very imprudent, and has deserved to lose Mr. Darcy's regard."

"Mr. Bingley does not know Mr. Wickham himself?"

"No; he never saw him till the other morning at Meryton."

"This account then must be what he has received from Mr. Darcy. But what does he say of the living?"

"He does not exactly recollect the circumstances, though he has heard them from Mr. Darcy more than once, but he believes that it was left to him conditionally only."

"I have not a doubt of Mr. Bingley's sincerity," said Elizabeth; "but you must excuse my not being convinced by assurances only. As Mr. Bingley is unacquainted with several parts of the story, and has learnt the rest from his friend, I shall venture to still think of both gentlemen as I did before."

She then changed the discourse to one more gratifying to each, and on which there could be no difference of sentiment. Elizabeth listened with delight to the happy, though modest hopes which Jane entertained of Mr. Bingley's regard, and said all in her power to heighten her confidence in it. On their being joined by Mr. Bingley himself, Elizabeth withdrew to Miss Lucas; to whose inquiry after the pleasantness of her last dance partner she had scarcely replied, before Mr. Collins came up to them, and told her with great exultation that he had just been so fortunate as to make a most important discovery.

"I have found out," said he, "by a singular accident, that there is now in the room a near relation of my patroness. I happened to overhear the gentleman himself mentioning to the young lady who does the honours of the house the names of his cousin Miss de Bourgh, and of her mother Lady Catherine. How wonderfully these sort of things occur! Who would have thought of my meeting with, perhaps, a nephew of Lady Catherine de Bourgh in this assembly! I am most thankful that the discovery is made in time for me to pay my respects to him, which I am now going to do, and trust he will excuse my not having done it before. My total ignorance of the connection must plead my apology."

"You are not going to introduce yourself to Mr. Darcy!" exclaimed Elizabeth.

"Indeed I am. I shall entreat his pardon for not having done it earlier. I believe him to be Lady Catherine's nephew. It will be in my power to assure him that her ladyship was quite well yesterday se'nnight."

Elizabeth tried to dissuade him from such a scheme, assuring him that Mr. Darcy would consider his addressing him without introduction as an impertinent freedom, rather than a compliment to his aunt; that it was not in the least necessary there should be any notice on either side; and that if it were, it must belong to Mr. Darcy, the superior in consequence, to begin the acquaintance. Mr. Collins listened to her with the determined air of following his own inclination, and, when she ceased speaking, replied thus:

"My dear Miss Elizabeth, I have the highest opinion in the world in your excellent judgment in all matters within the scope of your understanding; but permit me to say, that there must be a wide difference between the established forms of ceremony amongst the laity, and those which regulate the clergy; for, give me leave to observe that I consider the clerical office as equal in point of dignity with the highest rank in the kingdom—provided that a proper humility of behaviour is at the same time maintained. You must therefore allow me to follow the dictates of my conscience on this occasion, which leads me to perform what I look on as a point of duty. Pardon me for neglecting to profit by your advice, which on every other subject shall be my constant guide, though in the case before us I consider myself more fitted by education and habitual study to decide on what is right than a young lady like yourself."

And with a low bow he left her to attack Mr. Darcy, whose reception of his advances she watched, and whose astonishment at being so addressed was very evident. Her cousin prefaced his speech with a solemn bow and though she could not hear a word of it, she felt as if hearing it all, and saw in the motion of his lips the words "apology," "Hunsford," and "Lady Catherine de Bourgh." It vexed her to see him expose himself to such a man. Mr. Darcy was eyeing him with unrestrained wonder, and when at last Mr. Collins allowed him time to speak, replied with an air of distant civility. Mr. Collins, however, was not discouraged from speaking again, and Mr. Darcy's contempt seemed abundantly increasing with the length of his second speech, and at the end of it he only made him a slight bow, and moved another way. Mr. Collins then returned to Elizabeth.

"I have no reason, I assure you," said he, "to be dissatisfied with my reception. Mr. Darcy seemed much pleased with the attention. He answered me with the utmost civility, and even paid me the compliment of saying that he was so well convinced of Lady Catherine's discernment as to be certain she could never bestow a favour unworthily. It was really a very handsome thought. Upon the whole, I am much pleased with him."

Obliged as she was to hide any interest of her own at such an assembly, Elizabeth turned her attention almost entirely on her sister and Mr. Bingley; and the train of agreeable reflections which her observations gave birth to, made her perhaps almost as happy as Jane. She saw her sister in idea settled in that very house, in all the felicity which a marriage of true affection could bestow. Her mother's thoughts, she plainly saw, were also fixed on Jane's future prospects, and she determined not to venture near her, lest she might hear too much.

When they sat down to supper, therefore, she considered it a most unlucky perverseness which placed them within one of each other; and deeply was she vexed to find that her mother was talking to that one person (Lady Lucas) freely, openly, and of nothing else but her expectation that Jane would soon be married to Mr. Bingley. It was an animating subject, and Mrs. Bennet seemed incapable of fatigue while enumerating the advantages of the match. His being such a charming young man, and so rich, and living but three miles from them, were the first points of self-congratulation; and then it was such a comfort to think how fond the two sisters were of Jane, and to be certain that they must desire the connection as much as she could do. It was, moreover, such a promising thing for her younger daughters, as Jane's marrying so greatly must throw them in the way of other rich men; and lastly, it was so pleasant at her time of life to be able to consign her single daughters to the care of their sister, that she might not be obliged to go into company more than she liked. It was necessary to make this circumstance a matter of pleasure, because on such occasions it is the etiquette; but no one was less likely than Mrs. Bennet to find comfort in staying home at any period of her life. She concluded with many good wishes that Lady Lucas might soon be equally fortunate, though evidently and triumphantly believing there was no chance of it.

In vain did Elizabeth endeavour to check the rapidity of her mother's words, or persuade her to describe her felicity in a less audible whisper; for, to her inexpressible vexation, she could perceive that the chief of it was overheard by Mr. Darcy, who sat opposite to them. Her mother only scolded her for being nonsensical.

"What is Mr. Darcy to me, pray, that I should be afraid of him? I am sure we owe him no such particular civility as to be obliged to say nothing he may not like to hear."

"For heaven's sake, Madam, speak lower. What advantage can it be for you to offend Mr. Darcy? You will never recommend yourself to his friend by so doing!"

Nothing that she could say, however, had any influence. Her mother would talk of her views in the same intelligible tone. Elizabeth blushed and blushed again with shame and vexation. She could not help frequently glancing at Mr. Darcy, though every glance convinced her of what she dreaded; for though he was not always looking at her mother, she was convinced that his attention was invariably fixed on her. The expression of his face changed gradually from indignant contempt to a composed and steady gravity.

At length, however, Mrs. Bennet had no more to say; and Lady Lucas, who had been long yawning at the repetition of delights which she saw no likelihood of sharing, was left to the comforts of cold ham and chicken. Elizabeth now began to revive. But not long was the interval of tranquility; for, when supper was over, singing was talked of, and she had the mortification of seeing Mary, after very little entreaty, preparing to oblige the company. By many significant looks and silent entreaties, did she endeavour to prevent such a proof of complaisance, but in vain; Mary would not understand them; such an opportunity of exhibiting was delightful to her, and she began her song. Elizabeth's eyes were fixed on her with most painful sensations, and she watched her progress through the several stanzas with an impatience which was very ill rewarded at their close; for Mary, on receiving, amongst the thanks of the table, the hint of a hope that she might be prevailed on to favour them again, after the pause of half a minute began another. Mary's powers were by no means fitted for such a display; her voice was weak, and her manner affected. Elizabeth was in agonies. She looked at Jane, to see how she bore it; but Jane was very composedly talking to Bingley. She looked at Caroline, who was in a tête-à-tête with her London friend, and at Darcy, who continued imperturbably grave. She looked at her father to entreat his interference, lest Mary should be singing all night. He took the hint, and when Mary had finished her second song, said aloud, "That will do extremely well, child. You have delighted us long enough. Let the other young ladies have time to exhibit."

Mary, though pretending not to hear, was somewhat disconcerted; and Elizabeth, sorry for her, and sorry for her father's speech, was afraid her anxiety had done no good. Others of the party were now applied to.

"If I," said Mr. Collins, "were so fortunate as to be able to sing, I should have great pleasure, I am sure, in obliging the company with an air; for I consider music as a very innocent diversion, and perfectly compatible with the profession of a clergyman. I do not mean, however, to assert that we can be justified in devoting too much of our time to music, for there are certainly other things to be attended to. The rector of a parish has much to do. In the first place, he must make such an agreement for tithes as may be beneficial to himself and not offensive to his patron. He must write his own sermons; and the time that remains will not be too much for his parish duties, and the care and improvement of his dwelling, which he cannot be excused from making as comfortable as possible. And I do not think it of light importance that he should have attentive and conciliatory manners towards everybody, especially towards those to whom he owes his preferment. I cannot acquit him of that duty; nor could I think well of the man who should omit an occasion of testifying his respect towards anybody connected with the family." And with a bow to Mr. Darcy, he concluded his speech, which had been spoken so loud as to be heard by half the room. Many stared—many smiled; but no one looked more amused than Mr. Bennet himself, while his wife seriously commended Mr. Collins for having spoken so sensibly, and observed in a half-whisper to Lady Lucas, that he was a remarkably clever, good kind of young man.

To Elizabeth it appeared that, had her family made an agreement to expose themselves as much as they could during the evening, it would have been impossible for them to play their parts with more spirit or finer success; and happy did she think it for Bingley and Jane that some of the exhibition had escaped his notice, and that his feelings were not of a sort to be much distressed by the folly which he must have witnessed. That Miss Bingley and Mr. Darcy should have such an opportunity of observing her relations was bad enough, and she could not make up her mind whether the silent contempt of the gentleman, or the disinterested attitude of the lady, was worse.

The rest of the evening brought her little amusement. She was teased by Mr. Collins, who continued most perseveringly by her side, and though he could not prevail on her to dance with him again, put it out of her power to dance with others. In vain did she entreat him to stand up with somebody else, and offer to introduce him to any young lady in the room. He assured her, that as to dancing, he was perfectly indifferent to it; that his chief object was by delicate attentions to recommend himself to her and that he should therefore make a point of remaining close to her the whole evening. There was no arguing upon such a project. She owed her greatest relief to her Charlotte, who often joined them, and good-naturedly engaged Mr. Collins's conversation to herself.

She was at least free from the offense of Mr. Darcy's further notice; though often standing within a very short distance of her, quite disengaged, he never came near enough to speak. She felt it to be the probable consequence of her allusions to Mr. Wickham, and rejoiced in it. Less pleasure could be found, however, in Caroline Bingley's continued avoidance of her. She had destroyed any possibility of friendship between them by her lack of discretion, she knew; not that they had ever been likely candidates for true amiability.

The Longbourn party were the last of all the company to depart, and, by a maneuver of Mrs. Bennet, had to wait for their carriage a quarter of an hour after everybody else was gone, which gave them time to see how heartily they were wished away by some of the family. Mrs. Hurst scarcely opened her mouth, except to complain of fatigue, and was evidently impatient to have the house to herself. Caroline stood impassively at her side, neither agreeing with nor negating anything she said. Both sisters repulsed every attempt of Mrs. Bennet at conversation, and by so doing threw a languor over the whole party, which was very little relieved by the long speeches of Mr. Collins, who was complimenting Mr. Bingley and his sisters on the elegance of their entertainment, and the hospitality and politeness which had marked their behaviour to their guests. Darcy, like Caroline, said nothing at all. Mr. Bennet, in equal silence, was enjoying the scene. Mr. Bingley and Jane were standing together, a little detached from the rest, and talked only to each other. Elizabeth preserved as steady a silence as either Caroline or Darcy; and even Lydia was too much fatigued to utter more than the occasional exclamation of "Lord, how tired I am!" accompanied by a violent yawn.

When at length they arose to take leave, Mrs. Bennet was most pressingly civil in her hope of seeing the whole family soon at Longbourn, and addressed herself especially to Mr. Bingley, to assure him how happy he would make them by eating a family dinner with them at any time, without the ceremony of a formal invitation. Bingley was all grateful pleasure, and he readily engaged for taking the earliest opportunity of waiting on her, after his return from London, whither he was obliged to go the next day for a short time.

For her part, Mrs. Bennet was perfectly satisfied, and quitted the house under the delightful persuasion that, allowing for the necessary preparations of settlements, new carriages, and wedding clothes, she should undoubtedly see her daughter settled at Netherfield in the course of three or four months. Of having another daughter married to Mr. Collins, she thought with equal certainty, and with considerable, though not equal, pleasure. Elizabeth was the least dear to her of all her children; and though the man and the match were quite good enough, the worth of each was eclipsed by Mr. Bingley and Netherfield.

CHAPTER NINETEEN

The next day opened a new scene at Longbourn. Mr. Collins made his declaration in form. Having resolved to do it without loss of time, as his leave of absence extended only to the following Saturday, and having no feelings of diffidence to make it distressing to himself even at the moment, he set about it in a very orderly manner, with all the observances, which he supposed a regular part of the business. On finding Mrs. Bennet, Elizabeth, and one of the younger girls together, soon after breakfast, he addressed the mother in these words: "May I hope, Madam, for your interest with your fair daughter Elizabeth, when I solicit for the honour of a private audience with her in the course of this morning?"

Before Elizabeth had time for anything but a blush of surprise, Mrs. Bennet answered instantly, "Oh, dear—yes—certainly. I am sure Lizzy will be very happy—I am sure she can have no objection. Come, Kitty, I want you upstairs." And, gathering her work together, she was hastening away, when Elizabeth called out:

"Dear Madam, do not go. I beg you will not go. Mr. Collins must excuse me. He can have nothing to say to me that anybody need not hear. I am going away myself."

"No, no, nonsense, Lizzy. I desire you to stay where you are." And upon Elizabeth's seeming really, with vexed and embarrassed looks, about to escape, she added: "Lizzy, I insist upon your staying and hearing Mr. Collins."

Elizabeth would not oppose such an injunction—and a moment's consideration making her also sensible that it would be wisest to get it over as soon and as quietly as possible, she sat down again and tried to conceal, by incessant employment, the feelings which were divided between distress and diversion. Mrs. Bennet and Kitty walked off, and as soon as they were gone, Mr. Collins began.

"Believe me, my dear Miss Elizabeth, that your modesty, so far from doing you any disservice, rather adds to your other perfections. You would have been less amiable in my eyes had there not been this little unwillingness; but allow me to assure you, that I have your respected mother's permission for this address. You can hardly doubt the purport of my discourse, however your natural delicacy may lead you to dissemble; my attentions have been too marked to be mistaken. Almost as soon as I entered the house, I singled you out as the companion of my future life. But before I am run away with by my feelings on this subject, perhaps it would be advisable for me to state my reasons for marrying— and, moreover, for coming into Hertfordshire with the design of selecting a wife, as I certainly did."

The idea of Mr. Collins, with all his solemn composure, being run away with by his feelings, made Elizabeth so near laughing, that she could not use the short pause he allowed in any attempt to stop him further, and he continued:

"My reasons for marrying are, first, that I think it a right thing for every clergyman in easy circumstances (like myself) to set the example of matrimony in his parish; secondly, that I am convinced that it will add very greatly to my happiness; and thirdly—which perhaps I ought to have mentioned earlier, that it is the particular advice and recommendation of the very noble lady whom I have the honour of calling patroness. Twice has she condescended to give me her opinion (unasked too!) on this subject; and it was but the very Saturday night before I left Hunsford—between our pools at quadrille, while Mrs. Jenkinson was arranging Miss de Bourgh's footstool, that she said, 'Mr. Collins, you must marry. A clergyman like you must marry. Choose properly, choose a gentlewoman for my sake; and for your own, let her be an active, useful sort of person, not brought up high, but able to make a small income go a good way. This is my advice. Find such a woman as soon as you can, bring her to Hunsford, and I will visit her.' Allow me, by the way, to observe, my fair cousin, that I do not reckon the notice and kindness of Lady Catherine de Bourgh as among the least of the advantages in my power to offer. You will find her manners beyond anything I can describe; and your wit and vivacity, I think, must be acceptable to her, especially when tempered with the silence and respect which her rank will inevitably excite. Thus much for my general intention in favour of matrimony; it remains to be told why my views were directed towards Longbourn instead of my own neighbourhood, where I can assure you there are many amiable young women. But the fact is, that being, as I am, to inherit this estate after the death of your honoured father (who, however, may live many years longer), I could not satisfy myself without resolving to choose a wife from among his daughters, that the loss to them might be as little as possible, when the melancholy event takes place—which, however, as I have already said, may not be for several years. This has been my motive, my fair cousin, and I flatter myself it will not sink me in your esteem. And now nothing remains for me but to assure you in the most animated language of the violence of my affection. To fortune I am perfectly indifferent, and shall make no demand of that nature on your father, since I am well aware that it could not be complied with; and that one thousand pounds in the four per cents, which will not be yours till after your mother's decease, is all that you may ever be entitled to. On that head, therefore, I shall be uniformly silent; and you may assure yourself that no ungenerous reproach shall ever pass my lips when we are married."

It was absolutely necessary to interrupt him now.

"You are too hasty, sir," she said. "You forget that I have made no answer. Let me do it without further loss of time. Accept my thanks for the compliment you are paying me. I am very sensible of the honour of your proposals, but it is impossible for me to do otherwise than to decline them."

"I am not now to learn," replied Mr. Collins, with a formal wave of the hand, "that it is usual with young ladies to reject the addresses of the man whom they secretly mean to accept, when he first applies for their favour; and that sometimes the refusal is repeated a second, or even a third time. I am therefore by no means discouraged by what you have just said, and shall hope to lead you to the altar ere long."

"Upon my word, sir," said Elizabeth, "your hope is a rather extraordinary one after my declaration. I do assure you that I am not one of those young ladies (if such young ladies there are) who are so daring as to risk their happiness on the chance of being asked a second time. I am perfectly serious in my refusal. You could not make me happy, and I am convinced that I am the last woman in the world who could make you so. Nay, were your friend Lady Catherine to know me, I am persuaded she would find me in every respect ill qualified for the situation."

"Were it certain that Lady Catherine would think so," said Mr. Collins very gravely—"but I cannot imagine that her ladyship would at all disapprove of you. And you may be certain when I have the honour of seeing her again, I shall speak in the very highest terms of your modesty, economy, and other amiable qualification."

"Indeed, Mr. Collins, all praise of me will be unnecessary. You must give me leave to judge for myself, and pay me the compliment of believing what I say. I wish you very happy and very rich, and by refusing your hand, do all in my power to prevent your being otherwise. In making me the offer, you must have satisfied the delicacy of your feelings with regard to my family, and may take possession of Longbourn estate whenever it falls, without any self-reproach. This matter may be considered, therefore, as finally settled." And rising as she thus spoke, she would have quitted the room, had Mr. Collins not thus addressed her:

"When I do myself the honour of speaking to you next on the subject, I shall hope to receive a more favourable answer than you have now given me; though I am far from accusing you of cruelty at present, because I know it to be the established custom of your sex to reject a man on the first application, and perhaps you have even now said as much to encourage my suit as would be consistent with the true delicacy of the female character."

"Really, Mr. Collins," said Elizabeth with some warmth, "you puzzle me exceedingly. If what I have hitherto said can appear to you in the form of encouragement, I know not how to express my refusal in such a way as to convince you of its being one."

"You must give me leave to flatter myself, my dear cousin, that your refusal of my addresses is merely words of course. My reasons for believing it are briefly these: It does not appear to me that my hand is unworthy your acceptance, or that the establishment I can offer would be any other than highly desirable. My situation in life, my connections with the family of de Bourgh, and my relationship to your own, are circumstances highly in my favour; and you should take it into further consideration, that in spite of your manifold attractions, it is by no means certain that another offer of marriage may ever be made you. Your portion is unhappily so small that it will in all likelihood undo the effects of your loveliness and amiable qualifications. As I must therefore conclude that you are not serious in your rejection of me, I shall choose to attribute it to your wish of increasing my love by suspense, according to the usual practice of elegant females."

"I do assure you, sir, that I have no pretensions whatever to that kind of elegance which consists in tormenting a respectable man. I would rather be paid the compliment of being believed sincere. I thank you again and again for the honour you have done me in your proposals, but to accept them is absolutely impossible. My feelings in every respect forbid it. Can I speak plainer? Do not consider me now as an elegant female, intending to plague you, but as a rational creature, speaking the truth from her heart."

"You are uniformly charming!" cried he, with an air of awkward gallantry; "and I am persuaded that when sanctioned by the express authority of both your excellent parents, my proposals will not fail of being acceptable."

To such perseverance in willful self-deception Elizabeth would make no reply, and immediately and in silence withdrew; determined, if he persisted in considering her repeated refusals as flattering encouragement, to apply to her father, whose negative might be uttered in such a manner as to be decisive, and whose behaviour at least could not be mistaken for the affectation and coquetry of an elegant female.

CHAPTER TWENTY

M r. Collins was not left long to the silent contemplation of his successful love; for Mrs. Bennet, having dawdled about in the vestibule to watch for the end of the conference, no sooner saw Elizabeth open the door and with quick step pass her towards the staircase, than she entered the breakfast-room, and congratulated both him and herself in warm terms on the happy prospect or their nearer connection. Mr. Collins received and returned these felicitations with equal pleasure, and then proceeded to relate the particulars of their interview, with the result of which he trusted he had every reason to be satisfied, since the refusal which his cousin had steadfastly given him would naturally flow from her bashful modesty and the genuine delicacy of her character.

This information, however, startled Mrs. Bennet; she would have been glad to be equally satisfied that her daughter had meant to encourage him by protesting against his proposals, but she dared not believe it, and could not help saying so.

"But, depend upon it, Mr. Collins," she added, "that Lizzy shall be brought to reason. I will speak to her about it directly. She is a very headstrong, foolish girl, and does not know her own interest, but I will make her know it."

"Pardon me for interrupting you, Madam," cried Mr. Collins; "but if she is really headstrong and foolish, I know not whether she would altogether be a very desirable wife to a man in my situation, who naturally looks for happiness in the marriage state. If therefore she actually persists in rejecting my suit, perhaps it were better not to force her into accepting me, because if liable to such defects of temper, she could not contribute much to my felicity."

"Sir, you quite misunderstand me," said Mrs. Bennet, alarmed. "Lizzy is only headstrong in such matters as these. In everything else she is as good-natured a girl as ever lived. I will go directly to Mr. Bennet, and we shall very soon settle it with her, I am sure."

She would not give him time to reply, but hurrying instantly to her husband, called out as she entered the library, "Oh! Mr. Bennet, you are wanted immediately; we are all in an uproar. You must come and make Lizzy marry Mr. Collins, for she vows she will not have him, and if you do not make haste he will change his mind and not have her."

Mr. Bennet raised his eyes from his book as she entered, and fixed them on her face with a calm unconcern which was not in the least altered by her communication.

"I have not the pleasure of understanding you," said he, when she had finished her speech. "Of what are you talking?"

"Of Mr. Collins and Lizzy. Lizzy declares she will not have Mr. Collins, and Mr. Collins begins to say that he will not have Lizzy."

"And what am I to do on the occasion? It seems a hopeless business."

"Speak to Lizzy about it yourself. Tell her that you insist upon her marrying him."

"Let her be called down. She shall hear my opinion."

Mrs. Bennet rang the bell, and Miss Elizabeth was summoned to the library.

"Come here, child," said her father as she appeared. "I have sent for you on an affair of importance. I understand that Mr. Collins has made you an offer of marriage. Is it true?" Elizabeth replied that it was. "Very well—and this offer of marriage you have refused?"

"I have, sir."

"Very well. We now come to the point. Your mother insists upon your accepting it. Is it not so, Mrs. Bennet?"

"Yes, or I will never see her again."

"An unhappy alternative is before you, Elizabeth. From this day you must be a stranger to one of your parents. Your mother will never see you again if you do not marry Mr. Collins, and I will never see you again if you do."

Elizabeth could not but smile at such a conclusion of such a beginning, but Mrs. Bennet, who had persuaded herself that her husband regarded the affair as she wished, was excessively disappointed.

"What do you mean, Mr. Bennet, in talking this way? You promised me to insist upon her marrying him."

"My dear," replied her husband, "I have two small favours to request. First, that you will allow me the free use of my understanding on the present occasion; and secondly, of my room. I shall be glad to have the library to myself as soon as may be."

Not yet, however, in spite of her disappointment in her husband, did Mrs. Bennet give up the point. She talked to Elizabeth again and again; coaxed and threatened her by turns. She endeavoured to secure Jane in her interest; but Jane, with all possible mildness, declined interfering; and Elizabeth, sometimes with real earnestness, and sometimes with playful gaiety, replied to her attacks. Though her manner varied, however, her determination never did.

Mr. Collins, meanwhile, was meditating in solitude on what had passed. He thought too well of himself to comprehend on what motives his cousin could refuse him; and though his pride was hurt, he suffered in no other way. His regard for her was quite imaginary; and the possibility of her deserving her mother's reproach prevented his feeling any regret.

While the family were in this confusion, Charlotte Lucas came to spend the day with them. She was met in the vestibule by Lydia, who, flying to her, cried in a half whisper, "I am glad you are come, for there is such fun here! What do you think has happened this morning? Mr. Collins has made an offer to Lizzy, and she will not have him."

Charlotte hardly had time to answer, before they were joined by Kitty, who came to tell the same news; and no sooner had they entered the breakfast-room, where Mrs. Bennet was alone, than she likewise began on the subject, calling on Miss Lucas for her compassion, and entreating her to persuade her friend Lizzy to comply with the wishes of all her family. "Pray do, my dear Miss Lucas," she added in a melancholy tone, "for nobody is on my side, nobody takes part with me. I am cruelly used, nobody feels for my poor nerves."

Charlotte's reply was spared by the entrance of Jane and Elizabeth.

"Aye, there she comes," continued Mrs. Bennet, "looking as unconcerned as may be, and caring no more for us than if we were at York, provided she can have her own way. But I tell you, Miss Lizzy—if you take it into your head to go on refusing every offer of marriage in this way, you will never get a husband at all—and I am sure I do not know who is to maintain you when your father is dead. I shall not be able to keep you—and so I warn you. I have done with you from this very day. I told you in the library, you know, that I should never speak to you again, and you will find me as good as my word. I have no pleasure in talking to undutiful children. Not that I have much pleasure, indeed, in talking to anybody. People who suffer as I do from nervous complaints can have no great inclination for talking. Nobody can tell what I suffer! But it is always so. Those who do not complain are never pitied."

Her daughters listened in silence to this effusion, sensible that any attempt to reason with her or soothe her would only increase the irritation. She talked on, therefore, without interruption from any of them, till they were joined by Mr. Collins, who entered the room with an air more stately than usual, and on perceiving whom, she said to the girls, "Now, I do insist upon it, that you, all of you, hold your tongues, and let me and Mr. Collins have a little conversation together."

Elizabeth passed quietly out of the room, Jane and Kitty followed, but Lydia stood her ground, determined to hear all she could; and Charlotte, detained first by the civility of Mr. Collins, whose inquiries after herself and all her family were very minute, and then by not a little curiosity, satisfied herself with walking to the window and pretending not to hear. In a doleful voice Mrs. Bennet began the projected conversation: "Oh! Mr. Collins!"

"My dear madam," replied he, "let us be forever silent on this point. Far be it from me," he presently continued, in a voice that marked his displeasure, "to resent the behaviour of your daughter. Resignation to inevitable evils is the duty of us all; the peculiar duty of a young man who has been so fortunate as I have been in early preferment; and I trust I am resigned. Perhaps not the less so from feeling a doubt of my positive happiness had my fair cousin honoured me with her hand; for I have often observed that resignation is never so perfect as when the blessing denied begins to lose somewhat of its value in our estimation. You will not, I hope, consider me as showing any disrespect to your family, my dear madam, by thus withdrawing my pretensions to your daughter's favour, without having paid yourself and Mr. Bennet the compliment of requesting you to interpose your authority in my behalf.

My conduct may, I fear, be objectionable in having accepted my dismission from your daughter's lips instead of your own. But we are all liable to error. I have certainly meant well through the whole affair. My object has been to secure an amiable companion for myself, with due consideration for the advantage of all your family, and if my manner has been at all reprehensible, I here beg leave to apologise."

CHAPTER TWENTY-ONE

The discussion of Mr. Collins's offer was now nearly at an end, and Elizabeth had only to suffer from the uncomfortable feelings necessarily attending it, and occasionally from some peevish allusions of her mother. As for the gentleman himself, his feelings were chiefly expressed, not by embarrassment or dejection, or by trying to avoid her, but by stiffness of manner and resentful silence. He scarcely ever spoke to her, and the assiduous attentions which he had been so sensible of himself were transferred for the rest of the day to Miss Lucas, whose civility in listening to him was a seasonable relief to them all, and especially to her friend.

The morrow produced no abatement of Mrs. Bennet's ill-humour or ill health. Mr. Collins was also in the same state of angry pride. Elizabeth had hoped that his resentment might shorten his visit, but his plan did not appear in the least affected by it. He was always to have gone on Saturday, and to Saturday he meant to stay.

After breakfast, the girls walked to Meryton to inquire if Mr. Wickham were returned, with Lydia and Kitty lamenting the entire time over his absence from the Netherfield ball. He joined them on their entering the town, and attended them to their aunt's where his regret and vexation, and the concern of everybody, was well talked over. To Elizabeth, however, he voluntarily acknowledged that the necessity of his absence had been self-imposed.

"I found," said he, "as the time drew near that I had better not meet Mr. Darcy; that to be in the same room, the same party with him for so many hours together, might be more than I could bear, and that scenes might arise unpleasant to more than myself."

She approved his forbearance, and they had leisure for a discussion of it, and for the commendation which they civilly bestowed on each other, as Wickham and another officer walked back with them to Longbourn, and during the walk he particularly attended to her. His accompanying them was a double advantage; she felt the compliment it offered to herself, and it was most acceptable as an occasion of introducing him to her father and mother.

Soon after their return, a letter was delivered to Jane; it came from Netherfield. The envelope contained a sheet of elegant, hot-pressed paper, well covered with a lady's fair, flowing hand; and Elizabeth saw her sister's countenance change as she read it, and saw her dwelling intently on some particular passages. Jane recollected herself soon, and putting the letter away, tried to join with her usual cheerfulness in the general conversation; but Elizabeth felt an anxiety on the subject which drew off her attention from their visitors; and no sooner had Wickham and his companion taken leave, than a glance from Jane invited her to follow her upstairs.

When they had gained their own room, Jane, taking out the letter, said: "This is from Caroline Bingley; what it contains has surprised me a good deal. The whole party have left Netherfield by this time, and are on their way to town—and without any intention of coming back again."

"Gone?" repeated Elizabeth. This was not at all the news she had anticipated hearing from the Bingleys.

"Yes. You shall hear what she says."

She then read the first sentence aloud, which comprised the information of their having just resolved to follow their brother to town directly, and of their meaning to dine in Grosvenor Street, where Mr. Hurst had a house. The next was in these words: "I do not pretend to regret many things I shall leave behind in Hertfordshire; but I hope, at some future period, to enjoy many returns of the intercourse we have known, my friend, and in the meanwhile to continue our friendship through regular correspondence."

To these expressions Elizabeth listened without surprise—she had deemed it not unlikely that Caroline would return to London with her friends from the ball. But though her removal did seem sudden, Elizabeth saw nothing in it to seriously disturb Jane. It was not to be supposed that his sisters' absence from Netherfield would prevent Mr.

Bingley's being there; and as to the loss of their society, she was persuaded that Jane must cease to regard it, in the enjoyment of his.

"It is unlucky," said she, after a short pause, "that you should not be able to see your friends before they leave the country. But may we not hope that the period of future happiness to which Miss Bingley looks forward may arrive earlier than she is aware, and that the delightful intercourse you have known as friends will be renewed with yet greater satisfaction as sisters? Mr. Bingley will not be detained in London by them."

"Caroline decidedly says that none of the party will return into Hertfordshire this winter. I will read it to you: 'When my brother left us yesterday, he imagined that the business which took him to London might be concluded in three or four days; but as my sister believes that when Charles gets to town he will be in no hurry to leave it again, we have determined on following him, that he may not be obliged to spend his vacant hours in a hotel. Many of our acquaintances are already there for the winter; I wish I could hear that you, my dear friend, had any intention of making one of the crowd. But if you are unable to do so, I sincerely hope that your Christmas in Hertfordshire may abound in the gaieties which that season generally brings.'

"It is evident by this," added Jane, "that he comes back no more this winter."

"It is only evident that Miss Bingley does not expect that he will."

"You do not know all, Lizzy. I will read you the passage which particularly hurts me. I will have no reserves from you," added she, with emphasis.

Elizabeth felt herself colour at this seeming reference to her own decided lack of alacrity where matters of the heart were concerned.

Jane read: "Louisa and Mr. Darcy are impatient to see his sister; and I must admit, I am also eager to meet her again. I do not know whether I ever before mentioned this subject to you, but I did not want to leave the country without sharing this information: My brother admires Georgiana Darcy greatly, an admiration that I believe neither family would be averse to seeing grow. He will have frequent opportunity now of seeing her on the most intimate footing, and her relations all wish the connection as much as our own do. With all these circumstances to favour an attachment, and nothing to prevent it, am I wrong, my friend, in believing that you would want knowledge in advance of such a possibility?"

Jane stopped reading. "Well, what do you think of this, my dear Lizzy? Is it not clear enough? Does it not expressly declare that Caroline is convinced of her brother's indifference toward me; and that, as she suspects the nature of my feelings for him, she means (most kindly) to put me on my guard? Can there be any other opinion on the subject?"

"Yes, there can; for mine is different. Will you hear it?"

"Most willingly."

"Mr. Bingley's friends see that he is in love with you, but they are committed to his marrying Miss Darcy. Therefore, they are following him to town in hope of keeping him there, and Miss Bingley is writing in an attempt to persuade you that her brother does not care about you." This idea had risen as Jane read, and was now a near certitude in Elizabeth's mind. Miss Bingley, despite the occasional glimpse of interest and solicitude she had allowed Elizabeth, was the conniving, selfish woman she had initially shown herself to be, interested only in lifting the consequence of her family—and herself.

Jane shook her head.

"Indeed, Jane, you ought to believe me. No one who has ever seen you together can doubt his affection. But the case is this: We are not nearly rich enough or grand enough for them; besides which, Miss Bingley may be the more anxious to get Miss Darcy for her brother, from the notion that when there has been one intermarriage, there may be less trouble in achieving a second. But my dearest Jane, you cannot seriously imagine that because Miss Bingley tells you her brother greatly admires Miss Darcy, he is in the smallest degree less sensible of your merit than when he took leave of you on Tuesday, or that it will be in her power to persuade him that, instead of being in love with you, he is very much in love with her friend!"

"If we thought alike of Miss Bingley and the others," replied Jane, "your representation of all this might make me quite easy. But I know the foundation is unjust. They are incapable of willfully deceiving anyone; and all that I can hope in this case is that they are deceived themselves."

"That is right. You could not have started a more happy idea, since you will not take comfort in mine. Believe Mr. Bingley's sisters and Mr.

Darcy to be deceived, by all means. You have now done your duty by them, and must fret no longer."

"But, my dear sister, can I be happy, even supposing the best, in accepting a man whose sisters and friends are all wishing him to marry elsewhere?"

"You must decide for yourself," said Elizabeth; "and if, upon mature deliberation, you find that the misery of disobliging his connections is more than equivalent to the happiness of being his wife, I advise you by all means to refuse him."

"How can you talk so?" said Jane, faintly smiling. "You must know that though I should be exceedingly grieved at their disapprobation, I could not hesitate."

"I did not think you would; and that being the case, I cannot consider your situation with much compassion."

"But if he returns no more this winter, my choice will never be required. A thousand things may arise in six months!"

The idea of his returning no more Elizabeth treated with the utmost contempt. It appeared to her merely the suggestion of the interested wishes of others, and she could not for a moment suppose that those wishes, however openly or artfully spoken, could influence a young man so totally independent of everyone.

She represented to her sister as forcibly as possible what she felt on the subject, and had soon the pleasure of seeing its happy effect. Jane's temper was not desponding, and she was gradually led to hope, though the diffidence of affection sometimes overcame the hope, that Bingley would return to Netherfield and answer every wish of her heart.

"There is one more line you should hear," Jane said, worrying Caroline's letter on her lap. "Shall I read it?"

"Certainly." Elizabeth leaned forward, as something in her sister's manner told her the excerpt was intended for her.

Jane read: "If I may ask a favor of you in return, my friend, it would be to ask your sister Eliza to write to me at Grosvenor Street. If she does not choose to do so, I shall bear her no ill will. I only thought perhaps she matched me in believing our acquaintance yet unfinished."

Here Jane stopped and looked at Elizabeth with searching eyes that found no answer in her younger sister's quickly averted gaze. "Is she right? Is your acquaintance yet unfinished?"

Even if Elizabeth had thought to match Caroline's sentiments, she could not imagine caring to do so now. Caroline clearly afforded little regard for Jane, if she could set her aside so easily; the disgust she evidently bore toward Jane's connections, she must feel equally toward Elizabeth's, as they were the same. "No," answered she. "In fact, I can say in truth that I have no interest in forwarding any sort of relationship with Caroline Bingley."

"Oh, Lizzy," said Jane, "is it not high time you placed your trust in me?"

Elizabeth coloured, and stared, but did not answer.

"You know I love you best," added Jane warmly, "and wish for your happiness even more sincerely than my own."

This, Elizabeth knew, was entirely accurate. But would her sister continue to love her if she knew all? "To what, exactly, do you refer?"

"I would think it obvious," said Jane, folding the letter where it lay on her lap.

"Even if it were, I am not sure I would know where to begin."

"With Charlotte Lucas, perhaps?"

Elizabeth started. She had not expected shy Jane, sweet Jane, to challenge her so directly. Clearly her sister had no intention of leaving the matter be. With this realization, she began, haltingly, to tell Jane everything she had worked over the last few years to hide—how Charlotte had become increasingly important to her, and she to Charlotte; how their innocent friendship had slowly evolved into something else; how each had worried that there was something wrong with them before finally deciding that love could never be wrong, not even a love such as their own.

"On that count, I must agree with you," said Jane, leaning her head against Elizabeth's shoulder as they sat together on the bed. "I am so happy that you finally told me, dear Lizzy. How it has pained me to think of you alone with a secret of this magnitude!"

"How long have you known?"

"Since the summer, when I spied the two of you having a picnic by the lake. You believed you were quite on your own."

Elizabeth blanched, thinking how fortunate they were that it had been Jane who had discovered them, and not either of their mothers; or, worse, someone entirely unconnected to either family. And yet, the event they had always most feared had happened, and neither of them had even known it. Jane had not gone to their parents, or to the parish priest; Elizabeth and Charlotte had not been arrested or placed in the stocks, as habitually happened to men of their disposition. Life had continued on, mostly unaffected, except that Jane had known all these months that Elizabeth was lying to her by omitting to include her, in what might be considered the most important aspect of her daily life.

"You have told me of Charlotte, Lizzy, but what of Caroline Bingley?"

Elizabeth frowned. "There is nothing to tell."

"I thought for certain you disliked Caroline, at the outset."

"I did. I do."

"Do you? I rather thought she became somewhat less detestable, in your opinion, during our stay at Netherfield."

Elizabeth tossed her head. "Be that as it may, rest assured that I have no intention of writing to her."

"I beg of you, do not allow your conjectures of Caroline's attitude toward me, to affect your opinion of her. She is not all what she appears on the surface, you know; no more than you are."

"Nonsense, I am exactly the same person."

"I love you, Lizzy. Never worry yourself on that account, understood?"

"Understood. Thank you, Jane. A thousand times, thank you."

"You do not need to thank me, dear sister."

"Ah, but that is where you are wrong," said Elizabeth, thinking of the tension she had observed between Caroline and her ever-watchful elder sister.

After a pause, they returned to the letter, and discussed in earnest the dissemination of certain parts. They agreed that Mrs. Bennet should only hear of the departure of the family, without being alarmed on the score of the gentleman's conduct; but even this partial communication gave her a great deal of concern that evening, and she bewailed it as exceedingly unlucky that the ladies should happen to go away just as they were all getting so intimate together. At this comment, Jane sent Elizabeth such an uncharacteristically wicked look that she nearly choked on her dinner roll. Mr. Bennet noticed this exchange, and was intrigued. Mrs. Bennet, however, missed it entirely. After lamenting the loss of Mr.

Bingley's sisters at some length, she had the consolation that Mr. Bingley himself would be soon down again and soon dining at Longbourn, and the conclusion of all was the comfortable declaration, that though he had been invited only to a family dinner, she would take care to have two full courses.

CHAPTER TWENTY-TWO

T he Bennets were engaged to dine with the Lucases, and again during the chief of the day was Miss Lucas so kind as to listen to Mr. Collins. Elizabeth took an opportunity of thanking her. "It keeps him in good humour," said she, "and I am more obliged to you than I can express."

Charlotte assured her friend of her satisfaction in being useful, and that it amply repaid her for the little sacrifice of her time. This was very amiable, but Charlotte's kindness extended farther than Elizabeth had any conception of; its object was nothing else than to secure her from any return of Mr. Collins's addresses, by engaging them towards herself. Such was Miss Lucas's scheme; and appearances were so favourable, that when they parted at night, she would have felt almost secure of success if he had not been to leave Hertfordshire so very soon. But here she did injustice to the fire and independence of his character, for it led him to escape out of Longbourn House the next morning with admirable slyness, and hasten to Lucas Lodge to throw himself at her feet. He was anxious to avoid the notice of his cousins, from a conviction that if they saw him depart, they could not fail to conjecture his design, and he was not willing to have the attempt known till its success might be known likewise; for though feeling almost secure, and with reason, for Charlotte had been tolerably encouraging, he was comparatively diffident since the adventure of Wednesday. His reception, however, was of the most flattering kind. Miss Lucas perceived him from an upper window as he walked towards the house, and instantly set out to meet him accidentally in the lane. But little had she dared to hope that so much eloquence awaited her there.

In as short a time as Mr. Collins's long speeches would allow, everything was settled between them to the satisfaction of both; and as they entered the house he earnestly entreated her to name the day that was to make him the happiest of men; and though such a solicitation must be waived for the present, the lady felt no inclination to trifle with his happiness. The stupidity with which he was favoured by nature must guard his courtship from any charm that could make a woman wish for its continuance; and Miss Lucas, who accepted him solely from the pure and disinterested desire of an establishment, cared not how soon that establishment were gained. She had been content to let circumstances unfurl as they might, these past several years; but Mr. Collins had provided a most timely vehicle for her removal from Lucas Lodge and Hertfordshire. Aware that Mr. Collins was on the search for a wife, and knowing too that he would one day inherit Longbourn, where she had passed so many pleasant days and nights, Charlotte had set about directly to win his affection. Never had she supposed it would be so easy, nor so quick.

Sir William and Lady Lucas were speedily applied to for their consent; and it was bestowed with a most joyful alacrity. Mr. Collins's present circumstances made it a most eligible match for their daughter, to whom they could give little fortune; and his prospects of future wealth were exceedingly fair. Lady Lucas began directly to calculate, with more interest than the matter had ever excited before, how many years longer Mr. Bennet was likely to live; and Sir William gave it as his decided opinion, that whenever Mr. Collins should be in possession of the Longbourn estate, it would be highly expedient that both he and his wife should make their appearance at St. James's. The whole family, in short, was properly overjoyed on the occasion. The younger girls formed hopes of coming out a year or two sooner than they might otherwise have done; and the boys were relieved from their apprehension of Charlotte's dying an old maid. Charlotte herself was tolerably composed. She had gained her point, and had time to consider of it. Her reflections were in general satisfactory. Mr. Collins, to be sure, was neither sensible nor agreeable; his society was irksome, and his attachment to her must be imaginary. But still he would be her husband.

Without thinking highly either of men or matrimony, marriage had always been her object; it was the only provision for well-educated young women of small fortune, and however uncertain of giving happiness, must be their pleasantest preservative from want. This preservative she had now obtained; and at the age of twenty-five, she felt all the good luck of it. She had always believed that what Elizabeth and she shared was not a type of attachment that could survive outside their narrow domestic felicity. Still, the least agreeable circumstance in the business at hand was the disappointment it must occasion to Elizabeth, whose friendship she valued beyond that of any other person. Elizabeth would wonder, and probably would blame her for betraying their secret attachment; and though her resolution was not to be shaken, Charlotte's feelings must be hurt by such a disapprobation. She resolved to give Elizabeth the information herself, and therefore charged Mr. Collins, when he returned to Longbourn to dinner, to drop no hint of what had passed before any of the family. A promise of secrecy was of course very dutifully given, but it could not be kept without difficulty; for the curiosity excited by his long absence burst forth in such very direct questions on his return as required some ingenuity to evade, and he was at the same time exercising great self-denial, for he was longing to publish his prosperous love.

As he was to begin his journey too early on the morrow to see any of the family, the ceremony of leave-taking was performed when the ladies moved for the night; and Mrs. Bennet, with great politeness and cordiality, said how happy they should be to see him at Longbourn again, whenever his engagements might allow him to visit them.

"My dear madam," he replied, "this invitation is particularly gratifying, because it is what I have been hoping to receive; and you may be very certain that I shall avail myself of it as soon as possible."

They were all astonished; and Mr. Bennet, who could by no means wish for so speedy a return, immediately said: "But is there not danger of Lady Catherine's disapprobation here, my good sir? You had better neglect your relations than run the risk of offending your patroness."

"My dear sir," replied Mr. Collins, "I am particularly obliged to you for this friendly caution, and you may depend upon my not taking so material a step without her ladyship's concurrence."

"You cannot be too much upon your guard. Risk anything rather than her displeasure; and if you find it likely to be raised by your coming to us again, which I should think exceedingly probable, stay quietly at home, and be satisfied that we shall take no offence."

"Believe me, my dear sir, my gratitude is warmly excited by such affectionate attention; and depend upon it, you will speedily receive from me a letter of thanks for this, and for every other mark of your regard during my stay in Hertfordshire. As for my fair cousins, though my absence may not be long enough to render it necessary, I shall now take the liberty of wishing them health and happiness, not excepting my cousin Elizabeth."

With proper civilities the ladies then withdrew; all of them equally surprised that he meditated a quick return. Mrs. Bennet wished to understand by it that he thought of paying his addresses to one of her younger girls, and Mary might have been prevailed on to accept him. She rated his abilities much higher than any of the others; there was a solidity in his reflections which often struck her, and though by no means so clever as herself, she thought that if encouraged to read and improve himself by such an example as hers, he might become a very agreeable companion. But on the following morning, every hope of this kind was done away. Miss Lucas called soon after breakfast, and in a private conference with Elizabeth related the event of the day before.

The possibility of Mr. Collins's fancying himself in love with her friend had once occurred to Elizabeth within the last day or two; but that Charlotte could encourage him seemed almost as far from possibility as she could encourage him herself, and her astonishment and hurt were consequently so great that she could not help crying out: "Engaged to Mr. Collins! My dear Charlotte—impossible!"

The steady countenance which Miss Lucas had commanded in telling her story, gave way to a momentary confusion here on receiving so direct a reproach; though, as it was no more than she had expected, she soon regained her composure, and calmly replied: "Why should you be surprised, my dear Lizzy? Do you think it incredible that Mr. Collins should be able to procure any woman's good opinion, because he was not so happy as to succeed with you?"

"Not any woman's, Charlotte, but yours," said Elizabeth with not a little passion. Rising, she paced to the window. "Why ever would you do such a thing?"

"As I told you before, Lizzy, I believe marriage to be not only a woman's duty but her fate, whether there be love in the match or not.

You have always known that I wanted a home of my own, and children, should God see fit to bestow them."

This much was true. And yet, Elizabeth had never imagined that Charlotte was capable of such cool calculation toward an object of which she herself knew nothing; an end that would result in their certain separation. "But this means we will see no more of each other."

"Perhaps not exactly as we have done, but I will always be your friend, Lizzy, and you mine. Will you not?"

Elizabeth hardly knew how to answer this question. Could she remain Charlotte's stalwart friend, even as she watched her marry another? And yet, she could not imagine losing Charlotte entirely. While the distance between Hertfordshire and Hunsford was considerable, it was not insurmountable. What felt more insupportable by far was the detachment of affection Charlotte's actions had effectively occasioned.

"But Mr. Collins, of all people," said Elizabeth at last.

"Would you not rather have me as Longbourn's mistress, than some cold, unfeeling stranger? Lizzy, don't you see? I had to do this."

Elizabeth shook her head. "I see nothing of the sort."

"Come, now. What we have shared together has been lovely, the most pleasant, in fact, of idylls—in its own time. But you cannot pretend that it would have been enough, in the end."

Elizabeth sighed. "I wish it could have been."

"As do I. But you will see, Lizzy, this is truly the best possible course. This way, we will always be connected."

Elizabeth flung herself into Charlotte's willing arms, and the two friends embraced for some time, not a few tears shed between them. Finally Elizabeth recollected herself, and making a strong effort for it, was able to assure with tolerable sincerity that she wished Charlotte all imaginable happiness in her upcoming marriage.

"I see what you are feeling," replied Charlotte, brushing Elizabeth's hair back from her cheek. "But when you have had time to think it over, I hope you will be satisfied with what I have done. I am not sentimental like you, you know; I never was. I ask only a comfortable home; and considering Mr. Collins's character, connection, and situation in life, I am convinced that my chance of happiness with him is as fair as most people can boast on entering the marriage state."

Elizabeth quietly answered, "Undoubtedly;" and after an awkward pause, they returned to the rest of the family.

Charlotte did not stay much longer, and Elizabeth was then left to reflect on what she had heard. It would be a long time before she could become at all reconciled to the idea of so unsuitable a match. The strangeness of Mr. Collins's making two offers of marriage within three days was nothing in comparison of his being now accepted. She had always known that Charlotte's opinion of matrimony was somewhat more practical than her own, but she had not supposed it to be possible that, when called into action, she would sacrifice every better feeling to worldly advantage. Charlotte as the wife of Mr. Collins was a most distressing picture! To the pang of personal betrayal and lost esteem, was added the firm conviction that it would be impossible for her friend to ever be even tolerably happy in the lot she had chosen.

CHAPTER TWENTY-THREE

Elizabeth was sitting with her mother and sisters, reflecting on what she had heard, and doubting whether she was authorised to mention it, when Sir William Lucas himself appeared, sent by his daughter, to announce her engagement to the family. With many compliments to them, and much self-congratulation on the prospect of a connection between the houses, he unfolded the matter—to an audience not merely wondering, but incredulous; for Mrs. Bennet, with more perseverance than politeness, protested he must be entirely mistaken; and Lydia, always unguarded and often uncivil, boisterously exclaimed: "Good Lord! Sir William, how can you tell such a story? Do not you know that Mr. Collins wants to marry Lizzy?"

Nothing less than the complaisance of a courtier could have borne without anger such treatment; but Sir William's good breeding carried him through it all; and though he begged leave to be positive as to the truth of his information, he listened to all their impertinence with the most forbearing courtesy.

Elizabeth, feeling it incumbent on her to relieve him from so unpleasant a situation, now put herself forward to confirm his account, by mentioning her prior knowledge of it from Charlotte herself; and endeavoured to put a stop to the exclamations of her mother and sisters by the earnestness of her congratulations to Sir William, in which she was readily joined after a moment's hesitation by Jane, and by making a variety of remarks on the happiness that might be expected from the match, the excellent character of Mr. Collins, and the convenient distance of Hunsford from London.

Mrs. Bennet was in fact too much overpowered to say a great deal while Sir William remained; but no sooner had he left them than her feelings found a rapid vent. In the first place, she persisted in disbelieving the whole of the matter; secondly, she was very sure that Mr. Collins had been taken in; thirdly, she trusted that they would never be happy together; and fourthly, that the match might be broken off. Two inferences, however, were plainly deduced from the whole: one, that Elizabeth was the real cause of the mischief; and the other that she herself had been barbarously misused by them all; and on these two points she principally dwelt during the rest of the day. Nothing could console and nothing could appease her. Nor did that day wear out her resentment. A week elapsed before she could see Elizabeth without scolding her, a month passed away before she could speak to Sir William or Lady Lucas without being rude, and many months were gone before she could at all forgive their daughter.

Mr. Bennet's emotions were much more tranquil on the occasion, and such as he did experience he pronounced to be of a most agreeable sort; for it gratified him, he said, to discover that Charlotte Lucas, whom he had been used to think tolerably sensible, was as foolish as his wife, and more foolish than his daughter. Indeed, he was in fact gratified; for if he were not mistaken, Miss Lucas had just done Elizabeth the favor of removing herself as a competitor for Lizzy's affections, thereby clearing the way for a future, better-suited match. Charlotte Lucas was neither Lizzy's equal in beauty nor spirit, and Mr. Bennet hoped his favourite daughter would someday meet one who matched her in both.

Kitty and Lydia were far from envying Miss Lucas, for Mr. Collins was only a clergyman; and it affected them in no other way than as a piece of news to spread at Meryton. Jane confessed herself a little surprised at the match; but she said less of her astonishment than of her earnest desire for their happiness. Taking advantage of a brief pause in Mrs. Bennet's remonstrations on the subject, however, she added: "Lizzy, come upstairs with me, will you? I believe I have an idea for a new dress, and I would have your opinion."

Knowing well what was coming, Elizabeth followed Jane up to their room, where she threw herself on the bed and poured out her distress, while Jane held her hand and listened attentively.

"I simply cannot believe she would scheme so behind my back!"

"Perhaps it was not so much scheming as it was protecting your feelings, for she had to have been aware how uncommonly painful such a match would be to you."

"I hardly think my feelings were uppermost in her mind, Jane. Charlotte sees Mr. Collins as her best chance at worldly success."

"And is she wrong?"

"I do not care about right or wrong!" cried Elizabeth. And then, rubbing her eyes: "But she is likely perfectly justified."

"Does her desire to be married come as a surprise to you?"

"No, of course not. She has always wanted a house and a family of her own, on that she was quite clear."

"And you? Do you long for a house and a family to call your own?"

"Honestly? I much prefer a woman's company, Jane, I truly do. But I cannot imagine life without children. Unless, of course, I were to end up with miniature versions of Lydia and Mary, and then I should be most happy to remain barren."

"I see your wit at the expense of others has recovered."

"My best trait, is it not?"

"I would not say so, no."

"Oh, Jane," said Elizabeth, laying her cheek against her sister's shoulder. "Why does she not love me?"

"She loves you, I have seen it in her countenance. Perhaps she is just not as brave as you would have her be, Lizzy. For in order for such an attachment to endure, with all the world arrayed in opposition, it would have to be a powerfully brave love, I would imagine."

Briefly, Elizabeth found herself picturing Caroline Bingley, another woman such as she and Charlotte. During their first few meetings, Caroline had demonstrated a vexing conformity to the dictates of polite society; but on subsequent occasions, her willingness to trespass against what man deemed as natural and right had become increasingly apparent. Unfortunate that she had proven quite as willing to trample upon Jane's friendship—Elizabeth should have liked to have another friend such as herself; had the situation been different, she might even have written to Caroline in London. But as it was, the recollection of Caroline Bingley's character could not offer her any relief from her present agitation.

With Charlotte's engagement now public knowledge, Lady Lucas could not be insensible of triumph on being able to retort on Mrs. Bennet the comfort of having a daughter well married; and she called at Longbourn rather oftener than usual to say how happy she was, though

Mrs. Bennet's sour looks and ill-natured remarks might have been enough to drive happiness away.

Between Elizabeth and Charlotte there was a restraint which kept them mutually silent on the subject; and Elizabeth felt persuaded that no real confidence could ever subsist between them again. Her disappointment in Charlotte made her turn with fonder regard to her sister, of whose rectitude and delicacy she was sure her opinion could never be shaken, and for whose happiness she grew daily more anxious, as Bingley had now been gone a week and nothing more was heard of his return.

Jane had sent Miss Bingley an early answer to her letter, and was counting the days till she might reasonably hope to hear again. The promised letter of thanks from Mr. Collins arrived on Tuesday, addressed to their father, and written with all the solemnity of gratitude which a twelvemonth's abode in the family might have prompted. After discharging his conscience on that head, he proceeded to inform them, with many rapturous expressions, of his happiness in having obtained the affection of their amiable neighbour, Miss Lucas, and then explained that it was merely with the view of enjoying her society that he had been so ready to close with their kind wish of seeing him again at Longbourn, whither he hoped to be able to return on Monday fortnight; for Lady Catherine, he added, so heartily approved his marriage, that she wished it to take place as soon as possible, which he trusted would be an unanswerable argument with his amiable Charlotte to name an early day for making him the happiest of men.

Mr. Collins's return into Hertfordshire was no longer a matter of pleasure to Mrs. Bennet. On the contrary, she was as much disposed to complain of it as her husband. It was very strange that he should come to Longbourn instead of to Lucas Lodge; it was also very inconvenient and exceedingly troublesome. She hated having visitors in the house while her health was so indifferent, and lovers were of all people the most disagreeable. Such were the gentle murmurs of Mrs. Bennet, and they gave way only to the greater distress of Mr. Bingley's continued absence.

Neither Jane nor Elizabeth were comfortable on this subject. Day after day passed away without bringing any other tidings of him or his sister than the report which shortly prevailed in Meryton of their coming no more to Netherfield the whole winter; a report which highly incensed

Mrs. Bennet, and which she never failed to contradict as a most scandalous falsehood.

Even Elizabeth began to fear—not that Bingley was indifferent—but that his friends would be successful in keeping him away. Unwilling as she was to admit an idea so destructive of Jane's happiness, and so dishonorable to the stability of her lover, she could not prevent its frequently occurring. The united efforts of his determined sisters and of his overpowering friend, assisted by the attractions of Miss Darcy and the amusements of London, might be too much, she feared, for the strength of his attachment. A method of satisfying herself, and Jane, on this account, occurred at last to Elizabeth. After some consideration, she steeled herself to the task, and wrote a short letter to Caroline Bingley in which she inquired after the lady's plans—and those of her brother— with regard to Netherfield. As soon as she posted the letter, she regretted its existence. But there was nothing left to do but wait for an answer.

As for Jane, her anxiety under this suspense was, of course, more painful than Elizabeth's; but whatever she felt she was desirous of concealing, and between herself and Elizabeth, therefore, the subject was never alluded to. But as no such delicacy restrained their mother, an hour seldom passed in which she did not talk of Bingley, express her impatience for his arrival, or even require Jane to confess that if he did not come back she would think herself very ill used. It needed all Jane's steady mildness to bear these attacks with tolerable tranquility.

Mr. Collins returned most punctually on Monday fortnight, but his reception at Longbourn was not quite so gracious as it had been on his first introduction. He was too happy, however, to need much attention; and luckily for the others, the business of love-making relieved them from a great deal of his company. The chief of every day was spent by him at Lucas Lodge, and he sometimes returned to Longbourn only in time to make an apology for his absence before the family went to bed.

Mrs. Bennet was really in a most pitiable state. The very mention of anything concerning the match threw her into an agony of ill-humour, and wherever she went she was sure of hearing it talked of. The sight of Miss Lucas was odious to her. As her successor in that house, she regarded her with jealous abhorrence. Whenever Charlotte came to see them, she concluded her to be anticipating the hour of possession; and whenever she spoke in a low voice to Mr. Collins, was convinced that they were talking of the Longbourn estate, and resolving to turn herself and her daughters out of the house, as soon as Mr. Bennet were dead. She complained bitterly of all this to her husband.

"Indeed, Mr. Bennet," said she, "it is very hard to think that Charlotte Lucas should ever be mistress of this house, that I should be forced to make way for her, and live to see her take her place in it!"

"My dear, do not give way to such gloomy thoughts. Let us hope for better things. Let us flatter ourselves that I may be the survivor."

This was not very consoling to Mrs. Bennet, and therefore, instead of making any answer, she went on as before.

"I cannot bear to think that they should have all this estate. If it was not for the entail, I should not mind it."

"What should not you mind?"

"I should not mind anything at all."

"Let us be thankful that you are preserved from a state of such insensibility."

"I never can be thankful, Mr. Bennet, for anything about the entail. How anyone could have the conscience to entail away an estate from one's own daughters, I cannot understand; and all for the sake of Mr. Collins too! Why should he have it more than anybody else?"

"I leave it to yourself to determine," said Mr. Bennet.

CHAPTER TWENTY-FOUR

aroline's letter, addressed to Jane, finally arrived, and put an end to doubt. The very first sentence conveyed the assurance of their being all settled in London for the winter, and concluded with her brother's regret at not having had time to pay his respects to his friends in Hertfordshire before he left the country.

Hope was over, entirely over; and when Jane could attend to the rest of the letter, she found little, except the professed affection of the writer, that could give her any comfort. Miss Darcy had been spending a good deal of time with Mr. Bingley, as had been predicted in Caroline's previous letter, and the gentleman was in fact currently an inmate of Mr. Darcy's house. The letter did not, however, reference Elizabeth's message, nor did it refer to her at all except indirectly, in a general wish that Jane might convey the writer's greetings to her family.

Elizabeth, to whom Jane communicated all of this, heard it in silent indignation. Her heart was divided between concern for her sister, and resentment against all others. That Bingley was really fond of Jane, she doubted no more than she had ever done; and much as she had always been disposed to like him, she could not think without anger, hardly without contempt, on that easiness of temper, that want of proper resolution, which now made him the slave of his designing friends, and led him to sacrifice his own happiness to the caprice of their inclination. Had his own happiness, however, been the only sacrifice, he might have been allowed to sport with it in whatever manner he thought best, but her sister's was involved in it, as she thought he must recognise. This fact, in concert with Caroline's neglect of her letter, notably diminished Elizabeth's already low estimation of the Bingleys. Unfortunately, she could think of little else; and yet whether Bingley's regard for Jane had really died away, or was suppressed by his friends' interference; whether he had been aware of Jane's attachment, or whether it had escaped his observation; whether Caroline had any design of writing back to her, or not; whatever was the case, though her opinion of the Bingleys must be materially affected by the difference, her sister's situation remained the same, her peace equally wounded.

A day or two passed before Jane had opportunity to speak of her feelings to Elizabeth; but at last, on Mrs. Bennet's leaving them together, after a longer irritation than usual about Netherfield and its master, Jane could not help saying: "Oh, that my dear mother had more command over herself! She can have no idea of the pain she gives me by her continual reflections on him. But I will not repine. It cannot last long. He will be forgot, and we shall all be as we were before."

Elizabeth looked at her sister with incredulous solicitude, but said nothing.

"You doubt me," said Jane, slightly colouring; "indeed, you have no reason. He may live in my memory as the most amiable man of my acquaintance, but that is all. I have nothing either to hope or fear, and nothing to reproach him with. Thank God! I have not that pain. A little time, therefore—I shall certainly try to get the better." With a stronger voice she soon added, "I have this comfort immediately, that it has not been more than an error of fancy on my side, and that it has done no harm to anyone but myself."

"My dear Jane," exclaimed Elizabeth, "you are too good. Your sweetness and disinterestedness are really angelic; I do not know what to say to you. I feel as if I had never done you justice, or loved you as you deserve."

Miss Bennet eagerly disclaimed all extraordinary merit, and threw back the praise on her sister's warm affection.

"Nay," said Elizabeth, "this is not fair. You wish to think all the world respectable, and are hurt if I speak ill of anybody. I only want to think *you* perfect, and you set yourself against it. Do not be afraid of my running into any excess, of my encroaching on your privilege of universal good-will. You need not. There are few people whom I really love, and still fewer of whom I think well. The more I see of the world, the more am I dissatisfied with it; and every day confirms my belief of the inconsistency of all human characters, and of the little dependence that can be placed on the appearance of merit or sense. I have met with two instances lately, one I will not mention; the other is Charlotte's marriage. It is unaccountable! In every view it is unaccountable!"

"My dear Lizzy, do not give way to such feelings as these. They will ruin your happiness. You do not make allowance enough for difference of situation and temper. Consider Mr. Collins's respectability, and Charlotte's steady, prudent character. Remember that she is one of a large family; that as to fortune, it is a most eligible match; and be ready to believe, for everybody's sake, that she may feel something like regard and esteem for our cousin."

"To oblige you, I would try to believe almost anything, but no one else could be benefited by such a belief as this; for were I persuaded that Charlotte had any regard for him, I should only think worse of her understanding than I now do of her heart. My dear Jane, Mr. Collins is a conceited, pompous, narrow-minded, silly man; you know he is, as well as I do; and you must feel, as well as I do, that the woman who married him cannot have a proper way of thinking. You shall not defend her, though it is Charlotte Lucas. You shall not, for the sake of one individual, change the meaning of principle and integrity, nor endeavour to persuade yourself or me, that selfishness is prudence, and insensibility of danger security for happiness."

"I must think your language too strong in speaking of both," replied Jane. "But enough of this. You alluded to something else. You mentioned two instances. I entreat you, dear Lizzy, not to pain me by saying your opinion of *that person* is sunk. We must not be so ready to fancy ourselves intentionally injured. We must not expect a lively young man to be always so guarded and circumspect. It is very often nothing but our own vanity that deceives us. Women fancy admiration means more than it does."

"And men take care that they should."

"If it is designedly done, they cannot be justified; but I have no idea of there being so much design in the world as some persons imagine."

"I am far from attributing any part of Mr. Bingley's conduct to design," said Elizabeth; "but without scheming to do wrong, or to make others unhappy, there may be error, and there may be misery. Thoughtlessness, want of attention to other people's feelings, and want of resolution will do the business."

"And do you impute it to either of those?"

"Yes; to the last. But if I go on, I shall displease you by saying what I think of persons you esteem. Stop me whilst you can."

"You persist, then, in supposing his sisters influence him?"

"Yes, in conjunction with his friend. Miss Bingley and Mrs. Hurst have proven themselves to be arrogant and prideful, nearly as much so as Mr. Darcy."

"I am sure I do not agree with you. Why should they try to influence him? They can only wish his happiness; and if he is attached to me, no other woman can secure it."

"Your first position is false. They may wish many things besides his happiness; they may wish his increase of wealth and consequence; they may wish him to marry a girl who has all the importance of money, great connections, and pride."

"Beyond a doubt, they do wish him to choose Miss Darcy," replied Jane; "but this may be from better feelings than you are supposing. They have known her much longer than they have known me; no wonder if they love her better. But, whatever may be their own wishes, it is very unlikely they should have opposed their brother's. What sister would think herself at liberty to do it, unless there were something very objectionable? If they believed him attached to me, they would not try to part us; if he were so, they could not succeed. By presuming such an affection, you make everybody acting unnaturally and wrong, and me most unhappy. Do not distress me by the idea. I am not ashamed of having been mistaken—or, at least, it is light, it is nothing in comparison of what I should feel in thinking ill of him or his sisters. Let me take it in the best light, in the light in which it may be understood."

Elizabeth could not oppose such a wish; and from this time the Bingley name was scarcely ever mentioned between them.

Mrs. Bennet still continued to wonder and repine at his returning no more, and though a day seldom passed in which Elizabeth did not account for it clearly, there was little chance of her ever considering it with less perplexity. Her daughter endeavoured to convince her of what she did not believe herself, that his attentions to Jane had been merely the effect of a common and transient liking, which ceased when he saw her no more; but though the probability of the statement was admitted at the time, she had the same story to repeat every day. Mrs. Bennet's best comfort was that Mr. Bingley must be down again in the summer.

Mr. Bennet treated the matter differently. "So, Lizzy," said he one day, "your sister is crossed in love, I find. I congratulate her. Next to being married, a girl likes to be crossed a little in love now and then. It is something to think of, and it gives her a sort of distinction among her companions. When is your turn to come? You will hardly bear to be long outdone by Jane. Now is your time. Here are officers enough in Meryton to disappoint all the young ladies in the country. That Wickham is a pleasant enough fellow, and would jilt you creditably."

"Thank you, sir, but we must not all expect Jane's good fortune."

"True," said Mr. Bennet, "but it is a comfort to think that whatever of that kind may befall you, you have an affectionate mother who will make the most of it." He paused. "Then you are happy, Lizzy? You are not recently crossed in love yourself?"

Elizabeth looked at him quickly, thinking of Charlotte; but her father had as usual a book in one hand and appeared to be perusing it, with only half his attention reserved for her. "I am as happy, sir, as the situation warrants."

Nodding, he turned his full attention back to his book. Literature, he found, allowed far easier interaction than most people did—even those individuals he loved as much as he did his second eldest daughter.

Mr. Wickham's society was of material service in dispelling the gloom which the late perverse occurrences had thrown on many of the Longbourn family. They saw him often, and to his other recommendations was now added that of general unreserve. The whole of what Elizabeth had already heard, his claims on Mr. Darcy, and all that he had suffered from him, was now openly acknowledged and publicly canvassed; and everybody was pleased to know how much they had always disliked Mr. Darcy before they had known anything of the matter.

Jane was the only creature who could suppose there might be any extenuating circumstances in the case, unknown to the society of Hertfordshire; her mild and steady candour always pleaded for allowances, and urged the possibility of mistakes—but by everybody else Mr. Darcy was condemned as the worst of men. Elizabeth silently added Caroline Bingley's name to his. She would be just as happy never to see the pair of them, she was quite certain, again.

CHAPTER TWENTY-FIVE

After a week spent in professions of love and schemes of felicity, Mr. Collins was called from his amiable Charlotte by the arrival of Saturday. The pain of separation, however, might be alleviated on his side, by preparations for the reception of his bride; as he had reason to hope, that shortly after his return into Hertfordshire, the day would be fixed that was to make him the happiest of men. He took leave of his relations at Longbourn with as much solemnity as before; wished his fair cousins health and happiness again, and promised their father another letter of thanks.

On the following Monday, Mrs. Bennet had the pleasure of receiving her brother and his wife, who came as usual to spend the Christmas at Longbourn. Mr. Gardiner was a sensible, gentlemanlike man, greatly superior to his sister, as well by nature as education. The Netherfield ladies would have had difficulty in believing that a man who lived by trade, and within view of his own warehouses, could have been so well-bred and agreeable. Mrs. Gardiner, who was several years younger than Mrs. Bennet and Mrs. Phillips, was an amiable, intelligent, elegant woman, and a great favourite with all her Longbourn nieces. Between the two eldest and herself especially, there subsisted a particular regard. They had frequently been staying with her in town.

The first part of Mrs. Gardiner's business on her arrival was to distribute her presents and describe the newest fashions. When this was done she had a less active part to play. It became her turn to listen. Mrs. Bennet had many grievances to relate, and much to complain of. They had all been very ill-used since she last saw her sister. Two of her girls had been upon the point of marriage, and after all there was nothing in it.

"I do not blame Jane," she continued, "for Jane would have got Mr. Bingley if she could. But Lizzy! Oh, sister! It is very hard to think that she might have been Mr. Collins's wife by this time, had it not been for her own perverseness. He made her an offer in this very room, and she refused him. The consequence of it is, that Lady Lucas will have a daughter married before I have, and that the Longbourn estate is just as much entailed as ever. The Lucases are very artful people indeed, sister. They are all for what they can get. I am sorry to say it of them, but so it is. It makes me very nervous and poorly, to be thwarted so in my own family, and to have neighbours who think of themselves before anybody else. However, your coming just at this time is the greatest of comforts, and I am very glad to hear what you tell us, of long sleeves."

Mrs. Gardiner, to whom the chief of this news had been given before, in the course of Jane and Elizabeth's correspondence with her, made her sister a slight answer, and, in compassion to her nieces, turned the conversation.

When alone with Elizabeth afterwards, she spoke more on the subject. "It seems likely to have been a desirable match for Jane," said she. "I am sorry it went off. But these things happen so often! A young man, such as you describe Mr. Bingley, so easily falls in love with a pretty girl for a few weeks, and when accident separates them, so easily forgets her, that these sorts of inconsistencies are very frequent."

"An excellent consolation in its way," said Elizabeth, "but it will not do for us. We do not suffer by *accident*. It does not often happen that the interference of friends will persuade a young man of independent fortune to think no more of a girl whom he was violently in love with only a few days before."

"But that expression of 'violently in love' is so hackneyed, so doubtful, so indefinite, that it gives me very little idea. It is as often applied to feelings which arise from a half-hour's acquaintance, as to a real, strong attachment. Pray, how violent was Mr. Bingley's love?"

"I never saw a more promising inclination; he was growing quite inattentive to other people, and wholly engrossed by her. Every time they met, it was more decided and remarkable. At his own ball he offended two or three young ladies, by not asking them to dance; and I spoke to him twice myself, without receiving an answer. Could there be finer symptoms? Is not general incivility the very essence of love?"

"Oh, yes—of that kind of love which I suppose him to have felt. Poor Jane! I am sorry for her, because, with her disposition, she may not get over it immediately. It had better have happened to *you*, Lizzy; you would have laughed yourself out of it sooner. But do you think she would be prevailed upon to go back with us? Change of scene might be of service—and perhaps a little relief from home may be as useful as anything."

Elizabeth was exceedingly pleased with this proposal, and felt persuaded of her sister's ready acquiescence.

"I hope," added Mrs. Gardiner, "that no consideration with regard to this young man will influence her. We live in so different a part of town, all our connections are so different, and, as you well know, we go out so little, that it is very improbable that they should meet at all, unless he really comes to see her."

"And that is quite impossible; for he is now in the custody of his friend, and Mr. Darcy would no more suffer him to call on Jane in such a part of London! My dear aunt, how could you think of it? Mr. Darcy may perhaps have heard of such a place as Gracechurch Street, but he would hardly think a month's ablution enough to cleanse him from its impurities, were he once to enter it; and depend upon it, Mr. Bingley never stirs without him."

"So much the better. I hope they will not meet at all. But does not Jane correspond with his sister? *She* will not be able to help calling."

"She will likely drop the acquaintance entirely," said Elizabeth.

But in spite of the certainty which Elizabeth affected to place this point, as well as the still more interesting one of Bingley's being withheld from seeing Jane, she felt a solicitude on the subject which convinced her, on examination, that she did not consider it entirely hopeless. It was possible, and sometimes she thought it probable, that his affection might be reanimated, and the influence of his friends successfully combated by the more natural influence of Jane's attractions.

Miss Bennet accepted her aunt's invitation with pleasure; and the Bingleys were not otherwise in her thoughts at the same time, than as she hoped she might occasionally spend a morning with Caroline, if she could be guaranteed not to see her brother.

The Gardiners stayed a week at Longbourn; and what with the Phillipses, the Lucases, and the officers, there was not a day without its engagement. Mrs. Bennet had so carefully provided for the entertainment of her brother and sister, that they did not once sit down to a family dinner. When the engagement was for home, some of the officers always made part of it—of which officers Mr. Wickham was sure to be one; and on these occasions, Mrs. Gardiner, rendered suspicious by Elizabeth's commendation of him, narrowly observed them both. Without supposing them, from what she saw, to be in love, their preference of each other was plain enough to make her a little uneasy; and she resolved to speak to Elizabeth on the subject before she left Hertfordshire, and represent to her the imprudence of encouraging such an attachment.

To Mrs. Gardiner, Wickham had one means of affording pleasure, unconnected with his general powers. About ten or a dozen years ago, before her marriage, she had spent a considerable time in that very part of Derbyshire to which he belonged. They had, therefore, many acquaintances in common; and though Wickham had been little there since the death of Darcy's father, it was yet in his power to give her fresher intelligence of her former friends than she had been in the way of procuring.

Mrs. Gardiner had seen Pemberley, and known the late Mr. Darcy by character perfectly well. Here consequently was an inexhaustible subject of discourse. In comparing her recollection of Pemberley with the minute description which Wickham could give, and in bestowing her tribute of praise on the character of its late possessor, she was delighting both him and herself. On being made acquainted with the present Mr. Darcy's treatment of him, she tried to remember some of that gentleman's reputed disposition when quite a lad which might agree with it, and was confident at last that she recollected having heard Mr. Fitzwilliam Darcy formerly spoken of as a very proud, ill-natured boy.

CHAPTER TWENTY-SIX

Mrs. Gardiner's caution to Elizabeth was punctually and kindly given on the first favourable opportunity of speaking to her alone; after honestly telling her what she thought, she thus went on: "You are too sensible a girl, Lizzy, to fall in love merely because you are warned against it; and, therefore, I am not afraid of speaking openly. Seriously, I would have you be on your guard. Do not involve yourself or endeavour to involve him in an affection which the want of fortune would make so very imprudent. I have nothing to say against him; he is a most interesting young man; and if he had the fortune he ought to have, I should think you could not do better. But as it is, you must not let your fancy run away with you. You have sense, and we all expect you to use it. Your father would depend on your resolution and good conduct, I am sure. You must not disappoint your father."

Elizabeth tried not to show her amusement at this warning. "My dear aunt, this is being serious indeed."

"Yes, and I hope to engage you to be serious likewise."

"Well, then, you need not be under any alarm. I will take care of myself, and of Mr. Wickham too. He shall not be in love with me, if I can prevent it."

"Elizabeth, you are not serious now."

"I beg your pardon, I will try again. At present I am not in love with Mr. Wickham; no, I certainly am not. But he is a most agreeable man— and if he becomes really attached to me—I believe it will be better that he should not. I see the imprudence of it. While my father's opinion of me does me the greatest honour, and I should be miserable to forfeit it, I believe he is partial to Mr. Wickham. Still, my dear aunt, I should be very sorry to be the means of making any of you unhappy."

"Perhaps it will be as well if you discourage his coming here so very often. At least, you should not remind your mother of inviting him."

"As I did the other day," said Elizabeth with a conscious smile; "very true, it will be wise of me to refrain from that. But do not imagine that he is always here so often. It is on your account that he has been so frequently invited this week. You know my mother's ideas as to the necessity of constant company for her friends. But really, and upon my honour, I will try to do what I think to be the wisest; and now I hope you are satisfied."

Her aunt assured her that she was, and Elizabeth having thanked her for the kindness of her hints, they parted; a wonderful instance of advice being given on such a point, without being resented.

Mr. Collins returned into Hertfordshire soon after the Gardiners had returned to London with Jane; but as he took up his abode with the Lucases, his arrival was no great inconvenience to Mrs. Bennet. His marriage was now fast approaching, and she was at length so far resigned as to think it inevitable, and even repeatedly to say, in an ill-natured tone, that she "*wished* they might be happy."

Thursday was to be the wedding day, and on Wednesday Miss Lucas paid her farewell visit; and when she rose to take leave, Elizabeth, ashamed of her mother's ungracious and reluctant good wishes, and sincerely affected herself, accompanied her out of the room. As they went downstairs together, Charlotte said: "I shall depend on hearing from you very often, Eliza."

"*That* you certainly shall."

"And I have another favour to ask you. Will you come and see me?"

"We shall often meet, I hope, in Hertfordshire."

"I am not likely to leave Kent for some time. Promise me, therefore, to come to Hunsford."

Elizabeth could not refuse, though she foresaw little pleasure in the visit.

"My father and Maria are coming to me in March," added Charlotte, "and I hope you will consent to be of the party. Indeed, Eliza, you will be as welcome as either of them."

The wedding took place; the bride and bridegroom set off for Kent from the church door, and everybody had as much to say, or to hear, on the subject as usual. Elizabeth had reconciled herself to the loss of her friend, but even so, the day of the unhappy event was understandably affecting. She could still not quite entirely believe that her companion had forsaken her for a man such as Mr. Collins; but indeed Charlotte had done so, and the fact that she could had lessened Elizabeth's attachment significantly. Excepting a few tears on Charlotte's wedding night, she quite put the matter out of her mind, for it was not in her nature to dwell for long on unhappy events beyond her control.

Elizabeth soon heard from her friend; and their correspondence was nearly as regular as it had ever been; that it should be equally unreserved was impossible. Elizabeth could never address her without feeling that all the comfort of intimacy was over, and though determined not to slacken as a correspondent, it was for the sake of what had been, rather than what was. Charlotte's first letters were received with a good deal of eagerness; there could not but be curiosity to know how she would speak of her new home, how she would like Lady Catherine, and how happy she would dare pronounce herself to be; though, when the letters were read, Elizabeth felt that Charlotte expressed herself on every point exactly as she might have foreseen. She wrote cheerfully, seemed surrounded with comforts, and mentioned nothing which she could not praise. The house, furniture, neighbourhood, and roads, were all to her taste, and Lady Catherine's behaviour was most friendly and obliging. It was Mr. Collins's picture of Hunsford and Rosings rationally softened; and Elizabeth perceived that she must wait for her own visit there to know the rest.

Jane had already written a few lines to her sister to announce their safe arrival in London; and when she wrote again, Elizabeth hoped it would be in her power to say something of the Bingleys.

Her impatience for this second letter was as well rewarded as impatience generally is. Jane had been a week in town without either seeing or hearing from Caroline. She accounted for it, however, by supposing that her last letter to her friend from Longbourn had by some accident been lost.

"My aunt," she continued, "is going tomorrow into that part of the town, and I shall take the opportunity of calling in Grosvenor Street."

She wrote again when the visit was paid, and she had seen Miss Bingley. "I did not think Caroline in spirits," were her words, "but she was glad to see me, and reproached me for giving her no notice of my coming to London. I was right, therefore, my last letter had never reached her. I inquired after their brother, of course. He was well, but so much engaged with Mr. Darcy that they scarcely ever saw him. I found that Miss Darcy was expected to dinner. I wish I could see her. My visit was not long, as Caroline and Mrs. Hurst were going out. I dare say I shall see them soon here."

Elizabeth shook her head over this letter. It convinced her that accident only could discover to Mr. Bingley her sister's being in town.

Four weeks passed away, and Jane saw nothing of him. She endeavoured to persuade herself that she did not regret it; but she could no longer be blind to Miss Bingley's inattention. After waiting at home every morning for a fortnight, and inventing every evening a fresh excuse for her, the visitor did at last appear; but the shortness of her stay, and yet more, the alteration of her manner would allow Jane to deceive herself no longer. The letter which she wrote on this occasion to her sister will prove what she felt.

"My dearest Lizzy will, I am sure, be incapable of triumphing in her better judgment, at my expense, when I confess myself to have been entirely deceived in Miss Bingley's regard for me. But, my dear sister, though the event has proved you right, do not think me obstinate if I still assert that, considering what her behaviour was, my confidence was as natural as your suspicion. I do not at all comprehend her reason for wishing to be intimate with me; but if the same circumstances were to happen again, I am sure I should be deceived again. Caroline did not return my visit till yesterday; and not a note, not a line, did I receive in the meantime. When she did come, she made a slight, formal apology, for not calling before, said not a word of wishing to see me again, and was in every respect so altered a creature, that when she went away I was perfectly resolved to continue the acquaintance no longer. I pity her, because she must feel that she has been acting wrong, and because I am very sure that anxiety for her brother is the cause of it. I need not explain myself farther; and though *we* know this anxiety to be quite needless, yet if she feels it, it will easily account for her behaviour to me; and so deservedly dear as he is to his sister, whatever anxiety she must feel on his behalf is natural and amiable. I cannot but wonder, however, at her having any such fears now, because, if he had at all cared about me, we must have met, long ago. He must know of my being in town, I am certain of it. But I will endeavour to banish every painful thought, and think only of what will make me happy—your affection, and the invariable kindness of my dear uncle and aunt. Let me hear from you very soon. Miss Bingley said something of her brother's never returning to Netherfield again, of giving up the house, but not with any certainty. We had better not mention it. I am extremely glad that you have such pleasant accounts from our friends at Hunsford. Pray go to see them, with Sir William and Maria. I am sure you will be satisfied if you do.— Yours, etc."

This letter gave Elizabeth some pain; but her spirits returned as she considered that Jane would no longer be duped by the Bingleys. All expectation from the brother was now absolutely over. She would not even wish for a renewal of his attentions. His character sunk on every review of it; and as a punishment for him, as well as a possible advantage to Jane, she seriously hoped he might really soon marry Mr. Darcy's sister, as by Wickham's account, she would make him abundantly regret what he had thrown away.

Mrs. Gardiner about this time reminded Elizabeth of her promise concerning that gentleman, and required information; and Elizabeth had such to send as might give contentment to her aunt. His attentions were over; he was become the admirer of another. Elizabeth was watchful enough to see it all, but she could see it and write of it without material pain. Perhaps as a consequence of Charlotte's defection, she had briefly entertained ideas of a match with Wickham, a man with whom she shared so much natural affinity. But her heart had not been touched, and her vanity was satisfied with believing that the sudden acquisition of ten thousand pounds was the most remarkable charm of the young lady to whom he was now rendering himself agreeable. Elizabeth did not, however, quarrel with him for his wish of independence. Nothing, on the contrary, could be more natural; and while able to suppose that it cost him a few struggles to relinquish her, she was ready to allow it a wise and desirable measure for both, and could very sincerely wish him happy.

All this was acknowledged to Mrs. Gardiner; and after relating the circumstances, she thus went on: "I can admit to you, my dear aunt, that I had never been in love with Wickham. My feelings are not only cordial towards him, but they are even impartial towards Miss King. My watchfulness has been effectual; and though I certainly should be a more interesting object to all my acquaintances were I distractedly in love with him, I cannot say that I regret my comparative insignificance. Importance may sometimes be purchased too dearly. Kitty and Lydia take his defection much more to heart than I do. They are young in the ways of the world, and not yet open to the mortifying conviction that handsome young men must have something to live on as well as the plain."

CHAPTER TWENTY-SEVEN

With no greater events than these in the Longbourn family, and otherwise diversified by little beyond the walks to Meryton, sometimes dirty and sometimes cold, did January and February pass away. March was to take Elizabeth to Hunsford. She had not at first thought very seriously of going thither; but Charlotte, she soon found, was depending on the plan, and she gradually learned to consider it herself with greater pleasure as well as greater certainty. Absence had increased her desire of seeing Charlotte again, and weakened her disgust of Mr. Collins. There was novelty in the scheme, and as, with such a mother and such uncompanionable sisters, home could not be faultless, a little change was not unwelcome for its own sake. The journey would moreover give her a peep at Jane; and, in short, as the time drew near, she would have been very sorry for any delay. Everything, however, went on smoothly, and was finally settled according to Charlotte's first sketch. Elizabeth was to accompany Sir William and his second daughter. The improvement of spending a night in London was added in time, and the plan became perfect as plan could be.

The only pain was in leaving her father, who would certainly miss her, and who, when it came to the point, so little liked her going, that he told her to write to him, and almost promised to answer her letter.

The farewell between herself and Mr. Wickham was perfectly friendly; on his side even more. His present pursuit could not make him forget that Elizabeth had been the first to deserve his attention, the first to listen and to pity, the first to be admired; and in his manner of bidding her adieu, wishing her every enjoyment, reminding her of what she was to expect in Lady Catherine de Bourgh, and trusting their opinion of her—their opinion of everybody—would always coincide, there was a solicitude, an interest which she felt must ever attach her to him with a most sincere regard; and she parted from him convinced that, whether married or single, he must always be her model of the amiable and pleasing.

Her fellow-travelers the next day were not of a kind to make her think him less agreeable. Sir William Lucas and his daughter Maria, a good-humoured girl as empty-headed as himself, had nothing to say that could be worth hearing, and were listened to with about as much delight as the rattle of the chaise. Elizabeth loved absurdities, but she had known Sir William's too long. He could tell her nothing new of the wonders of his presentation and knighthood; and his civilities were worn out, like his information.

It was a journey of only twenty-four miles, and they began it so early as to be in Gracechurch Street by noon. As they drove to Mr. Gardiner's door, Jane was at a drawing-room window watching their arrival; when they entered the passage she was there to welcome them, and Elizabeth, looking earnestly in her face, was pleased to see it healthful and lovely as ever. On the stairs were a troop of little boys and girls, whose eagerness for their cousin's appearance would not allow them to wait in the drawing-room, and whose shyness, as they had not seen her for a twelvemonth, prevented their coming lower. All was joy and kindness. The day passed most pleasantly away; the morning in bustle and shopping, and the evening at one of the theatres.

Elizabeth then contrived to sit by her aunt. Their first object was her sister; and she was more grieved than astonished to hear, in reply to her minute inquiries, that though Jane always struggled to support her spirits, there were periods of dejection. It was reasonable, however, to hope that they would not continue long. Mrs. Gardiner gave her the particulars also of Miss Bingley's visit in Gracechurch Street, and repeated conversations occurring at different times between Jane and herself, which proved that the former had, from her heart, given up the acquaintance.

Mrs. Gardiner then turned the conversation to Wickham and the newest recipient of his attentions.

"My dear Elizabeth," she said, "what sort of girl is Miss King? I should be sorry to think our friend mercenary."

"Pray, my dear aunt, what is the difference in matrimonial affairs, between the mercenary and the prudent motive? Where does discretion end, and avarice begin? Last Christmas you were afraid of his marrying me, because it would be imprudent; and now, because he is trying to get a girl with only ten thousand pounds, you want to find out that he is mercenary."

"If you will only tell me what sort of girl Miss King is, I shall know what to think."

"She is a very good kind of girl, I believe. I know no harm of her."

"But he paid her not the smallest attention till her grandfather's death made her mistress of this fortune."

"No—why should he? If it were not allowable for him to gain *my* affections because I had no money, what occasion could there be for making love to a girl whom he did not care about, and who was equally poor?"

"But there seems an indelicacy in directing his attentions towards her so soon after this event."

"A man in distressed circumstances has not time for all those elegant decorums which other people may observe. If *she* does not object to it, why should we?"

"Her not objecting does not justify him. It only shows her being deficient in something herself—sense or feeling."

"Well," said Elizabeth, "have it as you choose. He shall be mercenary, and she shall be foolish."

"No, Lizzy, that is what I do *not* choose. I should be sorry, you know, to think ill of a young man who has lived so long in Derbyshire."

"If that is all, I have a very poor opinion of young people who have lived in Derbyshire; and their friends who live in Hertfordshire are not much better. I am sick of them all. Thank Heaven! I am going tomorrow where I shall find a man who has not one agreeable quality, who has neither manner nor sense to recommend him. Stupid men are the only ones worth knowing, after all."

"Take care, Lizzy; that speech savours strongly of disappointment."

Before they were separated by the conclusion of the play, she had the unexpected happiness of an invitation to accompany her uncle and aunt in a tour of pleasure which they proposed taking in the summer.

"We have not determined how far it shall carry us," said Mrs. Gardiner, "but, perhaps, to the Lakes."

No scheme could have been more agreeable to Elizabeth, and her acceptance of the invitation was most ready and grateful. "Oh, my dear, dear aunt," she rapturously cried, "what delight! What felicity! You give me fresh life and vigour. Adieu to disappointment and spleen. What are people to rocks and mountains? What hours of transport we shall spend! And when we *do* return, it shall not be like other travelers, without being able to give one accurate idea of anything. We *will* know where we have gone—we *will* recollect what we have seen. Lakes, mountains, and rivers shall not be jumbled together in our imaginations; nor when we attempt to describe any particular scene, will we begin quarreling about its relative situation. Let *our* first effusions be less insupportable than those of the generality of travelers."

Jane Austen *&* Kate Christie

CHAPTER TWENTY-EIGHT

Every object in the next day's journey was new and interesting to Elizabeth; and her spirits were in a state of enjoyment; for she had seen her sister looking so well as to banish all fear for her health, and the prospect of her northern tour was a constant source of delight.

When they left the high road for the lane to Hunsford, every eye was in search of the Parsonage, and every turning expected to bring it in view. The palings of Rosings Park was their boundary on one side. Elizabeth smiled at the recollection of all that she had heard of its inhabitants.

At length the Parsonage was discernible. The garden sloping to the road, the house standing in it, the green pales, and the laurel hedge, everything declared they were arriving. Mr. Collins and Charlotte appeared at the door, and the carriage stopped at the small gate which led by a short gravel walk to the house, amidst the nods and smiles of the whole party. In a moment they were all out of the chaise, rejoicing at the sight of each other. Mrs. Collins welcomed her friend with the liveliest pleasure, and Elizabeth was more and more satisfied with coming when she found herself so affectionately received. She saw instantly that her cousin's manners were not altered by his marriage; his formal civility was just what it had been, and he detained her some minutes at the gate to hear and satisfy his inquiries after all her family. They were then, with no other delay than his pointing out the neatness of the entrance, taken into the house; and as soon as they were in the parlour, he welcomed them a second time, with ostentatious formality to his humble abode, and punctually repeated all his wife's offers of refreshment.

Elizabeth was prepared to see him in his glory; and she could not help in fancying that in displaying the good proportion of the room, its aspect and its furniture, he addressed himself particularly to her, as if wishing to make her feel what she had lost in refusing him. But though everything seemed neat and comfortable, she was not able to gratify him by any sigh of repentance, and rather looked with wonder at her friend that she could have so cheerful an air with such a companion. When Mr. Collins said anything of which his wife might reasonably be ashamed, which certainly was not unseldom, she involuntarily turned her eye on Charlotte. Once or twice she could discern a faint blush; but in general Charlotte wisely did not hear. After sitting long enough to admire every article of furniture in the room, from the sideboard to the fender, to give an account of their journey, and of all that had happened in London, Mr. Collins invited them to take a stroll in the garden, which was large and well laid out, and to the cultivation of which he attended himself. To work in this garden was one of his most respectable pleasures; and Elizabeth admired the command of countenance with which Charlotte talked of the healthfulness of the exercise, and owned she encouraged it as much as possible. Here, leading the way through every walk and cross walk, and scarcely allowing them an interval to utter the praises he asked for, every view was pointed out with a minuteness which left beauty entirely behind. He could number the fields in every direction, and could tell how many trees there were in the most distant clump. But of all the views which his garden, or which the country or kingdom could boast, none were to be compared with the prospect of Rosings, afforded by an opening in the trees that bordered the park nearly opposite the front of his house. It was a handsome modern building, well situated on rising ground.

From his garden, Mr. Collins would have led them round his two meadows; but the ladies, not having shoes to encounter the remains of a white frost, turned back; and while Sir William accompanied him, Charlotte took her sister and friend over the house, extremely well pleased, probably, to have the opportunity of showing it without her husband's help. It was rather small, but well built and convenient; and everything was fitted up and arranged with a neatness and consistency of which Elizabeth gave Charlotte all the credit. When Mr. Collins could be forgotten, there was really an air of great comfort throughout, and by Charlotte's evident enjoyment of it, Elizabeth supposed he must be often forgotten.

She had already learnt that Lady Catherine was still in the country. It was spoken of again while they were at dinner, when Mr. Collins joining in, observed: "Yes, Miss Elizabeth, you will have the honour of seeing Lady Catherine de Bourgh on the ensuing Sunday at church, and I need not say you will be delighted with her. She is all affability and condescension, and I doubt not but you will be honoured with some portion of her notice when service is over. I have scarcely any hesitation in saying she will include you and my sister Maria in every invitation with which she honours us during your stay here. Her behaviour to my dear Charlotte is charming. We dine at Rosings twice every week, and are never allowed to walk home. Her ladyship's carriage is regularly ordered for us. I *should* say, one of her ladyship's carriages, for she has several."

"Lady Catherine is a very respectable, sensible woman indeed," added Charlotte, "and a most attentive neighbour."

"Very true, my dear, that is exactly what I say. She is the sort of woman whom one cannot regard with too much deference."

The evening was spent chiefly in talking over Hertfordshire news, and telling again what had already been written; and when it closed, Elizabeth, in the solitude of her chamber, had to meditate upon Charlotte's degree of contentment, to understand her address in guiding, and composure in bearing with, her husband, and to acknowledge that it was all done very well. She had also to anticipate how her visit would pass, the quiet tenor of their usual employments, the vexatious interruptions of Mr. Collins, and the gaieties of their intercourse with Rosings. A lively imagination soon settled it all tolerably. Any disappointment she had felt personally at Charlotte's defection had since ebbed, and from her current vantage point, she could see that their attachment had been almost too easy, too placid; that very serenity had made the level of connection difficult to sustain, in the end. She was relieved to find herself able to look on her former companion now with the genuine affection that had attended their long friendship.

About the middle of the next day, as she was in her room getting ready for a walk, a sudden noise below seemed to speak the whole house in confusion; and, after listening a moment, she heard somebody running up stairs in a violent hurry, and calling loudly after her. She opened the door and met Maria in the landing place, who, breathless with agitation, cried out: "Oh, my dear Eliza! Pray make haste and come into the dining-room, for there is such a sight to be seen! I will not tell you what it is. Make haste, and come down this moment."

Elizabeth asked questions in vain; Maria would tell her nothing more, and down they ran into the dining-room, which fronted the lane, in quest of this wonder. It was two ladies stopping in a low phaeton at the garden gate.

"And is this all?" cried Elizabeth. "I expected at least that the pigs were got into the garden, and here is nothing but Lady Catherine and her daughter."

"My dear," said Maria, quite shocked at the mistake, "it is not Lady Catherine. The old lady is Mrs. Jenkinson, who lives with them; the other is Miss de Bourgh. Only look at her. She is quite a little creature. Who would have thought that she could be so thin and small?"

"She is abominably rude to keep Charlotte out of doors in all this wind. Why does she not come in?"

"Oh, Charlotte says she hardly ever does. It is the greatest of favours when Miss de Bourgh comes in."

"I like her appearance," said Elizabeth, struck with other ideas. "She looks sickly and cross. Yes, she will do for him very well. She will make him a very proper wife."

Mr. Collins and Charlotte were both standing at the gate in conversation with the ladies; and Sir William, to Elizabeth's high diversion, was stationed in the doorway, in earnest contemplation of the greatness before him, and constantly bowing whenever Miss de Bourgh looked that way.

At length there was nothing more to be said; the ladies drove on, and the others returned into the house. Mr. Collins no sooner saw the two girls than he began to congratulate them on their good fortune, which Charlotte explained by letting them know that the whole party was asked to dine at Rosings the next day.

CHAPTER TWENTY-NINE

M r. Collins's triumph, in consequence of this invitation, was complete. The power of displaying the grandeur of his patroness to his wondering visitors, and of letting them see her civility towards himself and his wife, was exactly what he had wished for; and that an opportunity of doing it should be given so soon, was such an instance of Lady Catherine's condescension, as he knew not how to admire enough.

"I confess," said he, "that I should not have been at all surprised by her ladyship's asking us on Sunday to drink tea and spend the evening at Rosings. I rather expected, from my knowledge of her affability, that it would happen. But who could have foreseen such an attention as this? Who could have imagined that we should receive an invitation to dine there (an invitation, moreover, including the whole party) so immediately after your arrival!"

"I am the less surprised at what has happened," replied Sir William, "from that knowledge of what the manners of the great really are, which my situation in life has allowed me to acquire. About the court, such instances of elegant breeding are not uncommon."

Scarcely anything was talked of the whole day or next morning but their visit to Rosings. Mr. Collins was carefully instructing them in what they were to expect, that the sight of such rooms, so many servants, and so splendid a dinner, might not wholly overpower them.

When the ladies were separating for the toilette, he said to Elizabeth: "Do not make yourself uneasy, my dear cousin, about your apparel. Lady Catherine is far from requiring that elegance of dress in us which becomes herself and her daughter. I would advise you merely to put on whatever of your clothes is superior to the rest—there is no occasion for anything more. Lady Catherine will not think the worse of you for being simply dressed. She likes to have the distinction of rank preserved."

While they were dressing, he came two or three times to their different doors, to recommend their being quick, as Lady Catherine very much objected to be kept waiting for her dinner. Such formidable accounts of her ladyship, and her manner of living, quite frightened Maria Lucas who had been little used to company, and she looked forward to her introduction at Rosings with as much apprehension as her father had done to his presentation at St. James's.

As the weather was fine, they had a pleasant walk of about half a mile across the park. Every park has its beauty and its prospects; and Elizabeth saw much to be pleased with, though she could not be in such raptures as Mr. Collins expected the scene to inspire, and was but slightly affected by his enumeration of the windows in front of the house, and his relation of what the glazing altogether had originally cost Sir Lewis de Bourgh.

When they ascended the steps to the hall, Maria's alarm was every moment increasing, and even Sir William did not look perfectly calm. Elizabeth's courage did not fail her. She had heard nothing of Lady Catherine that spoke her awful from any extraordinary talents or miraculous virtue, and the mere stateliness of money or rank she thought she could witness without trepidation.

From the entrance-hall, of which Mr. Collins pointed out, with a rapturous air, the fine proportion and the finished ornaments, they followed the servants through an ante-chamber, to the room where Lady Catherine, her daughter, and Mrs. Jenkinson were sitting. Her ladyship, with great condescension, arose to receive them; and as Mrs. Collins had settled it with her husband that the office of introduction should be hers, it was performed in a proper manner, without any of those apologies and thanks which he would have thought necessary.

In spite of having been at St. James's, Sir William was so completely awed by the grandeur surrounding him that he had but just courage enough to make a very low bow, and take his seat without saying a word; and his daughter, frightened almost out of her senses, sat on the edge of her chair, not knowing which way to look. Elizabeth found herself quite equal to the scene, and could observe the three ladies before her composedly. Lady Catherine was a tall, large woman, with strongly-marked features, which might once have been handsome. Her air was not conciliating, nor was her manner of receiving them such as to make her visitors forget their inferior rank. She was not rendered formidable by silence; but whatever she said was spoken in so authoritative a tone, as marked her self-importance, and brought Mr. Wickham immediately to Elizabeth's mind; and from the observation of the day altogether, she believed Lady Catherine to be exactly what he represented.

When, after examining the mother, in whose countenance and deportment she soon found some resemblance of Mr. Darcy, she turned her eyes on the daughter, she could almost have joined in Maria's astonishment at her being so thin and so small. There was neither in figure nor face any likeness between the ladies. Miss de Bourgh was pale and sickly; her features, though not plain, were insignificant; and she spoke very little, except in a low voice, to Mrs. Jenkinson, in whose appearance there was nothing remarkable, and who was entirely engaged in listening to what she said, and placing a screen in the proper direction before her eyes.

After sitting a few minutes, they were all sent to one of the windows to admire the view, Mr. Collins attending them to point out its beauties, and Lady Catherine kindly informing them that it was much better worth looking at in the summer.

The dinner was exceedingly handsome, and there were all the servants and all the articles of plate which Mr. Collins had promised; and, as he had likewise foretold, he took his seat at the bottom of the table, by her ladyship's desire, and looked as if he felt that life could furnish nothing greater. He carved, and ate, and praised with delighted alacrity; and every dish was commended, first by him and then by Sir William, who was now enough recovered to echo whatever his son-in-law said, in a manner which Elizabeth wondered Lady Catherine could bear. But Lady Catherine seemed gratified by their excessive admiration, and gave most gracious smiles, especially when any dish on the table proved a novelty to them. The party did not supply much conversation. Elizabeth was ready to speak whenever there was an opening, but she was seated between Charlotte and Miss de Bourgh—the former of whom was engaged in listening to Lady Catherine, and the latter said not a word to her all dinner-time. Mrs. Jenkinson was chiefly employed in watching how little Miss de Bourgh ate, pressing her to try some other dish, and fearing she was indisposed. Maria thought speaking out of the question, and the gentlemen did nothing but eat and admire.

When the ladies returned to the drawing-room, there was little to be done but to hear Lady Catherine talk, which she did without any intermission till coffee came in, delivering her opinion on every subject in so decisive a manner, as proved that she was not used to have her judgment controverted. She inquired into Charlotte's domestic concerns familiarly and minutely, gave her a great deal of advice as to the management of them all; told her how everything ought to be regulated in so small a family as hers, and instructed her as to the care of her cows and her poultry. Elizabeth found that nothing was beneath this great lady's attention, which could furnish her with an occasion of dictating to others. In the intervals of her discourse with Mrs. Collins, she addressed a variety of questions to Maria and Elizabeth, but especially to the latter, of whose connections she knew the least, and who she observed to Mrs. Collins was a very genteel, pretty kind of girl. She asked her, at different times, how many sisters she had, whether they were older or younger than herself, whether any of them were likely to be married, whether they were handsome, where they had been educated, what carriage her father kept, and what had been her mother's maiden name? Elizabeth felt all the impertinence of her questions but answered them very composedly.

Lady Catherine then observed, "Your father's estate is entailed on Mr. Collins, I think. For your sake," turning to Charlotte, "I am glad of it; but otherwise I see no occasion for entailing estates from the female line. It was not thought necessary in Sir Lewis de Bourgh's family. Do you play and sing, Miss Bennet?"

"A little."

"Then sometime or other we shall be happy to hear you. Our instrument is a capital one, probably superior to—You shall try it some day. Do your sisters play and sing?"

"One of them does."

"Why did not you all learn? You ought all to have learned. The Miss Webbs all play, and their father has not so good an income as yours. Do you draw?"

"No, not at all."

"What, none of you?"

"Not one."

"That is very strange. But I suppose you had no opportunity. Your mother should have taken you to town every spring for the benefit of masters. Has your governess left you?"

"We never had any governess."

"No governess! How was that possible? Five daughters brought up at home without a governess! I never heard of such a thing. Your mother must have been quite a slave to your education."

Elizabeth could hardly help smiling as she assured her that had not been the case.

"Then, who taught you? Who attended to you? Without a governess, you must have been neglected."

"Compared with some families, I believe we were; but such of us as wished to learn never wanted the means. We were always encouraged to read, and had all the masters that were necessary. Those who chose to be idle, certainly might."

"Aye, no doubt; but that is what a governess will prevent, and if I had known your mother, I should have advised her most strenuously to engage one. I always say that nothing is to be done in education without steady and regular instruction, and nobody but a governess can give it. It is wonderful how many families I have been the means of supplying in that way. I am always glad to get a young person well placed out. Four nieces of Mrs. Jenkinson are most delightfully situated through my means; and it was but the other day that I recommended another young person, who was merely accidentally mentioned to me, and the family are quite delighted with her. Mrs. Collins, did I tell you of Lady Metcalf's calling yesterday to thank me? She finds Miss Pope a treasure. 'Lady Catherine,' said she, 'you have given me a treasure.' Are any of your younger sisters out, Miss Bennet?"

"Yes, Ma'am, all."

"All! What, all five out at once? Very odd! And you only the second. The younger ones out before the elder ones are married! Your younger sisters must be very young?"

"Yes, my youngest is not sixteen. Perhaps *she* is full young to be much in company. But really, Ma'am, I think it would be very hard upon younger sisters, that they should not have their share of society and amusement, because the elder may not have the means or inclination to marry early. The last-born has as good a right to the pleasures of youth at the first. And to be kept back on such a motive! I think it would not be very likely to promote sisterly affection or delicacy of mind."

"Upon my word," said her ladyship, "you give your opinion very decidedly for so young a person. Pray, what is your age?"

"With three younger sisters grown up," replied Elizabeth, smiling, "your ladyship can hardly expect me to own it."

Lady Catherine seemed quite astonished at not receiving a direct answer; and Elizabeth suspected herself to be the first creature who had ever dared to trifle with so much dignified impertinence.

"You cannot be more than twenty, I am sure, therefore you need not conceal your age."

"I am not one-and-twenty."

When the gentlemen had joined them, and tea was over, the card-tables were placed. Lady Catherine, Sir William, and Mr. and Mrs. Collins sat down to quadrille; and as Miss de Bourgh chose to play at cassino, the two girls had the honour of assisting Mrs. Jenkinson to make up her party. Their table was superlatively stupid. Scarcely a syllable was uttered that did not relate to the game, except when Mrs. Jenkinson expressed her fears of Miss de Bourgh's being too hot or too cold, or having too much or too little light. A great deal more passed at the other table. Lady Catherine was generally speaking—stating the mistakes of the three others, or relating some anecdote of herself. Mr. Collins was employed in agreeing to everything her ladyship said, thanking her for every fish he won, and apologising if he thought he won too many. Sir William did not say much. He was storing his memory with anecdotes and noble names.

When Lady Catherine and her daughter had played as long as they chose, the tables were broken up, the carriage was offered to Mrs. Collins, gratefully accepted and immediately ordered. The party then gathered round the fire to hear Lady Catherine determine what weather they were to have on the morrow. From these instructions they were summoned by the arrival of the coach; and with many speeches of thankfulness on Mr. Collins's side and as many bows on Sir William's, they departed. As soon as they had driven from the door, Elizabeth was called on by her cousin to give her opinion of all that she had seen at Rosings, which, for Charlotte's sake, she made more favourable than it really was. But her commendation, though costing her some trouble, could by no means satisfy Mr. Collins, and he was very soon obliged to take her ladyship's praise into his own hands.

CHAPTER THIRTY

Sir William stayed only a week at Hunsford, but his visit was long enough to convince him of his daughter's being most comfortably settled, and of her possessing such a husband and such a neighbour as were not often met with. While Sir William was with them, Mr. Collins devoted his morning to driving him out in his gig, and showing him the country; but when he went away, the whole family returned to their usual employments, and Elizabeth was thankful to find that they did not see more of her cousin by the alteration, for the chief of the time between breakfast and dinner was now passed by him either at work in the garden or in reading and writing, and looking out of the window in his own book-room, which fronted the road. The room in which the ladies sat was backwards. Elizabeth had at first rather wondered that Charlotte should not prefer the dining-parlour for common use; it was a better sized room, and had a more pleasant aspect; but she soon saw that her friend had an excellent reason for what she did, for Mr. Collins would undoubtedly have been much less in his own apartment, had they sat in one equally lively; and she gave Charlotte credit for the arrangement.

From the drawing-room they could distinguish nothing in the lane, and were indebted to Mr. Collins for the knowledge of what carriages went along, and how often especially Miss de Bourgh drove by in her phaeton, which he never failed coming to inform them of, though it happened almost every day. She not infrequently stopped at the Parsonage, and had a few minutes' conversation with Charlotte, but was scarcely ever prevailed upon to get out.

Very few days passed in which Mr. Collins did not walk to Rosings, and not many in which his wife did not think it necessary to go likewise; and till Elizabeth recollected that there might be other family livings to be disposed of, she could not understand the sacrifice of so many hours. Now and then they were honoured with a call from her ladyship, and nothing escaped her observation that was passing in the room during these visits. She examined into their employments, looked at their work, and advised them to do it differently; found fault with the arrangement of the furniture; or detected the housemaid in negligence; and if she accepted any refreshment, seemed to do it only for the sake of finding out that Mrs. Collins's joints of meat were too large for her family.

Elizabeth soon perceived, that though this great lady was not in commission of the peace of the county, she was a most active magistrate in her own parish, the minutest concerns of which were carried to her by Mr. Collins; and whenever any of the cottagers were disposed to be quarrelsome, discontented, or too poor, she sallied forth into the village to settle their differences, silence their complaints, and scold them into harmony and plenty.

The entertainment of dining at Rosings was repeated about twice a week; and, allowing for the loss of Sir William, and there being only one card-table in the evening, every such entertainment was the counterpart of the first. Their other engagements were few, as the style of living in the neighbourhood in general was beyond Mr. Collins's reach. This, however, was no evil to Elizabeth, and upon the whole she spent her time comfortably enough; there were half-hours of pleasant conversation with Charlotte, and the weather was so fine for the time of year that she had often great enjoyment out of doors. Her favourite walk, and where she frequently went while the others were calling on Lady Catherine, was along the open grove which edged the side of the park where there was a nice sheltered path, which no one seemed to value but herself, and where she felt beyond the reach of Lady Catherine's curiosity.

In this quiet way, the first fortnight of her visit soon passed away. Easter was approaching, and the week preceding it was to bring an addition to the family at Rosings, which in so small a circle must be important. Elizabeth had heard soon after her arrival that Mr. Darcy was expected there in the course of a few weeks, and though there were not many of her acquaintances whom she did not prefer, his coming would furnish one comparatively new to look at in their Rosings parties, and she might be amused in observing his behaviour to his cousin, for whom he was evidently destined by Lady Catherine, who talked of his coming with the greatest satisfaction, spoke of him in terms of the highest admiration, and seemed almost angry to find that he had already been frequently seen by Miss Lucas and herself.

His arrival was soon known at the Parsonage; for Mr. Collins was walking the whole morning within view of the lodges opening into Hunsford Lane, in order to have the earliest assurance of it, and after making his bow as the carriage turned into the Park, hurried home with the great intelligence. On the following morning he hastened to Rosings to pay his respects. There were two nephews of Lady Catherine to require them, for Mr. Darcy had brought with him a Colonel Fitzwilliam, the younger son of his uncle Lord ———, as well as a few other familiar faces: Mr. and Mrs. Hurst, and Miss Caroline Bingley.

To the great surprise of all the party, when Mr. Collins returned, the gentlemen and ladies accompanied him, excepting Mr. Hurst. Charlotte had seen them from her husband's room crossing the road, and immediately running into the other, told the girls what an honour they might expect, adding: "I may thank you, Eliza, for this piece of civility. Mr. Darcy and the ladies would never have come so soon to wait upon me."

"And which ladies are those?"

"Why, Miss Bingley and Mrs. Hurst."

"Miss Bingley?" repeated Elizabeth. But how could that be, with the London season only half gone?

She had scarcely time to formulate this question before the visitors' approach was announced by the door-bell, and shortly afterwards the gentlemen and ladies entered the room. Colonel Fitzwilliam, who led the way, was about thirty, not handsome, but in person and address most truly the gentleman. Mr. Darcy looked just as he had been used to look in Hertfordshire, while Miss Bingley appeared unusually reserved as her elder sister paid their compliments first to Mrs. Collins and then to Elizabeth, who returned the greeting coolly before smiling at Colonel Fitzwilliam with a gladness she did not feel. The gentleman met her with every appearance of liveliness, and Elizabeth curtseyed to him, noting with satisfaction Caroline's small frown at her purposeful slight.

The Colonel entered into conversation directly with the readiness and ease of a well-bred man, and talked very pleasantly; but his cousin, after having addressed a slight observation on the house and garden to

Mrs. Collins, sat for some time without speaking to anybody, while Mrs. Hurst watched Caroline, who sat quietly, hands folded on her lap. At length, Mr. Darcy's civility was so far awakened as to inquire of Elizabeth after the health of her family. She answered him in the usual way, and after a moment's pause, added: "My eldest sister has been in town these three months. Miss Bingley, I believe you saw her there on a few occasions?"

Mr. Darcy and Mrs. Hurst both looked at Caroline, who regarded Elizabeth evenly. "You are mistaken, Miss Bennet. Regrettably, I was only able to see your sister on a single instance in town, when she visited Grosvenor Street. I was most disappointed to be unable to return the favor."

Elizabeth tossed her head angrily, and was about to cast aspersions on the veracity of Caroline's statement, when she noticed the lady looking at her intently, seeming to attempt to transmit a message of some sort. At the last moment, Elizabeth changed course: "I am certain you felt the loss deeply. And you, Mr. Darcy? Had you occasion to see my sister?"

She was perfectly sensible that he never had; but she wished to see whether he would betray any consciousness of what had passed between the Bingleys and Jane. However, he looked perfectly composed as he answered that he had never been so fortunate as to meet Miss Bennet in town. The subject was pursued no farther, and the gentlemen and ladies soon afterwards went away.

As they left the room, Caroline appeared inclined to linger, but Mrs. Hurst rushed her out the door, turning to cast an antagonistic eye on Elizabeth, who viewed the entire episode with a degree of confusion that bordered on disbelief.

Their visitors gone, Charlotte gazed at Elizabeth and said: "Mrs. Hurst appeared surprised to discover you here."

Elizabeth had not paid any attention to Mrs. Hurst. "Did she, really?"

Before this line of inquiry could be pursued, Mr. Collins began to hold forth on the incredible kindness and respect the gentlemen and ladies had shewn him on coming to his home, a speech that took nearly the rest of the afternoon to deliver. His conversational meandering allowed Elizabeth time to reconsider the events of the morning. Why had Caroline denied seeing Jane? And what could be the reason for the tension between her and her elder sister? Except, of course, Elizabeth thought she might know one explanation for why Louisa guarded Caroline so attentively. At the Netherfield ball, Caroline had alluded to Louisa's hostility toward her disposition, had she not? Perhaps Mrs. Hurst's governance of Caroline was stricter than anyone knew; perhaps that was even why Elizabeth had failed to receive a reply to her letter.

Before her imagination could busy itself with excuses for Miss Bingley's past transgressions, Elizabeth recollected Caroline's recent treatment of Jane. Since first coming into Hertfordshire, the Bingleys had proven themselves unpardonably inconsistent in both action and affection; and no matter the explanation, there could be no satisfactory excuse for how they had abused Jane, who had been nothing but good to them all. Resolutely, Elizabeth turned her attention back to her needlepoint, while Mr. Collins droned on in tones of ever more self-important reverence.

Jane Austen & Kate Christie

CHAPTER THIRTY-ONE

olonel Fitzwilliam's manners were very much admired at the Parsonage, and the ladies all felt that he must add considerably to the pleasures of their engagements at Rosings. It was some days, however, before they received any invitation thither—for while there were visitors in the house, they could not be necessary; and it was not till Easter-day, almost a week after the arrival of Lady Catherine's guests, that they were honoured by such an attention, and then they were merely asked on leaving church to come there in the evening. For the last week they had seen very little of Lady Catherine or her daughter. Colonel Fitzwilliam had called at the Parsonage more than once during the time, but Mr. Darcy and the Bingley sisters they had seen only at church.

The invitation was accepted, of course, and at a proper hour they joined the party in Lady Catherine's drawing-room. Her ladyship received them civilly, but it was plain that their company was by no means so acceptable as when she could get nobody else; and she was, in fact, almost engrossed by her nephews, speaking to them, especially to Darcy, much more than to any other person in the room.

Colonel Fitzwilliam seemed really glad to see them; anything was a welcome relief to him at Rosings; and Mrs. Collins's pretty friend had moreover caught his fancy. He now seated himself by her, and talked so agreeably of Kent and Hertfordshire, of travelling and staying at home, of new books and music, that Elizabeth had never been half so well entertained in that room before; and they conversed with so much spirit and flow, as to draw the attention of Lady Catherine herself, as well as that of Miss Bingley, seated next to Charlotte. Caroline's eyes turned towards them frequently, Elizabeth could not help but notice; and her ladyship, who evidently shared the younger lady's interest, did not scruple to call out: "What is that you are saying, Fitzwilliam? What is it you are talking of? Let me hear what it is you are telling Miss Bennet."

"We are speaking of music, Madam," said he, when no longer able to avoid a reply.

"Of music! Then pray speak aloud. It is of all subjects my delight. I must have my share in the conversation if you are speaking of music. There are few people in England, I suppose, who have more true enjoyment of music than myself, or a better natural taste. If I had ever learnt, I should have been a great proficient. And so would Anne, if her health had allowed her to apply. I am confident that she would have performed delightfully. How does Georgiana get on, Darcy?"

Mr. Darcy spoke with affectionate praise of his sister's proficiency.

"I am very glad to hear such a good account of her," said Lady Catherine; "and pray tell her from me, that she cannot expect to excel if she does not practice a good deal."

"I assure you, Madam," he replied, "that she does not need such advice. She practises very constantly."

"So much the better. It cannot be done too much; and when I next write to her, I shall charge her not to neglect it on any account. I often tell young ladies that no excellence in music is to be acquired without constant practice. I have told Miss Bennet several times, that she will never play really well unless she practises more; and though Mrs. Collins has no instrument, she is very welcome, as I have often told her, to come to Rosings every day, and play on the pianoforte in Mrs. Jenkinson's room. She would be in nobody's way, you know, in that part of the house."

Mr. Darcy looked a little ashamed of his aunt's ill-breeding, and made no answer. But Caroline said, "I have heard Miss Bennet play, and I dare say she is one of the more accomplished ladies I know." And she smiled at Elizabeth while appearing not to notice the lowered brow of the lady of the house, at this notable refutation of her opinion. Elizabeth gazed coolly at her defender, hoping her agitation did not show on her face. Why should Caroline compliment her, at the risk of offending Darcy's powerful aunt? It did not make sense, not in the least.

When coffee was over, Colonel Fitzwilliam reminded Elizabeth of having promised to play for him; and she sat down directly to the instrument. He drew a chair near her. Lady Catherine listened to half a song, and then talked to Mrs. Hurst, who was seated beside her. With her elder sister's attention thus captured, Caroline made her way to the pianoforte and stationed herself so as to command a full view of the fair performer's countenance.

Elizabeth saw what she was doing, and at the first convenient pause, turned to her with a raised eyebrow, and said: "You mean to frighten me, Miss Bingley? I will not be alarmed, though you, I own, *are* the better musician."

"I will not say you have mistaken my purpose," replied she, "because you could not really believe me to entertain any design of alarming you; and I have had the pleasure of your acquaintance long enough to know that you find great enjoyment in occasionally professing opinions which in fact are not your own."

Despite her intention to remain cold, Elizabeth couldn't help laughing at this picture of herself, and said to Colonel Fitzwilliam, "Your cousin's friend will give you a very pretty notion of me, and teach you not to believe a word I say. Indeed, Miss Bingley, it is very impolitic in you to mention what you learned to my disadvantage in Hertfordshire, for it is provoking me to retaliate, and such things may come out as will shock your friends."

"Do your worse. I am not afraid," said she, smiling in challenge.

To her irritation, Elizabeth found herself longing to succumb to Caroline's charm, and turned instead to her other audience: "Well, Colonel Fitzwilliam, what do I play next? My fingers await your orders."

Here they were interrupted by Lady Catherine, who called out to know what they were talking of. Elizabeth immediately began playing again. Lady Catherine approached, and, after listening for a few minutes, said to Darcy, who had accompanied her: "Miss Bennet would not play at all amiss if she practised more, and could have the advantage of a London master. She has a very good notion of fingering, though her taste is not equal to Anne's. Anne would have been a delightful performer, had her health allowed her to learn."

Caroline, unbeknownst to Lady Catherine, gave Elizabeth such a look of amused derision that it was all the latter could do to hold in her laughter. To distract herself, she looked at Darcy to see how cordially he assented to his cousin's praise; but neither at that moment nor at any other could she discern any symptom of love.

Lady Catherine continued her remarks on Elizabeth's performance, mixing with them many instructions on execution and taste. Elizabeth received them with all the forbearance of civility, and, at the request of the gentlemen, remained at the instrument till her ladyship's carriage was ready to take them all home.

CHAPTER THIRTY-TWO

Elizabeth was sitting by herself the next morning, and writing to Jane while Mrs. Collins and Maria were gone on business into the village, when she was startled by a ring at the door, the certain signal of a visitor. As she had heard no carriage, she thought it not unlikely to be Lady Catherine, and under that apprehension was putting away her half-finished letter that she might escape all impertinent questions, when the door opened, and, to her very great surprise, Caroline Bingley entered the room, quite on her own.

She seemed astonished too on finding Elizabeth alone, and apologised for the intrusion by letting it be known that she had understood all the ladies were to be within.

They then sat down, and when the usual civilities had been exchanged, Elizabeth took a moment to shore up her resolve to remain impassive, for it had become clear the previous evening that her feelings were not as indifferent to Caroline as she might wish. Then she raised a topic that had been at the front of her mind since the unexpected renewal of their acquaintance: "How very suddenly you all quitted Netherfield last November, Miss Bingley. It must have been a most agreeable surprise to your brother to see you all after him so soon; for, if I recollect right, he went but the day before. He was quite well, I hope, when you left London?"

"Perfectly so, thank you."

"And why is he not here with your party?"

"He had business to attend to, but may join us yet."

"I think I have understood that Mr. Bingley has not much idea of ever returning to Netherfield again?"

"I have never heard him say so; but it is probable that he may spend very little of his time there in the future. He has many friends, and is at a time of life when friends and engagements are continually increasing."

"If he means to be but little at Netherfield, it would be better for the neighbourhood that he should give up the place entirely, for then we might possibly get a settled family there. But perhaps Mr. Bingley did not take the house so much for the convenience of the neighbourhood as for his own, and we must expect him to keep it or quit it on the same principle."

"I should not be surprised," said Caroline, "if he were to give it up as soon as any eligible purchase offers."

Elizabeth made no answer. She was afraid of her anger rising if they spoke any longer of Netherfield.

"This seems a very comfortable house," added Caroline. "Lady Catherine tells us that she did a great deal to it when Mr. Collins first came to Hunsford."

"I had heard that as well—and I am sure she could not have bestowed her kindness on a more grateful object."

"Mr. Collins appears to be very fortunate in his choice of a wife."

"Yes, indeed, his friends may well rejoice in his having met with one of the very few sensible women who would have accepted him. My friend has an excellent understanding—though I am not certain that I consider her marrying Mr. Collins to be the wisest thing she ever did. She seems happy enough, however, and in a prudential light it is certainly a very good match for her."

"It must be very agreeable for her to be settled within so easy a distance of her own family and friends."

"An easy distance, do you call it? It is nearly fifty miles."

"And what is fifty miles of good road? Little more than half a day's journey. Yes, I call it a *very* easy distance."

"I should never have considered the distance as one of the advantages of the match," said Elizabeth.

"It is a proof of your own attachment to Hertfordshire, or perhaps to the lady. Anything beyond the very neighbourhood of Longbourn, I suppose, would appear far."

As she spoke there was a type of knowing smile which Elizabeth fancied she understood; and she coloured as she answered: "I do not mean to say that a woman may not be settled too near her family. Where there is fortune to make the expenses of travelling unimportant, distance becomes no evil. But that is not the case *here*."

Caroline leaned a little nearer, and said, "You cannot have a right anymore to such a very strong attachment, surely."

Elizabeth withdrew slightly. "My attachments are my own business, Miss Bingley, and certainly none of yours."

Caroline experienced some change of feeling; she drew back her chair and said, in a cooler tone: "Are you pleased with Kent, then?"

A short dialogue on the subject of the country ensued, on either side calm and concise—and soon put an end to by the entrance of Charlotte and her sister, just returned from their walk. The tête-à-tête surprised them. Miss Bingley related the mistake which had occasioned her intruding on Miss Bennet, and after sitting a few minutes longer without saying much, went away. Maria left the room shortly after, and the two old friends were alone.

"What can be the meaning of this?" said Charlotte.

"I do not know what you mean."

"My dear Eliza, Miss Bingley would never have called on us in this familiar way if you were not here. It is you she wanted to see."

But when Elizabeth revealed the strained nature of their conversation, choosing not to share their brief debate over the distance of Hunsford from Hertfordshire, it did not seem very likely, even to Charlotte's mind, to be the case; and after various conjectures, they could at last only suppose her visit to proceed from the difficulty of finding anything to do, which was the more probable. Within doors there was Lady Catherine, books, and a billiard-table, but being within doors at Rosings was not always an entertaining experience, as they understood; and in the nearness of the Parsonage, or the pleasantness of the walk to it, or of the people who lived in it, Lady Catherine's visitors soon found a temptation they began to answer by walking thither almost every day. They called at various times of the morning, sometimes singly, sometimes in a group, and now and then accompanied by Lady Catherine herself. It was plain to them all that Colonel Fitzwilliam came because he had pleasure in their society, a persuasion which of course recommended him still more; and Elizabeth was reminded by her own satisfaction in being with him, as well as by his evident admiration of her, of her affection for George Wickham; and though, in comparing them, she saw there was less captivating softness in Colonel Fitzwilliam's manners, she believed he might have the best informed mind of the two.

But why Miss Bingley came so often to the Parsonage, it was more difficult to understand. It could not be for society, as she frequently sat there ten minutes together without opening her lips; and when she did speak, it seemed the effect of necessity rather than of choice—a sacrifice to propriety, not a pleasure. She seldom appeared really animated.

Mrs. Collins knew not what to make of this behavior. Mr. Darcy's occasionally poking fun at Caroline's reserve, proved that she was generally different, which Charlotte's own knowledge could not have told her; and as she suspected this change to be the effect of love, and the object of that love her friend Eliza, she set herself seriously to work to find it out. She watched Caroline whenever they were at Rosings, and whenever she came to Hunsford; but without much success. The lady certainly looked at her friend a great deal, but the expression of that look was disputable. It was an earnest, steadfast gaze, but she often doubted whether there were much admiration in it, and sometimes it seemed nothing but absence of mind.

She had once or twice suggested to Elizabeth the possibility of Miss Bingley's being partial to her, but Elizabeth always denied this; and Mrs. Collins did not think it right to press the subject, for she was a bit anxious, truthfully, that all her friend's purported dislike of the lady would vanish, if she could suppose Miss Bingley to be in her power.

In her solicitous schemes for Elizabeth, she occasionally planned her marrying Colonel Fitzwilliam. He was beyond comparison the most pleasant man; he certainly admired her, and his situation in life was most eligible. If only she could convince Elizabeth to settle down as she had; but on this subject as on the first, Elizabeth appeared disinclined to receive her opinion, an aversion Charlotte found in the end she could hardly begrudge her friend.

CHAPTER THIRTY-THREE

More than once did Elizabeth, in her ramble within the park, unexpectedly meet Miss Bingley. She felt all the perverseness of the mischance that should bring the lady where no one else was brought, and, to prevent its ever happening again, took care to inform her at first that it was a favourite haunt of hers. How it could occur a second time, therefore, was very odd! Yet it did, and even a third. It seemed like willful ill-nature, or a voluntary penance, for on these occasions it was not merely a few formal inquiries and an awkward pause and then away, but Caroline actually thought it necessary to turn back and walk with her. She never said a great deal, nor did Elizabeth give herself the trouble of talking or of listening much; but it struck her in the course of their third rencontre that Caroline was asking some odd unconnected questions—about her pleasure in being at Hunsford, her love of solitary walks, and her opinion of Mr. and Mrs. Collins's happiness. Had Charlotte been right? Was Caroline, in fact, enamored of her? Her spirits seemed set to rise at the thought; but then she pictured Jane waiting in vain at their aunt's house in town every morning for a fortnight, and she reminded herself that Caroline Bingley's feelings, like those of her brother's, had a history of capriciousness that did little to recommend her.

She was engaged one day as she walked, in perusing Jane's last letter, and dwelling on some passages which proved that Jane had not written in spirits, when, instead of being again surprised by Miss Bingley, she saw on looking up that Colonel Fitzwilliam was meeting her. Putting away the letter immediately and forcing a smile, she said: "I did not know before that you ever walked this way."

"I have been making the tour of the park," he replied, "as I generally do every year, and intend to close it with a call at the Parsonage. Are you going much farther?"

"No, I should have turned in a moment."

And accordingly she did turn, and they walked towards the Parsonage together.

"Do you certainly leave Kent on Saturday?" asked she.

"Yes—if Darcy does not put it off again. But I am at his disposal. He arranges the business just as he pleases."

"And if not able to please himself in the arrangement, he has at least pleasure in the great power of choice. I do not know anybody who seems more to enjoy the power of doing what he likes than Mr. Darcy."

"He likes to have his own way very well," replied Colonel Fitzwilliam. "But so we all do. It is only that he has better means of having it than many others, because he is rich, and many others are poor. I speak feelingly. A younger son, you know, must be inured to self-denial and dependence."

"In my opinion, the younger son of an earl can know very little of either. Seriously, what have you ever known of self-denial and dependence? When have you been prevented by want of money from going wherever you chose, or procuring anything you had a fancy for?"

"These are home questions—and perhaps I cannot say that I have experienced many hardships of that nature. But in matters of greater weight, I may suffer from want of money. Younger sons cannot marry where they like."

"Unless they like women of fortune, which I think they very often do."

"Our habits of expense make us too dependent, and there are not many in my rank of life who can afford to marry without some attention to money."

"Is this," thought Elizabeth, "meant for me?" She coloured at the idea; but, recovering herself, said in a lively tone, "And pray, what is the usual price of an earl's younger son? Unless the elder brother is very sickly, I suppose you would not ask above fifty thousand pounds."

He answered her in the same style, and the subject dropped. To interrupt a silence which might make him fancy her affected with what had passed, she soon afterwards said: "I imagine your cousin brought you and the others down with him chiefly for the sake of having someone at his disposal. I wonder he does not marry, to secure a lasting convenience of that kind. But, perhaps, his sister does as well for the present, and, as she is under his sole care, he may do what he likes with her."

"No," said Colonel Fitzwilliam, "that is an advantage which he must divide with me. I am joined with him in the guardianship of Miss Darcy."

"Are you indeed? And pray what sort of guardians do you make? Does your charge give you much trouble? Young ladies of her age are sometimes a little difficult to manage, and if she has the true Darcy spirit, she may like to have her own way."

As she spoke she observed him looking at her earnestly; and the manner in which he immediately asked her why she supposed Miss Darcy likely to give them any uneasiness, convinced her that she had somehow or other got pretty near the truth. She directly replied: "You need not be frightened. I never heard any harm of her; and I dare say she is one of the most tractable creatures in the world. She is a very great favourite with Mrs. Hurst and Miss Bingley."

"As well as an intimate friend of their brother, Mr. Bingley. I believe you said you know him as well? A most pleasant gentlemanlike man—he is a great friend of Darcy's."

"Oh, yes," said Elizabeth drily; "Mr. Darcy is uncommonly kind to Mr. Bingley, and takes a prodigious deal of care of him."

"Care of him! Yes, I really believe Darcy *does* take care of him in those points where he most wants care. From something that he told me in our journey hither, I have reason to think Bingley very much indebted to him. But I ought to beg his pardon, for I have no right to suppose that Bingley was the person meant. It was all conjecture."

"What is it you mean?"

"It is a circumstance which Darcy could not wish to be generally known, because if it were to get round to the lady's family, it would be an unpleasant thing."

"You may depend upon my not mentioning it."

"And remember that I have not much reason for supposing it to be Bingley. What he told me was merely this: that he congratulated himself on having helped save a friend from the inconveniences of a most imprudent marriage, but without mentioning names or any other particulars, and I only suspected it to be Bingley from believing him the kind of young man to get into a scrape of that sort, and from knowing them to have been together the whole of last summer. Besides which Darcy indicated that the main design of separation came from the man's sisters, and I could well imagine Miss Bingley and Mrs. Hurst to have a hand in such a scheme."

"Did Mr. Darcy give you reasons for this interference?"

"I understood that there were some very strong objections against the lady."

"And what arts did they use to separate them?"

"He did not talk to me of arts," said Fitzwilliam, smiling. "He only told me what I have now told you."

Elizabeth made no answer, and walked on, her heart swelling with indignation. After watching her a little, Fitzwilliam asked her why she was so thoughtful.

"I am thinking of what you have been telling me," said she. "Your cousin's conduct, and that of his friends, does not suit my feelings. Why did they feel the need to appoint themselves as judge?"

"You are rather disposed to call this interference officious?"

"I do not see what right Mr. Darcy or the man's sisters had to decide on the propriety of their friend's inclination, or why they were to determine and direct in what manner the friend was to be happy. But," she continued, recollecting herself, "as we know none of the particulars, it is not fair to condemn either Mr. Darcy or the sisters in question. It is not to be supposed that there was much affection in the case."

"That is not an unnatural surmise," said Fitzwilliam, "but it is a lessening of the honour of my cousin's triumph very sadly."

This was spoken jestingly; but it appeared to her so just a picture of Mr. Darcy, that she would not trust herself with an answer, and therefore, abruptly changing the conversation, talked on indifferent matters until they reached the Parsonage. There, shut into her own room, as soon as their visitor left them, she could think without interruption of all that she had heard. It was not to be supposed that any other people could be meant than those with whom she was connected. There could not exist in the world *two* men over whom Mr. Darcy could have such influence. That he had been concerned in the measures taken to separate Bingley and Jane she had never doubted; but to receive confirmation that Mrs. Hurst and Miss Bingley were responsible for the principal design and arrangement of them? Caroline, who Elizabeth had failed to convince herself was no more appealing than any other woman, was now confirmed without a doubt to be a principal cause of Jane's unhappiness. Caroline's pride and caprice, along with that of Mrs. Hurst and Mr. Darcy, were the cause of all that Jane had suffered, and still continued to suffer. Those three exalted individuals had helped ruin for a while every hope of happiness for the most affectionate, generous heart in the world; and no one could say how lasting an evil they might have inflicted.

"There were some very strong objections against the lady," were Colonel Fitzwilliam's words; and those strong objections probably were, her having one uncle who was a country attorney, and another who was in business in London.

"To Jane herself," she exclaimed, "there could be no possibility of objection; all loveliness and goodness as she is—her understanding excellent, her mind improved, and her manners captivating. Neither could anything be urged against my father, who, though with some peculiarities, has abilities Mr. Darcy himself need not disdain, and respectability which he will probably never reach." When she thought of her mother, her confidence gave way a little; but she would not allow that any objections *there* had material weight with Mr. Darcy or the Bingley sisters, whose pride, she was convinced, would receive a deeper wound from the want of importance in their friend's connections, than from any want of sense.

The agitation which the subject occasioned, brought on a headache; and it grew so much worse towards the evening that, added to her unwillingness to see any of Lady Catherine's guests, it determined her not to attend her cousins to Rosings, where they were engaged to drink tea. Mrs. Collins, seeing that she was really unwell, did not press her to go and as much as possible prevented her husband from pressing her; but Mr. Collins could not conceal his apprehension of Lady Catherine's being rather displeased by her staying at home.

CHAPTER THIRTY-FOUR

When they were gone, Elizabeth, as if intending to exasperate herself as much as possible against Miss Bingley, chose for her employment the examination of all the letters which Jane had written to her since her being in Kent. They contained no actual complaint, nor was there any revival of past occurrences, or any communication of present suffering. But in all, and in almost every line of each, there was a want of that cheerfulness which had been used to characterise her style, and which, proceeding from the serenity of a mind at ease with itself and kindly disposed towards everyone, had been scarcely ever clouded. Elizabeth noticed every sentence conveying the idea of uneasiness, with an attention which it had hardly received on the first perusal. Mr. Darcy's boast to his cousin of what misery he and his accomplices had been able to inflict, gave her a keener sense of her sister's sufferings. It was some consolation to think that Caroline and Darcy's visit to Rosings was to end on the day after the next—perhaps she could avoid seeing Lady Catherine's guests at all between now and then. A still greater consolation lay in the fact that, in less than a fortnight, Elizabeth should herself be with Jane again, and enabled to contribute to the recovery of her spirits, by all that affection could do.

While settling this point, she was suddenly roused by the sound of the door-bell, and her spirits were a little lifted by the idea of its being Colonel Fitzwilliam, who had once before called late in the evening, and might now come to inquire particularly after her. But this idea was soon banished, and her spirits were very differently affected, when, to her utter amazement, she saw Caroline Bingley walk into the room.

"What are you doing here?" demanded Elizabeth, colour rising in her cheeks as she stared at the very person she had wished most to avoid.

"I came to inquire after your health."

"You needn't have come."

"In fact, I did need to come." She paced the floor in front of Elizabeth.

"I cannot imagine why."

"You know exactly why." She dropped to her knees before Elizabeth, and reached for her hands. "It should not be so, but in vain have I struggled against my feelings for you. Against all reason, they will not be repressed."

Elizabeth's astonishment was beyond expression. She stared, blushed, doubted, and was silent. Caroline took this to be sufficient encouragement; and the avowal of all that she felt, and had long felt for Elizabeth, immediately followed. She spoke, too, of apprehension and anxiety regarding Elizabeth's sentiments toward her, but her countenance expressed real security. Such a circumstance was unlikely to recommend her suit, particularly given the history that existed between them.

"You must therefore allow me to tell you how ardently I love and admire you," she finished at last.

Colouring even more deeply, Elizabeth pulled her hands away and said: "I will allow no such thing." Her determination wavered momentarily after she said this, for she could not be entirely insensible to the compliment of the lady's affection. But then she felt the texture of the paper folded on her lap, and remembered her sister's disappointment upon receiving Caroline's letters the previous winter.

Her face going pale, Caroline rocked back on her heels. The disturbance of her mind was visible in every feature as she struggled for the appearance of composure; the resulting pause was to Elizabeth's feelings dreadful. But at length, with a voice of forced coolness, Caroline said: "I might, perhaps, wish to be informed why, with so little endeavour at civility, I am thus rejected."

"I do not intend to be uncivil. But even had not my feelings decided against you," said Elizabeth, "had they been indifferent, or had they even been favourable, do you think that any consideration would tempt me to accept the person who has been instrumental in ruining, perhaps forever, the happiness of a most beloved sister?"

As she pronounced these words, Miss Bingley changed colour; but she listened without attempting to interrupt Elizabeth while she continued: "I have every reason in the world to think ill of you. No motive can excuse the unjust and ungenerous part you acted there. You dare not, you cannot deny, that you have been a principal in the plot to divide them from each other—of exposing one to the censure of the world for caprice and instability, and the other to its derision for disappointed hopes, and involving them both in misery of the acutest kind."

She paused, and saw with no slight indignation that Caroline was listening with an air which proved her wholly unmoved by any feeling of remorse. She even looked back at Elizabeth with a smile of affected incredulity.

"Do you deny that you have done it?" Elizabeth repeated.

With assumed tranquility, Caroline replied: "I have no need of denying that I helped separate Charles from your sister. Towards *him* I have been kinder than towards myself."

Elizabeth disdained the appearance of noticing this civil reflection, but its meaning did not escape, nor was it likely to conciliate her.

"It is not merely this affair," she declared, "on which my dislike is founded. Your character unfolded from the start as one ruled by pride and vanity. Can you deny that you believe my family degraded, unworthy of connection to the Bingley name?"

"I cannot," said Caroline, rising to her feet and gazing down at Elizabeth.

"How perfect, to find that your one consistency should be your quite fantastic conceit."

"My *one* consistency? To what inconsistency do you refer?"

"I wrote to you," Elizabeth said, rising to face her, "and you did not answer. But why should this come as a surprise? Jane waited weeks for you to visit, and when you finally deigned to appear at Gracechurch Street, you were barely civil to her. Is that why you lied about visiting her at all? No matter—you have proven beyond a doubt that you are not capable of being a true and faithful friend, anymore than your brother could ever be."

Caroline shook her head. "And I suppose you would know all about truth and faithfulness, as you stand here in the house of your cousin and his wife—your lover!"

Elizabeth felt herself growing more angry every moment; yet she tried to the utmost to speak with composure when she said: "You are mistaken, Miss Bingley, if you suppose that your opinion on these matters affects me in any other way, than as it spares me the concern which I might have felt in refusing you, had you behaved more honourably."

She saw Caroline start at this, but as the lady said nothing, Elizabeth added: "From the very beginning of my acquaintance with you, your manners, impressing me with the fullest belief of your contemptible pride and conceit, were such as to form the groundwork of disapprobation on which succeeding events have built; and I had not known you a month before I felt that you were the last person in the world whom I could ever be prevailed upon to love."

"You have said quite enough," said Caroline, her features schooled now into an unreadable mask. "I perfectly comprehend your feelings, and have now only to be more ashamed of my own. Forgive me for having taken up so much of your time, and accept my best wishes for your health and happiness."

And with these words she quickly left the room, and Elizabeth heard her the next moment open the front door and quit the house.

The tumult of her mind was now painfully great. She knew not how to support herself, and from actual weakness sat down and cried for half-an-hour. Her astonishment, as she reflected on what had passed, was increased by every review of it. That she should receive a passionate avowal of love from Caroline Bingley! That Caroline should have been in love with her for so many months, so much in love as to wish to be with her in spite of all the objections which had made her prevent her brother's marrying Jane—and which must appear at least with equal force in her own case—was almost incredible! But Caroline's pride, that abominable pride, paired with her shameless refusal to apologise for the injury she had inflicted upon Jane, soon overcame the wonder which the consideration of her attachment had for a moment excited. Elizabeth continued in very agitated reflections till the sound of Lady Catherine's carriage made her feel how unequal she was to encounter Charlotte's observation, and hurried her away to her room.

CHAPTER THIRTY-FIVE

Elizabeth awoke the next morning to the same thoughts and meditations which had at length closed her eyes. She could not yet recover from the surprise of what had happened; it was impossible to think of anything else; and, totally indisposed for employment, she resolved, soon after breakfast, to indulge herself in air and exercise. She was proceeding directly to her favourite walk, when the recollection of Miss Bingley's sometimes coming there stopped her, and instead of entering the park, she turned up the lane, which led farther from the turnpike-road. The park paling was still the boundary on one side, and she soon passed one of the gates into the ground.

After walking two or three times along that part of the lane, she was lured, by the pleasantness of the morning, to stop at the gates and look into the park. The five weeks which she had now passed in Kent had made a great difference in the country, and every day was adding to the verdure of the early trees. She was on the point of continuing her walk, when she caught a glimpse of a lady within the sort of grove which edged the park; and, fearful of its being Miss Bingley, Elizabeth directly retreated. But the person who advanced was now near enough to see her, and stepping forward with eagerness, pronounced her name. She had turned away; but on hearing herself called, though in a voice which proved it to be Miss Bingley, she moved back towards the gate. Caroline had by that time reached it also, and, holding out a letter, which Elizabeth instinctively took, said, with an air of unusual formality, "I have been walking in the grove some time in the hope of meeting you. Will you do me the honour of reading that letter?" And then, with that slight bow of hers, she turned again into the plantation, and was soon out of sight.

With no expectation of pleasure, but with the strongest curiosity, Elizabeth opened the letter, and, to her still increasing wonder, perceived an envelope containing two sheets of letter-paper, written quite through, in a very close hand. The envelope itself was likewise full. Pursuing her way along the lane, she then began it. It was dated from Rosings, at eight o'clock in the morning, and was as follows:

"Please do not be concerned, Miss Eliza, that this letter will contain any resuscitation of the sentiments professed last night. It is not my intent to trouble you, nor to expose myself any further than I have already done, but I cannot rest easily until I address some among the considerations you raised in the course of our recent conversation. I only hope that you might be persuaded to pardon the presumption with which I am requesting your attention.

"You were not altogether wrong when you accused me of conceit, nor of pride. But while I did not deny last night the accusations you bestowed so liberally, this morning I find that I should like to offer a fairer accounting of my actions and motives. If, in the course of this explanation, I offend you, I pledge my sincere apologies. My aim is not to harm you in any way, only to remedy what I view to be the rather more affecting misunderstandings between us.

"It is true, I am aware, that I appear to believe myself and my connections far superior to those of others. In fact, I am overly conscious of the origins of my family's fortune. In school, and later, in town, I watched doors close and offers of friendship hastily be withdrawn wherever it was revealed that my father had come by his land and money through honest trade. To move in the society to which Louisa, Charles and I belong, it is difficult indeed to always be viewed as one who does not measure up. As a result, I have developed a carapace of sorts that I don in certain situations, a shield from the unkind whispers and demeaning manners of those individuals who believe me unremittingly inferior. I am distressed indeed to think that this defensive measure offended you, you who have been so engagingly forthright on most occasions. Perhaps almost too outspoken at times, given the events of last night.

"In regard to your sister's feelings toward my brother, I was apparently wrong in my estimation, as was Mr. Darcy. At the Netherfield ball, alerted by a comment from Sir Lucas, Darcy and I both perceived that Charles's partiality for Miss Bennet was beyond what either of us had previously witnessed in him. Your sister, however, while her look and manners were open, cheerful, and engaging as ever, seemed without any symptom of extraordinary regard. Thus were Darcy and I convinced that, though she received his attentions with pleasure, she did not feel the same degree of sentiment that Charles did. Believe me when I say that from all outward appearances, her heart did not appear so greatly invested. Add to that the vulgar behavior of your mother and younger sisters at Netherfield—pardon me for saying this, as I know it must offend you, although you and Jane are both entirely blameless of this charge, as you must be aware—Darcy and I agreed that Louisa's serious objections to the match were not entirely unfounded. This is why he and I went along with Louisa's plan to separate them, not merely owing to pride or superiority, but out of genuine love of and loyalty to my brother. Something, I suppose, of which you believe me incapable.

"Certain Charles was headed for a fall, we accordingly followed him to London, where Darcy engaged in pointing out to him the incommodity of such a match. While his remonstrance might have delayed my brother's determination, I do not believe that it would ultimately have prevented the marriage, had it not been for the assurance that Darcy gave of your sister's indifference. Charles had before believed Miss Bennet to return his affection with sincere, if not with equal regard. But he has great natural modesty, with a stronger dependence on the judgment of others, particularly that of Darcy, than on his own. To convince him that he had deceived himself was no very difficult task. Nor was persuading him against returning into Hertfordshire, once he believed Miss Bennet cared not for him.

"You may find fault, as I now do, with our decision to conceal from Charles your sister's being in town. He is even yet ignorant of her presence there. We decided to withhold this information primarily because of the belief that his regard did not seem enough extinguished for him to see her without some pain. Perhaps this concealment was beneath us; it was done, however, with all the best intentions. If we wounded your sister's feelings, as we so clearly must have done, we did so unknowingly; and though our motives may to you appear insufficient, I am not yet entirely prepared to condemn them.

"But charges of pride and malevolent scheming aside, you also accused me of faithlessness, to both you and Miss Bennet. What I would have you know is that, while my behavior has certainly seemed indicative of a lack of consistency in feeling, it cannot accurately reflect my sentiments, neither toward you nor your sister. On the matter of not writing back to you—please believe me when I say that your letter never reached me. Had I known, I would have responded immediately, for I very much wished us to become better acquainted. My lack of knowledge of your correspondence is related to a wider issue—namely, my place in my family. There is a reason that Louisa, Charles and I moved to Netherfield last year, one that has been hidden, for good reason, from public consumption. Therefore, I would beg you to keep what I am about to impart wholly to yourself. If you are unable to do so, please stop reading at once, and cast this letter into the fire directly upon returning to the Parsonage.

"If you are still reading, then I will assume you consent to the necessity for secrecy—a condition in which you have no doubt found yourself previously. So here it is, the information that Charles and Louisa would have no one outside ourselves ascertain: Last year, I entered into a friendship with a married woman, whose jealous husband threatened to publicly expose my 'unnatural tendencies' and, thereby, ruin the family, if I were not to leave Cumbria forever. Charles found Netherfield, and thither we went, with Louisa acting as my self-appointed guardian to ensure I would not advance any other opportunity of blackening the Bingley name. When she understood that Charles was becoming infatuated with your sister, and I with you, Louisa decided it was time to move back to town, where she confined me to Grosvenor Street and forbade me any contact with you or Jane. I can and do admit to a lack of courage, in allowing myself to be so managed by my sister, but the threat of being removed from the family and sent off to live on my own with neither fortune nor friend, a warning which Louisa leveled at me daily in London, was most affecting. I went to see your sister in direct violation of Louisa's wishes, and worried the entire visit what would happen if she were to find out. A woman of our class on her own in the world without money or connection—such a situation rarely ends well.

"Perhaps you can understand my cowardice? But then, you once led me to believe that your disposition, which I suspect to perfectly match my own, had been fairly received in your family, a situation I recall we agreed was most fortunate. In my own case, Louisa has become fixated on preventing me from ever forming another attachment, determining to keep me alone and miserable for the rest of my life. I have allowed her to exercise control over me—the primary reason we came with Darcy to Rosings was so that she could see me away from the influence of my crowd of 'unrepentant deviants,' as she terms my London friends. It seems, however, that there is danger wherever she takes me; for here you are, the person I had not been able to forget all these months.

"Pardon me—I do apologise, for that last comment drifts altogether far too near a renewal of the sentiments you find so repellent. In any case, I feel that I must thank you: Observing you as you are—happy, sociable, at perfect ease with yourself—has inspired me to try to emulate your example. I am determined to extricate myself from my sister's snare, and to leave her company for that of friends who will embrace me without censure or disgust. I am in your debt for the realization that I am not, in point of fact, obliged to live with the constant threat of loss or exposure, simply because my family abhors my preference for a particular type of companion.

"You may possibly wonder why I failed to tell you all of this last night; but I was not then master enough of my feelings to decide what ought to be revealed. For the truth of everything here related, I can appeal more particularly to the testimony of Mr. Darcy, who has been unavoidably acquainted with each of these transactions; and that you may have the possibility of consulting him, should you choose, I will endeavour to find some means of putting this letter in your hands in the course of the morning. I know that you do not think much of Mr. Darcy, possibly owing to your friendship with Mr. Wickham. But I once cautioned you against Wickham, and I must reiterate my warning: He is not a good man, and cannot be trusted. After the elder Mr. Darcy died, Wickham decided not to take orders, as had been planned, and applied to the younger Mr. Darcy for pecuniary assistance in the study of law. Darcy obliged with a sum many times the amount authorised in his father's will, only to watch Wickham waste the money on a life in town of dedicated idleness and dissipation. When he ran out of funds a few years on, he applied to Darcy for the living the elder Mr. Darcy had promised, should he take orders. When Darcy refused, Wickham repaid him by engaging in such nefarious behavior toward a member of Darcy's family that you would never think well of him again were you to know the particulars. If you take nothing else to heart from this letter, let it be that Mr. Wickham is a man in search of a fortune, any way he can find it.

"I will only add, may you remain healthy and happy today and all the days ahead.

"CAROLINE BINGLEY"

CHAPTER THIRTY-SIX

f Elizabeth, when Miss Bingley gave her the letter, did not expect it to contain a renewal of the previous evening's sentiments, she had formed no expectation at all of its contents. But such as they were, it may well be supposed how avidly she went through them, and what a contrariety of emotion they excited. Her feelings as she read were scarcely to be defined. With a strong prejudice against everything the lady might say, she began the letter, reading with an eagerness which hardly left her power of comprehension, and from impatience of knowing what the next sentence might bring, was incapable of attending to the sense of the one before her eyes. The lady's claim of encountering a marked lack of respect among certain social circles she instantly resolved to be false, along with her supposed belief of Jane's insensibility as the central motivation in wishing to separate the two lovers; and her account of the real, the worst objections to the match, made her too angry to have any wish of doing the author justice.

But when this subject was succeeded by Caroline's account of Louisa's treatment of her—when Elizabeth read with somewhat clearer attention a relation of events which, if true, must alarm anyone who, like her, shared the lady's particular affinity—her feelings were yet more acutely painful and more difficult to define. Apprehension afflicted her, that a sister would so willingly oppress and misuse her own blood. She wished to discredit the letter's claims, saying aloud, "This must be false." And when she had gone through the whole letter, though scarcely knowing anything of the last page or two, she put it hastily away, protesting that she would not regard it, that she would never look at it again.

In this perturbed state of mind, with thoughts that could rest on nothing, she walked on; but it would not do; in half a minute the letter was unfolded again, and collecting herself as well as she could, she again began the perusal of all that related to Mrs. Hurst, and commanded herself so far as to examine the meaning of every sentence. The account of the lady's role in separating her brother from Jane rang true, for Mrs. Hurst had not bothered to hide her contempt for the Bennets, particularly the night of the Netherfield Ball. It was only a small leap from interfering with a brother's happiness to exercising control over a disgraced sister, was it not? Caroline's explanations seemed to match what Elizabeth herself had observed of the Bingleys. Darcy, too—she did not understand how or why he could have had an intimate knowledge of all the events described in the letter, but she did believe him to bear Bingley genuine affection and friendship. The gentleman may have been unaccountably arrogant and unsociable, but he appeared to be a true friend to the Bingleys.

And yet, Caroline's slight against her own family was real and coldly given; and it seemed to offer a refutation of the more sympathetic passages of the letter. For a moment, she considered applying to Mr. Darcy for corroboration, but the idea was checked by the awkwardness of the application, and at length wholly banished by the conviction that Caroline would never have hazarded such a proposal had she not been well assured of Darcy's testimony. The closing bit about Wickham's attempts to extract money from Darcy, as well as his behaving badly toward a member of Darcy's family, reminded her of something, but she couldn't quite think what it might be.

She put down the letter, weighed every circumstance with what she meant to be impartiality—deliberated on the probability of each statement—with little success. Ultimately, it was only a series of assertions that she could choose to either believe or disbelieve. And yet, if she chose to believe what she read, the lines suggested that Caroline had been mostly innocent of the accusations which Elizabeth had so venomously cast at her the previous evening.

She grew absolutely ashamed of herself, unable to avoid the feeling that she had been blind, partial, prejudiced, absurd.

"How despicably I have acted," she thought; "I, who have prided myself on my discernment and abilities, who have often disdained the generous candour of my sister, and gratified my vanity in useless or blamable mistrust. Had I been in love, I could not have been more wretchedly blind! But vanity, not love, has been my folly. Since the very beginning of our acquaintance, I have courted prepossession and ignorance, and driven reason away, where Caroline Bingley was concerned. Till this moment I never knew myself."

From herself to Jane, from Jane to Bingley, her thoughts were in a line which soon brought to her recollection that Miss Bingley's explanation of their separation had appeared insufficient, and she read it again. Widely different was the effect of a second perusal. How could she deny that credit to her assertions in one instance, which she was obliged to give in the other? Caroline declared herself to have been totally unaware of her sister's attachment; and Elizabeth could not help remembering what Charlotte's opinion had always been. Neither could she deny the justice of the description of Jane. She felt that Jane's feelings, though fervent, were little displayed, and that there was a constant complacency in her air and manner not often united with great sensibility.

When she came to that part of the letter in which her family were mentioned in terms of such mortifying, yet merited reproach, her sense of shame was severe. The justice of the charge struck her too forcibly for denial, and the circumstances to which the letter particularly alluded as having passed at the Netherfield ball, could not have made a stronger impression on Caroline's mind than on hers. The compliment to herself and her sister was not unfelt. It soothed, but it could not console her for the contempt which had thus been self-attracted by the rest of her family; and as she considered that Jane's disappointment had in fact been the work of her nearest relations, and reflected how materially the credit of both must be hurt by such impropriety of conduct, she felt depressed beyond anything she had ever known before. The passage regarding Darcy and Wickham only added to her melancholy, for her mistrust of Caroline had undoubtedly contributed to her dislike of the proud gentleman who seemed always at her side. If she were to take Caroline's word for the other events described in the letter, didn't she almost have to rely on her version of Wickham's actions and character?

After wandering along the lane for two hours, giving way to every variety of thought—reconsidering events, determining probabilities, and reconciling herself, as well as she could, to a change so sudden and so important—fatigue, and a recollection of her long absence, made her at length return home; and she entered the house with the wish of appearing cheerful as usual, and the resolution of repressing such reflections as must make her unfit for conversation.

She was immediately told that two gentlemen from Rosings had called during her absence: Mr. Darcy, only for a few minutes, to take leave; and Colonel Fitzwilliam, who had sat with them at least an hour, hoping for her return, and almost resolving to walk after her till she could be found. Elizabeth could only just affect concern in missing him. Colonel Fitzwilliam was no longer any matter to her; she could think only of her letter.

CHAPTER THIRTY-SEVEN

ady Catherine's guests left Rosings the next morning, and Mr. Collins having been in waiting near the lodges, to make them his parting obeisance, was able to bring home the pleasing intelligence, of their appearing in very good health, and in as tolerable spirits as could be expected, after the melancholy scene so lately gone through at Rosings. To Rosings he then hastened, to console Lady Catherine and her daughter; and on his return brought back, with great satisfaction, a message from her ladyship, importing that she felt herself so dull as to make her very desirous of having them all to dine with her. An invitation which, of course, was accepted gratefully on all their behalf.

At dinner, their first subject was the diminution of the Rosings party. "I assure you, I feel it exceedingly," said Lady Catherine; "I believe no one feels the loss of friends so much as I do. But I am particularly attached to my nephews, and know them to be so much attached to me! They were excessively sorry to go! But so they always are. The dear Colonel rallied his spirits tolerably till just at last; but Darcy and his friend Miss Bingley seemed to feel it most acutely, more, I think, than last year. Darcy's attachment to Rosings certainly increases."

Mr. Collins had a compliment, and an allusion to throw in here, which were kindly smiled on by the mother and daughter.

Lady Catherine observed, after dinner, that Miss Bennet seemed out of spirits, and immediately accounting for it by herself, by supposing that she did not like to go home again so soon, she added: "But if that is the case, you must write to your mother and beg that you may stay a little longer. Mrs. Collins will be very glad of your company, I am sure."

"I am much obliged to your ladyship for your kind invitation," replied Elizabeth, "but it is not in my power to accept it. I must be in town next Saturday."

"Why, at that rate, you will have been here only six weeks. I expected you to stay two months. I told Mrs. Collins so before you came. There can be no occasion for your going so soon. Mrs. Bennet could certainly spare you for another fortnight."

"But my father cannot. He wrote last week to hurry my return."

"Oh, your father of course may spare you, if your mother can. Daughters are never of so much consequence to a father. And if you will stay another *month* complete, it will be in my power to take one of you as far as London, for I am going there early in June, for a week; and as Dawson does not object to the barouche-box, there will be very good room for one of you—and indeed, if the weather should happen to be cool, I should not object to taking you both, as you are neither of you large."

"You are all kindness, Madam; but I believe we must abide by our original plan."

Lady Catherine seemed resigned. "Mrs. Collins, you must send a servant with them. You know I always speak my mind, and I cannot bear the idea of two young women travelling post by themselves. It is highly improper. You must contrive to send somebody. I have the greatest dislike in the world to that sort of thing. Young women should always be properly guarded and attended, according to their situation in life. When my niece Georgiana went to Ramsgate last summer, I made a point of her having two men-servants go with her. Miss Darcy, the daughter of Mr. Darcy, of Pemberley, and Lady Anne, could not have appeared with propriety in a different manner. I am excessively attentive to all those things. You must send John with the young ladies, Mrs. Collins. I am glad it occurred to me to mention it; for it would really be discreditable to *you* to let them go alone."

"My uncle is to send a servant for us."

"Oh! Your uncle keeps a man-servant, does he? I am very glad you have somebody who thinks of these things. Where shall you change horses? Bromley, of course. If you mention my name at the Bell, you will be attended to."

Lady Catherine had many other questions to ask respecting their journey, and as she did not answer them all herself, attention was necessary, which Elizabeth believed to be lucky for her; or, with a mind so occupied, she might have forgotten where she was. Reflection must be reserved for solitary hours; whenever she was alone, she gave way to it as the greatest relief; and not a day went by without a solitary walk, in which she might indulge in all the delight of unpleasant recollections.

Miss Bingley's letter she was in a fair way of soon knowing by heart. She studied every sentence; and her feelings towards its writer were at times widely different. When she remembered the imperfect style of Caroline's pronouncement of love, she was still indignant; but when she considered how unjustly she had condemned and upbraided the lady, her anger was turned against herself; and Caroline's disappointed feelings became the object of compassion. Miss Bingley's attachment excited gratitude, her general character, now that it was more fully known, understanding; but Elizabeth could not for a moment repent her refusal, or feel more than a slight inclination ever to see the lady again. In her own past behaviour, there was a constant source of vexation and regret; and in the unhappy defects of her family, a subject of yet heavier chagrin. They were hopeless of remedy. Her father, contented with laughing at them, would never exert himself to restrain the wild giddiness of his youngest daughters; and her mother, with manners so far from right herself, was entirely insensible of the evil. Elizabeth had frequently united with Jane in an endeavour to check the imprudence of Catherine and Lydia; but while they were supported by their mother's indulgence, what chance could there be of improvement? Catherine, weak-spirited, irritable, and completely under Lydia's guidance, had been always affronted by their advice; and Lydia, self-willed and careless, would scarcely give them a hearing. Both girls were ignorant, idle, and vain. While there was an officer in Meryton, they would flirt with him; and while Meryton was within a walk of Longbourn, they would be going there forever.

Anxiety on Jane's behalf was another prevailing concern; and Miss Bingley's explanation, by restoring her brother to all of Elizabeth's former good opinion, heightened the sense of what Jane had lost. His affection was proved to have been sincere, and his conduct cleared of all blame, unless any could attach to the implicitness of his confidence in his friend. How grievous then was the thought that, of a situation so desirable in every respect, so replete with advantage, so promising for happiness, Jane had been deprived, by the folly and indecorum of her own family!

When to these recollections was added the behaviour of Mrs. Hurst and the business with Wickham, it may be easily believed that the happy spirits which had seldom been depressed before, were now so much affected as to make it almost impossible for her to appear tolerably cheerful.

Their engagements at Rosings were as frequent during the last week of her stay as they had been at first. The very last evening was spent there; and her ladyship again inquired minutely into the particulars of their journey, gave them directions as to the best method of packing, and was so urgent on the necessity of placing gowns in the only right way, that Maria thought herself obliged, on her return, to undo all the work of the morning, and pack her trunk afresh.

When they parted, Lady Catherine, with great condescension, wished them a good journey, and invited them to come to Hunsford again next year; and Miss de Bourgh exerted herself so far as to curtsey and hold out her hand to both.

CHAPTER THIRTY-EIGHT

n Saturday morning Elizabeth and Mr. Collins met for breakfast a few minutes before the others appeared; and he took the opportunity of paying the parting civilities which he deemed indispensably necessary.

"I know not, Miss Elizabeth," said he, "whether Mrs. Collins has yet expressed her sense of your kindness in coming to us; but I am very certain you will not leave the house without receiving her thanks for it. The favour of your company has been much felt, I assure you. We know how little there is to tempt anyone to our humble abode. Our plain manner of living, our small rooms and few domestics, and the little we see of the world, must make Hunsford extremely dull to a young lady like yourself; but I hope you will believe us grateful for the condescension, and that we have done everything in our power to prevent your spending your time unpleasantly."

Elizabeth was sincere in her thanks and assurances of happiness. She had spent six weeks with great enjoyment; and the pleasure of being with Charlotte, and the kind attentions she had received, must make *her* feel obliged.

Mr. Collins was gratified, and with a more smiling solemnity replied: "It gives me great pleasure to hear that you have passed your time not disagreeably. We have certainly done our best; and most fortunately having it in our power to introduce you to very superior society, and, from our connection with Rosings, the frequent means of varying the humble home scene, I think we may flatter ourselves that your Hunsford visit cannot have been entirely irksome. Our situation with regard to Lady Catherine's family is indeed the sort of extraordinary advantage and blessing which few can boast. You see on what a footing we are. You see how continually we are engaged there. In truth I must acknowledge that, with all the disadvantages of this humble parsonage, I should not think anyone abiding in it an object of compassion, while they are sharers of our intimacy at Rosings."

Words were insufficient for the elevation of his feelings; and he was obliged to walk about the room, while Elizabeth tried to unite civility and truth in a few short sentences.

"You may, in fact, carry a very favourable report of us into Hertfordshire, my dear cousin. I flatter myself at least that you will be able to do so. Lady Catherine's great attentions to Mrs. Collins you have been a daily witness of; and altogether I trust it does not appear that your friend has drawn an unfortunate—but on this point it will be as well to be silent. Only let me assure you, my dear Miss Elizabeth, that I can from my heart most cordially wish you equal felicity in marriage. My dear Charlotte and I have but one mind and one way of thinking. There is in everything a most remarkable resemblance of character and ideas between us. We seem to have been designed for each other."

Elizabeth, who had once, albeit not recently, believed that she and Charlotte had been designed for each other, took a calming breath. She could safely say to her cousin that it was a great happiness where that was the case, and with equal sincerity could add, that she firmly believed and rejoiced in his domestic comforts. She was not sorry, however, to have the recital of them interrupted by the lady from whom they sprang. Poor Charlotte! It was melancholy to leave her to such society. But she had chosen marriage to Mr. Collins with her eyes wide open; and though evidently regretting that her visitors were to go, she did not seem to ask for compassion. Her new home and her housekeeping, her parish and her poultry, and all their dependent concerns, had not yet lost their charm.

At length the chaise arrived, the trunks were fastened on, the parcels placed within, and it was pronounced to be ready. After an affectionate parting between the friends, Elizabeth was attended to the carriage by Mr. Collins, and as they walked down the garden he was commissioning her with his best respects to all her family, not forgetting his thanks for the kindness he had received at Longbourn in the winter, and his compliments to Mr. and Mrs. Gardiner, though unknown. He then handed her in, Maria followed, and the door was on the point of being closed, when he suddenly reminded them, with some consternation, that they had hitherto forgotten to leave any message for the ladies at Rosings.

"But," he added, "you will of course wish to have your humble respects delivered to them, with your grateful thanks for their kindness to you while you have been here."

Elizabeth made no objection; the door was then allowed to be shut, and the carriage drove off.

"Good gracious!" cried Maria, after a few minutes' silence, "it seems but a day or two since we first came! And yet how many things have happened!"

"A great many indeed," said her companion with a sigh.

"We have dined nine times at Rosings, besides drinking tea there twice! How much I shall have to tell!"

Elizabeth added privately, "And how much I shall have to conceal."

Their journey was performed without much conversation, or any alarm; and within four hours of their leaving Hunsford they reached Mr. Gardiner's house, where they were to remain a few days.

Jane looked well, and Elizabeth had little opportunity of studying her spirits, amidst the various engagements which the kindness of her aunt had reserved for them. But Jane was to go home with her, and at Longbourn there would be leisure enough for observation.

It was not without an effort, meanwhile, that she could wait even for Longbourn, before she told her sister of Miss Bingley's avowal of love. To know that she had the power of revealing what would so exceedingly astonish Jane, and must, at the same time, so highly gratify whatever of her own vanity she had not yet been able to reason away, was such a temptation to openness as nothing could have conquered but the fear that the revelation of the sister's sentiments might underscore the absence of the brother's, which would only grieve Jane further.

CHAPTER THIRTY-NINE

I t was the second week in May, in which the three young ladies set out together from Gracechurch Street for the town of ——, in Hertfordshire; and, as they drew near the appointed inn where Mr. Bennet's carriage was to meet them, they quickly perceived, in token of the coachman's punctuality, both Kitty and Lydia looking out of a dining-room upstairs. These two girls had been above an hour in the place, happily employed in visiting an opposite milliner, watching the sentinel on guard, and dressing a salad and cucumber.

After welcoming their sisters, they triumphantly displayed a table set out with such cold meat as an inn larder usually affords, exclaiming, "Is not this nice? Is not this an agreeable surprise?"

"And we mean to treat you all," added Lydia, "but you must lend us the money, for we have just spent ours at the shop out there." Then, showing her purchases—"Look here, I have bought this bonnet. I do not think it is very pretty; but I thought I might as well buy it as not. I shall pull it to pieces as soon as I get home, and see if I can make it up any better."

And when her sisters abused it as ugly, she added, with perfect unconcern, "Oh! But there were two or three much uglier in the shop; and when I have bought some prettier-coloured satin to trim it with fresh, I think it will be very tolerable. Besides, it will not much signify what one wears this summer, after the ——shire have left Meryton, and they are going in a fortnight."

"Are they indeed!" said Elizabeth, with the greatest satisfaction.

"They are going to be encamped near Brighton; and I do so want Papa to take us all there for the summer! It would be such a delicious scheme; and I dare say would hardly cost anything at all. Mamma would like to go too, of all things! Only think what a miserable summer else we shall have!"

"Yes," thought Elizabeth, "*that* would be a delightful scheme indeed, and completely do for us at once. Brighton, and a whole campful of soldiers, to us, who have been overset already by one poor regiment of militia, and the monthly balls of Meryton!"

"Now I have got some news for you," said Lydia, as they sat down at table. "What do you think? It is excellent news—capital news—and about a certain person we all like!"

Jane and Elizabeth looked at each other, and the waiter was told he need not stay. Lydia laughed, and said: "Aye, that is just like your formality and discretion. You thought the waiter must not hear, as if he cared! I dare say he often hears worse things said than I am going to say. But he is an ugly fellow! I am glad he is gone. I never saw such a long chin in my life. Well, but now for my news; it is about dear Wickham; too good for the waiter, is it not? There is no danger of Wickham's marrying Mary King. There's for you! She is gone down to her uncle at Liverpool: gone to stay. Wickham is safe."

"And Mary King is safe!" added Elizabeth, remembering Caroline Bingley's admonitions.

"She is a great fool for going away, if she liked him."

"But I hope there is no strong attachment on either side," said Jane.

"I am sure there is not on *his*. I will answer for it, he never cared three straws about her—who could about such a nasty little freckled thing?"

Elizabeth was dismayed to think that any of her own former sentiments could be reflected so coarsely in her younger sister. But as she reflected that it was Mary King's fortune that had undoubtedly attracted Wickham, Caroline's words returned to her: A man in search of a fortune, he had exhibited "nefarious behavior toward a member of Darcy's family." Elizabeth recollected, too, Colonel Fitzwilliam's uneasiness when she asked if Georgiana Darcy had ever given her guardians any difficulty. And all at once, she was sure she understood— Wickham's treachery and Georgiana Darcy's "trouble" were connected, most intimately. Wickham must have attempted to pursue Georgiana for her fortune, much as he had pursued Mary King for hers. Only he would not have been able to do so openly; Darcy would never have allowed such a thing. Wickham, then, must have attempted to seduce the girl, in secret, without her guardians' knowledge. Such perfidy would be more than enough to incur Darcy's outrage, and quite justifiably so.

Immediately Elizabeth longed to discuss the matter with Jane, to see if her sister saw the logic in her reasoning. But any conversation would have to wait until they were home again, and settled.

As soon as all had ate, and the elder ones paid, the carriage was ordered; and after some contrivance, the whole party, with all their boxes, work-bags, and parcels, and the unwelcome addition of Kitty's and Lydia's purchases, were seated in it.

"How nicely we are all crammed in," cried Lydia. "I am glad I bought my bonnet, if it is only for the fun of having another bandbox! Well, now let us be quite comfortable and snug, and talk and laugh all the way home. And in the first place, let us hear what has happened to you all since you went away. Have you seen any pleasant men? Have you had any flirting? I was in great hopes that one of you would have got a husband before you came back. Jane will be quite an old maid soon, I declare. She is almost three-and-twenty! Lord, how ashamed I should be of not being married before three-and-twenty! My aunt Phillips wants you so to get husbands, you can't think. She says Lizzy had better have taken Mr. Collins; but *I* do not think there would have been any fun in it. Lord! How I should like to be married before any of you; and then I would chaperone you about to all the balls. Dear me! We had such a good piece of fun the other day at Colonel Forster's. Kitty and me were to spend the day there, and Mrs. Forster promised to have a little dance in the evening (by the bye, Mrs. Forster and me are *such* friends!); and so she asked the two Harringtons to come, but Harriet was ill, and so Pen was forced to come by herself; and then, what do you think we did? We dressed up Chamberlayne in woman's clothes on purpose to pass for a lady, only think what fun! Not a soul knew of it, but Colonel and Mrs. Forster, and Kitty and me, except my aunt, for we were forced to borrow one of her gowns; and you cannot imagine how well he looked! When Denny, and Wickham, and Pratt, and two or three more of the men came in, they did not know him in the least. Lord! How I laughed! And so did Mrs. Forster. I thought I should have died. And *that* made the men suspect something, and then they soon found out what was the matter."

With such kinds of histories of their parties and good jokes, did Lydia, assisted by Kitty's hints and additions, endeavour to amuse her companions all the way to Longbourn. Elizabeth listened as little as she could, but there was no escaping the frequent mention of Wickham's name, which made her think of Darcy, which led her to Caroline, and thus to Bingley and Jane. She was well relieved when the carriage ride at last came to an end.

Their reception at home was most kind. Mrs. Bennet rejoiced to see Jane in undiminished beauty; and more than once during dinner did Mr. Bennet say voluntarily to Elizabeth: "I am glad you are come back, Lizzy."

Their party in the dining-room was large, for almost all the Lucases came to meet Maria and hear the news; and various were the subjects that occupied them: Lady Lucas was inquiring of Maria, after the welfare and poultry of her eldest daughter; Mrs. Bennet was doubly engaged, on one hand collecting an account of the present fashions from Jane, who sat some way below her, and, on the other, retailing them all to the younger Lucases; and Lydia, in a voice rather louder than any other person's, was enumerating the various pleasures of the morning to anybody who would hear her.

"Oh! Mary," said she, "I wish you had gone with us, for we had such fun! As we went along, Kitty and I drew up the blinds, and pretended there was nobody in the coach; and I should have gone so all the way, if Kitty had not been sick; and when we got to the George, I do think we behaved very handsomely, for we treated the other three with the nicest cold luncheon in the world, and if you would have gone, we would have treated you too. And then when we came away it was such fun! I thought we never should have got into the coach. I was ready to die of laughter. And then we were so merry all the way home! We talked and laughed so loud, that anybody might have heard us ten miles off!"

To this Mary very gravely replied, "Far be it from me, my dear sister, to depreciate such pleasures. They would doubtless be congenial with the generality of female minds. But I confess they would have no charms for *me*—I should infinitely prefer a book."

But of this answer Lydia heard not a word. She seldom listened to anybody for more than half a minute, and never attended to Mary at all.

In the afternoon Lydia was urgent with the rest of the girls to walk to Meryton, and to see how everybody went on; but Elizabeth steadily opposed the scheme. It should not be said that the Miss Bennets could not be at home half a day before they were in pursuit of the officers. There was another reason too for her opposition. She dreaded seeing Mr. Wickham again, now that she had guessed his trespass against the Darcys, and was resolved to avoid it as long as possible. The comfort to her of the regiment's approaching removal was indeed beyond expression. In a fortnight they were to go—and once gone, she hoped there would be nothing else for some time that would tempt further degradation of her younger sister's character.

She had not been many hours at home before she found that the Brighton scheme, of which Lydia had given them a hint at the inn, was under frequent discussion between her parents. Elizabeth saw directly that her father had not the smallest intention of yielding; but his answers were at the same time so vague and equivocal, that her mother, though often disheartened, had never yet despaired of succeeding at last.

CHAPTER FORTY

E lizabeth's impatience to acquaint Jane with what had happened could no longer be overcome; and at length, resolving to suppress every particular in which her sister was concerned, and preparing her to be surprised, she related to her the next morning the chief of the scene between Caroline Bingley and herself.

Miss Bennet's astonishment was soon lessened by the strong sisterly partiality which made any admiration of Elizabeth appear perfectly natural; and all surprise was shortly lost in other feelings, none of which outwardly appeared to be the hurt Elizabeth had worried her recitation might impart. Jane was only sorry that Caroline should have delivered her sentiments in a manner so little suited to recommend them, and still more grieved for the unhappiness her sister's refusal must have caused.

"Indeed," replied Elizabeth, "I am heartily sorry for her; but she has other feelings, which will probably soon drive away her regard for me. You do not blame me, however, for refusing her?"

"Blame you! Oh, no."

"But do you blame me for having accused her of inconsistency and disloyalty?"

"No—I do not know that you were wrong in saying what you did."

"But you *will* know it, when I tell you what happened the very next day."

She then spoke of the letter, repeating the whole of its contents as far as they concerned Mrs. Hurst's treatment of Caroline, which made Jane go pale and lament the family ties that could be so uncharitable. When Elizabeth shared the details of the financial transactions between Wickham and Darcy, along with what she believed to have happened to turn Darcy so resolutely against Wickham, Jane blanched even further. What a stroke this was for one who would willingly have gone through the world without believing such wickedness could exist. Most earnestly did she labour to prove the probability of error, and seek to clear the one without involving the other.

"This will not do," said Elizabeth; "you never will be able to make Darcy and Wickham both good and right, nor Caroline and Mrs. Hurst, for that matter. Take your choice, but you must be satisfied with only one. There is but such a quantity of merit between them in each case. For my part, I am inclined to believe it all Caroline's and Darcy's; but you shall do as you choose."

"Poor Wickham! There is such an expression of goodness in his countenance, such an openness and gentleness in his manner!"

"There certainly was some great mismanagement in the education of those two young men. One has got all the goodness, and the other all the appearance of it."

"I never thought Mr. Darcy deficient in goodness, as you did. Nor Caroline, either."

"And yet, I meant to be uncommonly clever in taking so decided a dislike to them both. It is such a spur to one's genius, such an opening for wit, to have a dislike of that kind. One may be continually abusive without saying anything just; but one cannot always be laughing at a person without now and then stumbling on something witty."

"Lizzy, when you first read that letter, I am sure you could not treat the matter as you do now."

"Indeed, I could not. I was uncomfortable enough, I may say unhappy. And with no one to speak to about what I felt, no Jane to comfort me and say that I had not been so very weak and vain and nonsensical as I knew I had! Oh, how I wanted you!"

"How unfortunate that you should have used such very strong expressions toward Caroline, for now your accusations do appear undeserved."

"It would seem that way. But the misfortune of speaking with bitterness is a most natural consequence of the prejudices I had been encouraging. There is one point on which I want your advice. I want to be told whether I ought, or ought not, to make our acquaintances in general understand Wickham's character."

Miss Bennet paused a little, and then replied, "Surely there can be no occasion for exposing him so dreadfully. What is your opinion?"

"That it ought not to be attempted. I am not even entirely certain that my conjectures are correct, though the evidence seems clear. Besides, Mr. Darcy's sister would be unduly harmed should the matter become public; and if I endeavour to undeceive people as to the general nature of Wickham's conduct, who will believe me? The prejudice against Mr. Darcy is so violent, that it would be the death of half the good people in Meryton to attempt to place him in an amiable light. I am not equal to it. Wickham will soon be gone; and therefore it will not signify to anyone here what he really is. Some time hence it will be all found out, and then we may laugh at their stupidity in not knowing it before. At present I will say nothing about it."

"You are quite right. To have his errors made public might ruin him forever. He is now, perhaps, sorry for what he has done, and anxious to re-establish a character. We must not make him desperate."

The tumult of Elizabeth's mind was allayed by this conversation. She had got rid of the secret which had weighed on her for a fortnight without appearing to wound Jane, and was certain of a willing listener in her sister, whenever she might wish to talk again. But there was still something lurking behind, of which prudence forbade the disclosure. She dared not relate the other half of Caroline's letter, nor explain to her sister how sincerely she had been valued by Bingley. Here was knowledge in which no one could partake; and she was sensible that nothing less than a perfect understanding between the parties could justify her in throwing off this last encumbrance of mystery.

"And then," said she, "if that very improbable event should ever take place, I shall merely be able to tell what Bingley may tell in a much more agreeable manner himself. The liberty of communication cannot be mine till it has lost all its value!"

She was now, on being settled at home, at leisure to observe the real state of her sister's spirits. Jane was not happy. She still cherished a very tender affection for Bingley. Having never even fancied herself in love before, her regard had all the warmth of first attachment, and, from her age and disposition, greater steadiness than most first attachments often boast; and so fervently did she value his remembrance, and prefer him to every other man, that all her good sense, and all her attention to the feelings of her friends, were requisite to check the indulgence of those regrets which must have been injurious to her own health and tranquility.

"Well, Lizzy," said Mrs. Bennet one day, "what is your opinion *now* of this sad business of Jane's? For my part, I am determined never to speak of it again to anybody. I told my sister Phillips so the other day. But I cannot find out that Jane saw anything of him in London. Well, he is a very undeserving young man—and I do not suppose there's the least chance in the world of her ever getting him now. There is no talk of his coming to Netherfield again in the summer; and I have inquired of everybody, too, who is likely to know."

"I do not believe he will ever live at Netherfield anymore."

"Oh well! It is just as he chooses. Nobody wants him to come. Though I shall always say he used my daughter extremely ill; and if I was her, I would not have put up with it. Well, my comfort is, I am sure Jane will die of a broken heart; and then he will be sorry for what he has done."

But as Elizabeth could not receive comfort from any such expectation, she made no answer.

"Well, Lizzy," continued her mother, soon afterwards, "and so the Collinses live very comfortable, do they? Well, well, I only hope it will last. And what sort of table do they keep? Charlotte is an excellent manager, I dare say. If she is half as sharp as her mother, she is saving enough. There is nothing extravagant in *their* housekeeping, I dare say."

"No, nothing at all."

"A great deal of good management, depend upon it. Yes, yes, they will take care not to outrun their income. They will never be distressed for money. Well, much good may it do them! And so, I suppose, they often talk of having Longbourn when your father is dead. They look upon it as quite their own, I dare say, whenever that happens."

"It was a subject which they could not mention before me."

"No; it would have been strange if they had; but I make no doubt they often talk of it between themselves. Well, if they can be easy with an estate that is not lawfully their own, so much the better. I should be ashamed of having one that was only entailed on me."

CHAPTER FORTY-ONE

The first week of their return was soon gone. The second began. It was the last of the regiment's stay in Meryton, and all the young ladies in the neighbourhood were drooping apace. The dejection was almost universal. The elder Miss Bennets alone were still able to eat, drink, sleep, and pursue the usual course of their employments. Very frequently were they reproached for this insensibility by Kitty and Lydia, whose own misery was extreme, and who could not comprehend such hard-heartedness in any of the family.

"Good Heaven, what is to become of us? What are we to do?" would they often exclaim in the bitterness of woe. "How can you be smiling so, Lizzy?"

Their affectionate mother shared all their grief; she remembered what she had herself endured on a similar occasion, five-and-twenty years ago.

"I am sure," said she, "I cried for two days together when Colonel Miller's regiment went away. I thought I should have broken my heart."

"I am sure I shall break mine," said Lydia.

"If one could but go to Brighton!" observed Mrs. Bennet.

"Oh, yes—if one could but go to Brighton! But Papa is so disagreeable."

"A little sea-bathing would set me up forever."

"And my aunt Phillips is sure it would do me a great deal of good," added Kitty.

Such were the kind of lamentations resounding perpetually through Longbourn House. Elizabeth tried to be diverted by them; but all sense of pleasure was lost in shame. She felt anew the justice of Caroline and Darcy's objections; and never had she been so much disposed to pardon their interference in Bingley's affairs.

But the gloom of Lydia's prospect was shortly cleared away; for she received an invitation from Mrs. Forster, the wife of the colonel of the regiment, to accompany her to Brighton. This invaluable friend was a very young woman, and very lately married. A resemblance in good humour and good spirits had recommended her and Lydia to each other, and out of their three months' acquaintance they had been intimate two.

The rapture of Lydia on this occasion, her adoration of Mrs. Forster, the delight of Mrs. Bennet, and the mortification of Kitty, could scarcely be described. Wholly inattentive to her sister's feelings, Lydia flew about the house in restless ecstasy, calling for everyone's congratulations, and laughing and talking with more violence than ever; whilst the luckless Kitty continued in the parlour repined at her fate in terms as unreasonable as her accent was peevish.

"I cannot see why Mrs. Forster should not ask me as well as Lydia," said she, "Though I am not her particular friend, I have just as much right to be asked, and more too, for I am two years older."

In vain did Elizabeth attempt to make her reasonable, and Jane to make her resigned. As for Elizabeth herself, this invitation was so far from exciting in her the same feelings as in her mother and Lydia, that she considered it as the death warrant of all possibility of common sense for the latter; and detestable as such a step must make her were it known, she could not help secretly advising her father not to let her go. She represented to him the little advantage Lydia could derive from the friendship of such a woman as Mrs. Forster, as well as the probability of her being yet more imprudent at Brighton, where the temptations must be greater than at home.

He heard her attentively, and then said: "Lydia will never be easy until she has exposed herself in some public place or other, and we can never expect her to do it with so little expense or inconvenience to her family as under the present circumstances."

"If you were aware," said Elizabeth, "of the very great disadvantage to us all which must arise from the public notice of Lydia's unguarded and imprudent manner—nay, which has already arisen from it, I am sure you would judge differently in the affair."

"Already arisen?" repeated Mr. Bennet. "What, has she frightened away some of your lovers? Poor little Lizzy! But do not be cast down. Such squeamish youths as cannot bear to be connected with a little absurdity are not worth a regret. Come, let me see the list of pitiful fellows who have been kept aloof by Lydia's folly."

"Indeed you are mistaken. I have no such injuries to resent. But if you, my dear father, will not take the trouble of checking her exuberant spirits, her character will be fixed, and she will, at sixteen, be the most determined flirt that ever made herself or her family ridiculous."

Despite Elizabeth's commitment to the subject, Mr. Bennet was not disposed to give in to her exhortations. Lydia reminded him a bit of himself at her age, though lacking in his native intelligence or strength of character; and far be it for him to judge her for her august interest in militia officers. He thought of reminding Elizabeth that her own disposition risked more injury to the family name than Lydia's silliness or propensity to flirt with any attractive man she met; but again, as he was hardly innocent of such charges himself, and as he had yet to confirm his daughter's attachment to a member of her own sex, he affectionately took her hand and said in reply: "Do not make yourself uneasy, my love—wherever you and Jane are known you must be respected and valued. But we shall have no peace at Longbourn if Lydia does not go to Brighton. Colonel Forster is a sensible man, and will keep her out of any real mischief; and she is luckily too poor to be an object of prey to anybody. At Brighton, the officers will find women better worth their notice. Let us hope that by being there, Lydia may comprehend her own insignificance. She cannot grow many degrees worse, without authorising us to lock her up for the rest of her life."

With this answer Elizabeth was forced to be content. It was not in her nature, however, to increase her vexations by dwelling on them. She was confident of having performed her duty, and to fret over unavoidable evils, or augment them by anxiety, was no part of her character.

Had Lydia and her mother known of her conference with her father, their indignation would hardly have found expression in their united volubility. In Lydia's imagination, a visit to Brighton comprised every possibility of earthly happiness. She saw, with the creative eye of fancy, the streets of that gay bathing-place covered with officers. She saw herself the object of attention, to tens and to scores of them at present unknown. She saw all the glories of the camp—its tents stretched forth in beauteous uniformity of lines, crowded with the young and the gay, and dazzling with scarlet; and, to complete the view, she saw herself seated beneath a tent, tenderly flirting with at least six officers at once.

Had she known her sister sought to tear her from such prospects and such realities as these, what would have been her sensations? They could have been understood only by her mother, who might have felt nearly the same. Lydia's going to Brighton was all that consoled her for her melancholy conviction of her husband's never intending to go there himself.

But they were entirely ignorant of what had passed; and their raptures continued, with little intermission, to the very day of Lydia's leaving home.

Elizabeth was now to see Mr. Wickham for the last time. Having been frequently in company with him since her return, any agitation she had felt was pretty well past. She had learnt to detect, in the very gentleness which had first delighted her, an affectation and a sameness to disgust and weary. In his present behaviour to herself, moreover, she had a fresh source of displeasure, for the inclination he soon testified of renewing those intentions which had marked the early part of their acquaintance could only serve, after what had since passed, to provoke her. She lost all concern for him in finding herself thus selected as the object of such idle and frivolous gallantry; and while she steadily repressed it, could not but feel the reproof contained in his believing, that however long, and for whatever cause, his attentions had been withdrawn, her vanity would be gratified, and her affection secured at any time by their renewal.

On the very last day of the regiment's remaining at Meryton, he dined, with other of the officers, at Longbourn; and so little was Elizabeth disposed to part from him in good humour, that on his making some inquiry as to the manner in which her time had passed at Hunsford, she mentioned Colonel Fitzwilliam's and Mr. Darcy's having both spent three weeks at Rosings, and asked him if he was acquainted with the former.

He looked surprised, displeased, alarmed, all of which encouraged her to put faith in her suppositions; but with a moment's recollection and a returning smile, replied that he had formerly seen him often; and, after observing that he was a very gentlemanlike man, asked her how she had liked him. Her answer was warmly in his favour. With an air of indifference he soon afterwards added: "How long did you say he was at Rosings?"

"Nearly three weeks."

"And you saw him frequently?"

"Yes, almost every day."

"His manners are very different from his cousin's."

"Yes, very different. But I think Mr. Darcy improves upon acquaintance."

"Indeed!" said Mr. Wickham with a look which did not escape her. "And pray, may I ask?—" But checking himself, he added, in a gayer tone, "Is it in address that he improves? Has he deigned to add aught of civility to his ordinary style?—For I dare not hope," he continued in a lower and more serious tone, "that he is improved in essentials."

"Oh, no!" said Elizabeth. "In essentials, I believe, he is very much what he ever was." While she spoke, Wickham looked as if scarcely knowing whether to rejoice over her words, or to distrust their meaning. There was something in her countenance that made him listen with an apprehensive and anxious attention, while she added: "When I said that he improved on acquaintance, I did not mean that his mind or his manners were in a state of improvement, but that, from knowing him better, his disposition was better understood."

Wickham's alarm now appeared in a heightened complexion and agitated look; for a few minutes he was silent, till, shaking off his embarrassment, he turned to her again, and said in the gentlest of accents: "You, who so well know my feeling towards Mr. Darcy, will readily comprehend how sincerely I must rejoice that he is wise enough to assume even the appearance of what is right. His pride, in that direction, may be of service, if not to himself, to many others, for it must only deter him from such foul misconduct as I have suffered by. I only fear that the sort of cautiousness to which you, I imagine, have been alluding, is merely adopted on his visits to his aunt, of whose good opinion and judgment he stands much in awe. His fear of her has always operated, I know, when they were together; and a good deal is to be imputed to his wish of forwarding the match with Miss de Bourgh, which I am certain he has very much at heart."

Elizabeth answered only by a slight inclination of the head. She saw that he wanted to engage her on the old subject of his grievances, and she was in no humour to indulge him. The rest of the evening passed with the appearance, on his side, of usual cheerfulness, but with no further attempt to distinguish Elizabeth; and they parted at last with mutual civility, and possibly a mutual desire of never meeting again.

When the party broke up, Lydia returned with Mrs. Forster to Meryton, from whence they were to set out early the next morning. The separation between her and her family was rather noisy than pathetic. Kitty was the only one who shed tears; but she did weep from vexation and envy. Mrs. Bennet was diffuse in her good wishes for the felicity of her daughter, and impressive in her injunctions that she should not miss the opportunity of enjoying herself as much as possible—advice which there was every reason to believe would be well attended to; and in the clamorous happiness of Lydia herself in bidding farewell, the more gentle adieus of her sisters were uttered without being heard.

CHAPTER FORTY-TWO

Had Elizabeth's opinion been all drawn from her own family, she could not have formed a very pleasing opinion of conjugal felicity or domestic comfort. Her father, attracted by that appearance of good humour which youth and beauty generally give, had married a woman whose weak understanding and illiberal mind had very early in their marriage put an end to any possibility of affection for her. Respect, esteem, and confidence had vanished for ever; and all his hopes for domestic contentment were overthrown. But Mr. Bennet was fond of the country and of books; and fond, too, of occasional trips to town for business and pleasure, especially when he was younger; and from these tastes had arisen his principal enjoyments. To his wife he was very little otherwise indebted, than as her ignorance and folly had contributed to his amusement. This is not the sort of happiness that a man would in general wish to owe to his wife; but where other powers of entertainment are wanting, the true philosopher will derive benefit from such as are given.

Elizabeth, however, had never been blind to the impropriety of her father's behaviour as a husband. She had always seen it with pain; but respecting his abilities, and grateful for his affectionate treatment of herself, she had endeavoured to forget what she could not overlook, and to banish from her thoughts that continual breach of conjugal obligation and decorum which, in exposing his wife to the contempt of her own children, was so highly reprehensible. But she had never felt so strongly as now the disadvantages which must attend the children of so unsuitable a marriage, nor ever been so fully aware of the evils arising from so ill-judged a direction of talents; talents, which, rightly used, might at least have preserved the respectability of his daughters, even if incapable of enlarging the mind of his wife.

While Elizabeth had celebrated Wickham's departure, she found little other cause for satisfaction in the loss of the regiment. Their parties abroad were less varied than before, and at home she had a mother and sister whose constant repinings at the dullness of everything around them threw a real gloom over their domestic circle; and, though Kitty might in time regain her natural degree of sense, since the disturbers of her brain were removed, her other sister, from whose disposition greater evil might be apprehended, was likely to be hardened in all her folly and assurance by a situation of such double danger as a watering-place and a camp. Upon the whole, therefore, she found, what has been sometimes found before, that an event to which she had been looking forward did not, in taking place, bring all the satisfaction she had promised herself. It was consequently necessary to name some other period for the commencement of actual felicity—to have some other point on which her wishes and hopes might be fixed, and by again enjoying the pleasure of anticipation, console herself for the present, and prepare for another disappointment. Her tour to the Lakes was now the object of her happiest thoughts; it was her best consolation for all the uncomfortable hours which the discontentedness of her mother and Kitty made inevitable; and could she have included Jane in the scheme, every part of it would have been perfect.

"But it is fortunate," thought she, "that I have something to wish for. Were the whole arrangement complete, my disappointment would be certain. But here, by carrying with me one ceaseless source of regret in my sister's absence, I may reasonably hope to have all my expectations of pleasure realised. A scheme of which every part promises delight can never be successful; and general disappointment is only warded off by the defence of some little peculiar vexation."

When Lydia went away she promised to write very often and very minutely to her mother and Kitty; but her letters were always long expected, and always very short. Those to her mother contained little else than that they were just returned from the library, where such and such officers had attended them, and where she had seen such beautiful ornaments as made her quite wild; that she had a new gown, or a new parasol, which she would have described more fully, but was obliged to leave off in a violent hurry, as Mrs. Forster called her, and they were going off to the camp; and from her correspondence with her sister, there was still less to be learnt—for her letters to Kitty, though rather longer, were much too full of lines under the words to be made public.

After the first fortnight or three weeks of her absence, health, good humour, and cheerfulness began to reappear at Longbourn. Everything wore a happier aspect. The families who had been in town for the winter came back again, and summer finery and summer engagements arose. Mrs. Bennet was restored to her usual querulous serenity; and, by the middle of June, Kitty was so much recovered as to be able to enter Meryton without tears; an event of such happy promise as to make Elizabeth hope that by the following Christmas she might be so tolerably reasonable as not to mention an officer above once a day, unless, by some cruel and malicious arrangement at the War Office, another regiment should be quartered in Meryton.

The time fixed for the beginning of their northern tour was now fast approaching, and a fortnight only was wanting of it, when a letter arrived from Mrs. Gardiner, which at once delayed its commencement and curtailed its extent. Mr. Gardiner would be prevented by business from setting out till a fortnight later in July, and must be in London again within a month, and as that left too short a period for them to go so far, and see so much as they had proposed, or at least to see it with the leisure and comfort they had built on, they were obliged to give up the Lakes, and substitute a more contracted tour, and, according to the present plan, were to go no farther northwards than Derbyshire. In that county there was enough to be seen to occupy the chief of their three weeks; and to Mrs. Gardiner it had a peculiarly strong attraction. The town where she had formerly passed some years of her life, and where they were now to spend a few days, was probably as great an object of her curiosity as all the celebrated beauties of Matlock, Chatsworth, Dovedale, or the Peak.

Elizabeth was excessively disappointed; she had set her heart on seeing the Lakes—the fact that the Bingleys came from the Lake District had nothing to do with her desire to visit the area, she was quite certain—and still thought there might have been time enough. But it was her business to be satisfied, and certainly her temper to be happy; and all was soon right again.

With the mention of Derbyshire there were many ideas connected. It was impossible for her to see the word without thinking of Pemberley and Mr. Darcy, a line of thought that necessarily led her to Caroline Bingley. "But surely," said she, "I may enter the county with impunity, and rob it of a few petrified spars without he or his friend perceiving me."

The period of expectation was now doubled. Four weeks were to pass away before her uncle and aunt's arrival. But they did pass away, and Mr. and Mrs. Gardiner, with their four children, did at length appear at Longbourn. The children, two girls of six and eight years old, and two younger boys, were to be left under the particular care of their cousin Jane, who was the general favourite, and whose steady sense and sweetness of temper exactly adapted her for attending to them in every way—teaching them, playing with them, and loving them.

The Gardiners stayed only one night at Longbourn, and set off the next morning with Elizabeth in pursuit of novelty and amusement. One enjoyment was certain—that of suitableness of companions; a suitableness which comprehended health and temper to bear inconveniences; cheerfulness to enhance every pleasure; and affection and intelligence, which might supply it among themselves if there were disappointments abroad.

It is not the object of this work to give a description of Derbyshire, nor of any of the remarkable places through which their route thither lay; Oxford, Blenheim, Warwick, Kenilworth, Birmingham, etc. are sufficiently known. A small part of Derbyshire is all the present concern. To the little town of Lambton, the scene of Mrs. Gardiner's former residence, and where she had lately learned some acquaintance still remained, they bent their steps, after having seen all the principal wonders of the country; and within five miles of Lambton, Elizabeth found from her aunt that Pemberley was situated nearby. It was not in their direct road, nor more than a mile or two out of it. In talking over their route the evening before, Mrs. Gardiner expressed an inclination to see the place again. Mr. Gardiner declared his willingness, and Elizabeth was applied to for her approbation.

"My love, should not you like to see a place of which you have heard so much?" said her aunt. "A place, too, with which so many of your acquaintances are connected."

Elizabeth felt that she had no business at Pemberley, the owner of which being such an intimate of the Bingleys, and was obliged to assume a disinclination for seeing it. She must own that she was tired of seeing great houses; after going over so many, she really had no pleasure in fine carpets or satin curtains.

"If it were merely a fine house richly furnished," said Mrs. Gardiner, "I should not care about it myself; but the grounds are delightful. They have some of the finest woods in the country."

Elizabeth said no more—but her mind could not acquiesce. The possibility of meeting Mr. Darcy, while viewing the place, instantly occurred. It would be unfortunate, as the gentleman would undoubtedly inform Miss Bingley of her presence, and then Caroline would wonder at her impertinence, visiting the home of one of her intimate friends; or perhaps she might even think that Elizabeth was visiting in the hope of meeting her. What if, after all, Caroline were visiting Pemberley? Elizabeth blushed at the very idea, and thought it would be better to speak openly to her aunt than to take the risk. But against this there were objections; and she finally resolved that it could be the last recourse, if her private inquiries to the absence of the family were unfavourably answered.

Accordingly, when she retired at night, she asked the chambermaid whether Pemberley were not a very fine place? What was the name of its proprietor? And, with no little alarm, whether the family or friends were down for the summer? A most welcome negative followed the last question—and her alarms now being removed, she was at leisure to feel a great deal of curiosity to see the house herself; and when the subject was revived the next morning, and she was again applied to, could readily answer, and with a proper air of indifference, that she had not really any dislike to the scheme. To Pemberley, therefore, they were to go.

CHAPTER FORTY-THREE

Elizabeth, as they drove along, watched for the first appearance of Pemberley Woods with some perturbation. The lodge's park was very large, and contained great variety of ground. They entered it in one of its lowest points, and drove for some time through a beautiful wood stretching over a wide extent.

Her mind was too occupied for conversation, but she saw and admired every remarkable spot and point of view. They gradually ascended for half-a-mile, and then found themselves at the top of a considerable eminence, where the wood ceased, and the eye was instantly caught by Pemberley House, situated on the opposite side of a valley, into which the road with some abruptness wound. It was a large, handsome stone building, standing well on rising ground, and backed by a ridge of high woody hills; and in front, a stream of some natural importance was swelled into greater, but without any artificial appearance. Elizabeth had never seen a place for which nature had done more, or where natural beauty had been so little counteracted by an awkward taste.

They descended the hill, crossed the bridge, and drove to the door; and, while examining the nearer aspect of the house, all her apprehension of meeting its owner or his friend returned. She dreaded lest the chambermaid had been mistaken. On applying to see the place, they were admitted into the hall; and Elizabeth, as they waited for the housekeeper, had leisure to wonder at being where she was.

The housekeeper came: a respectable-looking elderly woman, much less fine, and more civil, than she had any notion of finding her. They followed her into the dining-parlour. It was a large, well proportioned room, handsomely fitted up. Elizabeth, after slightly surveying it, went to a window to enjoy its prospect. The hill, crowned with wood, which they had descended, receiving increased abruptness from the distance, was a beautiful object. Every aspect of the ground was good; and she looked on the whole scene, the river, the trees scattered on its banks and the winding of the valley, as far as she could trace it, with delight. As they passed into other rooms these objects were taking different positions; but from every window there were beauties to be seen. The rooms were lofty and handsome, and their furniture suitable to the fortune of its proprietor; but Elizabeth saw, with admiration of his taste, that it was neither gaudy nor uselessly fine; with less of splendour, and more real elegance, than the furniture of Rosings.

She longed to inquire of the housekeeper whether her master was really absent, but had not the courage for it. At length, however, the question was asked by her uncle; and Mrs. Reynolds replied that he was, adding, "But we expect him tomorrow, with a large party of friends."

How rejoiced was Elizabeth that their own journey had not by any circumstance been delayed a day, for the party of friends, she had no doubt, must include Caroline Bingley.

Her aunt now called her to look at a picture. She approached and saw the likeness of Mr. Wickham, suspended, amongst several other miniatures, over the mantelpiece. Her aunt asked her, smilingly, how she liked it. The housekeeper came forward, and told them it was a picture of a young gentleman, the son of her late master's steward, who had been brought up by him at his own expense.

"He is now gone into the army," she added; "but I am afraid he has turned out very wild."

Mrs. Gardiner looked at her niece with a smile, but Elizabeth could not return it.

"And that," said Mrs. Reynolds, pointing to another of the miniatures, "is my master—and very like him. It was drawn at the same time as the other."

"I have heard much of your master's fine person," said Mrs. Gardiner, looking at the picture; "it is a handsome face. But, Lizzy, you can tell us whether it is like or not."

Mrs. Reynolds's respect for Elizabeth seemed to increase on this intimation of her knowing her master.

"Does the young lady know Mr. Darcy?"

Elizabeth said: "A little."

"And do not you think him a very handsome gentleman, Ma'am?"

"Yes, he is tolerably handsome."

"I am sure I know none so handsome; but in the gallery upstairs you will see a finer picture of him than this. This room was my late master's favourite room, and these miniatures are just as they used to be then."

This accounted to Elizabeth for Wickham's being among them.

Mrs. Reynolds then directed their attention to one of Miss Darcy, drawn when she was only eight years old.

"And is Miss Darcy as handsome as her brother?" said Mrs. Gardiner.

"Oh, yes—the handsomest young lady that ever was seen; and so accomplished! She plays and sings all day long. In the next room is a new instrument just come down for her—a present from my master; she comes here tomorrow with him."

"Is your master much at Pemberley in the course of the year?"

"Not so much as I could wish, sir; but I dare say he may spend half his time here; and Miss Darcy is always down for the summer months."

"Except," thought Elizabeth, "when she goes to Ramsgate."

"If your master would marry, you might see more of him."

"Yes, sir; but I do not know when *that* will be. I do not know who is good enough for him."

Mr. and Mrs. Gardiner smiled. Elizabeth could not help saying, "It is very much to his credit, I am sure, that you should think so."

"I say no more than the truth, and everybody will say that knows him," replied the other. Elizabeth thought this was going pretty far; and she listened with astonishment as the housekeeper added, "I have never known a cross word from him in my life, and I have known him ever since he was four years old."

This was praise, of all others most extraordinary, most opposite to her ideas. That he was not a good-tempered man had been her firmest opinion. But then, she had gotten so much wrong about Darcy and the Bingleys; his perceived ill humor might simply be another instance of bad judgment on her side.

"There are very few people of whom so much can be said," Mr. Gardiner noted. "You are lucky in having such a master."

"Yes, sir, I know I am. If I were to go through the world, I could not meet with a better. But I have always observed, that they who are good-natured when children, are good-natured when they grow up; and he was always the sweetest-tempered, most generous-hearted boy in the world."

Mrs. Reynolds moved on to the subjects of the pictures, the dimensions of the rooms, and the price of the furniture. They then proceeded together up the great staircase. On reaching the spacious lobby above they were shown into a very pretty sitting-room, lately fitted up with greater elegance and lightness than the apartments below; and were informed that it was but just done to give pleasure to Miss Darcy, who had taken a liking to the room when last at Pemberley.

"Mr. Darcy is certainly a good brother," said Elizabeth, as she walked towards one of the windows, remembering as she did the letters that Darcy had always seemed to be writing at Netherfield.

"This is always the way with him," said Mrs. Reynolds. "Whatever can give his sister any pleasure is sure to be done in a moment. There is nothing he would not do for her."

The picture-gallery, and two or three of the principal bedrooms, were all that remained to be shown. In the former were many good paintings; but Elizabeth knew nothing of the art; and from such as had been already visible below, she had willingly turned to look at some drawings of Miss Darcy's, whose subjects were usually more interesting, and also more intelligible.

In the gallery there were many family portraits, but they could have little to fix the attention of a stranger. Elizabeth wandered in search of the only face whose features would be known to her, and at last beheld a striking resemblance to Mr. Darcy, with such a smile over the face as she thought she had only ever seen directed at Miss Bingley. What lay between Darcy and Caroline? It had occurred to her to wonder before, but never so avidly as at this moment, in the gentleman's home. In the beginning, Elizabeth had believed Caroline wanted Darcy for a husband, and viewed herself as a rival for his affections. Clearly that had never been the case. Caroline had written that Darcy knew everything there was to know about the details in the letter; and yet he remained a steadfast, intimate friend. As she gazed at his likeness, she remembered a moment at the Netherfield ball, when Caroline had proposed that men of their persuasion had a more difficult time than women, given the necessity of living a public life, and had fixed a curious look upon Darcy. Had she meant that Darcy—but it could not be, could it? And yet it would explain so much if Darcy, like Caroline and Elizabeth, preferred the company of his own sex.

As she gazed at Darcy's likeness, there was certainly at this moment, in Elizabeth's mind, a more open sensation towards the original than she had ever felt at the height of their acquaintance. To think that he may in fact share her own nature, was a compelling enough reason to release what little remained of her former dislike of the man. The commendation bestowed on him by Mrs. Reynolds was of no trifling nature, either. What praise is more valuable than the praise of an intelligent servant? Elizabeth had misjudged so much, and almost now wished for the opportunity to share with Caroline her new understanding. But Miss Bingley would not, could not want to see her again, not after the way she had behaved at their last meeting. She still blushed to think of it, though her feelings for the lady had long since reconstituted themselves into something tolerably close to genuine regard.

When all of the house that was open to general inspection had been seen, they returned downstairs, and, taking leave of the housekeeper, were consigned over to the gardener, who met them at the hall-door. As they walked across the hall towards the river, Elizabeth turned back to look again; her uncle and aunt stopped also, and while the former was conjecturing as to the date of the building, the owner of it himself suddenly came forward from the road, which led behind it to the stables. They were within twenty yards of each other, and so abrupt was his appearance, that it was impossible to avoid his sight. Their eyes instantly met, and he absolutely started, and for a moment seemed immovable from astonishment; but shortly recovering himself, advanced towards the party, and spoke to Elizabeth with perfect civility: "Good day, Miss Bennet. What a welcome surprise to see you again."

She had instinctively turned away; but stopping on his approach, now received his compliments with careful composure. "Thank you, Mr. Darcy. And you, as well." She coloured a bit, realizing that as they were currently at his home, the surprise was rather more inclined to belong to him. Her blush was not only due to her choice in words, however. With her new insight, she could not doubt that he was aware of at least the general gist of her scene with his friend, if not particular details, and now looked closely to see if his gaze held even a hint of censure. It did not, only a generally welcoming earnestness and perhaps, if she read him correctly, a spark of interest.

Had his first appearance, or his resemblance to the picture they had just been examining, been insufficient to assure the other two that they now saw Mr. Darcy, the gardener's expression of surprise on beholding his master must immediately have told it. They stood a little aloof while he was talking to their niece, who answered calmly his civil inquiries after her family. But her calm was forced; every idea of the impropriety of her being found there recurring to her mind, the few minutes in which they continued were in fact decidedly uncomfortable. Darcy, however, seemed much at ease, inquiring after the time of her having left Longbourn, and of her having stayed in Derbyshire, with such solicitude, as left her wondering at the direction of his thoughts.

At length a servant approached from the house, and Mr. Darcy took his leave, wishing Elizabeth well on her journey.

The others then joined her, and expressed admiration of his figure; but Elizabeth only followed them in silence. Her coming there was the most unfortunate thing in the world. How strange it must appear to him, as if she had purposely thrown herself in his way—in Caroline's way, for that was how it must seem. Had they been only ten minutes sooner, they should have been beyond the reach of his discrimination; for it was plain that he was that moment arrived. She blushed over the perverseness of the meeting. And his kind, attentive behaviour toward her—what could it mean? That he should even wish to speak to her was amazing after her previous behavior, but to speak with such civility? She knew not what to think, or how to account for it. Surely if Caroline had detested her, Darcy must as well, given the binds of loyalty. But he had allowed not a hint of disapprobation to show.

They had now entered a beautiful walk by the side of the water, and every step was bringing forward a nobler fall of ground, or a finer reach of the woods to which they were approaching; but it was some time before Elizabeth was sensible of much of it; and, though she answered mechanically to the repeated appeals of her uncle and aunt, and seemed to direct her eyes to such objects as they pointed out, she distinguished no part of the scene. Her thoughts were all fixed on that one spot of the country, wherever it might be, where Miss Caroline Bingley then was. She longed to know what at that moment was passing in Miss Bingley's mind—in what manner Caroline thought of her, if at all, and whether, in defiance of everything, she still held Elizabeth dear. Perhaps Darcy had been civil only because he felt himself at ease; yet there had been something in his voice which was not like ease, something of a pleased interest in unexpectedly beholding her again that she knew could not extend from any personal stake.

At length, however, the remarks of her companions on her absence of mind roused her, and she felt the necessity of appearing more like herself.

They entered the woods, and bidding adieu to the river for a while, ascended some of the higher grounds. Mr. Gardiner expressed a wish of going round the whole park, but feared it might be beyond a walk. With a triumphant smile, the gardener explained that it was ten miles round. The matter settled, they pursued the accustomed circuit; which brought them again, after some time, in a descent among hanging woods, to the edge of the water, and one of its narrowest parts. They crossed it by a simple bridge, in character with the general air of the scene; it was a spot less adorned than any they had yet visited; and the valley, here contracted into a glen, allowed room only for the stream, and a narrow walk amidst the rough coppice-wood which bordered it. Elizabeth longed to explore its windings; but when they had crossed the bridge, and perceived their distance from the house, Mrs. Gardiner, who was not a great walker, could go no farther, and thought only of returning to the carriage as quickly as possible. Her niece was, therefore, obliged to submit, and they took their way towards the house on the opposite side of the river, in the nearest direction; but their progress was slow, for Mr. Gardiner, though seldom able to indulge the taste, was very fond of fishing, and was so much engaged in watching the occasional appearance of some trout in the water, and talking to the man about them, that he advanced but little.

Whilst wandering on in this slow manner, they were again surprised, and Elizabeth's astonishment was quite equal to what it had been at first, by the sight of Mr. Darcy approaching them, and at no great distance. The walk here being here less sheltered than on the other side, allowed them to see him before they met. Elizabeth, however startled, resolved to appear and to speak with calmness again, if he really intended to meet them. He did. With a glance, she saw that he had lost none of his recent civility, nor the hint of amused curiosity; and, to imitate his politeness, she began, as they met, to admire the beauty of the place.

Mrs. Gardiner was standing a little behind; and when Elizabeth paused, Darcy asked her if she would do him the honour of introducing him to her friends. This was a stroke of civility for which she was quite unprepared, as he undoubtedly shared Caroline's repugnance toward her connections. "What will be his surprise," thought she, "when he knows who they are? He takes them now for people of fashion."

The introduction, however, was immediately made; and as she named their relationship to herself, she stole a sly look at him to see how he bore it, and was not without the expectation of his decamping as fast as he could from such disgraceful companions. That he was surprised by the connection was evident; he sustained it, however, with fortitude, and so far from going away, turned back with them, and entered into conversation with Mr. Gardiner. Elizabeth could not but be pleased. It was consoling that he should know she had some relations for whom there was no need to blush; he might well be expected to pass on this information to Caroline. She listened most attentively to all that passed between them, and gloried in every expression, every sentence of her uncle, which marked his intelligence, his taste, or his good manners.

The conversation soon turned upon fishing; and she heard Mr. Darcy invite Mr. Gardiner, with the greatest civility, to fish there as often as he chose while he continued in the neighbourhood, offering at the same time to supply him with fishing tackle, and pointing out those parts of the stream where there was usually most sport. Mrs. Gardiner, who was walking arm-in-arm with Elizabeth, gave her a look expressive of wonder. Elizabeth said nothing. Her astonishment, however, was not minor, and continually was she repeating, "Why is he so altered? It cannot be for Caroline's sake that his manners are thus softened. It is impossible that she should still love me."

After walking some time in this way, the two ladies in front, the two gentlemen behind, on resuming their places, after descending to the brink of the river for the better inspection of some curious water-plant, there chanced to be a little alteration. It originated in Mrs. Gardiner, who, fatigued by the exercise of the morning, found Elizabeth's arm inadequate to her support, and consequently preferred her husband's. Mr. Darcy took her place by her niece, and they walked on together.

Elizabeth spoke first: "Your arrival earlier was very unexpected, for your housekeeper informed us that you would certainly not be here till tomorrow; and indeed, before we left Bakewell, we understood that you were not immediately expected in the country."

He acknowledged the truth of it all, and said that business with his steward had occasioned his coming forward a few hours before the rest of the party with whom he had been travelling. "They will join me early tomorrow," he continued, "and among them are some who will claim an acquaintance with you—Mr. Bingley and one of his sisters."

She tried to resist what she knew to be a purposeful bait, but found she could not. "And which sister would that be?"

"Miss Caroline Bingley," said he, his voice deepened by suppressed laughter.

Vainly did she attempt to ignore his triumph. "Is Mrs. Hurst not a member of the party, then?"

"She is not. The good lady and her husband were persuaded to return north some time ago."

Caroline and Bingley, without Louisa, then—Elizabeth recalled a line from the letter, scrawled in the lady's flowing hand: "I am determined to extricate myself from my sister's snare, and to leave her company for that of friends who will embrace me without censure or disgust." It seemed she had managed to do so, after all. Elizabeth could not hold back a small smile of satisfaction.

"You appear to take pleasure in this news," said Darcy. "Could it be, you are not a particular admirer of Mrs. Hurst's?"

"I am not." Elizabeth lifted her chin and looked into his eyes. "And I believe you know my reasons."

"Indeed," he answered with a slight bow, more serious now. "I verily do. There is also one other person in the party," he continued after a pause, " who I am aware wishes to be known to you. Will you allow me to introduce my sister to your acquaintance during your stay at Lambton?"

The surprise of such an application was great indeed; it was too great for her to know in what manner she acceded to it. She immediately felt that whatever desire Miss Darcy might have of being acquainted with her must be the work of Miss Bingley. It was gratifying to know that

Caroline must not think very ill of her if one of her favourites wished to make Elizabeth's acquaintance.

They now walked on in silence, the warm day offering plentiful bird song and a breeze that carried with it the sweet scent of honeysuckle. They soon outstripped the others, and when they had reached the carriage, Mr. and Mrs. Gardiner were half a quarter of a mile behind.

He then asked her to walk into the house—but she declared herself not tired, and they stood together on the lawn, again without speaking. He seemed to know that her mind was full of questions about the months since they had last met, and he waited, giving her more than ample opportunity to loose her tongue. But she could not. Caroline even now was making her way to Pemberley, and would be here on this very spot the following day. This fact seemed almost too much to grasp. The event which Elizabeth had dreaded only this morning now appeared as an occasion to which she actually believed she might be looking forward. Or possibly not. Oh, how she had disgraced herself the last time she was in Caroline's presence! And yet here was an intimate of the lady's treating her with a diffidence and a courtesy that seemed to argue against any great bitterness on Caroline's part.

At such a time much might have been said, and Elizabeth in fact wished to talk, but she considered one subject after another, universally finding that the topics her mind provided were unseemly. As she did not want to remind the gentleman of her more vulgar connections, she at last introduced the topic of travelling, and they talked of Matlock and Dove Dale with great perseverance. Yet time and her aunt moved slowly—and her patience and her ideas were nearly worn out before the tête-à-tête was over. On Mr. and Mrs. Gardiner's coming up, they were all pressed to go into the house and take some refreshment; but this was declined, and they parted on each side with utmost politeness. Mr. Darcy handed the ladies into the carriage; and when it drove off, Elizabeth saw him walking quickly towards the house. Presumably he was eager to send word of this development to the party even now making its way northward from London.

The observations of her uncle and aunt now began; and each of them pronounced Darcy to be infinitely superior to anything they had expected. "He is perfectly well behaved, polite, and unassuming," said her uncle.

"There *is* something a little stately in him, to be sure," replied her aunt, "but it is confined to his air, and is not unbecoming. I can now say with the housekeeper, that though some people may call him proud, I have seen nothing of it."

"I was never more surprised than by his behaviour to us. It was more than civil; it was really attentive; and there was no necessity for such attention. His acquaintance with Elizabeth was very trifling."

"To be sure, Lizzy," said her aunt, "he is not so handsome as Wickham; or, rather, he has not Wickham's countenance, for his features are perfectly good. But how came you to tell me that he was so disagreeable?"

Elizabeth excused herself as well as she could; said that she had liked him better when they had met in Kent than before, and that she had never seen him so pleasant as this morning.

"But perhaps he may be a little whimsical in his civilities," replied her uncle. "Your great men often are; and therefore I shall not take him at his word, as he might change his mind another day, and warn me off his grounds."

Elizabeth felt that they had entirely misunderstood his character, but said nothing.

"From what we have seen of him," continued Mrs. Gardiner, "I really should not have thought that he could have behaved in so cruel a way by anybody as he has done by poor Wickham. He has not an ill-natured look. On the contrary, there is something of dignity in his countenance that gives one a favourable idea of his heart. To be sure, the good lady who showed us his house did give him a most flaming character! I could hardly help laughing aloud sometimes. But he is a liberal master, I suppose, and *that* in the eye of a servant comprehends every virtue."

Elizabeth here felt herself called on to say something in vindication of his behaviour; and therefore gave them to understand, in as guarded a manner as she could, that by what she had heard from his relations in Kent, his actions toward Wickham were capable of a very different construction; and that his character was by no means so faulty, nor Wickham's so amiable, as they had been considered in Hertfordshire. In confirmation of this, she related the particulars of all the pecuniary transactions in which they had been connected, without actually naming her authority, but stating it to be such as might be relied on.

Mrs. Gardiner was surprised and concerned; but as they were now approaching the scene of her former pleasures, every idea gave way to the charm of recollection; and she was too much engaged in pointing out to her husband all the interesting spots in its environs to think of anything else. Fatigued as she had been by the morning's walk, they had no sooner dined than she set off again in quest of her former acquaintance, and the evening was spent in the satisfactions of an intercourse renewed after many years' discontinuance.

The occurrences of the day were too full of interest to leave Elizabeth much attention for any of these new friends; and she could do nothing but think of Pemberley's beauty and Mr. Darcy's civility, and, above all, of Caroline Bingley's arrival on the morrow.

CHAPTER FORTY-FOUR

r. Darcy had suggested he bring his sister and other "interested guests" to visit Elizabeth the day after the party reached Pemberley. But on the very day of their arrival, the visitors came to Lambton in search of her. Elizabeth had been walking about the place with her aunt and uncle and some of their new friends; and they were just returning to the inn to dress themselves for dining with the same family when the sound of a coach drew them to a window, where they spied a carriage driving up the street. Elizabeth, immediately recognizing the livery, guessed what it meant, and imparted no small degree of her surprise to her relations by acquainting them with the honour which she expected. Her uncle and aunt were all amazement; and her discomposure as she spoke, joined to the circumstance itself, and many of the circumstances of the preceding day, opened to them a new idea on the business. Nothing had ever suggested it before, but they felt that there was no other way of accounting for such attentions from such a quarter than by supposing a partiality for their niece. While these newly-born notions were passing in their heads, the perturbation of Elizabeth's feelings was at every moment increasing. She had not expected to see Caroline Bingley until the following day, and now she could not remember how the meeting might ever have had the least power of recommending itself to her.

She retreated from the window, fearful of being seen; and as she walked up and down the room, endeavouring to compose herself, saw such looks of inquiring surprise in her uncle and aunt as made everything worse.

Soon the sound of steps could be heard on the stairs, and Elizabeth smoothed her dress, waiting. Caroline Bingley appeared in the doorway first, her face that haughty mask she seemed capable of assuming at will; but as her eyes met Elizabeth's, a slight smile softened her countenance.

"Miss Bingley," said Elizabeth, cursing the flush that must signal to all her decided lack of composure on the occasion.

"Miss Bennet," said Caroline, nodding calmly. "What a pleasure it is to see you again."

Elizabeth did not have a chance to reply before Miss Darcy and her brother entered the room, and introductions took place all around. Elizabeth redirected her gaze from Caroline who, she noted, looked as impressive as ever in a dress of the latest fashion, and focused instead on Darcy's sister. Miss Darcy was tall too, but on a larger scale than she or Caroline; and, though little more than sixteen, her figure was formed, her appearance womanly and graceful. Since arriving in Lambton, Elizabeth had heard that Miss Darcy was exceedingly proud; but the observation of a very few minutes convinced her that she was only exceedingly shy.

Risking a glance at Caroline, Elizabeth found herself the subject of a curiously intent gaze. But upon intercepting the look, Caroline turned away to engage Mrs. Gardiner in, if not animated, at least convivial, conversation on the topic of the previous season's tendency toward ever more sizable headgear.

They had not long been together before Mr. Darcy told Elizabeth that Mr. Bingley was also coming to wait on her; and she had barely time to express her satisfaction, and prepare for such a visitor, when Bingley's approach could be heard, and in a moment he entered the room. Elizabeth's anger against him had been long done away; but had she still felt any, it could hardly have stood its ground against the unaffected cordiality with which he expressed himself on seeing her again. He inquired in a friendly, though general way, after her family, and looked and spoke with the same good-humoured ease that he had ever done.

To Mr. and Mrs. Gardiner he was scarcely a less interesting personage than to herself. They had long wished to see him. The whole party before them, indeed, excited a lively attention. The suspicions which had just arisen of Mr. Darcy and their niece directed their observation towards each with an earnest though guarded inquiry; but though they watched the interaction with care, they were unable to detect more than an average sensation from either side.

Elizabeth, for her part, had much to do. She wanted to ascertain the feelings of each of her visitors; she wanted to compose her own, and to make herself agreeable to all; and in the latter object, where she feared most to fail, she was most sure of success, for those to whom she endeavoured to give pleasure were prepossessed in her favour. Bingley was ready, Georgiana was eager, and even Caroline was open to being pleased.

The latter watched Elizabeth, too, noting with approval the kindness with which she worked to draw out the shy Miss Darcy, wondering at the occasional blushing looks cast her way. Seeing Elizabeth as she was now, Caroline couldn't help but wonder if her written words of explication and justification might have had the desired effect on their reader. Darcy had claimed that Miss Bennet's attitude had seemed much changed since their last meeting at Rosings, and Caroline could see that he was right—Elizabeth had about her a softer, more diffident air, her countenance decidedly lacking the general sense of antagonism of previous encounters. The change, Darcy had insisted, must be owed entirely to Caroline, and to no one else. Tempting as it was to believe his interpretation, Caroline could not forget the last time she had seen Elizabeth. She didn't dare hope that Miss Bennet had reconsidered her views on everything that had happened—or, more importantly, her feelings toward Caroline. Being told that she was the last person in the world Elizabeth could ever love had left Caroline, who suffered the misfortune of loving Elizabeth better than any woman she had ever known, somewhat less inclined to hope for a revolution in the other's sentiments.

In seeing Mr. Bingley, Elizabeth found her thoughts shifting from Caroline to Jane; and how ardently did she long to know whether any of his were transported in a like manner. Sometimes she could fancy that he talked less than on former occasions, and once or twice pleased herself with the notion that, as he looked at her, he was trying to trace a resemblance. But, though this might be imaginary, she could not be deceived as to his behaviour to Miss Darcy, who had been set up as a possible rival to Jane. No look appeared on either side that spoke particular regard, and nothing occurred between them that could justify the charge. On this point she was soon satisfied; and two or three little circumstances occurred ere they parted, which, in her anxious interpretation, denoted a recollection of Jane not untinctured by tenderness, and a wish of saying more that might lead to the mention of her, had he dared.

He observed to her, at a moment when the others were talking together, and in a tone which had something of real regret, that it was "a very long time since he had had the pleasure of seeing her;" and, before she could reply, he added, "It is above eight months. We have not met since the 26th of November, when we were all dancing together at Netherfield."

She was pleased to find his memory so exact; and he afterwards took occasion to ask her, when unattended to by any of the rest, whether *all* her sisters were at Longbourn. There was not much in the question, nor in the preceding remark; but there was a look and a manner which gave to them meaning, and to her, hope on her sister's behalf.

It was not often during the short visit that Elizabeth had occasion to turn her eyes on Caroline; but, whenever she did catch a glimpse, she saw an expression of general complaisance, and in all that the lady said Elizabeth heard an accent so removed from hauteur or superiority, as convinced her that Caroline's manners had undergone a similar shift to those of Pemberley's master. When she saw the lady thus courting the good opinion of her relations, and recollected their last lively scene in Hunsford Parsonage—the difference, the change was so great, and struck so forcibly on her mind, that she could hardly restrain her astonishment from being visible. Never had she seen Caroline so desirous to please, so free from self-consequence, as now, when no importance could result from the success of her endeavours.

Their visitors stayed with them above half-an-hour; and when they arose to depart, Mr. Darcy called on his sister to join him in expressing their wish of seeing Mr. and Mrs. Gardiner, and Miss Bennet, to dinner at Pemberley, before they left the country. Miss Darcy, though with a diffidence which marked her little in the habit of giving invitations, readily obeyed, while in the background Miss Bingley looked out the window and worried the thin fabric of her travelling gown. Mrs. Gardiner looked at her niece, desirous of knowing how *she*, whom the invitation most concerned, felt disposed as to its acceptance, but

Elizabeth had turned away her head. Presuming however, that this studied avoidance spoke rather a momentary embarrassment than any dislike of the proposal, and seeing in her husband, who was fond of society, a perfect willingness to accept it, she ventured to engage for her attendance, and the day after the next was fixed on.

Bingley expressed great pleasure in the certainty of seeing Elizabeth again, having still a great deal to say to her, and many inquiries to make after all their Hertfordshire friends. Elizabeth, construing all this into a wish of hearing her speak of her sister, was pleased, and on this account as well as some others, including the manner in which Caroline smiled graciously at her on the way out of the room, found herself, when their visitors had left them, capable of considering the last half-hour with some satisfaction; though while it was passing, the enjoyment of it had been little. Eager to be alone, and fearful of inquiries or hints from her uncle and aunt, she stayed with them only long enough to hear their favourable opinion of the Bingleys and Miss Darcy, and then hurried away to dress.

But she had no reason to fear Mr. and Mrs. Gardiner's curiosity; it was not their wish to force her communication. It was evident that she was much better acquainted with Mr. Darcy than they had before any idea of; but the precise nature of the acquaintance still remained uncertain. They saw much to interest, but nothing to justify inquiry.

As for Elizabeth, her thoughts were at Pemberley this evening more than the last; and the evening, though as it passed it seemed long, was not long enough to determine her feelings towards *one* in that mansion; and she lay awake two whole hours endeavouring to make them out. She certainly did not hate Caroline. No; hatred had vanished long ago, and she had almost as long been ashamed of ever feeling a dislike against her. The respect created by the conviction of her valuable qualities, though at first unwillingly admitted, had for some time ceased to be repugnant to her feelings; and it was now heightened into somewhat of a friendlier nature, by the amiability the lady had displayed on meeting again. But above all, above respect and esteem, there was a feeling within her of gratitude; gratitude, not merely for having once loved her, but for loving her still well enough to forgive all the petulance and acrimony of Elizabeth's manner in rejecting her, and all the unjust accusations accompanying that rejection. She who, Elizabeth had been persuaded, would avoid her as her greatest enemy, seemed, on this accidental meeting, content to preserve the acquaintance, and without any indelicate display of regard, or any peculiarity of manner, where their two selves only were concerned, was soliciting the good opinion of her friends, and seemed bent on making her better known to her own. Elizabeth respected, she esteemed, she was grateful to Caroline, she felt a real interest in the lady's welfare; and she only wanted to know how far she wished that welfare to depend upon herself, and how far it would be for the happiness of both that she should employ the power, which her fancy told her she still possessed, of bringing on her the renewal of Caroline's addresses.

It had been settled in the evening between the aunt and the niece, that such a striking civility as Miss Darcy's in coming to see them on the very day of her arrival at Pemberley, for she had reached it only to a late breakfast, ought to be imitated, though it could not be equaled, by some exertion of politeness on their side; and, consequently, that it would be highly expedient to wait on her at Pemberley the following morning. They were, therefore, to go. Elizabeth was pleased; though when she asked herself the reason, she had very little to say in reply.

CHAPTER FORTY-FIVE

n the morning, upon reaching Pemberley, Elizabeth and Mrs. Gardiner were shown through the hall into the saloon, whose northern aspect rendered it delightful for summer. Its windows opening to the ground, admitted a most refreshing view of the high woody hills behind the house, and of the beautiful oaks and Spanish chestnuts which were scattered over the intermediate lawn.

In this house they were received by Miss Darcy, who was sitting there with Mrs. Annesley, the lady with whom she lived in London, and Miss Bingley. Georgiana's reception of them was very civil, but attended with all the embarrassment which, though proceeding from shyness and the fear of doing wrong, would easily give to those who felt themselves inferior the belief of her being proud and reserved. Mrs. Gardiner and her niece, however, did her justice, and pitied her.

By Miss Bingley they were noticed by a polite curtsey; and, on ascertaining the coolness in the lady's regard, Elizabeth wondered if she might not have been mistaken in her thoughts the previous evening. On their being seated, a pause, awkward as such pauses must always be, succeeded for a few moments. It was first broken by Mrs. Annesley, a genteel, agreeable-looking woman, whose endeavour to introduce some kind of discourse proved her to be more truly well-bred than either of the others; and between her and Mrs. Gardiner, with occasional help from Elizabeth, the conversation was carried on. Miss Darcy looked as if she wished for courage enough to join in it; and sometimes did venture a short sentence when there was least danger of its being heard.

After a few minutes, Elizabeth steeled herself and said to Caroline: "Mr. Darcy tells me your sister has returned home for the summer."

At this, Caroline's coolness waned, and she smiled a little. "My sister allowed herself to be convinced that her attentions were needed elsewhere, and so she left my brother and I to one another's charge."

"Indeed." Elizabeth inclined her head. "I must offer congratulations, then, on achieving a goal close to your heart."

Caroline looked quickly at Miss Darcy, who appeared occupied in pouring more tea for the gathered party.

Elizabeth lowered her voice. "She does not know?"

"Not of my situation."

"And her brother?"

Caroline's brow furrowed briefly. "What of him?"

"Does he know of your situation?"

"Oh. Yes, he knows all." And here she fixed a serious look upon Elizabeth, a faint frown still darkening her countenance.

Elizabeth was saved from the need to say anything further by the entrance of servants with cold meat, cake, and a variety of all the finest fruits in season; but this did not take place till after many a significant look and smile from Mrs. Annesley to Miss Darcy had been given, to remind her of her post. There was now employment for the whole party—for though they could not all talk, they could all eat; and the beautiful pyramids of grapes, nectarines, and peaches soon collected them round the table.

While the ladies were thus engaged, Mr. Darcy and a gentleman Elizabeth did not recognize entered the room. They were laughing as they came in, Darcy's hand on the other man's shoulder, and Elizabeth was struck by the sense of ease apparent in the master of the house, his very real happiness evident as he introduced his friend to the party. Monsieur de Laurent, a handsome man with delicate features and a warm smile, was an intimate friend with whom Darcy had only recently been reunited in London, where the Frenchman had been forced to flee to avoid the trouble on the continent. Elizabeth, watching them together, began to entreat suspicions of her own, much along the line of those of her aunt and uncle; though with a far different pairing in mind.

Darcy, unlike previous occasions in Elizabeth's experience, proved most talkative as the two men joined the party. He and his friend had been some time with Mr. Gardiner, who, with two or three other gentlemen from the house, was engaged by the river; and they had left the fishermen only upon learning that the ladies of the family intended a visit to Georgiana that morning. No sooner did Darcy appear than Caroline glanced from him to Elizabeth, her expression seeming marked by the very opposite humour from his. Elizabeth, who could not account for Miss Bingley's vagaries of temperament, resolved to be perfectly easy and unembarrassed; a resolution the more necessary to be made, but perhaps not the more easily kept. Miss Darcy, on her brother's entrance, exerted herself much more to talk, and Elizabeth saw that he seemed to be encouraging his sister to get better acquainted with her, and helpfully forwarded every attempt at conversation on either side. Miss Bingley saw all this likewise; and, Elizabeth noted, grew more thoughtful as the visit wore on. After a few minutes, Monsieur de Laurent pulled Caroline to one side and engaged her in what Elizabeth felt to be a remarkably familiar manner; causing Elizabeth, similarly, to become more pensive than social.

While she was trying not to watch Caroline in her tête-à-tête with the Frenchman, Elizabeth overheard her aunt mention to Mrs. Annesley, with whom she had been discussing the fighting between Napoleon and what seemed to be nearly the entirety of the world, that the ——shire Militia had recently stayed some months in Meryton, where Elizabeth's family made their home.

Elizabeth felt a blush steal across her face at this reminder of her younger sisters' "vulgar behavior," as Caroline had termed it in her letter. An involuntary glance showed her Miss Darcy also with a heightened complexion, overcome with confusion and unable to lift up her eyes. Caroline was looking at the young lady, too, with a look of such pity that Elizabeth immediately knew her suspicions of Wickham's behavior toward the girl to be accurate. Mrs. Annesley's quick change of topic further underscored the exactness of her suppositions, while Mrs. Gardiner appeared not to notice the veer away from territory she could have no idea was fraught with danger. After a moment, Caroline seemed to become aware that Elizabeth was watching Georgiana, and her eyes grew a bit darker as her mind supplied her with the cause of this observation. Elizabeth's collected behaviour, however, soon quieted Miss Bingley's anxiety; and as the conversation turned to lighter things, Georgiana also recovered in time, though not enough to be able to speak any more.

Their visit did not continue long after this episode; and when it came time to take their leave, Caroline gave Elizabeth a bow and a slight smile that had the latter smiling in return and clasping her hand in real affection for a moment, before releasing her fingers quickly and turning away. The memory of Hunsford Parsonage again intruding, Elizabeth fixed her attention on Mr. Darcy, his sister, and the Frenchman, treating them rather more warmly than she might have otherwise. The last thing she wished for was to stir up any remembrance of hurt in Caroline, which she must do if she appeared to encourage her previous attachment after so cruelly rejecting her—even if rejection was no longer such a fixture in her own mind.

Caroline, meanwhile, lingering in the saloon afterward, could not help saying to Georgiana: "How very pretty Miss Eliza looks this morning. She is quite altered since the winter, and not a little brown from her summertime travels under the sun. But I find it brings a glow of health to her features, contrary to the general opinion."

Smiling at her affectionately, Georgiana, who, like her brother, was far more at ease in the company of intimates, said: "You would think so, would you not?" with a pertness that brought a smile of surprise to the lips of her companion. Perhaps Georgiana was not as innocent or unaware as she seemed, after all.

Caroline saw Mrs. Annesley eyeing them curiously, and said quickly, "Well, of course—I remember, when we first knew her in Hertfordshire, how when we all discovered that she was a reputed beauty, the general consensus was in agreement. But I particularly recollect your brother saying one night, after they had been dining at Netherfield, '*She* a beauty! I should as soon call her mother a wit.' But afterwards she seemed to improve on him, and I believe even he thought her rather pretty at one time."

Georgiana quirked an eyebrow at her. "'Rather pretty'? A compliment, indeed, coming from my brother."

"Indeed," echoed Caroline, and looked toward the window, where sunlight poured in unobstructed.

Mrs. Gardiner and Elizabeth talked of all that had occurred during their visit, as they returned, except what had particularly interested the latter. The look and behaviour of everybody they had seen were discussed, except of the person who had mostly engaged Elizabeth's attention. They talked of Darcy's sister, Mrs. Annesley, Mr. Darcy and Monsieur de Laurent, the house, the food—of everything but Miss Bingley; yet Elizabeth was longing to know what Mrs. Gardiner thought of her, and Mrs. Gardiner would not have been alarmed by her niece's beginning the subject, given her misplaced suspicions of Elizabeth's affections.

CHAPTER FORTY-SIX

Elizabeth had been a good deal disappointed in not finding a letter from Jane on their first arrival at Lambton; and this disappointment had been renewed on each of the mornings that had now been spent there; but on the third her repining was over, and her sister justified, by the receipt of two letters from her at once, on one of which was marked that it had been missent elsewhere. Elizabeth was not surprised at it, as Jane had written the direction remarkably ill.

They had just been preparing to walk as the letters came in; and her uncle and aunt, leaving her to enjoy them in quiet, set off by themselves. The one missent must first be attended to; it had been written five days ago. The beginning contained an account of all their little parties and engagements, with such news as the country afforded; but the latter half, which was dated a day later, and written in evident agitation, gave more important intelligence. It was to this effect:

"Since writing the above, dearest Lizzy, something has occurred of a most unexpected and serious nature; but I am afraid of alarming you— be assured that we are all well. What I have to say relates to poor Lydia. An express came at twelve last night, just as we were all gone to bed, from Colonel Forster, to inform us that she was gone off to Scotland with one of his officers; to own the truth, with Wickham! Imagine our surprise. To Kitty, however, it does not seem so wholly unexpected. I am very, very sorry. So imprudent a match on both sides! But I am willing to hope the best, and that his character has been misunderstood. Thoughtless and indiscreet I can easily believe him, but this step (and let us rejoice over it) marks nothing bad at heart. His choice is disinterested at least, for he must know my father can give her nothing. Our poor mother is sadly grieved. My father bears it better. How thankful am I that we never let them know what has been said against him; we must forget it ourselves. They were off Saturday night about twelve, as is conjectured, but were not missed till yesterday morning at eight. The express was sent off directly. My dear Lizzy, they must have passed within ten miles of us. Colonel Forster gives us reason to expect him here soon. Lydia left a few lines for his wife, informing her of their intention. I must conclude, for I cannot be long from my poor mother. I am afraid you will not be able to make it out, but I hardly know what I have written."

Without allowing herself time for consideration, and scarcely knowing what she felt, Elizabeth on finishing this letter instantly seized the other, written a day after the first, and opening it with the utmost impatience, read as follows:

"By this time, my dearest sister, you have received my hurried letter; I wish this may be more intelligible, but though not confined for time, my head is so bewildered that I cannot answer for being coherent. Dearest Lizzy, I hardly know what I would write, but I have bad news for you, and it cannot be delayed. Imprudent as the marriage between Mr. Wickham and our poor Lydia would be, we are now anxious to be assured it has taken place, for there is but too much reason to fear they are not gone to Scotland. Colonel Forster came yesterday, having left Brighton the day before, not many hours after the express. Though Lydia's short letter to Mrs. F. gave them to understand that they were going to Gretna Green, something was dropped by Denny expressing his belief that W. never intended to go there, or to marry Lydia at all, which was repeated to Colonel F., who, instantly taking the alarm, set off from B. intending to trace their route. He did trace them easily to Clapham, but no further; for on entering that place, they removed into a hackney coach, and dismissed the chaise that brought them from Epsom. All that is known after this is, that they were seen to continue the London road. I know not what to think. After making every possible inquiry on that side London, Colonel F. came on into Hertfordshire, anxiously renewing them at all the turnpikes, and at the inns in Barnet and Hatfield, but without any success—no such people had been seen to pass through. With the kindest concern he came on to Longbourn, and broke his apprehensions to us in a manner most creditable to his heart. I am sincerely grieved for him and Mrs. F., but no one can throw any blame on them. Our distress, my dear Lizzy, is very great. My father and mother believe the worst, but I cannot think so ill of him. Many circumstances might make it more eligible for them to be married privately in town than to pursue their first plan; and even if *he* could form such a design against a young woman of Lydia's connections, which is not likely, can I suppose her so lost to everything? Impossible! I grieve to find, however, that Colonel F. is not disposed to depend upon their marriage; he shook his head when I expressed my hopes, and said he feared W. was not a man to be trusted. My poor mother is really ill, and keeps her room. Could she exert herself, it would be better; but this is not to be expected. And as to my father, I never in my life saw him so affected. Poor Kitty has anger for having concealed their attachment; but as it was a matter of confidence, one cannot wonder. I am truly glad, dearest Lizzy, that you have been spared something of these distressing scenes; but now, as the first shock is over, shall I own that I long for your return? I am not so selfish, however, as to press for it, if inconvenient. Adieu! I take up my pen again to do what I have just told you I would not; but circumstances are such that I cannot help earnestly begging you all to come here as soon as possible. I know my dear uncle and aunt so well, that I am not afraid of requesting it, though I have still something more to ask of the former. My father is going to London with Colonel Forster instantly, to try to discover her. What he means to do I am sure I know not; but his excessive distress will not allow him to pursue any measure in the best and safest way, and Colonel Forster is obliged to be at Brighton again to-morrow evening. In such an exigency, my uncle's advice and assistance would be everything in the world; he will immediately comprehend what I must feel, and I rely upon his goodness."

"Oh! Where, where is my uncle?" cried Elizabeth, darting from her seat as she finished the letter, in eagerness to follow him, without losing a moment of the time so precious; but as she reached the door it was opened by a servant, and Miss Bingley appeared. Elizabeth's pale face and impetuous manner made her visitor start, and before she could recover enough to speak, Elizabeth, in whose mind every idea was superseded by Lydia's situation, hastily exclaimed, "I beg your pardon, but I must leave you. I must find Mr. Gardiner this moment, on business that cannot be delayed; I have not an instant to lose."

"My God! What is the matter?" asked she, with more feeling than politeness; then recollecting herself, "I will not detain you; but let me, or let the servant go after Mr. and Mrs. Gardiner. You cannot go yourself; you are not well enough."

Elizabeth hesitated, but her knees trembled under her and she felt how little would be gained by her attempting to pursue them. Calling back the servant, therefore, she commissioned him, though in so breathless an accent as made her almost unintelligible, to fetch his master and mistress home instantly.

On his quitting the room she sat down, unable to support herself, and looking so miserably ill, that it was impossible for Caroline to leave her, or to refrain from saying, in a tone of gentleness and commiseration, "Let me call your maid. Is there nothing you could take to give you relief? A glass of wine; shall I get you one?"

"No, I thank you," she replied, endeavouring to recover herself. "There is nothing the matter with me. I am quite well; I am only distressed by some dreadful news which I have just received from Longbourn."

For a few minutes she could not speak another word. Caroline, in wretched suspense, could only offer an indistinct concern, and observe her in compassionate silence.

At length Elizabeth spoke again. "I have just had a letter from Jane, with such dreadful news. It cannot be concealed from anyone. My younger sister has left all her friends—has eloped; has thrown herself into the power of Mr. Wickham. They are gone off together from Brighton. *You* know him too well to doubt the rest. She has no money, no connections, nothing that can tempt him to—she is lost forever."

Caroline was fixed in astonishment.

"When I consider," Elizabeth added in a yet more agitated voice, "that I might have prevented it! I, who knew what he was. Had I but explained some part of it only—some part of what you told me, to my own family! Had his character been known, this could not have happened. But it is all—all too late now."

"I am grieved indeed," said Caroline. "But is it certain—absolutely certain?"

"Oh, yes! They left Brighton together on Sunday night, and were traced almost to London, but not beyond; they are certainly not gone to Scotland."

"And what has been done, what has been attempted, to recover her?"

"My father is gone to London, and Jane has written to beg my uncle's immediate assistance; and we shall be off, I hope, in half-an-hour. But nothing can be done—I know very well that nothing can be done. How is such a man to be worked on? How are they even to be discovered? I have not the smallest hope. It is in every way horrible!"

Caroline shook her head in silent acquiescence.

"When my eyes were opened to his real character—oh! Had I known what I ought, what I dared to do! But I knew not—I was afraid of doing too much. Wretched, wretched mistake!"

Caroline made no answer. She seemed scarcely to hear, and was pacing the room, her mood disturbed. Elizabeth soon observed, and instantly understood it. Her own power was sinking; everything must sink under such a proof of family weakness, such an assurance of the deepest disgrace. She could neither wonder nor condemn, but the belief of Caroline's self-conquest brought nothing consolatory to her bosom, afforded no palliation of her distress. It was, on the contrary, exactly calculated to make her understand her own wishes; and never had she so honestly felt that she could have loved Caroline Bingley, as now, when all love must be in vain.

But self, though it would intrude, could not engross her. Lydia—the humiliation, the misery she was bringing on them all, must swallow up every private care, and Elizabeth was soon lost to everything else; and, after a pause of several minutes, was only recalled to a sense of her situation by the voice of her companion, who, in a manner which, though it spoke compassion, spoke likewise restraint, said, "I am afraid you have been long desiring my absence, nor have I anything to plead in excuse of my stay, but real, though unavailing concern. How I wish that anything could be either said or done on my part that might offer consolation—but I will not torment you with vain wishes. This unfortunate affair will, I fear, prevent our having the pleasure of seeing you at Pemberley today?"

"Oh, yes. Be so kind as to apologise for us to Mr. and Miss Darcy. Say that urgent business calls us home immediately. Conceal the unhappy truth as long as it is possible, I know it cannot be long."

Caroline readily assured her of the utmost secrecy; again expressed sorrow for her distress, wished it a happier conclusion than there was at present reason to hope, and leaving her compliments for her relations, with only one serious, parting look, went away.

As she quitted the room, Elizabeth felt how improbable it was that they should ever see each other again on such terms of cordiality as had marked their several meetings in Derbyshire; and as she threw a retrospective glance over the whole of their acquaintance, so full of contradictions and varieties, sighed at the perverseness of those feelings which would now have promoted its continuance, and would formerly have rejoiced in its termination.

If gratitude and esteem are good foundations of affection, Elizabeth's change of sentiment will be neither improbable nor faulty. But if otherwise—if regard springing from such sources is unreasonable or unnatural, in comparison of what is so often described as arising on a first interview with its object, and even before two words have been exchanged, nothing can be said in her defence. Be that as it may, she saw Caroline go with regret; and in this early example of what Lydia's infamy must produce, found additional anguish as she reflected on that wretched business. Never, since reading Jane's second letter, had she entertained a hope of Wickham's meaning to marry her. No one but Jane, she thought, could flatter herself with such an expectation. Surprise was the least of her feelings on this development. While the contents of the first letter remained in her mind, she was all surprise—all astonishment that Wickham should marry a girl whom it was impossible he could marry for money; and how Lydia could ever have attached him had appeared incomprehensible. But now it was all too natural. For such an attachment as this she might have sufficient charms; and though she did not suppose Lydia to be deliberately engaging in an elopement without the intention of marriage, she had no difficulty in believing that neither her virtue nor her understanding would preserve her from falling an easy prey.

She had never perceived, while the regiment was in Hertfordshire, that Lydia had any partiality for him; but she was convinced that Lydia wanted only encouragement to attach herself to anybody. Sometimes one officer, sometimes another, had been her favourite, as their attentions raised them in her opinion. Her affections had continually been fluctuating but never without an object. The mischief of neglect and mistaken indulgence towards such a girl—oh! How acutely did she now feel it!

She was anxious to be at home—to hear, to see, to be upon the spot to share with Jane in the cares that must now fall upon her in a family so distressed, a father absent, a mother incapable of exertion, and requiring constant attendance; and though almost persuaded that nothing could be done for Lydia, her uncle's interference seemed of the utmost importance, and till he entered the room her impatience was severe. Mr. and Mrs. Gardiner had hurried back in alarm, supposing by the servant's account that their niece was taken suddenly ill; but satisfying them instantly on that head, she eagerly communicated the cause of their summons, reading the two letters aloud, and dwelling on the postscript of the last with trembling energy. Though Lydia had never been a favourite with them, Mr. and Mrs. Gardiner could not but be deeply afflicted. Not Lydia only, but all were concerned in it; and after the first exclamations of surprise and dismay, Mr. Gardiner promised every assistance in his power. Elizabeth, though expecting no less, thanked him with tears of gratitude; and all three being actuated by one spirit, everything relating to their journey was speedily settled. They were to be off as soon as possible.

"But what is to be done about Pemberley?" asked Mrs. Gardiner. "John told us Miss Bingley was here when you sent for us; was it so?"

"Yes; and I told her we should not be able to keep our engagement. *That* is all settled."

"What is all settled?" repeated the other, as she ran into her room to prepare. "Oh, that I knew how it was!"

But wishes were vain, or at least could only serve to amuse her in the hurry and confusion of the following hour. Had Elizabeth been at leisure to be idle, she would have remained certain that all employment was impossible to one so miserable as herself; but she had her share of business as well as her aunt, and amongst the rest there were notes to be written to all their friends at Lambton, with false excuses for their sudden departure. An hour, however, saw the whole completed; and Mr.

Gardiner meanwhile having settled his account at the inn, nothing remained to be done but to go; and Elizabeth, after all the despair of the morning, found herself, in a shorter space of time than she could have supposed, seated in the carriage, and on the road to Longbourn.

CHAPTER FORTY-SEVEN

have been thinking it over again, Elizabeth," said her uncle, as they drove from the town; "and really, upon serious consideration, I am much more inclined than I was to judge as your eldest sister does on the matter. It appears to me so very unlikely that any young man should form such a design against a girl who is by no means unprotected or friendless, and who was actually staying in his colonel's family, that I am strongly inclined to hope the best. Could he expect that her friends would not step forward? Could he expect to be noticed again by the regiment, after such an affront to Colonel Forster? His temptation is not adequate to the risk!"

"Do you really think so?" asked Elizabeth, brightening up for a moment.

"Upon my word," said Mrs. Gardiner, "I begin to be of your uncle's opinion. It is really too great a violation of decency, honour, and interest, for him to be guilty of. I cannot think so very ill of Wickham. Can you yourself, Lizzy, so wholly give him up, as to believe him capable of it?"

"Not, perhaps, of neglecting his own interest; but of every other neglect I can believe him capable. If, indeed, it should be so! But I dare not hope it. Why should they not go on to Scotland if that had been the case?"

"In the first place," replied Mr. Gardiner, "there is no absolute proof that they are not gone to Scotland."

"But their removing from the chaise into a hackney coach is such a presumption! And, besides, no traces of them were to be found on the Barnet road."

"Well, then—supposing them to be in London. They may be there, though for the purpose of concealment, for no more exceptional purpose. It is not likely that money should be very abundant on either side; and it might strike them that they could be more economically, though less expeditiously, married in London than in Scotland."

"But why all this secrecy? Why any fear of detection? Why must their marriage be private? Oh, no, no—this is not likely. His most particular friend, you see by Jane's account, was persuaded of his never intending to marry her. Wickham will never marry a woman without some money. He cannot afford it. And what claims has Lydia—what attraction has she beyond youth, health, and good humour that could make him, for her sake, forego every chance of benefiting himself by marrying well? As to what restraint the apprehensions of disgrace in the corps might throw on a dishonourable elopement with her, I am not able to judge; for I know nothing of the effects that such a step might produce. But as to your other objection, I am afraid it will hardly hold good. Lydia has no brothers to step forward; and he might imagine, from my father's behaviour, from his indolence and the little attention he has ever seemed to give to what was going forward in his family, that he would do as little, and think as little about it, as any father could do, in such a matter."

"But can you think that Lydia is so lost to everything but love of him as to consent to live with him on any terms other than marriage?"

"It does seem, and it is most sorrowful indeed," replied Elizabeth, "that a sister's sense of decency and virtue in such a point should admit of doubt. But, really, I know not what to say. Perhaps I am not doing her justice. But she is very young; she has never been taught to think on serious subjects; and for the last half-year, nay, for a twelvemonth—she has been given up to nothing but amusement and vanity. She has been allowed to dispose of her time in the most idle and frivolous manner, and to adopt any opinions that came in her way. Since the ——shire were first quartered in Meryton, nothing but love, flirtation, and officers have been in her head. She has been doing everything in her power by thinking and talking on the subject, to give greater—what shall I call it?—susceptibility to her feelings; which are naturally lively enough. And we all know that Wickham has every charm of person and address that can captivate a woman who is open to being captivated."

"But you see that Jane," said her aunt, "does not think so very ill of Wickham as to believe him capable of the attempt."

"Of whom does Jane ever think ill? And who is there, whatever might be their former conduct, that she would think capable of such an attempt, till it were proved against them? But Jane knows, as well as I do, what Wickham really is. We both know that he has been profligate in every sense of the word; that he has neither integrity nor honour; that he is as false and deceitful as he is insinuating."

"And do you really know all this?" asked Mrs. Gardiner, whose curiosity as to the mode of her intelligence was all alive.

"I do indeed," replied Elizabeth, colouring. "I told you, the other day, of his behaviour to Mr. Darcy; and you yourself, when last at Longbourn, heard in what manner he spoke of the man who had behaved with such forbearance and liberality towards him. And there are other circumstances which I am not at liberty—which it is not worthwhile to relate; but his lies about the whole Pemberley family are endless. From what he said of Miss Darcy I was thoroughly prepared to see a proud, reserved, disagreeable girl. Yet he knew to the contrary himself. He must know that she was as amiable and unpretending as we have found her."

"But does Lydia know nothing of this? Can she be ignorant of what you and Jane seem so well to understand?"

"Oh, yes! That, that is the worst of all. Till I was in Kent, I was ignorant of the truth myself. And when I returned home, the ——shire was to leave Meryton in a week or fortnight's time. As that was the case, neither Jane, to whom I related the whole, nor I, thought it necessary to make our knowledge public; for of what use could it apparently be to any one, that the good opinion which all the neighbourhood had of him should then be overthrown? And even when it was settled that Lydia should go with Mrs. Forster, the necessity of opening her eyes to his character never occurred to me. That she could be in any danger from the deception never entered my head. That such a consequence as this could ensue, you may easily believe, was far enough from my thoughts."

"When they all removed to Brighton, therefore, you had no reason, I suppose, to believe them fond of each other?"

"Not the slightest. I can remember no symptom of affection on either side; and had anything of the kind been perceptible, you must be aware that ours is not a family on which it could be thrown away. When first he entered the corps, she was ready enough to admire him; but so was everyone else. Nearly each girl in or near Meryton was out of her senses about him for the first two months; but he never distinguished *her* by any particular attention; and, consequently, after a moderate period of extravagant and wild admiration, her fancy for him gave way, and others of the regiment, who treated her with more distinction, again became her favourites."

If only she had known, then perhaps this disastrous situation could have been avoided. But such regrets could be of little use, and only added to her anxiety as the carriage continued on toward Longbourn.

***

It may be easily believed, that however little of novelty could be added to their fears, hopes, and conjectures, on this interesting subject, by its repeated discussion, no other could detain them from it long, during the whole of the journey. From Elizabeth's thoughts it was never absent. Fixed there by the keenest of all anguish, self-reproach, she could find no interval of ease or forgetfulness.

They travelled as expeditiously as possible, and, sleeping one night on the road, reached Longbourn by dinner time the next day. It was a comfort to Elizabeth to consider that Jane could not have been wearied by long expectations.

The little Gardiners, attracted by the sight of a chaise, were standing on the steps of the house as they entered the paddock; and, when the carriage drove up to the door, the joyful surprise that lighted up their faces, and displayed itself over their whole bodies, in a variety of capers and frisks, was the first pleasing earnest of their welcome.

Elizabeth jumped out; and, after giving each of them a hasty kiss, hurried into the vestibule, where Jane, who came running down from her mother's apartment, immediately met her.

Elizabeth, as she affectionately embraced her, lost not a moment in asking whether anything had been heard of the fugitives.

"Not yet," replied Jane. "But now that my dear uncle is come, I hope everything will be well."

"Is my father in town?"

"Yes, he went on Tuesday, as I wrote you word."

"And have you heard from him?"

"We have heard only twice. He wrote me a few lines on Wednesday to say that he had arrived in safety, and to give me his directions, which I particularly begged him to do. He merely added that he should not write again till he had something of importance to mention."

"And my mother—how is she? How are you all?"

"My mother is tolerably well, I trust; though her spirits are greatly shaken. She is upstairs and will have great satisfaction in seeing you all. She does not yet leave her dressing-room. Mary and Kitty, thank Heaven, are quite well."

"But you—how are you?" asked Elizabeth. "You look pale. How much you must have gone through!"

Her sister, however, assured her of her being perfectly well; and their conversation, which had been passing while Mr. and Mrs. Gardiner were engaged with their children, was now put to an end by the approach of the whole party. Jane ran to her uncle and aunt, and welcomed and thanked them both, with alternate smiles and tears.

When they were all in the drawing-room, the questions that Elizabeth had already asked were of course repeated by the others, and they soon found that Jane had no intelligence to give. The sanguine hope of good, however, which the benevolence of her heart suggested, had not yet deserted her; she still expected that it would all end well, and that every morning would bring some letter, either from Lydia or her father, to explain their proceedings, and, perhaps, announce their marriage.

Mrs. Bennet, to whose apartment they all repaired after a few minutes' conversation together, received them exactly as might be expected; with tears and lamentations of regret, invectives against the villainous conduct of Wickham, and complaints of her own sufferings and ill-usage; blaming everybody but the person to whose ill-judging indulgence the errors of her daughter must principally be owing.

"If I had been able," said she, "to carry my point in going to Brighton, with all my family, *this* would not have happened; but poor dear Lydia had nobody to take care of her. Why did the Forsters ever let her go out of their sight? I am sure there was some great neglect or other on their side, for she is not the kind of girl to do such a thing if she had been well looked after. I always thought they were very unfit to have the charge of her; but I was overruled, as I always am. Poor dear child! And now here's Mr. Bennet gone away, and I know he will fight Wickham, wherever he meets him and then he will be killed, and what is to become of us all? The Collinses will turn us out before he is cold in his grave, and if you are not kind to us, brother, I do not know what we shall do."

They all exclaimed against such terrific ideas; and Mr. Gardiner, after general assurances of his affection for her and all her family, told her that he meant to be in London the very next day, and would assist Mr. Bennet in every endeavour for recovering Lydia.

"Do not give way to useless alarm," added he; "though it is right to be prepared for the worst, there is no occasion to look on it as certain. It is not quite a week since they left Brighton. In a few days more we may gain some news of them; and till we know that they are not married, and have no design of marrying, do not let us give the matter over as lost. As soon as I get to town I shall go to my brother, and make him come home with me to Gracechurch Street; and then we may consult together as to what is to be done."

"My dear brother," replied Mrs. Bennet, "that is exactly what I could most wish for. And now do, when you get to town, find them out, wherever they may be; and if they are not married already, *make* them marry. And as for wedding clothes, do not let them wait for that, but tell Lydia she shall have as much money as she chooses to buy them, after they are married. And, above all, keep Mr. Bennet from fighting. Tell him what a dreadful state I am in, that I am frighted out of my wits— and have such tremblings, such flutterings, all over me—such spasms in my side and pains in my head, and such beatings at heart, that I can get no rest by night nor by day. And tell my dear Lydia not to give any directions about her clothes till she has seen me, for she does not know which are the best warehouses. Oh, brother, how kind you are! I know you will contrive it all."

But Mr. Gardiner, though he assured her again of his earnest endeavours in the cause, could not avoid recommending moderation to her, as well in her hopes as her fear; and after talking with her in this manner till dinner was on the table, they all left her to vent all her feelings on the housekeeper, who attended in the absence of her daughters.

Though her brother and sister were persuaded that there was no real occasion for such a seclusion from the family, they did not attempt to oppose it, for they knew that she had not prudence enough to hold her tongue before the servants, while they waited at table, and judged it better that one only of the household, and the one whom they could most trust, should comprehend all her fears and solicitude on the subject.

In the dining-room they were soon joined by Mary and Kitty, who had been too busily engaged in their separate apartments to make their appearance before. One came from her books, and the other from her toilette. The faces of both, however, were tolerably calm; and no change was visible in either, except that the loss of her favourite sister, or the anger that she had herself incurred in this business, had given more of fretfulness than usual to the accents of Kitty.

As for Mary, she was mistress enough of herself to whisper to Elizabeth, with a countenance of grave reflection, soon after they were seated at table: "This is a most unfortunate affair, and will probably be much talked of. But we must stem the tide of malice and pour into the wounded bosoms of each other the balm of sisterly consolation."

Then, perceiving in Elizabeth no inclination of replying, she added, "Unhappy as the event must be for Lydia, we may draw from it this useful lesson: that loss of virtue in a female is irretrievable; that one false step involves her in endless ruin; that her reputation is no less brittle than it is beautiful; and that she cannot be too much guarded in her behaviour towards the undeserving of the other sex."

Elizabeth lifted up her eyes in amazement, but was too much oppressed to make any reply. Mary, however, continued to console herself with such kind of moral extractions from the evil before them.

In the afternoon, the two elder Miss Bennets were able to be for half-an-hour by themselves; and Elizabeth instantly availed herself of the opportunity of making any inquiries, which Jane was equally eager to satisfy. After joining in general lamentations over the dreadful sequel of this event, which Elizabeth considered as all but certain, and Miss Bennet could not assert to be wholly impossible, the former continued the subject, by saying, "But tell me all and everything about it which I have not already heard. Give me further particulars. What did Colonel Forster say? Had they no apprehension of anything before the elopement took place? They must have seen them together forever."

"Colonel Forster did own that he had often suspected some partiality, especially on Lydia's side, but nothing to give him any alarm. I am so grieved for him! His behaviour was attentive and kind to the utmost. He was coming to us to assure us of his concern, before he had any idea of their not being gone to Scotland; when that apprehension first got abroad, it hastened his journey."

"And was Denny convinced that Wickham would not marry? Did he know of their intending to go off? Had Colonel Forster seen Denny himself?"

"Yes; but when questioned, Denny denied knowing anything of their plans, and would not give his real opinion about it. He did not repeat his persuasion of their not marrying—and from *that*, I am inclined to hope, he might have been misunderstood before."

"And till Colonel Forster came himself, not one of you entertained a doubt, I suppose, of their being really married?"

"How was it possible that such an idea should enter our brains? I felt a little uneasy—a little fearful of my sister's happiness with him in marriage, because I knew that his conduct had not been always quite right. My father and mother knew nothing of that; they only felt how imprudent a match it must be. Kitty then owned, with a very natural triumph on knowing more than the rest of us, that in Lydia's last letter she had prepared her for such a step. She had known, it seems, of their being in love with each other, many weeks."

"But not before they went to Brighton?"

"No, I believe not."

"And did Colonel Forster appear to think well of Wickham himself? Does he know his real character?"

"I must confess that he did not speak so well of Wickham as he formerly did. He believed him to be imprudent and extravagant. And since this sad affair has taken place, it is said that he left Meryton greatly in debt; but I hope this may be false."

"Oh, Jane, had we been less secret, had we told what we knew of him, this could not have happened!"

"Perhaps it would have been better," replied her sister. "But to expose the former faults of any person without knowing what their present feelings were, seemed unjustifiable. We acted with the best intentions."

"Could Colonel Forster repeat the particulars of Lydia's note to his wife?"

"He brought it with him for us to see."

Jane then took it from her pocket-book, ĩ
These were the contents:

"MY DEAR HARRIET,

"You will laugh when you know where I am
laughing myself at your surprise tomorrow mo
missed. I am going to Gretna Green, and if you c
shall think you a simpleton, for there is but one n
and he is an angel. I should never be happy witho
harm to be off. You need not send them word
going, if you do not like it, for it will make the surp
I write to them and sign my name 'Lydia Wickhai
it will be! I can hardly write for laughing. Pray mak
for not keeping my engagement, and dancing wi
him I hope he will excuse me when he knows all;
dance with him at the next ball we meet, with great
for my clothes when I get to Longbourn; but I wish
to mend a great slit in my worked muslin gown bef
up. Good-bye. Give my love to Colonel Forster. I ho
our good journey.

"Your affectionate friend,

"LYDIA BENNET."

"Thoughtless, thoughtless Lydia," said Elizabetl
finished it. "What a letter is this, to be written at such
least it shows that *she* was serious on the subject
Whatever he might afterwards persuade her to, it was i
scheme of infamy. My poor father! How he must have fe

"I never saw anyone so shocked. He could not speal
ten minutes. My mother was taken ill immediately, and
in such confusion!"

"Oh, Jane," said Elizabeth, "was there a servant belor
did not know the whole story before the end of the day?"

"I do not know. I hope there was. But to be guarded at
very difficult. Our mother was in hysterics, and though I e
give her every assistance in my power, I am afraid I did no
as I might have done! But the horror of what might poš
almost took from me my faculties."

ur attendance upon her has been too much for you. You do not
ll. Oh, that I had been with you! You have had every care and
upon yourself alone."

ry and Kitty have been very kind, and would have shared in
atigue, I am sure; but I did not think it right for either of them.
s slight and delicate; and Mary studies so much, that her hours of
should not be broken in on. My aunt Phillips came to Longbourn
esday, after Father went away; and was so good as to stay till
day. She was of great use and comfort to us all. Lady Lucas also has
ery kind; she walked here on Wednesday morning to condole with
d offered her services, or any of her daughters', if they should be of
us."

he had better have stayed at home," said Elizabeth; "perhaps she
well, but under such a misfortune as this, one cannot see too little
e's neighbours. Assistance is impossible; condolence insufferable.
em triumph over us at a distance, and be satisfied."

he then proceeded to inquire into the measures which her father
ntended to pursue, while in town, for the recovery of his daughter.

He meant, I believe," replied Jane, "to go to Epsom, the place where
last changed horses, see if anything could be made out from the
lions. His principal object must be to discover the number of the
ney coach that took them from Clapham. It had come with a fare
 London; and as he thought that the circumstance of a gentleman
lady's removing from one carriage into another might be remarked,
eant to make inquiries at Clapham. If he could anyhow discover at
t house the coachman had before set down his fare, he determined to
e inquiries there, and hoped it might not be impossible to find out
stand and number of the coach. I do not know of any other designs
 he had formed; but he was in such a hurry to be gone, and his spirits
greatly discomposed, that I had difficulty in finding out even so much
his."

CHAPTER FORTY-EIGHT

The whole party were in hopes of a letter from Mr. Bennet the next morning, but the post came in without bringing a single line from him. His family knew him to be, on all common occasions, a most negligent and dilatory correspondent; but at such a time they had hoped for exertion. They were forced to conclude that he had no pleasing intelligence to send; but even of that they would have been glad to be certain. Mr. Gardiner had waited only for the letters before he set off.

When he was gone, they were certain at least of receiving constant information of what was going on, and their uncle promised, at parting, to prevail on Mr. Bennet to return to Longbourn, as soon as he could, to the great consolation of his sister, who considered it as the only security for her husband's not being killed in a duel.

Mrs. Gardiner and the children were to remain in Hertfordshire a few days longer, as the former thought her presence might be serviceable to her nieces. She shared in their attendance on Mrs. Bennet, and was a great comfort to them in their hours of freedom. Their other aunt also visited them frequently, and always, as she said, with the design of cheering and heartening them—though, as she never came without reporting some fresh instance of Wickham's extravagance or irregularity, she seldom went away without leaving them more dispirited than she had found them.

All Meryton seemed striving to blacken the man who, but three months before, had been almost an angel of light. He was declared to be in debt to every tradesman in the place, and his intrigues, all honoured with the title of seduction, had been extended into every tradesman's family. Everybody declared that he was the wickedest young man in the world; and everybody began to find out that they had always distrusted the appearance of his goodness. Elizabeth, though she did not credit above half of what was said, believed enough to make her former assurance of her sister's ruin more certain; and even Jane, who believed still less of it, became almost hopeless, more especially as the time was now come when, if they had gone to Scotland, which she had never before entirely despaired of, they must in all probability have gained some news of them.

Mr. Gardiner left Longbourn on Sunday; on Tuesday his wife received a letter from him; it told them that, on his arrival, he had immediately found out his brother, and persuaded him to come to Gracechurch Street; that Mr. Bennet had been to Epsom and Clapham, before his arrival, but without gaining any satisfactory information; and that he was now determined to inquire at all the principal hotels in town, as Mr. Bennet thought it possible they might have gone to one of them, on their first coming to London, before they procured lodgings. Mr. Gardiner himself did not expect any success from this measure, but as his brother was eager in it, he meant to assist him in pursuing it. He added that Mr. Bennet seemed wholly disinclined at present to leave London and promised to write again very soon. There was also a postscript to this effect:

"I have written to Colonel Forster to desire him to find out, if possible, from some of the young man's intimates in the regiment, whether Wickham has any relations or connections who would be likely to know in what part of town he has now concealed himself. If there were anyone that one could apply to with a probability of gaining such a clue as that, it might be of essential consequence. At present we have nothing to guide us. Colonel Forster will, I dare say, do everything in his power to satisfy us on this head. But, on second thoughts, perhaps, Lizzy could tell us what relations he has now living, better than any other person."

Elizabeth was at no loss to understand from whence this deference to her authority proceeded; but it was not in her power to give any information of so satisfactory a nature as the compliment deserved. She had never heard of his having had any relations, except a father and mother, both of whom had been dead many years. It was possible, however, that some of his companions in the ——shire might be able to give more information; and though she was not very sanguine in expecting it, the application was a something to look forward to.

Every day at Longbourn was now a day of anxiety; but the most anxious part of each was when the post was expected. The arrival of letters was the grand object of every morning's impatience. Through letters, whatever of good or bad was to be told would be communicated, and every succeeding day was expected to bring some news of importance.

But before they heard again from Mr. Gardiner, a letter arrived for their father, from a different quarter, from Mr. Collins; which, as Jane had received directions to open all that came for him in his absence, she accordingly read; and Elizabeth, who knew what curiosities his letters always were, looked over her shoulder, and read it likewise. It was as follows:

"MY DEAR SIR,

"I feel myself called upon, by our relationship, and my situation in life, to condole with you on the grievous affliction you are now suffering under, of which we were yesterday informed by a letter from Hertfordshire. Be assured, my dear sir, that Mrs. Collins and myself sincerely sympathise with you and all your respectable family, in your present distress, which must be of the bitterest kind, because proceeding from a cause which no time can remove. No arguments shall be wanting on my part that can alleviate so severe a misfortune—or that may comfort you, under a circumstance that must be of all others the most afflicting to a parent's mind. The death of your daughter would have been a blessing in comparison of this. And it is the more to be lamented, because there is reason to suppose, as my dear Charlotte informs me, that this licentiousness of behaviour in your daughter has proceeded from a faulty degree of indulgence; though, at the same time, for the consolation of yourself and Mrs. Bennet, I am inclined to think that her own disposition must be naturally bad, or she could not be guilty of such an enormity, at so early an age. Howsoever that may be, you are grievously to be pitied; in which opinion I am not only joined by Mrs. Collins, but likewise by Lady Catherine and her daughter, to whom I have related the affair. They agree with me in apprehending that this false step in one daughter will be injurious to the fortunes of all the others; for who, as Lady Catherine herself says, will connect themselves with such a family? And this consideration leads me moreover to reflect, with augmented satisfaction, on a certain event of last November; for had it been otherwise, I must have been involved in all your sorrow and disgrace. Let me then advise you, dear sir, to console yourself as much as possible, to throw off your unworthy child from your affection forever, and leave her to reap the fruits of her own heinous offense.

"I am, dear sir, etc., etc."

Mr. Gardiner did not write again till he had received an answer from Colonel Forster; and then he had nothing of a pleasant nature to send. It was not known that Wickham had a single relationship with whom he kept up any connection, and it was certain that he had no near one living. His former acquaintances had been numerous; but since he had been in the militia, it did not appear that he was on terms of particular friendship with any of them. There was no one, therefore, who could be pointed out as likely to give any news of him. And in the wretched state of his own finances, there was a very powerful motive for secrecy, in addition to his fear of discovery by Lydia's relations, for it had just transpired that he had left gaming debts behind him to a very considerable amount. Colonel Forster believed that more than a thousand pounds would be necessary to clear his expenses at Brighton. He owed a good deal in town, but his debts of honour were still more formidable. Mr. Gardiner did not attempt to conceal these particulars from the Longbourn family.

Jane heard them with horror. "A gamester!" she said. "This is wholly unexpected. I had not an idea of it."

Mr. Gardiner added in his letter, that they might expect to see their father at home on the following day, which was Saturday. Rendered spiritless by the ill-success of all their endeavours, he had yielded to his brother-in-law's entreaty that he would return to his family, and leave it to him to do whatever occasion might suggest to be advisable for continuing their pursuit. When Mrs. Bennet was told of this, she did not express so much satisfaction as her children expected, considering what her anxiety for his life had been before.

"What, is he coming home, and without poor Lydia?" she cried. "Surely he will not leave London before he has found them. Who is to fight Wickham, and make him marry her, if he comes away?"

As Mrs. Gardiner began to wish to be at home, it was settled that she and the children should go to London, at the same time that Mr. Bennet came from it. The coach, therefore, took them the first stage of their journey, and brought its master back to Longbourn.

Mrs. Gardiner went away in all the perplexity about Elizabeth and her Derbyshire friend that had attended her from that part of the world. Mr. Darcy's name had never been voluntarily mentioned before them by her niece; and the kind of half-expectation which Mrs. Gardiner had formed, of their being followed by a letter from him, had ended in nothing. Elizabeth had received none since her return that could come from Pemberley.

The present unhappy state of the family rendered any other excuse for the lowness of her spirits unnecessary; though Elizabeth, who was by this time tolerably well acquainted with her own feelings, was perfectly aware that, had she known nothing of Caroline, she could have borne the dread of Lydia's infamy somewhat better. It would have spared her, she thought, one sleepless night out of two.

When Mr. Bennet arrived, he had all the appearance of his usual philosophic composure. He said as little as he had ever been in the habit of saying; made no mention of the business that had taken him away, and it was some time before his daughters had courage to speak of it.

It was not till the afternoon, when he had joined them at tea, that Elizabeth ventured to introduce the subject; and then, on her briefly expressing her sorrow for what he must have endured, he replied, "Say nothing of that. Who should suffer but myself? It has been my own doing, and I ought to feel it."

"You must not be too severe upon yourself," replied Elizabeth.

"You may well warn me against such an evil. Human nature is so prone to fall into it! No, Lizzy, let me once in my life feel how much I have been to blame. I am not afraid of being overpowered by the impression. It will pass away soon enough."

"Do you suppose them to be in London?"

"Yes; where else can they be so well concealed?"

"And Lydia used to want to go to London," added Kitty.

"She is happy then," said her father drily; "and her residence there will probably be of some duration."

Then after a short silence he continued: "Lizzy, I bear you no ill-will for being justified in your advice to me last May, which, considering the event, shows some greatness of mind."

They were interrupted by Miss Bennet, who came to fetch her mother's tea.

"This is a parade," he said, "that does one good; it gives such an elegance to misfortune! Another day I will do the same; I will sit in my library, in my nightcap and powdering gown, and give as much trouble as I can; or, perhaps, I may defer it till Kitty runs away."

"I am not going to run away, Papa," said Kitty fretfully. "If I should ever go to Brighton, I would behave better than Lydia."

"*You* go to Brighton—I would not trust you so near it as Eastbourne for fifty pounds! No, Kitty, I have learnt to be cautious with my daughters, and you will feel the effects of it. No officer is ever to enter into my house again, nor even to pass through the village. Balls will be absolutely prohibited, unless you stand up with one of your sisters. And you are never to stir out of doors till you can prove that you have spent ten minutes of every day in a rational manner."

Kitty, who took all these threats in a serious light, began to cry.

"Well, well," said he, "do not make yourself unhappy. If you are a good girl for the next ten years, I will take you to a review at the end of them."

CHAPTER FORTY-NINE

wo days after Mr. Bennet's return, as Jane and Elizabeth were walking together in the shrubbery behind the house, they saw the housekeeper coming towards them, and, concluding that she came to call them to their mother, went forward to meet her; but, instead of the expected summons, when they approached her, she said to Miss Bennet, "I beg your pardon, Madam, for interrupting you, but I was in hopes you might have got some good news from town, so I took the liberty of coming to ask."

"What do you mean, Hill? We have heard nothing from town."

"Dear Madam," said Mrs. Hill, in great astonishment, "don't you know there is an express come for master from Mr. Gardiner? He has been here this half-hour, and master has had a letter."

Away hurried the girls, too eager to have time for speech. They ran through the vestibule into the breakfast-room; from thence to the library; their father was in neither; and they were on the point of seeking him upstairs with their mother, when they were met by the butler, who said: "If you are looking for my master, Ma'am, he is walking towards the little copse."

Upon this information, they instantly passed through the hall once more, and ran across the lawn after their father, who was deliberately pursuing his way towards a small wood on one side of the paddock.

Jane, who was not so light nor so much in the habit of running as Elizabeth, soon lagged behind, while her sister, panting for breath, came up with him, and eagerly cried out: "Oh, Papa, what news—what news? Have you heard from our uncle?"

"Yes, I have had a letter from him by express."

"Well, and what news does it bring—good or bad?"

"What is there of good to be expected?" said he, taking the letter from his pocket. "But perhaps you would like to read it."

Elizabeth impatiently caught it from his hand. Jane now came up.

"Read it aloud," said their father, "for I hardly know myself what it is about."

"Gracechurch Street, Monday, August 2.

"MY DEAR BROTHER,

"At last I am able to send you some tidings of my niece, and such as, upon the whole, I hope it will give you satisfaction. Soon after you left me on Saturday, I was fortunate enough to find out in what part of London they were. The particulars I reserve till we meet; it is enough to know they are discovered. I have seen them both—"

"Then it is as I always hoped," cried Jane; "they are married!"

Elizabeth read on:

"I have seen them both. They are not married, nor can I find there was any intention of being so; but if you are willing to perform the engagements which I have ventured to make on your side, I hope it will not be long before they are. All that is required of you is, to assure to your daughter, by settlement, her equal share of the five thousand pounds secured among your children after the decease of yourself and my sister; and, moreover, to enter into an engagement of allowing her, during your life, one hundred pounds per annum. These are conditions which, considering everything, I had no hesitation in complying with, as far as I thought myself privileged, for you. I shall send this by express, that no time may be lost in bringing me your answer. You will easily comprehend, from these particulars, that Mr. Wickham's circumstances are not so hopeless as they are generally believed to be. The world has been deceived in that respect; and I am happy to say there will be some little money, even when all his debts are discharged, to settle on my niece, in addition to her own fortune. If, as I conclude will be the case, you send me full powers to act in your name throughout the whole of this business, I will immediately give directions to Haggerston for preparing a proper settlement. There will not be the smallest occasion for your coming to town again; therefore stay quiet at Longbourn, and depend on my diligence and care. Send back your answer as fast as you can, and be careful to write explicitly. We have judged it best that my niece should be married from this house, of which I hope you will approve. She comes to us today. I shall write again as soon as anything more is determined on. Yours, etc.,

"EDW. GARDINER."

"Is it possible?" cried Elizabeth, when she had finished. "Can it be possible that he will marry her?"

"Wickham is not so undeserving, then, as we thought him," said her sister. "My dear father, I congratulate you."

"And have you answered the letter?" asked Elizabeth.

"No; but it must be done soon."

"My dear father," she said, "come back and write immediately. Consider how important every moment is in such a case."

"Let me write for you," said Jane, "if you dislike the trouble yourself."

"I dislike it very much," he replied; "but it must be done."

And so saying, he turned back with them, and walked towards the house.

"And may I ask—" said Elizabeth; "but the terms, I suppose, must be complied with."

"Complied with! I am only ashamed of his asking so little."

"And they *must* marry, yet he is such a man!"

"Yes, yes, they must marry. There is nothing else to be done. But there are two things that I want very much to know; one is, how much money your uncle has laid down to bring it about; and the other, how am I ever to pay him."

"Money!" said Jane. "What do you mean, sir?"

"I mean that no man in his senses would marry Lydia on so slight a temptation as one hundred a year during my life, and fifty after I am gone."

"That is very true," said Elizabeth, "though it had not occurred to me before. His debts to be discharged, and something still to remain! It must be our uncle's doing! Generous, good man, I am afraid he has distressed himself. A small sum could not do all this."

"No," said her father. "Wickham's a fool if he takes her with a farthing less than five thousand pounds. I should be sorry to think so ill of him, in the very beginning of our relationship."

"Five thousand pounds! How is half such a sum to be repaid?"

Mr. Bennet made no answer, and each of them, deep in thought, continued silent till they reached the house. Their father then went on to the library to write, and the girls walked into the breakfast-room.

"They are really to be married!" said Elizabeth, as soon as they were by themselves. "And for this we are to be thankful. That they should marry, small as is their chance of happiness, and wretched as is his character, we are forced to rejoice."

"I comfort myself with thinking," replied Jane, "that he certainly would not marry Lydia if he had not a real regard for her. Though our kind uncle has done something towards clearing him, I cannot believe that five thousand pounds, or anything like it, has been advanced. He has children of his own, and may have more. How could he spare five thousand pounds?"

"If he were ever able to learn what Wickham's debts have been," said Elizabeth, "and how much is settled on his side on our sister, we shall exactly know what Mr. Gardiner has done for them, because Wickham has not sixpence of his own. The kindness of my uncle and aunt can never be requited. Their taking her home, and affording her their personal protection and countenance, is such a sacrifice to her advantage as years of gratitude cannot enough acknowledge. By this time she is actually with them. If such goodness does not make her miserable now, she will never deserve to be happy. What a meeting for her, when she first sees my aunt!"

"We must endeavour to forget all that has passed on either side," said Jane. "I hope and trust they will yet be happy. His consenting to marry her is a proof, I will believe, that he is come to a right way of thinking. Their mutual affection will steady them; and I flatter myself they will settle so quietly, and live in so rational a manner, as may in time make their past imprudence forgotten."

"Their conduct has been such," replied Elizabeth, "as neither you, nor I, nor anybody can ever forget. It is useless to talk of it."

It now occurred to the girls that their mother was in all likelihood perfectly ignorant of what had happened. They went to the library, therefore, and asked their father whether he would not wish them to make it known to her. He was writing and, without raising his head, coolly replied: "Just as you please."

"May we take my uncle's letter to read to her?"

"Take whatever you like, and get away."

Elizabeth took the letter from his writing-table, and they went upstairs together. Mary and Kitty were both with Mrs. Bennet; one communication would, therefore, do for all. After a slight preparation for good news, the letter was read aloud. Mrs. Bennet could hardly contain herself. As soon as Jane had read Mr. Gardiner's hope of Lydia's being soon married, her joy burst forth, and every following sentence added to its exuberance. She was now in an irritation as violent from delight, as she had ever been fidgety from alarm and vexation. To know that her daughter would be married was enough. She was disturbed by no fear for her felicity, nor humbled by any remembrance of her misconduct.

"My dear, dear Lydia!" she cried. "This is delightful indeed! She will be married! I shall see her again! She will be married at sixteen! My good, kind brother! I knew how it would be. I knew he would manage everything! How I long to see her, and to see dear Wickham, too! But the clothes, the wedding clothes! I will write to my sister Gardiner about them directly. Lizzy, my dear, run down to your father, and ask him how much he will give her. Stay, stay, I will go myself. Ring the bell, Kitty, for Hill. I will put on my things in a moment. My dear, dear Lydia! How merry we shall be together when we meet!"

Her eldest daughter endeavoured to give some relief to the violence of these transports, by leading her thoughts to the obligations which Mr. Gardiner's behaviour laid them all under.

"For we must attribute this happy conclusion," she added, "in a great measure to his kindness. We are persuaded that he has pledged himself to assist Mr. Wickham with money."

"Well," cried her mother, "it is all very right; who should do it but her own uncle? If he had not had a family of his own, I and my children must have had all his money, you know; and it is the first time we have ever had anything from him, except a few presents. Well! I am so happy! In a short time I shall have a daughter married. Mrs. Wickham! How well it sounds! And she was only sixteen last June. My dear Jane, I am in such a flutter, that I am sure I can't write; so I will dictate, and you write for me. We will settle with your father about the money afterwards; but the things should be ordered immediately."

She was then proceeding to all the particulars of calico, muslin, and cambric, and would shortly have dictated some very plentiful orders, had not Jane, though with some difficulty, persuaded her to wait till her father was at leisure to be consulted. One day's delay, she observed, would be of small importance; and her mother was too happy to be quite so obstinate as usual. Other schemes, too, soon came into her head.

"I will go to Meryton," said she, "as soon as I am dressed, and tell the good, good news to my sister Phillips. And as I come back, I can call on Lady Lucas and Mrs. Long. Kitty, run down and order the carriage. An airing would do me a great deal of good, I am sure. Girls, can I do anything for you in Meryton? Oh! Here comes Hill! My dear Hill, have you heard the good news? Miss Lydia is going to be married; and you shall all have a bowl of punch to make merry at her wedding."

Mrs. Hill began instantly to express her joy. Elizabeth received her congratulations amongst the rest, and then, sick of this folly, took refuge in her own room, that she might think with freedom.

Poor Lydia's situation must, at best, be bad enough; but that it was no worse, she had need to be thankful. She felt it so; and though, in looking forward, neither rational happiness nor worldly prosperity could be justly expected for her sister, in looking back to what they had feared, only two hours ago, she felt all the advantages of what they had gained. After a moment, she remembered vowing to Charlotte these many months past that she should never marry a person she did not love, and would sooner run away with one she did; and closed her eyes in shame, that she should ever have considered such an ill-advised action. To do so would surely sink her family's standing irretrievably; and she could no sooner imagine betraying Jane or her father, than she could imagine knowingly submitting to a doomed marriage, such as the union into which Lydia was on the verge of entering.

CHAPTER FIFTY

M r. Bennet had very often wished before this period of his life that, instead of spending his whole income, he had laid by an annual sum for the better provision of his children, and of his wife, if she survived him. He now wished it more than ever. Had he done his duty in that respect, Lydia need not have been indebted to her uncle for whatever of honour or credit could now be purchased for her. The satisfaction of prevailing on one of the most worthless young men in Great Britain to be her husband might then have rested in its proper place.

He was seriously concerned that a cause of so little advantage to anyone should be forwarded at the sole expense of his brother-in-law, and he was determined, if possible, to find out the extent of his assistance, and to discharge the obligation as soon as he could.

When first Mr. Bennet had married, economy was held to be perfectly useless, for, of course, they were to have a son. The son was to join in cutting off the entail, as soon as he should be of age, and the widow and younger children would by that means be provided for. Five daughters successively entered the world, but yet the son was to come; and Mrs. Bennet, for many years after Lydia's birth, had been certain that he would. This event had at last been despaired of, but it was then too late to be saving. Mrs. Bennet had no turn for economy, and her husband's love of independence had alone prevented their exceeding their income.

Five thousand pounds was settled by marriage articles on Mrs. Bennet and the children. But in what proportions it should be divided amongst the latter depended on the will of the parents. This was one point, with regard to Lydia, at least, which was now to be settled, and Mr. Bennet could have no hesitation in acceding to the proposal before him. In terms of grateful acknowledgment for the kindness of his brother, though expressed most concisely, he then delivered on paper his perfect approbation of all that was done, and his willingness to fulfill the engagements that had been made for him. He had never before supposed that, could Wickham be prevailed on to marry his daughter, it would be done with so little inconvenience to himself as by the present arrangement. He would scarcely be ten pounds a year the loser by the hundred that was to be paid them; for, what with her board and pocket allowance, and the continual presents in money which passed to her through her mother's hands, Lydia's expenses had been very little within that sum.

That it would be done with such trifling exertion on his side, too, was another very welcome surprise; for his wish at present was to have as little trouble in the business as possible. When the first transports of anger which had produced his activity in seeking her were over, he naturally returned to all his former indolence. His letter was soon dispatched; for, though dilatory in undertaking business, he was quick in its execution. He begged to know further particulars of what he was indebted to his brother, but was too angry with Lydia to send any message to her.

The good news spread quickly through the house, and with proportionate speed through the neighbourhood. It was borne in the latter with decent philosophy. To be sure, it would have been more for the advantage of conversation had Miss Lydia Bennet come upon the town; or, as the happiest alternative, been secluded from the world, in some distant farmhouse. But there was much to be talked of in marrying her; and the good-natured wishes for her well-doing that had proceeded before from all the spiteful old ladies in Meryton lost but a little of their spirit in this change of circumstances, because with such a husband her misery was considered certain.

It was a fortnight since Mrs. Bennet had been downstairs; but on this happy day she again took her seat at the head of her table, and in spirits oppressively high. No sentiment of shame gave a damp to her triumph. The marriage of a daughter, which had been the first object of her wishes since Jane was sixteen, was now on the point of accomplishment, and her thoughts and her words ran wholly on those attendants of elegant nuptials, fine muslins, new carriages, and servants. She was busily searching through the neighbourhood for a proper situation for her daughter, and, without knowing or considering what their income might be, rejected many as deficient in size and importance.

"Haye Park might do," said she, "if the Gouldings could quit it—or the great house at Stoke, if the drawing-room were larger; but Ashworth is too far off! I could not bear to have her ten miles from me; and as for Pulvis Lodge, the attics are dreadful."

Her husband allowed her to talk on without interruption while the servants remained. But when they had withdrawn, he said to her: "Mrs. Bennet, before you take any or all of these houses for your son and daughter, let us come to a right understanding. Into *one* house in this neighbourhood they shall never have admittance. I will not encourage the impudence of either by receiving them at Longbourn."

A long dispute followed this declaration; but Mr. Bennet was firm. It soon led to another; and Mrs. Bennet found, with amazement and horror, that her husband would not advance a guinea to buy clothes for his daughter. He protested that she should receive from him no mark of affection whatever on the occasion. Mrs. Bennet could hardly comprehend it. That his anger could be carried to such a point of inconceivable resentment as to refuse his daughter a privilege without which her marriage would scarcely seem valid, exceeded all she could believe possible. She was more alive to the disgrace that her want of new clothes must reflect on her daughter's nuptials, than to any sense of shame at her eloping and living with Wickham a fortnight before they took place.

Elizabeth was now most heartily sorry that she had, from the distress of the moment, been led to make Miss Bingley acquainted with their fears for her sister; for since her marriage would so shortly give the proper termination to the elopement, they might hope to conceal its unfavourable beginning from all those who were not immediately on the spot.

She had no fear of its spreading farther through the lady's means. There were few people on whose secrecy she would have more confidently depended; but, at the same time, there was no one whose knowledge of a sister's frailty would have mortified her so much—not, however, from any fear of disadvantage from it individually to herself, for, at any rate, there seemed a gulf impassable between them. Had

Lydia's marriage been concluded on the most honourable terms, it was not to be supposed that Miss Bingley would allow herself to be connected with a family where, to every other objection, would now be added an alliance and relationship of the nearest kind with a man whom she and her closest friends could not tolerate.

The lady's desire to secure her regard, which Elizabeth had fancied was the case in Derbyshire, could not in rational expectation survive such a blow as this. Elizabeth was humbled, she was grieved; she repented, though she hardly knew of what. She became jealous of Caroline's esteem, when she could no longer hope to be benefited by it. She wanted to hear news of her, when there seemed the least chance of gaining intelligence. She was convinced that she could have been happy with Caroline, now that it was no longer likely they should meet.

What a triumph for Miss Bingley, she often thought, could she know that the attachment Elizabeth had proudly spurned only four months ago, would now have been most gladly and gratefully received! She was a generous woman, Elizabeth doubted not; but while she was mortal, there must be triumph.

She began now to comprehend that Caroline was exactly the woman who, in disposition and talents, would most suit her. The lady's understanding and temper, though unlike her own, would have answered all her wishes. It was a partnership that must have been to the advantage of both; by Elizabeth's ease and liveliness, Caroline's manner might have been softened, her independence from the rancor of her family increased; and from Caroline's judgment and knowledge of the world, Elizabeth must have received benefit of greater importance. But no such happy union could now teach either the felicity of a perfectly balanced match.

An alliance of a different tendency was soon to be formed in Elizabeth's family. How Wickham and Lydia were to be supported in tolerable independence, she could not imagine. But how little of permanent happiness could belong to a couple who were only brought together because their passions were stronger than their character, she could easily conjecture.

***

Mr. Gardiner soon wrote again to his brother. To Mr. Bennet's acknowledgments he briefly replied, with assurance of his eagerness to promote the welfare of any of his family; and concluded with entreaties that the subject might never be mentioned to him again. The principal purport of his letter was to inform them that Mr. Wickham had resolved on quitting the militia.

"It was greatly my wish that he should do so," he added, "as soon as his marriage was fixed on. And I think you will agree with me, in considering the removal from that corps as highly advisable, both on his account and my niece's. It is Mr. Wickham's intention to go into the regulars; and among his former friends, there are still some who are able and willing to assist him in the army. He has the promise of an ensigncy in General ———'s regiment, now quartered in the North. It is an advantage to have it so far from this part of the kingdom. He promises fairly; and I hope among different people, where they may each have a character to preserve, they will both be more prudent. I have written to Colonel Forster to inform him of our present arrangements, and to request that he will satisfy the various creditors of Mr. Wickham in and near Brighton, with assurances of speedy payment, for which I have pledged myself. And will you give yourself the trouble of carrying similar assurances to his creditors in Meryton, of whom I shall subjoin a list according to his information? He has given in all his debts; I hope at least he has not deceived us. Haggerston has our directions, and all will be completed in a week. They will then join his regiment, unless they are first invited to Longbourn; and I understand from Mrs. Gardiner, that my niece is very desirous of seeing you all before she leaves the South. She is well, and begs to be dutifully remembered to you and her mother.—Yours, etc.,

"E. GARDINER."

Mr. Bennet and his daughters saw all the advantages of Wickham's removal from the ———shire as clearly as Mr. Gardiner could do. But Mrs. Bennet was not so well pleased with it. Lydia's being settled in the North, just when she had expected most pleasure and pride in her company, for she had by no means given up her plan of their residing in Hertfordshire, was a severe disappointment; and, besides, it was such a pity that Lydia should be taken from a regiment where she was acquainted with everybody, and had so many favourites.

"She is so fond of Mrs. Forster," said she, "it will be quite shocking to send her away! And there are several of the young men, too, that she likes very much. The officers may not be so pleasant in General ———'s regiment."

His daughter's request, for such it might be considered, of being admitted into her family again before she set off for the North, received at first an absolute negative. But Jane and Elizabeth, who agreed in wishing, for the sake of their sister's feelings and consequence, that she should be noticed on her marriage by her parents, urged their father so earnestly yet so rationally and so mildly, to receive her and her husband at Longbourn as soon as they were married, that he was prevailed on to think as they thought, and act as they wished. And their mother had the satisfaction of knowing that she would be able to show her married daughter in the neighbourhood before she was banished to the North. When Mr. Bennet wrote again to his brother, therefore, he sent his permission for them to come; and it was settled, that as soon as the ceremony was over, they should proceed to Longbourn. Elizabeth was surprised, however, that Wickham should consent to such a scheme, and had she consulted only her own inclination, any meeting with him would have been the last object of her wishes.

CHAPTER FIFTY-ONE

Their sister's wedding day arrived; and Jane and Elizabeth felt for her probably more than she felt for herself. The carriage was sent to meet them at ——, and they were to return in it by dinner-time. Their arrival was dreaded by the elder Miss Bennets, and Jane more especially, who gave Lydia the feelings which would have attended herself, had she been the culprit, and was wretched in the thought of what her sister must endure.

They came. The family were assembled in the breakfast room to receive them. Smiles decked the face of Mrs. Bennet as the carriage drove up to the door; her husband looked impenetrably grave; her daughters, alarmed, anxious, uneasy.

Lydia's voice was heard in the vestibule; the door was thrown open, and she ran into the room. Her mother stepped forwards, embraced her, and welcomed her with rapture; gave her hand, with an affectionate smile, to Wickham, who followed his lady; and wished them both joy with an alacrity which offered no doubt of their happiness.

Their reception from Mr. Bennet, to whom they then turned, was not quite so cordial. His countenance rather gained in austerity; and he scarcely opened his lips. The easy assurance of the young couple, indeed, was enough to provoke him. Elizabeth was disgusted, and even Miss Bennet was shocked. Lydia was Lydia still; untamed, unabashed, wild, noisy, and fearless. She turned from sister to sister, demanding their congratulations; and when at length they all sat down, looked eagerly round the room, took notice of some little alteration in it, and observed, with a laugh, that it was a great while since she had been there.

Wickham was not at all more distressed than herself, but his manners were always so pleasing, that had his character and his marriage been exactly what they ought, his smiles and his easy address, while he claimed their relationship, would have delighted them all. Elizabeth had not before believed him quite equal to such assurance; but she sat down, resolving within herself to draw no limits in future to the impudence of an impudent man. She blushed, and Jane blushed; but the cheeks of the two who caused their confusion suffered no variation of colour.

There was no want of discourse. The bride and her mother could neither of them talk fast enough; and Wickham, who happened to sit near Elizabeth, began inquiring after his acquaintance in that neighbourhood, with a good-humoured ease which she felt very unable to equal in her replies. They seemed each of them to have the happiest memories in the world. Nothing of the past was recollected with pain; and Lydia led voluntarily to subjects which her sisters would not have alluded to for the world.

"Only think of its being three months," she cried, "since I went away; it seems but a fortnight I declare; and yet there have been things enough happened in the time. Good gracious! When I went away, I am sure I had no more idea of being married till I came back again! Though I thought it would be very good fun if I was."

Her father lifted up his eyes. Jane was distressed. Elizabeth looked expressively at Lydia; but she, who never heard nor saw anything of which she chose to be insensible, gaily continued, "Oh, Mamma, do the people hereabouts know I am married today? I was afraid they might not; and we overtook William Goulding in his curricle, so I was determined he should know it, and so I let down the side-glass next to him, and took off my glove, and let my hand just rest upon the window frame, so that he might see the ring, and then I bowed and smiled like anything."

Elizabeth could bear it no longer. She got up and left the room; and returned no more, till she heard them passing through the hall to the dining parlour. She then joined them soon enough to see Lydia, with anxious parade, walk up to her mother's right hand, and hear her say to her eldest sister, "Ah! Jane, I take your place now, and you must go lower, because I am a married woman."

It was not to be supposed that time would give Lydia that embarrassment from which she had been so wholly free at first. Her ease and good spirits increased. She longed to see Mrs. Phillips, the Lucases, and all their other neighbours, and to hear herself called "Mrs.

Wickham" by each of them; and in the mean time, she went after dinner to show her ring, and boast of being married, to Mrs. Hill and the two housemaids.

"Well, Mamma," said she, when they all returned to the breakfast room, "and what do you think of my husband? Is not he a charming man? I am sure my sisters must all envy me. I only hope they may have half my good luck. They must all go to Brighton. That is the place to get husbands. What a pity it is, Mamma, we did not all go."

"Very true; and if I had my will, we should. But my dear Lydia, I don't at all like your going such a way off. Must it be so?"

"Oh, lord! Yes, there is nothing in that. I shall like it of all things. You and Papa, and my sisters, must come and see us. We shall be at Newcastle all the winter, and I dare say there will be some balls, and I will take care to get good partners for them all."

"I should like it beyond anything!" said her mother.

"And then when you go away, you may leave one or two of my sisters behind you; and I dare say I shall get husbands for them before the winter is over."

"I thank you for my share of the favour," said Elizabeth; "but I do not particularly like your way of getting husbands."

Lydia paid the comment little attention, and continued on just as she had before.

Their visitors were not to remain above ten days with them. Mr. Wickham had received his commission before he left London, and he was to join his regiment at the end of a fortnight.

No one but Mrs. Bennet regretted that their stay would be so short; and she made the most of the time by visiting about with her daughter, and having very frequent parties at home. These parties were acceptable to all; to avoid a family circle was even more desirable to such as did think, than such as did not.

Wickham's affection for Lydia was just what Elizabeth had expected to find it; not equal to Lydia's for him. She had scarcely needed her present observation to be satisfied, from the reason of things, that their elopement had been brought on by the strength of her love, rather than by his; and she would have wondered why, without violently caring for her, he chose to elope with her at all, had she not felt certain that his flight was rendered necessary by distress of circumstances; and if that were the case, he was not the young man to resist an opportunity of having a companion.

Lydia was exceedingly fond of him. He was her dear Wickham on every occasion; no one was to be put in competition with him. He did everything best in the world; and she was sure he would kill more birds on the first of September, than anybody else in the country.

One morning, soon after their arrival, as she was sitting with her two elder sisters, she said to Elizabeth: "Lizzy, *you* were not by when I told Mamma and the others about my wedding, I believe. Are not you curious to hear how it was managed?"

"No, really," replied Elizabeth. "I think there cannot be too little said on the subject."

"La! You are so strange! But I must tell you how it went off. We were married, you know, at St. Clement's, because Wickham's lodgings were in that parish. And it was settled that we should all be there by eleven o'clock. My uncle and aunt and I were to go together; and the others were to meet us at the church. Well, Monday morning came, and I was in such a fuss! I was so afraid, you know, that something would happen to put it off, and then I should have gone quite distracted. And there was my aunt, all the time I was dressing, preaching and talking away just as if she was reading a sermon. However, I did not hear above one word in ten, for I was thinking, you may suppose, of my dear Wickham. I longed to know whether he would be married in his blue coat.

"Well, and so we breakfasted at ten as usual; I thought it would never be over; for, by the bye, you are to understand, that my uncle and aunt were horrid unpleasant all the time I was with them. If you'll believe me, I did not once put my foot out of doors, though I was there a fortnight. Not one party, or scheme, or anything. To be sure London was rather thin, but, however, the Little Theatre was open. Well, and so just as the carriage came to the door, my uncle was called away upon business to that horrid man Mr. Stone. And then, you know, when once they get together, there is no end of it. Well, I was so frightened I did not know what to do, for my uncle was to give me away; and if we were beyond the hour, we could not be married all day. But, luckily, he came back again in ten minutes' time, and then we all set out. However, I recollected afterwards that if he had been prevented going, the wedding need not be put off, for Mr. Darcy might have done as well."

"Mr. Darcy!" repeated Elizabeth, in utter amazement.

"Oh, yes! He was to come there with Wickham, you know. But gracious me! I quite forgot! I ought not to have said a word about it. I promised them so faithfully! What will Wickham say? It was to be such a secret!"

"If it was to be secret," said Jane, "say not another word on the subject. You may depend upon my seeking no further."

"Certainly," said Elizabeth, though burning with curiosity; "we will ask you no questions."

"Thank you," said Lydia, "for if you did, I should certainly tell you all, and then Wickham would be angry."

On such encouragement to ask, Elizabeth was forced to put it out of her power, by taking immediate leave.

But to live in ignorance on such a point was impossible; or at least it was impossible not to try for information. Mr. Darcy had been at her sister's wedding. It was exactly a scene where he had apparently least temptation to go. Conjectures as to the meaning of it hurried into her brain; but she was satisfied with none. Those that best pleased her, all of which included some version of Caroline's requesting his assistance due to her regard for Elizabeth, seemed most improbable. She could not bear such suspense; and hastily seizing a sheet of paper, wrote a short letter to her aunt, to request an explanation of what Lydia had dropt, if it were compatible with the secrecy which had been intended.

"You may readily comprehend," she added, "what my curiosity must be to know how a person unconnected with any of us, and (comparatively speaking) a stranger to our family, should have been amongst you at such a time. Pray write instantly, and let me understand it—unless it is, for very cogent reasons, to remain in the secrecy which Lydia seems to think necessary; and then I must endeavour to be satisfied with ignorance."

"Not that I *shall* be," she added to herself as she finished the letter; "and my dear aunt, if you do not tell me in an honourable manner, I shall certainly be reduced to tricks and stratagems to find it out."

Jane's delicate sense of honour would not allow her to speak to Elizabeth privately of what Lydia had let fall; Elizabeth was glad of it; till it appeared whether her inquiries would receive any satisfaction, she had rather be without a confidante.

CHAPTER FIFTY-TWO

E lizabeth had the satisfaction of receiving an answer to her letter as soon as she possibly could. She was no sooner in possession of it than, hurrying into the little copse, where she was least likely to be interrupted, she sat down on one of the benches and prepared to be happy; for the length of the letter convinced her that it did not contain a denial.

"Gracechurch street, Sept. 6.

"MY DEAR NIECE,

"I have just received your letter, and shall devote this whole morning to answering it, as I foresee that a little writing will not comprise what I have to tell you. I must confess myself surprised by your application; I did not expect it from you. Don't think me angry, however, for I only mean to let you know that I had not imagined such inquiries to be necessary on *your* side. If you do not choose to understand me, forgive my impertinence. Your uncle is as much surprised as I am—and nothing but the belief of your being a party concerned would have allowed him to act as he has done. But if you are really innocent and ignorant, I must be more explicit.

"On the very day of my coming home from Longbourn, your uncle had a most unexpected visitor. Mr. Darcy called, and was shut up with him several hours. It was all over before I arrived; so my curiosity was not so dreadfully racked as yours seems to have been. He came to tell Mr. Gardiner that he had found out where your sister and Mr. Wickham were, and that he had seen and talked with them both; Wickham repeatedly, Lydia once. From what I can collect, he left Derbyshire only one day after ourselves, and came to town with the resolution of hunting for them. The motive professed was his conviction of its being owing to himself that Wickham's worthlessness had not been so well known as to make it impossible for any young woman of character to love or confide in him. He generously imputed the whole to his mistaken pride, and confessed that he had before thought it beneath him to lay his private actions open to the world. He called it, therefore, his duty to endeavour to remedy an evil which had been brought on by himself. If he had another motive, I am sure it would never disgrace him. He had been some days in town, before he was able to discover them; but he had something to direct his search, which was more than we had; and the consciousness of this was another reason for his resolving to follow us.

"There is a lady, it seems, a Mrs. Younge, who was some time ago governess to Miss Darcy, and was dismissed from her charge on some cause of disapprobation, though he did not say what. She then took a large house in Edward-street, and has since maintained herself by letting lodgings. This Mrs. Younge was, he knew, intimately acquainted with Wickham; and he went to her for intelligence of him as soon as he got to town. But it was two or three days before he could get from her what he wanted. She would not betray her trust, I suppose, without bribery and corruption, for she really did know where her friend was to be found. Wickham indeed had gone to her on their first arrival in London, and had she been able to receive them into her house, they would have taken up their abode with her. At length, however, our kind friend procured the wished-for direction. They were in —— street. He saw Wickham, and afterwards insisted on seeing Lydia. His first object with her, he acknowledged, had been to persuade her to quit her present disgraceful situation, and return to her friends as soon as they could be prevailed on to receive her, offering his assistance, as far as it would go. But he found Lydia absolutely resolved on remaining where she was. She cared for none of her friends; she wanted no help of his; she would not hear of leaving Wickham. She was sure they should be married some time or other, and it did not much signify when. Since such were her feelings, it only remained, he thought, to secure and expedite a marriage, which, in his very first conversation with Wickham, he easily learnt had never been intended. He confessed himself obliged to leave the regiment on account of some debts of honour, which were very pressing; and scrupled not to lay all the ill-consequences of Lydia's flight on her own folly alone. He meant to resign his commission immediately; and as to his future situation, he could conjecture very little about it. He must go somewhere, but he did not know where, and he knew he should have nothing to live on.

"They met several times, for there was much to be discussed. Wickham of course wanted more than he could get; but at length was reduced to be reasonable.

"Everything being settled between them, Mr. Darcy's next step was to make your uncle acquainted with it, and he first called in Gracechurch street the evening before I came home. But Mr. Gardiner could not be seen, and Mr. Darcy found, on further inquiry, that your father was still with him, but would quit town the next morning. He did not judge your father to be a person whom he could so properly consult as your uncle, and therefore readily postponed seeing him till after the departure of the former. He did not leave his name, and till the next day it was only known that a gentleman had called on business.

"On Saturday he came again. Your father was gone, your uncle at home, and, as I said before, they had a great deal of talk together.

"They met again on Sunday, and then I saw him too. It was not all settled before Monday. As soon as it was, the express was sent off to Longbourn. But our visitor was very obstinate. I fancy, Lizzy, that obstinacy is the real defect of his character, after all. He has been accused of many faults at different times, but *this* is the true one. Nothing was to be done that he did not do himself; though I am sure (and I do not speak it to be thanked, therefore say nothing about it), your uncle would most readily have settled the whole.

"At last your uncle was forced to yield, and instead of being allowed to be of use to his niece, was forced to accept only having the probable credit of it, which went sorely against the grain; and I really believe your letter this morning gave him great pleasure, because it required an explanation that would rob him of his borrowed feathers, and give the praise where it was due. But, Lizzy, this must go no farther than yourself, or Jane at most.

"You know pretty well, I suppose, what has been done for the young people. His debts are to be paid, amounting, I believe, to considerably more than a thousand pounds, another thousand in addition to her own settled upon her, and his commission purchased. The reason why all this was to be done by him alone, was such as I have given above. Perhaps there was some truth in this. But in spite of all this fine talking, my dear

Lizzy, you may rest perfectly assured that your uncle would never have yielded, if we had not given him credit for another interest in the affair.

"When all this was resolved on, he returned again to his friends, who were still staying at Pemberley; but it was agreed that he should be in London once more when the wedding took place, and all money matters were then to receive the last finish.

"I believe I have now told you everything. It is a relation which you tell me is to give you great surprise; I hope at least it will not afford you any displeasure. Lydia came to us; and Wickham had constant admission to the house. He was exactly what he had been when I knew him in Hertfordshire; but I would not tell you how little I was satisfied with her behaviour while she stayed with us, if I had not perceived, by Jane's letter last Wednesday, that her conduct on coming home was exactly of a piece with it, and therefore what I now tell you can give you no fresh pain. I talked to her repeatedly in the most serious manner, representing to her all the wickedness of what she had done, and all the unhappiness she had brought on her family. If she heard me, it was by good luck, for I am sure she did not listen. I was sometimes quite provoked, but then I recollected my dear Elizabeth and Jane, and for their sakes had patience with her.

"Mr. Darcy was punctual in his return, and as Lydia informed you, attended the wedding. He and Miss Bingley, who was also in town, dined with us the next day, and were to leave town again on Wednesday or Thursday. Will you be very angry with me, my dear Lizzy, if I take this opportunity of saying (what I was never bold enough to say before) how much I like Mr. Darcy? His behaviour to us has, in every respect, been as pleasing as when we were in Derbyshire. His understanding and opinions all please me; he wants nothing but a little more liveliness, and that, if he marries *prudently*, his wife may teach him. I thought him very sly—he hardly ever mentioned your name. But slyness seems the fashion.

"Pray forgive me if I have been very presuming, or at least do not punish me so far as to exclude me from P. I shall never be quite happy till I have been all round the park. A low phaeton, with a nice little pair of ponies, would be the very thing.

"But I must write no more. The children have been wanting me this half hour.

"Yours, very sincerely,

289

"M. GARDINER."

The contents of this letter threw Elizabeth into a flutter of spirits, in which it was difficult to determine whether pleasure or pain bore the greatest share. The vague and unsettled suspicions her uncertainty had produced of what Mr. Darcy might have been doing to forward her sister's match, which she had feared to encourage as an exertion of goodness too great to be probable, and at the same time dreaded to be just, from the pain of obligation, were proved beyond their greatest extent to be true! On what must have been Caroline's instigation, he had followed Lydia and Wickham to town and taken on the trouble and mortification attendant on such a research; in which supplication had been necessary to a woman whom he must abominate and despise, and where he was reduced to frequently meet, reason with, persuade, and finally bribe the man whose very name it was punishment to him to pronounce. He had done all this, at Caroline's entreaty, for a girl whom neither could possibly regard or esteem. Her heart did whisper that the lady had done it for her. But it was a hope shortly checked by other considerations, and she soon felt that even her vanity was insufficient, when required to depend on Caroline's affection for her—for a woman who had already refused her—as able to persuade Darcy to overcome a sentiment so natural as abhorrence against any connection with Wickham.

While Caroline had undoubtedly informed Darcy of Wickham's latest descent into scandal, Darcy was the one who had taken action. Given that he seemed much changed since their first meeting, and that those who knew him swore by his goodness and generosity, Elizabeth knew she had better believe the reasons he had offered for his interference, which asked no extraordinary stretch of belief. It was reasonable that he should feel he had been wrong; he had liberality, and he had the means of exercising it; and though she would not cast it as the principal inducement, she could, perhaps, believe that Darcy's sympathy to Caroline's former partiality toward her might have contributed in his decision to assist in a cause where her peace of mind must be materially concerned. It was painful, exceedingly painful, to know that her family was under obligation to persons who could never receive a return. They owed the restoration of Lydia, her character, everything, to Darcy and Caroline. How heartily did Elizabeth now grieve over every ungracious sensation she had ever encouraged regarding the two friends, every saucy speech she had ever directed toward either. For herself she was humbled; but she was grateful to Caroline and Darcy for their assistance in resolving a matter that would never elicit the approbation so clearly deserved.

She read over her aunt's commendation of Darcy again, wondering if she should discourage the false assumptions of an attachment between the gentleman and herself. She was sensible of some regret on finding how steadfastly her aunt and uncle had been persuaded that affection and confidence subsisted between Mr. Darcy and herself, while, all along, the attachment lay in quite another area. Had they known of Caroline's professions of love at Hunsford Parsonage, what would have been their reaction? Certainly not a cheerful reference to someday visiting their shared home for a turn about the park. Were Elizabeth and Caroline to choose each other above all others, such a choice would have to remain secret; an open secret to friends, family, and even strangers, perhaps, but an unspoken secret nonetheless. Romantic friendship between women of their class was a grudgingly tolerated tradition, as the example of the Ladies of Llangollen, the celebrated Welsh couple, had proven. But even Eleanor Butler and Sarah Ponsonby stringently denied any intimacy that went beyond the accepted boundaries of friendship.

Neither Elizabeth nor Charlotte, both amply pleased by the physical nature of their own love, had ever believed the Ladies' claims to innocence. In the early months of their attachment, they had read everything on the Ladies they could find, imagining a future for themselves based on just such a model. Or, at least, Elizabeth had pictured herself living in pastoral bliss with Charlotte, far from the notice of those who would have them settled in unwanted marriages. Her friend had been contemplating a very different type of life, as her actions clearly attested. What, wondered Elizabeth, did Caroline Bingley want? To be rescued from society's censure, like Charlotte, by entering into a marriage of expediency? Or did she, as Elizabeth had once done, dream of running away with the woman she loved?

In the wake of her sister's elopement, Elizabeth's old dream had lost any possible remaining shine of nobility or appeal. After considering further the pain Lydia's actions had inflicted, she was convinced that she could never exact from her family the significant toll required should she give in to the longing to share her life with the person of her preference. Perhaps Charlotte had been right to sacrifice real affection for respectability, after all. If only they were not required to make such a choice—but it was useless, and not in Elizabeth's character, to waste time wishing for such a revolution in social mores.

She was roused from her seat, and her reflections, by someone's approach; and before she could strike into another path, she was overtaken by Wickham.

"I am afraid I interrupt your solitary ramble, my dear sister?" said he, as he joined her.

"You certainly do," she replied politely; "but it does not follow that the interruption must be unwelcome."

"I should be sorry indeed, if it were. We were always good friends; and now we are better."

"Are the others coming out?"

"I do not know. Mrs. Bennet and Lydia are going in the carriage to Meryton. And so, my dear sister, I find, from our uncle and aunt, that you have actually seen Pemberley."

She replied in the affirmative.

"I almost envy you the pleasure, and yet I believe it would be too much for me, or else I could take it in my way to Newcastle. And you saw the old housekeeper, I suppose? Poor Reynolds, she was always very fond of me. But of course she did not mention my name to you."

"Yes, she did."

"And what did she say?"

"That you were gone into the army, and she was afraid had—not turned out well. At such a distance as that, you know, things are strangely misrepresented."

"Certainly," he replied, biting his lip. Elizabeth hoped she had silenced him; but he soon afterwards said: "I was surprised to see Darcy in town last month. We passed each other several times. I wonder what he can be doing there."

"Perhaps preparing for his marriage with Miss de Bourgh," said Elizabeth. "It must be something particular, to take him there at this time of year."

"Undoubtedly. Did you see him while you were at Lambton? I thought I understood from the Gardiners that you had."

"Yes; he introduced us to his sister."

"And do you like her?"

"Very much."

"I have heard, indeed, that she is uncommonly improved within this year or two. When I last saw her, she was not very promising. I am very glad you liked her. I hope she will turn out well."

"I dare say she will; she has got over the most trying age."

"Did you go by the village of Kympton?"

"I do not recollect that we did."

"I mention it because it is the living which I ought to have had. A most delightful place! Excellent Parsonage House! It would have suited me in every respect."

"How should you have liked making sermons?"

"Exceedingly well. I should have considered it as part of my duty, and the exertion would soon have been nothing. One ought not to repine; but, to be sure, it would have been such a thing for me! The quiet, the retirement of such a life would have answered all my ideas of happiness. But it was not to be. Did you ever hear Darcy mention the circumstance, when you were in Kent?"

"I have heard from authority, which I thought as good, that it was left you conditionally only, and at the will of the present patron."

"You have. Yes, there was something in that; I told you so from the first, you may remember."

"I did hear, too, that there was a time when sermon-making was not so palatable to you as it seems to be at present; that you actually declared your resolution of never taking orders, and that the business had been compromised accordingly."

"You did! And it was not wholly without foundation. You may remember what I told you on that point, when first we talked of it."

They were now almost at the door of the house, for she had walked fast to get rid of him; and unwilling, for her sister's sake, to provoke him, she only said in reply, with a good-humoured smile: "Come, Mr. Wickham, we are brother and sister, you know. Do not let us quarrel about the past. In future, I hope we shall be always of one mind."

She held out her hand; he kissed it with affectionate gallantry, though he hardly knew how to look, and they entered the house.

CHAPTER FIFTY-THREE

r. Wickham was so perfectly satisfied with this conversation that he never again distressed himself, or provoked his dear sister Elizabeth, by introducing the subject of it; and she was pleased to find that she had said enough to keep him quiet.

The day of his and Lydia's departure soon came, and Mrs. Bennet was forced to submit to a separation that, as her husband by no means entered into her scheme of their all going to Newcastle, was likely to continue at least a twelvemonth.

"Oh, my dear Lydia," she cried, "when shall we meet again?"

"Oh, lord! I don't know. Not these two or three years, perhaps."

"Write to me very often, my dear."

"As often as I can. But you know married women have never much time for writing. My sisters may write to *me*. They will have nothing else to do."

Mr. Wickham's adieus were much more affectionate than his wife's. He smiled, looked handsome, and said many pretty things.

"He is as fine a fellow," said Mr. Bennet, as soon as they were out of the house, "as ever I saw. He simpers, and smirks, and makes love to us all. I am prodigiously proud of him. I defy even Sir William Lucas himself to produce a more valuable son-in-law."

The loss of her daughter made Mrs. Bennet very dull for several days.

"I often think," said she, "that there is nothing so bad as parting with one's friends. One seems so forlorn without them."

"This is the consequence, you see, Madam, of marrying a daughter," said Elizabeth. "It must make you better satisfied that your other four are single."

"It is no such thing. Lydia does not leave me because she is married, but only because her husband's regiment happens to be so far off. If that had been nearer, she would not have gone so soon."

But the spiritless condition which this event threw her into was shortly relieved, and her mind opened again to the agitation of hope, by an article of news which then began to be in circulation. The housekeeper at Netherfield had received orders to prepare for the arrival of her master, who was coming down in a day or two, to shoot there for several weeks. When Mrs. Phillips first brought her the news, Mrs. Bennet was quite in the fidgets. She looked at Jane, and smiled and shook her head by turns.

"Well, well, and so Mr. Bingley is coming down, sister. Well, so much the better. Not that I care about it, though. He is nothing to us, you know, and I am sure *I* never want to see him again. But, however, he is very welcome to come to Netherfield, if he likes it. And who knows what may happen? But that is nothing to us. You know, sister, we agreed long ago never to mention a word about it. And so, is it quite certain he is coming?"

"You may depend on it," replied the other, "for Mrs. Nicholls was in Meryton last night; I saw her passing by, and went out myself on purpose to know the truth of it; and she told me that it was certain true. He comes down on Thursday at the latest, very likely on Wednesday. She was going to the butcher's, she told me, on purpose to order in some meat on Wednesday, and she has got three couple of ducks just fit to be killed."

Miss Bennet had not been able to hear of his coming without changing colour. It was many months since she had mentioned his name to Elizabeth; but now, as soon as they were alone together, she said: "I saw you look at me today, Lizzy, when my aunt told us of the present report; and I know I appeared distressed. But don't imagine it was from any silly cause. I was only confused for the moment because I felt that I should be looked at. I do assure you that the news does not affect me either with pleasure or pain."

Elizabeth did not know what to make of it. Had she not seen him in Derbyshire, she might have supposed him capable of coming there with no other view than what was acknowledged; but she still thought him partial to Jane, and she wavered as to the greater probability of his coming there *with* his friend's permission, or being bold enough to come without it. The one question she longed to ask, of course, was whether he would come alone, or be accompanied by his sister.

"Yet it is hard," she sometimes thought, "that this poor man cannot come to a house which he has legally hired, without raising all this speculation! I will leave him to himself."

Despite this resolution, the idea that she might soon see Caroline Bingley caused her sentiments more than their share of perturbation. And in spite of what her sister declared, and really believed to be her feelings in the expectation of Bingley's arrival, Elizabeth could easily perceive that her spirits were affected by it, too. They were more disturbed, more unequal, than she had often seen them.

The subject which had been so warmly canvassed between their parents the previous winter was now brought forward again.

"As soon as ever Mr. Bingley comes, my dear," said Mrs. Bennet, "you will wait on him of course."

"No, no. You forced me into visiting him last year, and promised, if I went to see him, he should marry one of my daughters. But it ended in nothing; I will not be sent on a fool's errand again."

His wife represented to him how absolutely necessary such an attention would be from all the neighbouring gentlemen, on his returning to Netherfield.

"'Tis an etiquette I despise," said he. "If he wants our society, let him seek it. He knows where we live. I will not spend my hours in running after my neighbours every time they go away and come back again."

"Well, all I know is that it will be abominably rude if you do not wait on him. But, however, that shan't prevent my asking him to dine here, I am determined. We must have Mrs. Long and the Gouldings soon. That will make thirteen with ourselves, so there will be just room at table for him."

Consoled by this resolution, she was the better able to bear her husband's incivility; though it was very mortifying to know that her neighbours might all see Mr. Bingley, in consequence of it, before *they* did.

As the day of his arrival drew near, Jane said to her sister: "I begin to be sorry that he comes at all. It would be nothing; I could see him with perfect indifference, but I can hardly bear to hear it thus perpetually talked of. My mother means well; but she does not know, no one can know, how much I suffer from what she says. Happy shall I be, when his stay at Netherfield is over!"

"I wish I could say something to comfort you," replied Elizabeth, who had been unable to uncover any intelligence regarding Caroline's accompaniment; "but it is wholly out of my power. You must feel it; and the usual satisfaction of preaching patience to a sufferer is denied me, because you have always so much."

Mr. Bingley arrived. Mrs. Bennet, through the assistance of servants, contrived to have the earliest tidings of it, that the period of anxiety and fretfulness on her side might be as long as it could. She counted the days that must intervene before their invitation could be sent; hopeless of seeing him before. But on the third morning after his arrival in Hertfordshire, she saw him, from her dressing-room window, enter the paddock and guide his chaise towards the house.

Her daughters were eagerly called to partake of her joy. Jane resolutely kept her place at the table; but Elizabeth, to satisfy her mother, went to the window—she looked—she saw Miss Bingley and Mr. Darcy with him, and quickly went to sit down again by her sister. Caroline Bingley was here, now, at Longbourn. What could it mean?

"His sister is with him, Mamma," said Kitty, "and a gentleman, too; who can it be?"

"Good gracious! Mr. Darcy! Well, any friend of Mr. Bingley's will always be welcome here, to be sure; but else I must say that I hate the very sight of him."

Jane looked at Elizabeth with surprise and concern. She knew but little of her sister's stay in Derbyshire, and therefore felt for the awkwardness which must attend Elizabeth in seeing Caroline almost for the first time since receiving her explanatory letter. Both sisters were uncomfortable enough. Each felt for the other, and of course for themselves; and their mother talked on, of her dislike of Mr. Darcy and Miss Bingley alike, and her resolution to be civil to them only as Mr. Bingley's friends, without being heard by either of them. But Elizabeth had sources of uneasiness which could not be suspected by Jane, to whom she had never yet had courage to show Mrs. Gardiner's letter, or to relate her own change of sentiment towards Caroline. To Jane, Miss Bingley could be only a woman whose love Elizabeth had rejected, and whose merit she had undervalued; but to her own more extensive information, Caroline was the woman whom she regarded herself with an interest, if not quite so tender, at least as reasonable and just as what Jane felt for Bingley. Her astonishment at her coming—to Netherfield, to Longbourn, and voluntarily seeking her again, was almost equal to what she had known on first witnessing her altered behaviour in Derbyshire.

The colour which had been driven from her face, returned for half a minute with an additional glow, and a smile of delight added luster to her eyes, as she thought for that space of time that the lady's affection and wishes must still be unshaken. But she would not be secure.

"Let me first see how she behaves," said she; "it will then be early enough for expectation."

She sat intently at work, striving to be composed, and without daring to lift up her eyes, till anxious curiosity carried them to the face of her sister as the servant was approaching the door. Jane looked a little paler than usual, but more sedate than Elizabeth had expected. On the gentlemen and lady's appearing, her colour increased; yet she received them with tolerable ease, and with a propriety of behaviour equally free from any symptom of resentment or any unnecessary complaisance.

Elizabeth said as little to the guests as civility would allow, and sat down again to her work, with an eagerness which it did not often command. She had ventured only one glance at Caroline. She looked calm, as usual; and, she thought, more as she had been used to look in Hertfordshire, than as she had seemed at Pemberley. For Darcy, the same was true. But perhaps they could not either be as easy in her mother's presence as they were with her uncle and aunt. It was a painful, but not improbable, conjecture.

Bingley, she had likewise seen for an instant, and in that short period saw him looking both pleased and embarrassed. He was received by Mrs. Bennet with a degree of civility which made her two daughters ashamed, especially when contrasted with the cold and ceremonious politeness of her curtsey and address to his friends. Elizabeth, particularly, who knew that her mother owed to Darcy and Caroline the preservation of her favourite daughter from irremediable infamy, was hurt and distressed to a most painful degree by a distinction so ill-applied.

Darcy, after inquiring of Mrs. Bennet how Mr. and Mrs. Gardiner did, a question which she could not answer without confusion, said scarcely anything. Caroline was not seated beside her, but near Jane, to whom she spoke with cautious affection, as if mindful of Jane's disappointment the last time they had met. Jane responded as warmly as ever, and when Elizabeth occasionally, unable to resist the impulse of curiosity, raised her eyes to Caroline's face, she more often found their guest looking at Jane than at herself. More thoughtfulness and less anxiety to please than when they last met were plainly expressed in Caroline's countenance. Elizabeth found she was disappointed, and was immediately angry with herself for being so.

"Could I expect it to be otherwise!" said she. "Yet why did she come?"

She was in no humour for conversation with anyone but Caroline, who she longed to thank for her part in Lydia's retrieval; yet to her she had not nearly enough courage to speak.

"It is a long time, Mr. Bingley, since you went away," said Mrs. Bennet.

He readily agreed to it.

"I began to be afraid you would never come back again. People *did* say you meant to quit the place entirely at Michaelmas; but, however, I hope it is not true. A great many changes have happened in the neighbourhood, since you went away. Miss Lucas is married and settled. And one of my own daughters. I suppose you have heard of it; indeed, you must have seen it in the papers. It was in The Times and The Courier, I know; though it was not put in as it ought to be. It was only said, 'Lately, George Wickham, Esq. to Miss Lydia Bennet,' without there being a syllable said of her father, or the place where she lived, or anything. It was my brother Gardiner's drawing up, too, and I wonder how he came to make such an awkward business of it. Did you see it?"

Bingley replied that he had, and made his congratulations. Elizabeth dared not lift up her eyes. How Caroline or Mr. Darcy looked, therefore, she could not tell.

"It is a delightful thing, to be sure, to have a daughter well married," continued her mother, "but at the same time, Mr. Bingley, it is very hard to have her taken such a way from me. They are gone to Newcastle, a place quite northward, it seems, and there they are to stay I do not know how long. His regiment is there; for I suppose you have heard of his leaving the ——shire, and of his being gone into the regulars. Thank Heaven he has *some* friends, though perhaps not so many as he deserves."

Elizabeth, who knew this to be leveled at Mr. Darcy, was in such misery of shame, that she could hardly keep her seat. It drew from her, however, the exertion of speaking, which nothing else had so effectually done before; and she asked Bingley whether he meant to make any stay in the country at present, keeping her eyes carefully fixed on his visage rather than that of his sister's. A few weeks, he believed.

"When you have killed all your own birds, Mr. Bingley," said her mother, "I beg you will come here, and shoot as many as you please on Mr. Bennet's manor. I am sure he will be vastly happy to oblige you, and will save all the best of the covies for you."

Elizabeth's misery increased at such unnecessary, such officious attention! Were the same fair prospect to arise at present as had flattered them a year ago, everything, she was persuaded, would be hastening to the same vexatious conclusion. At that instant, she felt that years of happiness could not make Jane or herself amends for moments of such painful confusion.

"The first wish of my heart," said she to herself, "is never more to be in company with any of our visitors. Their society can afford no pleasure that will atone for such wretchedness as this!"

Yet the misery, for which years of happiness were to offer no compensation, received soon afterwards material relief, from observing how much the beauty of her sister rekindled the admiration of her former lover. When first he came in, he had spoken to her but little; but every five minutes seemed to be giving her more of his attention. He found her as handsome as she had been last year; as good-natured, and as unaffected, though not quite so chatty. Jane was anxious that no difference should be perceived in her at all, and was really persuaded that she talked as much as ever. But her mind was so busily engaged, that she did not always know when she was silent.

For her part, Caroline was struggling to prevent herself from following the example set by her smitten-anew brother. She had told herself that she would see how Miss Bennet seemed, and allow her to establish the tenor of their interaction. But other than a heightened complexion, Caroline could not see that her presence had any impact on the lady at all. Elizabeth was so focused on her needlework that she seemed quite unaware of Caroline's presence in her drawing-room.

When their guests rose to go, Mrs. Bennet was mindful of her intended civility, and invited the trio to dine at Longbourn in a few days time.

"You are quite a visit in my debt, Mr. Bingley," she added, "for when you went to town last winter, you promised to take a family dinner with us, as soon as you returned. I have not forgot, you see; and I assure you, I was very much disappointed that you did not come back and keep your engagement."

Bingley looked a little silly at this reflection, and said something of his concern at having been prevented by business. Miss Bingley glanced at Elizabeth, whose attention remained steadfastly at her work, even as her blush increased at her mother's lack of manners. The visitors then made their farewells and went away.

Mrs. Bennet had been strongly inclined to ask them to stay and dine there that day; but, though she always kept a very good table, she did not think anything less than two courses could be good enough for a man on whom she had such anxious designs, or satisfy the appetite and pride of one who had ten thousand a year.

CHAPTER FIFTY-FOUR

As soon as they were gone, Elizabeth walked out to recover her spirits; or in other words, to dwell without interruption on those subjects that must deaden them more. Miss Bingley's behaviour astonished and vexed her.

"Why, if she came only to be polite and indifferent," thought Elizabeth, "did she come at all?"

She could settle it in no way that gave her pleasure.

"She could be still amiable, still pleasing, to my uncle and aunt, and now to my sister; and why not to me? If she fears me, why come hither? If she no longer cares for me, why ignore me? Teasing, teasing, woman! I will think no more about her."

Her resolution was for a short time involuntarily kept by the approach of her sister, who joined her with a cheerful look, which showed her better satisfied with their visitors, than Elizabeth.

"Now," said she, "that this first meeting is over, I feel perfectly easy. I know my own strength, and I shall never be embarrassed again by his coming. I am glad he dines here on Tuesday. It will then be publicly seen that, on both sides, we meet only as common and indifferent acquaintances."

"Yes, very indifferent indeed," said Elizabeth, laughingly. "Oh, Jane, take care."

"My dear Lizzy, you cannot think me so weak as to be in danger now?"

"I think you are in very great danger of making him as much in love with you as ever."

***

They did not see the gentlemen and lady again till Tuesday; and Mrs. Bennet, in the meanwhile, was giving way to all the happy schemes, which the good humour and common politeness of Bingley, in half an hour's visit, had revived.

On Tuesday there was a large party assembled at Longbourn; and the three who were most anxiously expected were in very good time. When they repaired to the dining-room, Elizabeth watched to see whether Bingley would take the place, which, in all their former parties, had belonged to him, by her sister. Her prudent mother, occupied by the same ideas, forbore to invite him to sit by herself. On entering the room, he seemed to hesitate; but Jane happened to look round, and happened to smile: It was decided. He placed himself by her.

Elizabeth, with a triumphant sensation, looked towards his friends. Caroline and Darcy both bore it with noble indifference, and she would have imagined that Bingley had received their sanction to be happy, had she not seen his eyes likewise turned towards Mr. Darcy in particular, with an expression of half-laughing alarm.

Bingley's behaviour to Jane was such, during dinner time, as showed an admiration of her, which, though more guarded than formerly, persuaded Elizabeth that, if left wholly to himself, Jane's happiness—and his own—would be speedily secured. Though she dared not depend upon the consequence, she yet received pleasure from observing his behaviour. It gave her all the animation that her spirits could boast; for she was in no cheerful humour. Miss Bingley and Mr. Darcy were seated together almost as far from her as the table could divide them. Darcy was on one side of her mother. She knew how little such a situation would give pleasure to either, or make either appear to advantage. She was not near enough to hear any of their discourse, but she could see how seldom they spoke to each other, and how formal and cold was their manner whenever they did. Her mother's ungraciousness made the sense of what they owed him more painful to Elizabeth's mind; and she would, at times, have given anything to be privileged to tell Darcy and Caroline that their kindness was neither unknown nor unfelt by the whole of the family.

She was in hopes that the evening would afford some opportunity of bringing her and Caroline together; that the whole of the visit would not pass away without enabling them to enter into something more of conversation than the mere ceremonious salutation attending Miss Bingley's entrance. But the period that passed in the drawing-room before the gentlemen came afforded no such opportunity, as Elizabeth found herself set upon by a group of local ladies who desired to hear of her travels with her aunt and uncle. Caroline, who had seemed about to approach, instead veered toward another cluster that contained Jane and several of the Lucases. Elizabeth found this request for her performance burdensome to a degree that almost made her uncivil, and decided that a clearer opportunity to converse with Caroline would likely arise when the gentlemen joined them, when the other ladies would be distracted. Therefore she looked to their entrance as the point on which all her chance of pleasure for the evening must depend.

"If she does not come to me *then*," said she, "I shall give her up forever."

The gentlemen came; and she thought Caroline looked as if she would have answered her hopes; but, alas! The other ladies had crowded round the table where Jane and Elizabeth were pouring out the tea and coffee, in so close a confederacy that there was not a single vacancy near them that would admit of a chair.

Soon the gentlemen approached, hemming in the Bennet sisters even further. One of the girls moved closer to Elizabeth, and said in a whisper: "The men shan't come and part us, I am determined. We want none of them; do we?"

While this was true enough, however, the clutch caused Caroline to remove to another part of the room. Elizabeth followed her with her eyes, envied everyone to whom she spoke, had scarcely patience enough to help anybody to coffee; and then was enraged against herself for being so silly!

"A woman who has once been refused! How could I ever be foolish enough to expect a renewal of her affection? Is there one among either sex who would not protest against such a weakness?"

She was a little revived, however, by Caroline's bringing back her coffee cup herself; and she seized the opportunity of saying: "Are you also to stay at Netherfield for some three or four weeks?"

"Not at all," said Caroline. "Darcy and I are wanted at Pemberley shortly, though we hope to be back down in good time. That is, if my brother is still here." And she smiled faintly, her eye finding her brother lingering in the space near Jane, patiently awaiting her attentions.

"Ah," said Elizabeth, feeling her spirits sink at this information. "Is Miss Darcy at Pemberley still?"

"Yes, she will remain there till Christmas."

"And quite alone?"

"Mrs. Annesley is with her. Monsieur de Laurent is there as well." She paused, her eyes searching Elizabeth's face, and seemed as if she would say more. But Sir William Lucas approached just then and engaged them both in conversation about recent occurrences in the neighborhood, including the letting of another estate near Meryton to a Belgian family that had only just quit the continent.

Elizabeth responded as civilly as she could manage, her mind whirling with conjectures of what Caroline might have been about to tell her. But Darcy soon came over and joined the party, and then the two gentlemen and the lady walked away together as Elizabeth gazed after them in disappointment.

When the tea-things were removed, and the card-tables placed, the ladies all rose, and Elizabeth was then hoping to find her way to Caroline's side to continue their conversation, when all her views were overthrown by seeing her fall a victim to Mrs. Bennet's rapacity for whist players. Elizabeth now lost every expectation of pleasure. They were confined for the evening at different tables, and she had nothing to hope, but that Caroline's eyes were so often turned toward her side of the room, as to make the lady play as unsuccessfully as herself.

Mrs. Bennet had designed to keep the Netherfield party to supper; but their carriage was unluckily ordered before any of the others, and she had no opportunity of detaining them. When Caroline said goodnight, her gaze fixed briefly and troublingly on Elizabeth's face before she accompanied her friends from the house. Elizabeth only half paid attention to the rest of their guests, her spirits sunk lower than they had been in recent memory.

"Well, girls," said Mrs. Bennet, as soon as they were left to themselves, "what say you to the day? I think everything has passed off uncommonly well, I assure you. The dinner was as well dressed as any I ever saw. The venison was roasted to a turn—and everybody said they never saw so fat a haunch. The soup was fifty times better than what we had at the Lucases' last week; and even Mr. Darcy acknowledged, that the partridges were remarkably well done; and I suppose he has two or three French cooks at least. And, my dear Jane, I never saw you look in greater beauty. Mrs. Long said so too, for I asked her whether you did not. And what do you think she said besides? 'Ah! Mrs. Bennet, we shall have her at Netherfield at last.' She did indeed. I do think Mrs. Long is as good a creature as ever lived—and her nieces are very pretty behaved girls, and not at all handsome: I like them prodigiously."

Mrs. Bennet, in short, was in very great spirits; she had seen enough of Bingley's behaviour to Jane, to be convinced that she would get him at last; and her expectations of advantage to her family, when in a happy humour, were so far beyond reason, that she was quite disappointed at not seeing him there again the next day, to make his proposals.

"It has been a very agreeable day," said Jane to Elizabeth. "The party seemed so well selected, so suitable one with the other. I hope we may often meet again."

Elizabeth smiled.

"Lizzy, you must not do that. You must not suspect me. It mortifies me. I assure you that I have now learnt to enjoy his conversation as an agreeable and sensible young man, without having a wish beyond it. I am perfectly satisfied, from what his manners now are, that he never had any design of engaging my affection. It is only that he is blessed with greater sweetness of address, and a stronger desire of generally pleasing, than any other man."

"You are very cruel," said her sister; "you will not let me smile, yet are provoking me to it every moment."

"How hard it is in some cases to be believed!"

"And how impossible in others!"

"But why should you wish to persuade me that I feel more than I acknowledge?"

"That is a question which I hardly know how to answer. We all love to instruct, though we can teach only what is not worth knowing. Forgive me; and if you persist in indifference, do not make me your confidante."

CHAPTER FIFTY-FIVE

A few days after this visit, Mr. Bingley called again, alone. His friends had left him that morning, but were to return in ten days time. He sat with them above an hour, and was in remarkably good spirits. Mrs. Bennet invited him to dine with them; but, with many expressions of concern, he confessed himself engaged elsewhere.

"Next time you call," said she, "I hope we shall be more lucky."

He should be particularly happy at any time, etc. etc.; and if she would give him leave, would take an early opportunity of waiting on them.

"Can you come tomorrow?"

Yes, he had no engagement at all for tomorrow; and her invitation was accepted with alacrity.

He came, and in such very good time that the ladies were none of them dressed. In ran Mrs. Bennet to her daughter's room, in her dressing gown, and with her hair half-finished, crying out: "My dear Jane, make haste and hurry down. He is come—Mr. Bingley is come. He is, indeed. Make haste, make haste. Here, Sarah, come to Miss Bennet this moment, and help her on with her gown. Never mind Miss Lizzy's hair."

"We will be down as soon as we can," said Jane; "but I dare say Kitty is forwarder than either of us, for she went upstairs half an hour ago."

"Oh, hang Kitty! What has she to do with it? Come be quick, be quick! Where is your sash, my dear?"

But when her mother was gone, Jane would not be prevailed on to go down without one of her sisters.

The same anxiety to get them by themselves was visible again in the evening. After tea, Mr. Bennet retired to the library, as was his custom, and Mary went up stairs to her instrument. Two obstacles of the five being thus removed, Mrs. Bennet sat looking and winking at Elizabeth and Catherine for a considerable time, without making any impression on them. Elizabeth would not observe her; and when at last Kitty did, she very innocently said, "What is the matter, Mamma? What do you keep winking at me for? What am I to do?"

"Nothing child, nothing. I did not wink at you." She then sat still five minutes longer; but unable to waste such a precious occasion, she suddenly got up, and saying to Kitty, "Come here, my love, I want to speak to you," took her out of the room. Jane instantly gave a look at Elizabeth which spoke her distress at such premeditation, and her entreaty that she would not give in to it. In a few minutes, Mrs. Bennet half-opened the door and called out: "Lizzy, my dear, I want to speak with you."

Elizabeth was forced to go.

"We may as well leave them by themselves, you know," said her mother, as soon as she was in the hall. "Kitty and I are going upstairs to sit in my dressing-room."

Elizabeth made no attempt to reason with her mother, but remained quietly in the hall, till she and Kitty were out of sight, then returned into the drawing-room.

Mrs. Bennet's schemes for this day were ineffectual. Bingley was everything that was charming, except the professed lover of her daughter. His ease and cheerfulness rendered him a most agreeable addition to their evening party; and he bore with the ill-judged officiousness of the mother, and heard all her silly remarks with a forbearance and command of countenance particularly grateful to the daughter. Elizabeth found herself meditating on how his features resembled those of his sister, and contented herself with gazing upon his countenance rather more than was typical of a disinterested observer. But he seemed not to notice anyone but Jane, and so Elizabeth could continue her secret vigil at will.

He scarcely needed an invitation to stay for supper; and before he went away, an engagement was formed, chiefly through his own and Mrs. Bennet's means, for his coming in a few days to shoot with her husband. He had business in London on the morrow, he told them, but would be back the following evening at the latest, and would be happy to join Mr. Bennet the morning after his return.

After this day, Jane said no more of her indifference. Not a word passed between the sisters concerning Bingley; but Elizabeth went to bed in the happy belief that all must speedily be concluded, unless Mr. Darcy and Miss Bingley returned within the stated time. Seriously, however, she felt tolerably persuaded that all this must have taken place with that gentleman and lady's concurrence.

Bingley was punctual to his appointment; and he and Mr. Bennet spent the designated morning together. The latter was much more agreeable than his companion expected. There was nothing of presumption or folly in Bingley that could provoke his ridicule, or disgust him into silence; and Mr. Bennet was more communicative, and less eccentric, than the other had ever seen him. Bingley of course returned with him to dinner; and in the evening Mrs. Bennet's invention was again at work to get everybody away from him and her daughter. Elizabeth, who had a letter to write, went into the breakfast room for that purpose soon after tea; for as the others were all going to sit down to cards, she could not be wanted to counteract her mother's schemes.

But on returning to the drawing-room, when her letter was finished, she saw, to her infinite surprise, there was reason to fear that her mother had been too ingenious for her. On opening the door, she perceived her sister and Bingley standing together over the hearth, as if engaged in earnest conversation; and had this led to no suspicion, the faces of both, as they hastily turned round and moved away from each other, would have told it all. Their situation was awkward enough; but *hers* she thought was still worse. Not a syllable was uttered by either; and Elizabeth was on the point of going away again, when Bingley, who as well as the other had sat down, suddenly rose, and whispering a few words to her sister, quickly exited the room.

Jane could have no reserves from Elizabeth, where confidence would give pleasure; and instantly embracing her, acknowledged, with the liveliest emotion, that she was the happiest creature in the world.

"'Tis too much!" she added. "By far, too much! I do not deserve it. Oh! Why is not everybody as happy?"

Elizabeth's congratulations were given with a sincerity, a warmth, a delight, which words could but poorly express. Every sentence of kindness was a fresh source of happiness to Jane. But she would not allow herself to stay with her sister, or say half that remained to be said for the present.

"I must go instantly to my mother!" she cried. "I would not on any account trifle with her affectionate solicitude; or allow her to hear it from anyone but myself. He is gone to my father already. Oh, Lizzy, to know that what I have to relate will give such pleasure to all my dear family! How shall I bear so much happiness!"

She then hastened away to her mother, who had purposely broken up the card party, and was sitting upstairs with Kitty.

Elizabeth, who was left by herself, now smiled at the rapidity and ease with which an affair was finally settled, that had given them so many previous months of suspense and vexation. And yet part of her regretted, too, that no such announcement of happiness on her part would likely ever bring a corresponding pleasure to her family. But as this was Jane's moment of joy, she shook away the uneasy thought. She had much rather to be happy for a beloved sister than aggrieved over a situation she was powerless to alter.

In a few minutes she was joined by Bingley, whose conference with Mr. Bennet had been short and to the purpose.

"Where is your sister?" said he hastily, as he opened the door.

"With my mother upstairs. She will be down in a moment, I dare say."

He then shut the door, and, coming up to her, claimed the good wishes and affection of a sister. Elizabeth honestly and heartily expressed her delight in the prospect of their relationship. They shook hands with great cordiality; and then, till her sister came down, she had to listen to all he had to say of his own happiness, and of Jane's perfections; and in spite of his being a lover, Elizabeth really believed all his expectations of felicity to be rationally founded, because they had for basis the excellent understanding, and super-excellent disposition of Jane, and a general similarity of feeling and taste between her and himself.

It was an evening of no common delight to them all; the satisfaction of Jane's mind gave a glow of such sweet animation to her face, as made her look handsomer than ever. Kitty simpered and smiled, and hoped her turn was coming soon. Mrs. Bennet could not give her consent or speak her approbation in terms warm enough to satisfy her feelings, though she talked to Bingley of nothing else for half an hour; and when

Mr. Bennet joined them at supper, his voice and manner plainly showed how really happy he was.

Not a word, however, passed his lips in allusion to it, till their visitor took his leave for the night; but as soon as he was gone, he turned to his daughter, and said: "Jane, I congratulate you. You will be a very happy woman."

Jane went to him instantly, kissed him, and thanked him for his goodness.

"You are a good girl," he replied, "and I have great pleasure in thinking you will be so happily settled. I have not a doubt of your doing very well together. Your tempers are by no means unlike. You are each of you so complying, that nothing will ever be resolved on; so easy, that every servant will cheat you; and so generous, that you will always exceed your income."

"I hope not. Imprudence or thoughtlessness in money matters would be unpardonable in me."

"Exceed their income! My dear Mr. Bennet," cried his wife, "what are you talking of? Why, he has four or five thousand a year, and very likely more." Then addressing her daughter, "My dear, dear Jane, I am so happy! I am sure I shan't get a wink of sleep all night. I knew how it would be. I always said it must be so, at last. I was sure you could not be so beautiful for nothing! I remember, as soon as ever I saw him, when he first came into Hertfordshire last year, I thought how likely it was that you should come together. Oh, he is the handsomest young man that ever was seen!"

Wickham, Lydia, were all forgotten. Jane was beyond competition her favourite child. At that moment, she cared for no other.

Jane's younger sisters soon began to make interest with her for objects of happiness which she might in future be able to dispense. Mary petitioned for the use of the library at Netherfield, while Kitty begged very hard for a few balls there every winter.

Bingley, from this time, was of course a daily visitor at Longbourn; coming frequently before breakfast, and always remaining till after supper; unless when some barbarous neighbour, who could not be enough detested, had given him an invitation to dinner which he thought himself obliged to accept.

Elizabeth had now but little time for conversation with her sister; for while he was present, Jane had no attention to bestow on anyone else; but she found herself considerably useful to both of them in those hours of separation that must sometimes occur. In the absence of Jane, he always attached himself to Elizabeth, for the pleasure of talking of her; and when Bingley was gone, Jane constantly sought the same means of relief.

"He has made me so happy," said she, one evening, "by telling me that he was totally ignorant of my being in town last spring! I had not believed it possible."

"I suspected as much," replied Elizabeth. "But how did he account for it?"

"It must have been his friends' doing. They were certainly not enamored of his acquaintance with me, which I cannot wonder at, since he might have chosen so much more advantageously in many respects. But when they see, as I trust they will, that their brother is happy with me, they will learn to be contented, and we shall be on good terms again. Would you believe it, Lizzy, that when he went to town last November, he really loved me, and nothing but a persuasion of *my* being indifferent would have prevented his coming down again?"

"He made a little mistake to be sure; but it is to the credit of his modesty," said she, recalling Caroline's words on the subject with a nostalgia that immediately irritated her. The lady had clearly given her up; she must do the same.

Elizabeth's statement naturally introduced a panegyric from Jane on Bingley's diffidence, and the little value he put on his own good qualities. Elizabeth was pleased to find that he had not betrayed the interference of his friends; for, though Jane had the most generous and forgiving heart in the world, Elizabeth knew it was a circumstance which must prejudice her against them.

"I am certainly the most fortunate creature that ever existed!" cried Jane. "Oh, Lizzy, why am I thus singled from my family, and blessed above them all! If I could but see *you* as happy! If there were but such another for you!"

"Even then, I never could be so happy as you. Till I have your disposition, your goodness, I never can have your happiness. No, no, let me shift for myself; and, perhaps, if I have very good luck, I may meet another Charlotte in time."

The situation of affairs in the Longbourn family could not be long a secret. Mrs. Bennet was privileged to whisper it to Mrs. Phillips, and she ventured, without any permission, to do the same by all her neighbours in Meryton.

The Bennets were speedily pronounced to be the luckiest family in the world, though only a few weeks before, when Lydia had first run away, they had been generally proved to be marked out for misfortune.

CHAPTER FIFTY-SIX

One morning, about a week after Bingley's engagement with Jane had been formed, as he and the females of the family were sitting together in the dining-room, their attention was suddenly drawn to the window, by the sound of a carriage; and they perceived a chaise and four driving up the lawn. It was too early in the morning for visitors, and besides, the equipage did not answer to that of any of their neighbours. The horses were post; and neither the carriage, nor the livery of the servant who preceded it, were familiar to them. As it was certain, however, that somebody was coming, Bingley instantly prevailed on Miss Bennet to avoid the confinement of such an intrusion, and walk away with him into the shrubbery. They both set off, and the conjectures of the remaining three continued, though with little satisfaction, till the door was thrown open and their visitor entered. It was Lady Catherine de Bourgh.

They were of course all intending to be surprised; but their astonishment was beyond their expectation; and on the part of Mrs. Bennet and Kitty, though she was perfectly unknown to them, even inferior to what Elizabeth felt.

She entered the room with an air more than usually ungracious, made no other reply to Elizabeth's salutation than a slight inclination of the head, and sat down without saying a word. Elizabeth had mentioned her name to her mother on her ladyship's entrance, though no request of introduction had been made.

Mrs. Bennet, all amazement, though flattered by having a guest of such high importance, received her with the utmost politeness. After sitting for a moment in silence, she said very stiffly to Elizabeth, "I hope you are well, Miss Bennet. That lady, I suppose, is your mother."

Elizabeth replied very concisely that she was.

"And *that* I suppose is one of your sisters."

"Yes, Madam," said Mrs. Bennet, delighted to speak to Lady Catherine. "She is my youngest girl but one. My youngest of all is lately married, and my eldest is somewhere about the grounds, walking with a young man who, I believe, will soon become a part of the family."

"You have a very small park here," returned Lady Catherine after a short silence.

"It is nothing in comparison of Rosings, my lady, I dare say; but I assure you it is much larger than Sir William Lucas's."

"This must be a most inconvenient sitting room for the evening, in summer; the windows are full west."

Mrs. Bennet assured her that they never sat there after dinner, and then added: "May I take the liberty of asking your ladyship whether you left Mr. and Mrs. Collins well?"

"Yes, very well. I saw them the night before last."

Elizabeth now expected that she would produce a letter for her from Charlotte, as it seemed the only probable motive for her calling. But no letter appeared, and she was completely puzzled.

Mrs. Bennet, with great civility, begged her ladyship to take some refreshment; but Lady Catherine very resolutely, and not very politely, declined eating anything; and then, rising up, said to Elizabeth, "Miss Bennet, there seemed to be a prettyish kind of a little wilderness on one side of your lawn. I should be glad to take a turn in it, if you will favour me with your company."

"Go, my dear," said her mother, "and show her ladyship about the different walks. I think she will be pleased with the hermitage."

Elizabeth obeyed, and going into her own room for her parasol, attended her noble guest downstairs. As they passed through the hall, Lady Catherine opened the doors into the dining-parlour and drawing-room, and pronouncing them, after a short survey, to be decent looking rooms, walked on.

Her carriage remained at the door, and Elizabeth saw that her waiting-woman was in it. They proceeded in silence along the gravel walk that led to the copse; Elizabeth was determined to make no effort for conversation with a woman who was now more than usually insolent and disagreeable.

"How could I ever think Darcy a bit like her?" thought she, as she looked in her face.

As soon as they entered the copse, Lady Catherine began in the following manner: "You can be at no loss, Miss Bennet, to understand the reason of my journey hither. Your own heart, your own conscience, must tell you why I come."

Elizabeth looked with unaffected astonishment.

"Indeed, you are mistaken, Madam. I have not been at all able to account for the honour of seeing you here."

"Miss Bennet," replied her ladyship, in an angry tone, "you ought to know, that I am not to be trifled with. But however insincere *you* may choose to be, you shall not find me so. My character has ever been celebrated for its sincerity and frankness, and in a cause of such moment as this, I shall certainly not depart from it. A report of a most alarming nature reached me two days ago. I was told that not only your sister was on the point of being most advantageously married, but that you, Miss Elizabeth Bennet, would, in all likelihood, be soon afterwards united to my nephew, my own nephew, Mr. Darcy. Though I know it must be a scandalous falsehood, though I would not injure him so much as to suppose the truth of it possible, I instantly resolved on setting off for this place, that I might make my sentiments known to you."

For a moment Elizabeth could not respond, so great was her astonishment. Darcy, marry her? What a preposterous notion. He was far more likely to marry Caroline—if he were to marry at all, which she supposed he probably would, given the obligations of his lineage. "If you believed it impossible to be true," said she, colouring with disdain, "I wonder you took the trouble of coming so far. What could your ladyship propose by it?"

"At once to insist upon having such a report universally contradicted."

"Your coming to Longbourn, to see me and my family, will be rather a confirmation of it," said Elizabeth coolly, her mind working through the particulars; "if, indeed, such a report is in existence."

"If! Do you then pretend to be ignorant of it? Has it not been industriously circulated by yourselves? Do you not know that such a report is spread abroad?"

"I never heard that it was."

"And can you likewise declare, that there is no foundation for it?"

"I do not pretend to possess equal frankness with your ladyship. You may ask questions which I shall not choose to answer." While Elizabeth found it nearly impossible to believe that such a proud gentleman would ever seek to unite himself with her, she had also never expected the kindness he had shown her family over the Wickham affair. Darcy, it seemed, was nowhere near as concerned with the customary way of doing things as Elizabeth had believed when she first made his acquaintance.

"This is not to be borne. Miss Bennet, I insist on being satisfied. Has he, has my nephew, made you an offer of marriage?"

"Your ladyship has declared it to be impossible."

"It ought to be so; it must be so, while he retains the use of his reason. But your arts and allurements may, in a moment of infatuation, have made him forget what he owes to himself and to all his family. You may have drawn him in."

The absurdity of such an accusation almost made her laugh. "If I have, I shall be the last person to confess it."

"Miss Bennet, do you know who I am? I have not been accustomed to such language as this. I am almost the nearest relation he has in the world, and am entitled to know all his dearest concerns."

"But you are not entitled to know mine; nor will such behaviour as this, ever induce me to be explicit."

"Let me be rightly understood. This match, to which you have the presumption to aspire, can never take place. No, never. Mr. Darcy is engaged to my daughter. Now what have you to say?"

"Only this; that if he is so, you can have no reason to suppose he will make an offer to any other."

Lady Catherine hesitated for a moment, and then replied: "The engagement between them is of a peculiar kind. From their infancy, they have been intended for each other. It was the favourite wish of his mother, as well as of hers. While in their cradles, we planned the union: and now, at the moment when the wishes of both sisters would be accomplished in their marriage, to be prevented by a young woman of inferior birth, of no importance in the world, and wholly unallied to the family! Are you lost to every feeling of propriety and delicacy? Have you not heard me say that from his earliest hours he was destined for his cousin?"

"Yes, and I had heard it before. But what is that to me? You and his aunt both did as much as you could in planning your children's marriage. Its completion depends on others. If Mr. Darcy is neither by honour nor inclination confined to his cousin, why is not he to make another choice? And if I am that choice, why may not I accept him?" The idea was still absurd, but Lady Catherine's indefatigable contempt was sorely trying Elizabeth's temper.

"Because honour, decorum, prudence, nay, interest, forbid it. Yes, Miss Bennet, interest; for do not expect to be noticed by his family or friends, if you willfully act against the inclinations of all. You will be censured, slighted, and despised, by everyone connected with him. Your alliance will be a disgrace; your name will never even be mentioned by any of us."

"These are heavy misfortunes," replied Elizabeth. "But the wife of Mr. Darcy must have such extraordinary sources of happiness necessarily attached to her situation, that she could, upon the whole, have no cause to repine."

"Obstinate, headstrong girl! I am ashamed of you! Is this your gratitude for my attentions to you last spring? Is nothing due to me on that score? Let us sit down. You are to understand, Miss Bennet, that I came here with the determined resolution of carrying my purpose; nor will I be dissuaded from it. I have not been used to submit to any person's whims. I have not been in the habit of brooking disappointment."

"That will make your ladyship's situation at present more pitiable; but it will have no effect on me."

"I will not be interrupted. Hear me in silence. My daughter and my nephew are formed for each other. They are descended, on the maternal side, from the same noble line; and, on the father's, from respectable, honourable, and ancient—though untitled—families. Their fortune on both sides is splendid. They are destined for each other by the voice of every member of their respective houses; and what is to divide them? The upstart pretensions of a young woman without family, connections, or fortune. Is this to be endured! But it must not, shall not be. If you were sensible of your own good, you would not wish to quit the sphere in which you have been brought up."

"In marrying your nephew, I should not consider myself as quitting that sphere. He is a gentleman; I am a gentleman's daughter; so far we are equal."

"You are a gentleman's daughter. But who was your mother? Who are your uncles and aunts? Do not imagine me ignorant of their condition."

"Whatever my connections may be," said Elizabeth, "if your nephew does not object to them, they can be nothing to you."

"Tell me once for all, are you engaged to him?"

Though Elizabeth would not, for the mere purpose of obliging Lady Catherine, have answered this question, she could not but say, after a moment's deliberation: "I am not."

Lady Catherine seemed momentarily pleased. "And will you promise me, never to enter into such an engagement?"

"I will make no promise of the kind."

"Miss Bennet, I am shocked and astonished. I expected to find a more reasonable young woman. But do not deceive yourself into a belief that I will ever recede. I shall not go away till you have given me the assurance I require."

"And I certainly never shall give it. I am not to be intimidated into anything so wholly unreasonable. Your ladyship wants Mr. Darcy to marry your daughter; but would my giving you the wished-for promise make their marriage at all more probable? Allow me to say, Lady Catherine, that the arguments with which you have supported this extraordinary application have been as frivolous as the application was ill-judged. You have widely mistaken my character, if you think I can be worked on by such persuasions as these. How far your nephew might approve of your interference in his affairs, I cannot tell; but you have certainly no right to concern yourself in mine. I must beg, therefore, to be importuned no further on the subject."

"Not so hasty, if you please. I have by no means done. To all the objections I have already urged, I have still another to add. I am no stranger to the particulars of your youngest sister's infamous elopement. I know it all; that the young man's marrying her was a patched-up business, at the expense of your father and uncles. And is such a girl to be my nephew's sister? Is her husband, is the son of his late father's steward, to be his brother? Heaven and earth! Of what are you thinking? Are the shades of Pemberley to be thus polluted?"

"You can now have nothing further to say," Elizabeth answered resentfully. "You have insulted me in every possible method. I must beg to return to the house."

And she rose as she spoke. Lady Catherine rose also, and they turned back. Her ladyship was highly incensed.

"You have no regard, then, for the honour and credit of my nephew! Unfeeling, selfish girl! Do you not consider that a connection with you must disgrace him in the eyes of everybody?"

"Lady Catherine, I have nothing further to say. You know my sentiments."

"You are then resolved to have him?"

"I have said no such thing. I am only resolved to act in that manner which will, in my own opinion, constitute my happiness, without reference to you or to any person so wholly unconnected with me."

"You refuse, then, to oblige me. You refuse to obey the claims of duty, honour, and gratitude. You are determined to ruin him in the opinion of all his friends, and make him the contempt of the world."

"Neither duty, nor honour, nor gratitude," replied Elizabeth, "have any possible claim on me, in the present instance. And with regard to the resentment of Mr. Darcy's family, or the indignation of the world, if the former were excited by his marrying me, it would not give me one moment's concern—and the world in general would have too much sense to join in the scorn."

"And this is your real opinion! This is your final resolve! Very well. I shall now know how to act. Do not imagine, Miss Bennet, that your ambition will ever be gratified. I came to try you. I hoped to find you reasonable; but, depend upon it, I will carry my point."

In this manner Lady Catherine talked on, till they were at the door of the carriage, when, turning hastily round, she added, "I take no leave of you, Miss Bennet. I send no compliments to your mother. You deserve no such attention. I am most seriously displeased."

Elizabeth made no answer; and without attempting to persuade her ladyship to return into the house, walked quickly into it herself. She heard the carriage drive away as she proceeded upstairs. Her mother impatiently met her at the door of the dressing-room, to ask why Lady Catherine would not come in again and rest herself.

"She did not choose it," said her daughter shortly; "she would go."

"She is a very fine-looking woman! And her calling here was prodigiously civil, for she only came, I suppose, to tell us the Collinses were well. She is on her road somewhere, I dare say, and so, passing through Meryton, thought she might as well call on you. I suppose she had nothing particular to say to you, Lizzy?"

Elizabeth was forced to give into a little falsehood here; for to acknowledge the substance of their conversation was impossible. She could hardly believe what had occurred herself.

CHAPTER FIFTY-SEVEN

The discomposure of spirits which this extraordinary visit threw Elizabeth into, could not be easily overcome; nor could she, for many hours, learn to think of it less than incessantly. Lady Catherine, it appeared, had actually taken the trouble of this journey from Rosings, for the sole purpose of breaking off her supposed engagement with Mr. Darcy. It was a rational scheme, to be sure! But from what the report of their engagement could originate, Elizabeth was at a loss to imagine; till she decided that *his* being the intimate friend of Bingley, and *her* being the sister of Jane, might prove to be motivation enough at a time when the expectation of one wedding made everybody eager for another. She had not herself neglected to note that the marriage of her sister must bring her and Darcy—and Caroline, more importantly—frequently together. And her neighbours at Lucas Lodge, therefore (for through their communication with the Collinses, the report, she concluded, must have reached Lady Catherine), had likely set that eventuality down as almost certain. That must be it, for there was no other explanation that made as much sense.

The surprise of the rest of the family, on hearing who their visitor had been, was very great; but they obligingly satisfied it with the same kind of supposition which had appeased Mrs. Bennet's curiosity; and Elizabeth was spared from much teasing on the subject.

But the very next morning, as she was going downstairs, she was met by her father, who came out of his library with a letter in his hand.

"Lizzy," said he, "I was going to look for you; come into my room."

She followed him thither; and her curiosity to know what he had to tell her was heightened by the supposition of its being in some manner connected with the letter he held. It suddenly struck her that it might be from Lady Catherine; and she anticipated with dismay all the consequent explanations.

As she followed her father to the fire place, where they both sat down, he said: "I have received a letter this morning that has astonished me exceedingly. As it principally concerns yourself, you ought to know its contents. I did not know before, that I had two daughters on the brink of matrimony. Let me congratulate you on a very important conquest."

The colour now rushed into Elizabeth's cheeks. Never before had she resented his propensity toward ill-favoured humour than at that moment. Lady Catherine's words were undoubtedly as acrimonious and genuinely cruel on the page as they had been in person. As her father, was it not his duty to defend her, rather than mock her?

"You look conscious," added Mr. Bennet. "Young ladies have great penetration in such matters as these; but I think I may defy even *your* sagacity, to discover the name of your admirer. This letter is from Mr. Collins."

Elizabeth stared. "Mr. Collins! And what can *he* have to say?"

"Something very much to the purpose, of course. He begins with congratulations on the approaching nuptials of my eldest daughter, of which, it seems, he has been told by some of the good-natured, gossiping Lucases. I shall not sport with your impatience, by reading what he says on that point. What relates to yourself is as follows: 'Having thus offered you the sincere congratulations of Mrs. Collins and myself on this happy event, let me now add a short hint on the subject of another; of which we have been advertised by the same authority. Your daughter Elizabeth, it is presumed, will not long bear the name of Bennet, after her elder sister has resigned it, and the chosen partner of her fate may be reasonably looked up to as one of the most illustrious personages in this land.'

"Can you possibly guess, Lizzy, who is meant by this?" 'This young gentleman is blessed, in a peculiar way, with everything the heart of mortal can most desire—splendid property, noble kindred, and extensive patronage. Yet in spite of all these temptations, let me warn my cousin Elizabeth, and yourself, of what evils you may incur by a precipitate closure with this gentleman's proposals, which, of course, you will be inclined to take immediate advantage of.'

"Have you any idea, Lizzy, who this gentleman is? But now it comes out: 'My motive for cautioning you is as follows. We have reason to imagine that his aunt, Lady Catherine de Bourgh, does not look on the match with a friendly eye.' *Mr. Darcy*, you see, is the man! Now, Lizzy, I think I have surprised you. Could he, or the Lucases, have pitched on any man within the circle of our acquaintance, whose name would have given the lie more effectually to what they related? Mr. Darcy, who never looks at any woman but to see a blemish, and who probably never looked at you in his life! It is admirable!"

Elizabeth tried to join in her father's pleasantry, but could only force one most reluctant smile. Rarely had his wit been directed in a manner so little agreeable to her.

"Are you not diverted?"

"Oh, yes. Pray read on."

"'After mentioning the likelihood of this marriage to her ladyship last night, she immediately, with her usual condescension, expressed what she felt on the occasion; when it became apparent, that on the score of some family objections on the part of my cousin, she would never give her consent to what she termed so disgraceful a match. I thought it my duty to give the speediest intelligence of this to my cousin, that she and her noble admirer may be aware of what they are about, and not run hastily into a marriage which has not been properly sanctioned.' Mr. Collins moreover adds, 'I am truly rejoiced that my cousin Lydia's sad business has been so well hushed up, and am only concerned that their living together before the marriage took place should be so generally known. I must not, however, neglect the duties of my station, or refrain from declaring my amazement at hearing that you received the young couple into your house as soon as they were married. It was an encouragement of vice; and had I been the rector of Longbourn, I should very strenuously have opposed it. You ought certainly to forgive them, as a Christian, but never to admit them in your sight, or allow their names to be mentioned in your hearing.' That is his notion of Christian forgiveness! The rest of his letter is only about his dear Charlotte's situation, and his expectation of a young olive-branch. But, Lizzy, you look as if you did not enjoy it. You are not going to be missish, I hope, and pretend to be affronted at an idle report. For what do we live, but to make sport for our neighbours, and laugh at them in our turn?"

"Oh," said Elizabeth, "I am excessively diverted. But it is so strange."

"Yes—that is what makes it amusing. Had they fixed on any other man it would have been nothing; but your mutual indifference to each other makes it so delightfully absurd! Much as I abominate writing, I would not give up Mr. Collins's correspondence for any consideration. Nay, when I read a letter of his, I cannot help giving him the preference even over Wickham, much as I value the impudence and hypocrisy of my son-in-law. And pray, Lizzy, what said Lady Catherine about this report? Did she call to refuse her consent?"

To this question his daughter replied only with a laugh; and as it had been asked without the least suspicion, she was not distressed by his repeating it. She soon excused herself and wandered the grounds at some length, pondering the future that awaited her with an interest she had not previously thought to entertain.

CHAPTER FIFTY-EIGHT

r. Bingley was able to bring Darcy and Caroline with him to Longbourn before many days had passed after Lady Catherine's visit. The party arrived early; and, before Mrs. Bennet had time to tell Darcy of their having seen his aunt, of which her daughter sat in momentary dread, Bingley, who wanted to be alone with Jane, proposed their all walking out. It was agreed to. Mrs. Bennet and Kitty were not in the habit of walking; Mary could never spare time; but the remaining five set off together. Bingley and Jane, however, soon allowed the others to outstrip them. They lagged behind, while Elizabeth, Caroline, and Darcy kept pace with each other. Very little was said at first; Elizabeth was secretly forming a desperate resolution, as was Caroline; and perhaps he might be doing the same.

They walked towards the Lucases, but continued past without stopping. As soon as the house was lost to sight, Elizabeth decided the moment was right for her resolution to be executed, and, while her courage was high, she immediately said: "I am a very selfish creature; and, for the sake of giving relief to my own feelings, care not how much I may be wounding either of yours. I can no longer help thanking you both for your unexampled kindness to my poor sister. Ever since I have known it, I have been most anxious to acknowledge to each of you how gratefully I feel it. Were it known to the rest of my family, I should not have merely my own gratitude to express."

Caroline did not say anything, only looked to Darcy.

"I did not think Mrs. Gardiner was so little to be trusted," replied he, in a tone of surprise.

"You must not blame my aunt. Lydia's thoughtlessness first betrayed to me that you, Mr. Darcy, had been concerned in the matter; and, of course, I could not rest till I knew the particulars. Let me thank you both again and again, in the name of all my family, for that generous compassion which induced you to take so much trouble for the sake of discovering them."

"Do not thank me," said Darcy, "for it was Miss Bingley's none-too-gentle reminders of my duty that led to such an involvement in the matter—I may well have turned my back on Wickham's latest deceit if she had not persuaded me of my own culpability in the matter. But while I was responsible for the negotiations, any pecuniary settlement did not originate from me." And he looked at Caroline.

She frowned and shook her head slightly at him, but it was too late. Elizabeth had comprehended all in a moment, and now she touched Caroline's arm hesitantly. "You? It was you?"

"Yes, but I am sorry, exceedingly sorry, that you have been informed of what may, in a mistaken light, give you any uneasiness."

"Uneasiness!" repeated Elizabeth. "Far from it. You have rescued my family from a certain fall. On their behalf, as well as my own, I cannot thank you enough."

"If you would thank me," she replied, her countenance quite serious, "let it be for yourself alone. Your family owe me nothing. Much as I respect them, I must confess, I was thinking only of *you*."

Elizabeth glanced at Darcy, who was watching them with an air of amused interest that reminded her of her father—perhaps the two gentlemen had more in common than was obvious at first glance. She said, entreatingly: "Miss Bingley, I would talk to you alone if I could."

Caroline nodded, and they both looked to Darcy. He only offered an enigmatic smile, bowed slightly, and turned back toward the lovers. After he had gone a little ways, Caroline gazed at Elizabeth and said: "Before we continue, Miss Eliza, I must share a piece of news with you. The truth of the matter is that I, well, you see—" She paused, appearing quite affected. "I must inform you that I was in London last week to attend a wedding. My own, as it were." And as she spoke, she removed her glove, revealing an ancient, ornate diamond ring.

Not this again, thought Elizabeth in dismay. Not another ill-advised marriage; not Caroline, too. Her colour rose, and she bit her lip. Were those tears rising? Embarrassed, she picked up her skirts and rushed away, her need to escape the present scene leading her into the park that belonged to their new Belgian neighbours.

Caroline stared in astonishment, then lifted her own skirts and started after her. She finally caught Elizabeth in a clearing alongside a pretty little stream that burbled and bubbled quietly under the autumn sky. "Miss Eliza—Lizzy—wait!" And she reached out a hand to stop her friend's headlong dash.

Elizabeth hurriedly wiped a hand across her eyes, letting herself, at the same time, be turned to face the surprised eyes of her companion.

"Is that—are you crying?" Caroline asked, touching her face.

Elizabeth was too much embarrassed to say a word. After a short pause, Caroline added, "You are too generous to trifle with me. If your feelings are still what they were last April, tell me so at once. For despite my marriage vows, my affections and wishes are unchanged; one word from you, however, will silence me on this subject forever."

"I do not wish you to be silenced," Elizabeth said, reaching for her hands. She felt the ring, and held up the traitorous finger. "But you are married. You belong to another."

"You do not wish me to be silenced?" Caroline repeated, a slight smile beginning to emerge. "Come now, Elizabeth Bennet, I happen to know that your mother schooled you better than that in the art of language, even with so many daughters still at home. If not silenced, then how, exactly, might I go on? What subject could I choose that would interest you?"

Her temper rising, Elizabeth relinquished Caroline's hand. "It is hardly a matter of amusement," said she, "that I find myself in love with you, just as you pledge yourself to another in lawful matrimony."

Caroline clapped her hands in delight. "You, in love with me?"

Unable to prevent a matching smile, Elizabeth cast her eyes upward. "Heaven help me, yes. But I do not even know your name, do I? What shall I call you, Madam—?"

"Madame de Laurent," Caroline said, her spirits falling just a bit at the reminder of her new station.

"Darcy's friend?"

"The very one."

"And do you love him?"

"You know I do not."

"Does he love you?"

"Of course, he does not," Caroline said, frowning. "He loves Darcy; they love one another, and have for many years, though they were forced to live apart for some time. Did you truly not know?"

"I had thought, and conjectured; but I did not know." She paused. "Then it is a marriage of expediency?"

"Entirely. By marrying me, he and Darcy receive respectability. And by marrying him, I gain my fortune, which, according to the papers we had drawn up, he is not eligible to receive except upon my death."

"I did not know you were in such high need of your fortune. Did your sister threaten you again?"

"No," Caroline said, and turned away to walk to the stream. "What a lovely spot to which you made me give chase. Are we in any danger of being discovered by the Belgians?"

But Elizabeth would not be so easily distracted. She thought for a moment, her mind hastening from one conjecture to another, and then she said: "It was for Wickham! You married Darcy's Frenchman so that you could pay my new brother's debts. You foolish woman. You wonderful, foolish woman." And she began to cry again.

"Pardon me," Caroline said, walking back to her side and gently wiping away her tears, "but I take exception to the charge of foolishness. The other I do not mind, because it convinces me that your feelings do, in fact, match mine perfectly."

"They do," Elizabeth said miserably, "they really do."

"Oh, love," Caroline said, and put her arm around her friend's shoulders; "it will all work out for the best, I promise. You see, I have a plan."

"A plan?" Elizabeth's eyes narrowed. "Does it perchance involve my marrying Darcy?"

Caroline started. "How did you know?"

"We had a visitor a few days ago—Lady Catherine herself, come to warn me to keep my 'arts and allurements' away from her sainted nephew." And she described the old lady's mannerisms and turns of speech so accurately that Caroline was soon laughing aloud.

"Oh! Wait until Darcy hears!"

"You cannot tell him," protested Elizabeth. "I could never face him if he knew."

"He is really not as austere as he seems. Beneath that lordly countenance, he has the heart of a good boy. You would be amazed at just how sweet a man he can be."

They began to walk back to the road now, knowing the others would miss them soon and eager to prevent any worry in their friends.

"But tell me," said Caroline, looping her arm through Elizabeth's, "just how this transformation in your sentiments came about. I must admit, while I had hoped it would be the case, I am still somewhat astonished that you could love me."

"It is I who am amazed that you could still love me," said Elizabeth; but feeling a gentle tug on her arm, she began to attempt an explanation as to how her sentiments had undergone so material a change. The happiness which this supplication produced was such as Caroline had never felt before, and an expression of heartfelt delight, diffused over her face, made her lovelier than Elizabeth had ever seen her.

They walked on, without knowing in what direction. There was too much to be thought, and felt, and said, for attention to any other objects. She soon learnt that Darcy had suggested the double marriage as a means of allowing them all to protect themselves within society, yet without the burden of an unequal marriage. By following his plan of action, Darcy had insisted, he and Rémy could be together, and she and Elizabeth could, as well. Besides, she and Elizabeth were the only women he truly liked, other than his own sister. If he were to marry—and, naturally, such a duty was expected of someone of his station—it would have to be to one of them. As Caroline already had a fortune and Elizabeth did not, the choice, he believed, was quite clear.

"At first I was not convinced," confessed Caroline. "I had rather thought he and I would marry."

"I knew you were plotting for Darcy's hand!"

"It would make sense, would it not? We are alike in many ways, although Lady Catherine would probably not entirely approve of my connections, either."

"At least your family have not distinguished themselves in quite so gratuitous a fashion, as mine have done."

"Well said." Caroline dodged the well-placed elbow Elizabeth aimed toward her ribs. "Honestly, I believe Darcy will like the plan all the better as soon as he learns of his aunt's feelings on the matter."

"Two declared obstinates, then—what a wonderful couple we would make."

"Indeed; you are two of my favourite people."

"And how many favourites do you have, pray tell?"

"Not as many as you might imagine."

"What of the married friend whose jealous husband drove you from your own home?"

"Only a friend, nothing more, though the husband would not believe the truth of the matter."

"And the tart—that is, the lady from the ball at Netherfield? Each time I looked for you, I found you in such a tête-à-tête with her that I was certain you must be in love with her."

"I was, once," admitted Caroline. "But it was only a schoolgirl fancy long since outgrown. We will always be dear friends, but that is all. You need not worry, Elizabeth. I have thought of no one else since almost our first meeting."

"Which cannot have made you very happy," said Elizabeth; "you, who are used to sophisticated ladies, not country girls who are only tolerably pretty."

"I was only ignorant of the charms of this portion of the country. But what of you and your Mrs. Collins? What have you to recommend in defence of yourself?"

"You cannot believe that I would continue on with her after her marriage."

"Why ever not? You intend to continue on with me after my marriage, do you not? At least, I hope you will."

Elizabeth frowned. "The situations are very different. I believe your phrase, 'a schoolgirl fancy,' applies equally well to my attachment to Charlotte. With you, however, my sentiments are based on something far greater than familiarity. If I were to marry Darcy, an idea you both seem to have taken much to heart, both parties would have matching expectations from the union, as is true for you and your husband, but cannot possibly be for the Collinses."

"But even as a partner in a marriage of mere convenience," Caroline said, "Darcy would treat you with respect and honour. I could not endorse the notion if I believed otherwise."

"I must admit, my opinion of him has improved, over the course of these many months. But I wouldn't have thought he would ever dream of connecting himself in marriage to Wickham, whom he so greatly detests."

Caroline waved a hand. "He does not detest Wickham, much as he wishes he could. One can almost never truly hate the first person one loves, no matter how badly the affair might end."

Elizabeth clutched her arm more tightly. "You don't mean... Darcy and Wickham?"

"I do indeed. You of all people, Lizzy, must know what little entertainment there is to be had in the country." And she smiled wickedly.

After some moments, Elizabeth recovered sufficiently to shake her head. "I cannot believe I ever thought Wickham to be Darcy's superior."

"Wickham may have charm, but Darcy has all the character in that pairing. Do you know, he offered to pay Wickham's debts and commission himself?"

"Why did you not let him? It would have been such a lovely dower gift."

"Because you will be my wife, will you not? Perhaps not in name, but in every other way."

"And you, mine," Elizabeth said. "And we shall reside together in one wing of Pemberley, and the boys will live in another, and we will all dine together now and again and throw lovely parties where we dance with one another's husbands, and no one will ever be the wiser."

"Except our dearest friends. And the servants, more than likely."

"It is most fortunate, then, that the Pemberley staff appear to dote on Darcy more than might be deserved."

"In any case, we will have our husband's children, so who would question anything then? What fun we will have! I absolutely adore babies."

Elizabeth stopped walking. "Our husband's children?"

"Do not worry yourself. You are likely quite fertile, a tall, healthy country girl like yourself. And if done correctly, the act with a man does not have to be unpleasant."

Elizabeth's eyes grew even wider, and Caroline laughed, the sound carrying on the breeze.

A little while later, they returned to the subject of the distance they had traversed since that infamous day at Hunsford Parsonage. Elizabeth offered her sincere apologies for the abominable abuse she had wielded, but Caroline would not accept.

"What did you say of me that I did not deserve? For, though your accusations were formed on mistaken premises, my behaviour to you at the time was unpardonable. I cannot think of it without abhorrence."

"We will not quarrel for the greater share of blame annexed to that evening," said Elizabeth. "The conduct of neither, if strictly examined, will be irreproachable; but since then we have both, I hope, improved in civility."

"I cannot be so easily reconciled. The recollection of my conduct, my manners, my expressions during the whole of it, is still painful to me. Your reproof, I shall never forget: 'You are the last person in the world whom I could ever be prevailed upon to love.' Those were your words. You know not, you can scarcely conceive how they have tortured me—it was some time, I confess, before I was reasonable enough to allow the justice of anything else you said that day."

"I certainly did not expect my words to make so strong an impression. I had not the smallest idea of their being ever felt in such a way."

"I can easily believe it. You thought me then devoid of every proper feeling, I am sure. I shall never forget your countenance as you said that I could not have addressed you in any possible way that would induce you to accept me."

"Oh! Do not repeat what I then said. These recollections will not do at all. I assure you that I have long been most heartily ashamed of my conduct."

Caroline mentioned the letter. "Did it," said she, "soon make you think better of me? Did you give any credit to its contents?"

Elizabeth explained what its effect on her had been, and how gradually all her former prejudices had been removed.

"I knew," said Caroline, "that what I wrote must give you pain, but it was necessary. I hope you have destroyed the letter. I can remember some expressions which might justly make you hate me."

"The letter shall certainly be burnt, if you believe it essential to the preservation of my regard; but, though we both have reason to think my opinions not entirely unalterable, they are not, I hope, quite so easily changed as that implies."

"When I wrote that letter," said Caroline, "I believed myself perfectly calm and cool, but I am since convinced that it was written in a dreadful bitterness of spirit."

"The letter, perhaps, began in bitterness, but it did not end so. The adieu is charity itself. But think no more of the letter. The feelings of the person who wrote, and the person who received it, are now so widely different from what they were then that every unpleasant circumstance attending it ought to be forgotten. You must learn some of my philosophy. Think only of the past as its remembrance gives you pleasure."

"I cannot give you credit for any philosophy of the kind. Your retrospections must be so totally void of reproach, that the contentment arising from them is not of philosophy, but, what is much better, of innocence. But with me, it is not so. Painful recollections will intrude which cannot, which ought not, to be repelled. I have been a selfish being all my life, in practice though not in principle. Such I was, from eight to twenty; and such I might still have been but for you, dearest, loveliest Elizabeth! You taught me a lesson, hard indeed at first, but most advantageous. You showed me how insufficient were all my pretensions to please a woman worthy of being pleased."

"Had you then persuaded yourself that I should?"

"Indeed I had. What will you think of my vanity? I believed you to be wishing, expecting my addresses."

"My manners must have been in fault, but not intentionally, I assure you. I never meant to deceive you, but my spirits might often lead me wrong. How you must have hated me after that evening?"

"Hate you! I was angry perhaps at first, but my anger soon began to take a proper direction."

"I am almost afraid of asking what you thought of me, when we met at Pemberley. You blamed me for being there?"

"No, indeed; I felt nothing but surprise."

"Your surprise could not be greater than mine in being noticed by you. My conscience told me that I deserved no extraordinary politeness, and I confess that I did not expect to receive more than my due."

"My object then," replied Caroline, "was to show you, by every civility in my power, that I was not so mean as to resent the past; and I hoped to obtain your forgiveness, to lessen your ill opinion, by letting you see that your reproofs had been attended to. How soon any other wishes introduced themselves I can hardly tell, but I believe in about half an hour after I had seen you."

Caroline then described Georgiana Darcy's delight in Elizabeth's acquaintance, and her disappointment at its sudden interruption; which, naturally leading to the cause of that interruption, she admitted that the resolution of enlisting Darcy's assistance in quest of Lydia and Wickham had been formed before she had even quitted the inn, and that her gravity and thoughtfulness there had arisen from no other struggles than what such a purpose must comprehend.

Elizabeth expressed her gratitude again, but it was too painful a subject to each, to be dwelt on further.

After walking several miles in a leisurely manner, and too busy to know anything about it, they found at last, on examining their watches, that it was time to be at home.

"What could become of Mr. Bingley and Jane!" was a wonder which introduced the discussion of their affairs. Caroline was delighted with their engagement; her brother had given her the earliest information of it.

"I must ask whether you were surprised?" said Elizabeth.

"Not at all. When Darcy and I went away, I felt that it would soon happen."

"That is to say, you had both given your blessing. I guessed as much." And though Caroline exclaimed at the term, Elizabeth found that it had been pretty much the case.

"On the evening before Darcy and I went to London," said she, "I made a confession to my brother, which I believe I ought to have made long ago. I told him of all that had occurred to make any former interference in his affairs absurd and impertinent. His surprise was great. He had never had the slightest suspicion. I told him, moreover, that I believed Darcy and myself mistaken in supposing, as we had done, that your sister was indifferent to him; and as I could easily perceive that his attachment to her was unabated, I felt no doubt of their happiness together."

"Did you speak from your own observation," asked Elizabeth, "when you told him that my sister loved him, or merely from my information last spring?"

"From the former. Darcy and I had each narrowly observed her during the two visits we had lately made here; and we were both convinced of her affection."

"And your assurance of it, I suppose, carried immediate conviction to him."

"As you are aware, Charles is most unaffectedly modest. His diffidence had prevented his depending on his own judgment in so anxious a case, but his reliance on someone else's made everything easy. I was obliged to confess one thing, which for a time, and not unjustly, offended him. I could not allow myself to conceal that your sister had been in town three months last winter, that I had known it, and purposely kept it from him. He was angry, briefly. My brother's anger, I am persuaded, lasted no longer than he remained in any doubt of your sister's sentiments. He has heartily forgiven me now."

"And what did he think of your sudden nuptials?"

"He was surprised, of course, but understanding. He came to London for the ceremony, an event which was hardly worth the term."

That, then, was what had taken Darcy and Caroline to Pemberley, and Bingley to London: Caroline's wedding to Rémy, Darcy's Frenchman. For a moment Elizabeth's spirits were in danger of sinking, but then she remembered that Caroline loved her, and she loved Caroline, unequivocal facts that only encouraged her usual conviction that all would somehow turn out well.

One last question occurred to her: "How in the world did you manage to convince Louisa to leave off her persecution of you?"

"Charles happened to overhear her threatening me quite recklessly one afternoon in London, and privately entreated of me if this scene were representative of her behaviour toward me since quitting Cumbria. While sharing her belief that a speedy removal from our family's home last year had been advisable, he had not known or approved of the extent of her treachery. When I allowed that Louisa's treatment had been growing steadily more objectionable, and that I had commensurately been growing my resolve to quit her company, and therefore that of my family, he offered to intercede. I do not know by what means he persuaded her to remove to her husband's home in the north, only that he was successful."

"His intercession makes me even more satisfied that your brother will soon be mine, too."

"He truly is a most agreeable person, as is your sister. It is, indeed, quite a match in temperaments."

In anticipating the happiness of Bingley and Jane, which of course was to be inferior only to their own, they continued the conversation till they reached the house. In the hall, they reluctantly parted, each wishing to share the reason for her happiness with the others, but knowing such an action was impossible. Caroline promised to inform Darcy of Elizabeth's willingness to discuss his proposal, and they agreed to try to find time to be alone again at the earliest convenience.

CHAPTER FIFTY-NINE

My dear Lizzy, where can you have been walking to?" was a question which Elizabeth received from Jane as soon as she entered their room, and from all the others when they sat down to table. She had only to say in reply, that they had wandered about, till she was beyond her own knowledge. She coloured as she spoke; but neither that, nor anything else, awakened a suspicion of the truth in anyone other than Jane, who was so overcome by her own happiness that she did not dwell long on her younger sister's distraction. Darcy, meanwhile, had greeted both ladies upon their return with an extraordinary politeness that Elizabeth soon decided must arise from a form of anxiety. Could he be worried she might refuse his proposal? And if so, was the concern for his vanity, or for the sake of his friend?

The evening passed quietly, unmarked by anything extraordinary. The acknowledged lovers talked and laughed, while the unacknowledged worked to avoid giving themselves away, a constraint to which both had grown accustomed with prior attachments. Elizabeth, in addition to recognizing the customary imperative for secrecy, could not help but acknowledge that there were other evils before them. She anticipated what would be felt in the family if she were to accept Darcy's proposal; she was aware that no one liked him but Jane; and even worried that with the others it was a dislike which not all his fortune and consequence might do away.

At night she opened her heart to Jane. Though suspicion was very far from Miss Bennet's general habits, she was absolutely incredulous here.

"You are joking, Lizzy. This cannot be! In love with Caroline Bingley! No, no, you shall not deceive me. I know it to be impossible."

"This is a wretched beginning indeed! My sole dependence was on you; no one else can know how it really is. Yet, indeed, I am in earnest. I speak nothing but the truth. She still loves me, and has proposed a manner in which we may always be together."

Jane looked at her doubtingly. "Oh, Lizzy! It cannot be. I know how much you dislike Miss Bingley."

"You know nothing of the matter. *That* is all to be forgot. Perhaps I did not always love her so well as I do now; but in such cases as these, a good memory is unpardonable. And in fact, she is no longer Miss Bingley."

"Do you mean—like Charlotte?"

"Not entirely." And she proceeded to explain the complicated arrangement Caroline and Darcy were proposing. Jane, whose nature it was to look for the positive in any undertaking, at first could only stare at her sister in shock. But as Elizabeth went on, Jane's countenance slowly lost its astonished appearance, and she even began to nod.

"It might work," she said at last. "That is, if you are all of a mind to do so, this might be your only chance at achieving happiness. But are you certain, truly certain, that your feelings for Caroline are so great that you would be willing to marry a man you do not even like?"

"I believe they might be; but fortunately, that is not the case. I have grown to like Mr. Darcy far more than I ever had before, for reasons some of which you will soon comprehend." Here at last was the inducement to confess to Jane the gentleman's—and lady's—involvement in Lydia's marriage to Wickham.

Miss Bennet looked all amazement. "Good Heaven! Can it be really so?"

Elizabeth very seriously assured her it was.

"Now I must believe you," said Jane. "My dear, dear Lizzy, I would—I do congratulate you—but are you certain? Forgive the question—are you quite certain that you can be happy with her?"

"There can be no doubt of that. It is settled between us already, that we are to be the happiest couple in the world. But are you pleased, Jane? Shall you like to have such a sister and brother?"

"Very, very much. She is already destined to be my sister, and the addition of Mr. Darcy to the family could only give Charles more delight. Do you really like him quite well enough? Oh, Lizzy! Do anything rather than marry without friendship. Are you quite sure that you feel what you ought to do?"

"Yes. You will only think I feel more than I ought to do, when I tell you all."

"What do you mean?"

"Why, I must confess that I like Darcy better than I do Bingley. I am afraid you will be angry."

"My dearest sister, now be serious. I want to talk very seriously. Let me know everything that I am to know, without delay. Will you tell me how long you have loved Caroline, and ceased to dislike Darcy?"

"Both have been coming on so gradually, that I hardly know when either began. But I believe I must date my regard for the gentleman from my first seeing his beautiful grounds at Pemberley."

Another entreaty that she would be serious, however, produced the desired effect; and she soon satisfied Jane by her solemn assurances of genuine regard for both Caroline, her beloved, and Darcy, her possible betrothed. When convinced on that article, Miss Bennet had nothing further to wish.

"Now I am quite happy," said she, "for you will be as happy as myself. I always had a value for Caroline. Were it for nothing but her love of you, I must always have esteemed her; and now, as Bingley's sister and your beloved, there can be only Charles and yourself more dear to me. But Lizzy, you have been very sly, very reserved with me. How little did you tell me of what passed at Pemberley and Lambton! I owe all that I know of it to another, not to you."

Elizabeth told her the motives of her secrecy. She had been unwilling to mention Bingley; and the unsettled state of her own feelings had made her equally avoid the name of his sister. But now she would no longer conceal anything from Jane. All was acknowledged, and half the night spent in conversation.

***

"Good gracious!" cried Mrs. Bennet, as she stood at a window the next morning, "if that disagreeable Mr. Darcy is not coming here again with our dear Bingley! What can he mean by being so tiresome as to be always coming here? I had no notion but he would go a-shooting, or something or other, and not disturb us with his company. What shall we do with him? Lizzy, you must walk out with him, that he may not be in Bingley's way."

Elizabeth could hardly help laughing at so convenient a proposal; yet was vexed that her mother should be always giving him such an epithet.

As soon as they entered, Bingley looked at her so expressively, and shook hands with such warmth, as left no doubt of his feelings on the proposal being proffered.

"My dear Miss Eliza," said he, "please accept tidings from my sister. She awakened with a head-ache this morning, but asks that if you are not too busy later, might you not be able to find time to visit her at Netherfield?"

"Certainly," Elizabeth said, outwardly calm but inwardly excited at the thought of being alone with Caroline for the space of an entire afternoon. What luxury—the same as awaited them at Pemberley nearly every day ahead, should she marry Darcy.

Bingley inclined his head with a smile, and soon afterwards added, "Mrs. Bennet, have you no more lanes hereabouts in which Lizzy may lose her way again today?"

"I advise Mr. Darcy, and Lizzy, and Kitty," said Mrs. Bennet, "to walk to Oakham Mount this morning. It is a nice long walk, and Mr. Darcy has never seen the view."

"It may do very well for the others," replied Bingley; "but I am sure it will be too much for Kitty. Won't it, Kitty?" Kitty owned that she had rather stay at home. Darcy professed a great curiosity to see the view from the Mount, and Elizabeth silently consented.

As she went upstairs to get ready, Mrs. Bennet followed her, saying: "I am quite sorry, Lizzy, that you should be forced to have that disagreeable man all to yourself. But I hope you will not mind it. It is all for Jane's sake, you know; and there is no occasion for talking to him, except just now and then. So, do not put yourself to inconvenience."

They had not gone far down the lane when Darcy said: "And so, Miss Bennett? Caroline tells me that you and she had quite a tête-à-tête yesterday."

"Indeed. She tells me that she is married to your friend, Monsieur de Laurent."

He inclined his head. "A perfect match, if I may say so. As for the other matter, have you given it consideration, or would you prefer more time to weigh your options?"

"Come now, Mr. Darcy," said Elizabeth. "Surely you can ask for a woman's hand in a more agreeable manner than that. You must know that all women dream of being proposed to in gallant fashion."

"Even those with little interest in marriage?"

"Perhaps some among us."

"In that case," said Darcy, bowing deeply, "Miss Elizabeth Bennet, will you do me the honour of accepting my proposal of marriage?"

"I will," she said after only a slight pause; "on the condition that we openly acknowledge our union to be based on friendship and shared interest, entirely devoid of romantic love."

"Of course," he agreed, nodding at her with real warmth. "I must say, I am happy that you trust my intentions enough to agree to this alliance of our interests. I can assure you that you will be very well cared for and supported, and all of your material needs attended to, as my wife."

"I do not have any doubts on that account."

"I imagine, however, that was not always the case?"

"No more than it could have been on your side."

"What luck that we have both allowed our mutual esteem to grow, then."

"What luck, indeed," said Elizabeth, looking up at him. His wife, she thought; my husband. Not words she had ever thought to utter in such proximity to Darcy's name, let alone his person.

He offered his arm to her, and they walked on, both of their minds full of what her assent might materially mean. In any other situation, Elizabeth would have accepted her companion's arm merely from politeness; but this morning she leaned rather heavily on her future husband as they discussed the details of their engagement. A week before she had had no idea of marriage to Mr. Darcy, but now it seemed to be happening quickly. She wondered if all brides-to-be felt the same curious sense of dislocation. Her future life had long been a mystery, open to interpretation and marked by a certain freedom of choice. But this was a decision that could not be undone without much pain and mortification; a decision that would decide the course of her entire life. And yet, she imagined herself at Pemberley with Caroline and Darcy and Rémy and Georgiana, with Jane and Bingley and Mr. and Mrs. Gardiner as their frequent guests, and the tumultuous nature of her thoughts immediately quieted. This was the life she had only dreamed of having, and the man beside her was making it all possible. She had not lied to Jane, after all. Despite her early impressions, she really did like Darcy better than Bingley. Which was a good thing, given she had just agreed to marry him.

During their walk, it was resolved that Mr. Bennet's consent should be asked after the mid-day meal. Elizabeth reserved to herself the application for her mother's that evening. She could not determine how her mother would take it; sometimes doubting whether all his wealth and grandeur would be enough to overcome her abhorrence of the man. But whether she were violently set against the match, or violently delighted with it, it was certain that her manner would be equally ill-adapted to do credit to her sense; and Elizabeth could no more bear that Darcy should hear the first raptures of her mother's joy, than the first vehemence of her disapprobation.

***

In the afternoon, soon after Mr. Bennet withdrew to the library, she saw Mr. Darcy rise also and follow him, and her agitation on seeing it rose commensurately. She did not fear her father's opposition, but he was going to be made unhappy; and that it should be through her means—that she, his favourite child, should distress him by her choice—was an unhappy reflection, and she sat in silent worry till Mr. Darcy appeared again, when, looking at him, she was a little relieved by his smile. In a few minutes he approached the table where she was sitting with Kitty; and, while pretending to admire her work said in a whisper, "Go to your father; he wants you in the library." She was gone directly.

Her father was walking about the room, looking grave and anxious. "Lizzy," said he, "what are you doing? Are you out of your senses, to be accepting this man? Have not you always hated him?"

How earnestly did she then wish that her former opinions had been more reasonable, her expressions more moderate! It would have spared her from explanations and professions which it was exceedingly awkward to give; but they were now necessary, and she assured him, with some confusion, of her affection for Mr. Darcy.

"Or, in other words, you are determined to have him. He is rich, to be sure, and you may have more fine clothes and fine carriages than Jane. But will they make you happy?"

"Have you any other objection," said Elizabeth, "than your belief of my indifference?"

"None at all. We all know him to be a proud, unpleasant sort of man; but this would be nothing if you really liked him."

"I do like him," she replied, "and he is in a position to offer me a type of happiness I doubted I should ever attain. Indeed he has no improper pride. He is perfectly amiable. You do not know what he really is."

"Lizzy," said her father, "I have given him my consent. He is the kind of man, indeed, to whom I should never dare refuse anything which he condescended to ask. I now give it to you, if you are resolved on having this match. But let me advise you to think better of it. I know your disposition, Lizzy. I know that you could be neither happy nor respectable, unless you truly esteemed your husband. Your lively talents would place you in the greatest danger in an unequal marriage. My child, let me not have the grief of seeing *you* unable to respect your partner in life. You know not what you are about."

"But I do know, Father," said she; "for we are absolutely equal in our affection toward one another, possibly even more so than Jane and Bingley. We have a perfect accord, and I do indeed esteem him. It pains me to think that you would worry about my contentment, so let me say this: My marriage to Mr. Darcy will afford me the means of obtaining genuine happiness."

Her earnestness was evident to her father, and as he considered her language—she had not once claimed to love him, only to like and esteem him; the marriage would offer her the opportunity to be happy, not in fact make her happy in and of itself—another idea occurred to him: Elizabeth was marrying Darcy in order to realize the very arrangement he, her father, had hoped she would find. Who, then, was the lucky young lady? He flashed on the fashionable Miss Bingley, with whom Lizzy had walked away the previous day. Could it be true? Had Caroline Bingley fallen in love with his daughter? But then, why should she not? Lizzy may not be nearly as polished as Miss Bingley, but Mr. Bennet liked to think she offered considerably more wit and heart at once than any of the other young women he knew.

Which left only the question of Darcy's role in all of this. Of course, now that he thought about it, Mr. Bennet believed he might have noticed something in the line of the young man's breeches; perhaps a certain impudence in his gaze. If such were the case, then Elizabeth was likely to be far happier in her union to Fitzwilliam Darcy than Mr. Bennet had been in his own marriage.

"Are you certain, Lizzy? I want only for you to be sure before you make such a weighty decision."

Elizabeth was earnest and solemn in her reply; and at length, by repeated assurances that Darcy was really the object of her choice, by explaining the gradual change which her estimation of him had undergone, and enumerating with energy all his good qualities, she did conquer her father's incredulity, and reconcile him to the match. To complete the favourable impression, she then told him what Darcy had done for Lydia, giving him the credit for Caroline's contributions, as she could hardly reveal the lady's support, much as she might wish to. Her father heard her with astonishment.

"This is a day of wonders, indeed! And so, Darcy did everything; made up the match, gave the money, paid the fellow's debts, and got him his commission! So much the better. It will save me a world of trouble and economy. Had it been your uncle's doing, I must and *would* have paid him; but these young men carry everything their own way. I shall offer to pay him tomorrow; he will refuse; and there will be an end of the matter."

He then recollected Mr. Collins's letter; and after laughing at his own fallacy for some time, allowed her at last to go—saying, as she quitted the room, "If any young men come for Mary or Kitty, do send them in, for I am quite at leisure."

Elizabeth's mind was now relieved of a heavy weight, and she was able to join the others with tolerable composure. Everything was too recent for gaiety, but there was no longer anything material to be dreaded, and the comfort of ease and familiarity would come in time.

"Mr. Darcy," said she, "would you be kind enough to escort me to Netherfield? I am of a mind to look in on Miss Bingley." She nearly tripped over the name, knowing it as she did to be false.

"Of course," said Darcy, who had risen when she entered the room. "I would be happy to attend you in the brief journey. Unless you have any objection, Mrs. Bennet?"

The lady waved her hand permissively, only too happy, Elizabeth judged, to be rid of Darcy's company.

In the carriage, they each discussed what had transpired. Just before they reached Netherfield, Darcy asked: "Are you quite sure this arrangement is amenable to you, Miss Bennet?"

"I am. And as such, I believe it is time you called me by my Christian name."

"Eliza," he said, seeming to test the name.

"Darcy," she returned. "I am sorry, but I do not think I can call you Fitzwilliam."

"I will admit to being mortified if you should," he replied. And they both smiled, their diffidence toward one another beginning to give way to a tentative friendliness.

Inside, the housekeeper led her to Caroline's dressing-room, where the two ladies spent several happy hours together talking and making love. The happiness they enjoyed was new, but had taken so long to establish itself that it did not feel in the least bit fragile. Elizabeth left just before dinnertime, but not before persuading Caroline and Darcy both to return to Longbourn with her, where a perfectly tranquil evening passed overly quickly, in her estimation.

When her mother went up to her dressing-room at night, Elizabeth followed her, and made the important communication. Its effect was most extraordinary; for on first hearing it, Mrs. Bennet sat quite still, unable to utter a syllable. Nor was it under many, many minutes that she could comprehend what she heard; though not in general backward to credit what was for the advantage of her family, or that came in the shape of a lover to any of them. She began at length to recover, to fidget about in her chair, get up, sit down again, wonder, and bless herself.

"Good gracious! Lord bless me! Only think, dear me! Mr. Darcy! Who would have thought it! And is it really true? Oh, my sweetest Lizzy! How rich and how great you will be! What pin-money, what jewels, what carriages you will have! Jane's is nothing to it—nothing at all. I am so pleased—so happy. Such a charming man! So handsome! So tall! Oh, my dear Lizzy! Pray apologise for my having disliked him so much before. I hope he will overlook it. Dear, dear Lizzy. A house in town! Everything that is charming! Three daughters married! Ten thousand a year! Oh, Lord! What will become of me? I shall go distracted."

This was enough to prove that her approbation need not be doubted: and Elizabeth, rejoicing that such an effusion was heard only by herself, soon went away. But before she had been three minutes in her own room, her mother followed her.

"My dearest child," she cried, "I can think of nothing else! Ten thousand a year, and very likely more! 'Tis as good as a Lord! And a special licence. You must and shall be married by a special licence. But my dearest love, tell me what dish Mr. Darcy is particularly fond of, that I may have it tomorrow."

This was a sad omen of what her mother's behaviour to the gentleman himself might be; and Elizabeth found that, though in the certain possession of his promise, and secure of her relations' consent, there was still something to be wished for. But the morrow passed off much better than she expected; for Mrs. Bennet luckily stood in such awe of her intended son-in-law that she ventured not to speak to him, unless it was in her power to offer him any attention, or mark her deference for his opinion. Besides, with Caroline beside her once again, Elizabeth's happiness could only have been diverted by some great calamity. Fortunately, none presented itself.

Elizabeth even had the satisfaction of seeing her father taking pains to get better acquainted with both Darcy and Caroline; and Mr. Bennet soon assured her that the gentleman was rising every hour in his esteem.

"I admire all my three sons-in-law highly," said he. "Wickham, perhaps, is my favourite; but I think I shall like *your* husband even better than Jane's."

CHAPTER SIXTY

Elizabeth's spirits soon rising to playfulness again, when next they were alone together, she wanted Caroline to account for having ever fallen in love with her. "How could you begin?" said she. "I can comprehend your going on charmingly, when you had once made a beginning; but what could set you off in the first place?"

"I cannot fix on the hour, or the spot, or the look, or the words, which laid the foundation. It is too long ago. I was in the middle before I knew that I *had* begun."

"My beauty you had early withstood, and as for my manners—my behaviour to you was at least always bordering on the uncivil, and I never spoke to you without rather wishing to give you pain than not. Now be sincere; did you admire me for my impertinence?"

"For the liveliness of your mind, I did," said Caroline.

"You may as well call it impertinence at once. It was very little less. The fact is, I roused, and interested you, because I was so unlike the decorous, officious, dull ladies from town to whom you were accustomed. There—I have saved you the trouble of accounting for it; and really, all things considered, I begin to think it perfectly reasonable. To be sure, you knew no actual good of me—but nobody thinks of *that* when they fall in love."

"Was there no good in your affectionate behaviour to Jane while she was ill at Netherfield?"

"Dearest Jane! Who could have done less for her? But make a virtue of it, by all means. My good qualities are under your protection, and you are to exaggerate them as much as possible; and, in return, it belongs to me to find occasions for teasing and quarrelling with you as often as may be; and I shall begin directly by asking you what made you so unwilling to come to the point at last. What made you so shy of me, when you first called, and afterwards dined here? Why, especially, when you called, did you look as if you did not care about me?"

"Because you were grave and silent, and gave me no encouragement, of course," said Caroline.

"But I was embarrassed."

"As was I!"

"You might have talked to me more when you came to dinner."

"One who had felt less, might."

"How unlucky that you should have a reasonable answer to give, and that I should be so reasonable as to admit it. But I wonder how long you would have gone on, if you had been left to yourself. My resolution of thanking you for your kindness to Lydia had certainly great effect. But what becomes of the moral, if our comfort springs from a breach of promise?"

"The moral will be perfectly fair," said Caroline; "I am not indebted for my present happiness to your desire of expressing your gratitude."

"But tell me, what did you come down to Netherfield for?" asked Elizabeth. "Was it merely to ride to Longbourn and be embarrassed? Or had you intended any more serious consequence?"

"My real purpose was to see *you*," said she, "and to judge, if I could, whether I might ever hope to make you love me. My avowed one, or what I avowed to myself, was to see whether your sister were still partial to Charles, and if she were, to make the confession to my brother which I have since made."

"Shall you ever have courage to announce to Louisa what has happened to her little sister?"

"I am more likely to want time than courage, Lizzy. But it ought to be done, and if you will give me a sheet of paper, it shall be done directly."

"And if I had not a letter to write myself, I might sit by you and admire the evenness of your writing. But I have an aunt, who must not be longer neglected."

From an unwillingness to confess how much her intimacy with Mr. Darcy had been over-rated, Elizabeth had never yet answered Mrs. Gardiner's long letter; but now, having that to communicate which she knew would be not be unwelcome, she wrote as follows:

"I would have thanked you before, my dear aunt, as I ought to have done, for your long, kind, satisfactory, detail of particulars; but to say the truth, I was too cross to write. You supposed more than really existed. Now, things are different, and I thank you, again and again, for not going to the Lakes, but to P. instead. Your idea of the ponies is delightful. We will go round the Park every day with my friend Miss Bingley. I am the happiest creature in the world. Perhaps other people have said so before, but not one with such justice. I am happier even than Jane; she only smiles, I laugh. Mr. Darcy sends his kind greetings, as does Miss Bingley. You are all to come to Pemberley at Christmas. Yours, etc."

Mr. Darcy also had a letter to write to his aunt, Lady Catherine, though in a quite different style; and still different from either was what Mr. Bennet sent to Mr. Collins, in reply to his last.

"DEAR SIR,

"I must trouble you once more for congratulations. Elizabeth will soon be the wife of Mr. Darcy. Console Lady Catherine as well as you can. But, if I were you, I would stand by the nephew. He has more to give.

"Yours sincerely, etc."

The joy which Miss Darcy expressed on receiving the news of her brother's engagement, made Elizabeth feel most guilty until Caroline explained that Georgiana was aware of the arrangement between Darcy and Rémy, and had long feared her brother's eventual choice of a bride whom she would find intolerable. Two sides of paper were barely enough to contain her earnest assurances of affection for her new sister.

Before any answer could arrive from Mr. Collins, or any congratulations to Elizabeth from his wife, the Longbourn family heard that the Collinses were come themselves to Lucas Lodge. The reason of this sudden removal was soon evident. Lady Catherine had been rendered so exceedingly angry by the contents of her nephew's letter, that Charlotte, rejoicing in the match, was anxious to get away till the storm was blown over. At such a moment, the arrival of her friend was a sincere pleasure to Elizabeth, though in the course of their meetings she must sometimes think the pleasure dearly bought, when she saw both Caroline and Darcy exposed to all the parading and obsequious civility of Charlotte's husband. They bore it, however, with admirable calmness.

Darcy even listened politely to Sir William Lucas, when he complimented him on carrying away the brightest jewel of the country, and expressed his hopes of their all meeting frequently at St. James's, with very decent composure. If he did shrug his shoulders at Caroline, it was not till Sir William was out of sight.

Mrs. Phillips's vulgarity was another, and perhaps a greater, tax on Darcy's forbearance; and though Mrs. Phillips, as well as her sister, stood in too much awe of him to speak with the familiarity which Bingley's good humour encouraged, yet, whenever she did speak, she must be vulgar. Caroline confided teasingly to Elizabeth that there were some advantages to being her lover in secret, after all. Elizabeth shushed her and did all she could to shield Darcy from the frequent notice of either relation, and was ever anxious to surround him with those of her family with whom he might converse without mortification; and though the uncomfortable feelings arising from all of this maneuvering took some of the pleasure from her courtship with Caroline, it added to the hope of the future; and she looked forward with delight to the time when they should be removed from society so little pleasing, to the comfort and elegance of their own family party at Pemberley.

CHAPTER SIXTY-ONE

Happy for all her maternal feelings was the day on which Mrs. Bennet got rid of her two most deserving daughters. With what delighted pride she afterwards visited Mrs. Bingley, and talked of Mrs. Darcy, may be guessed. I wish I could say, for the sake of her family, that the accomplishment of her earnest desire in the establishment of so many of her children produced so happy an effect as to make her a sensible, amiable, well-informed woman for the rest of her life; though perhaps it was lucky for her husband, who might not have relished domestic felicity in so unusual a form, that she still was occasionally nervous and invariably silly.

Mr. Bennet missed Elizabeth exceedingly; his affection for her drew him oftener from home than anything else could do. He delighted in going to Pemberley, especially when he was least expected, and soon fancied he understood the arrangement between the two couples. His happiness for his second eldest daughter was surpassed only by his envy at her ability to successfully manage her domestic life in a fashion that had eluded him. But a father always wishes a better life for his children than for himself, and Mr. Bennet was no different on that score, particularly where Elizabeth was concerned.

Mr. Bingley and Jane remained at Netherfield only a twelvemonth. So near a vicinity to her mother and Meryton relations was not desirable even to his easy temper, or her affectionate heart. The original wish of his sisters was then gratified; he bought an estate in a neighbouring county to Derbyshire, and Jane and Elizabeth, in addition to every other source of happiness, were within thirty miles of each other.

Kitty, to her very material advantage, spent the chief of her time with her eldest sister. In society so superior to what she had generally known, her improvement was great. She was not of so ungovernable a temper as

Lydia; and, removed from the influence of Lydia's example, she became, by proper attention and management, less irritable, less ignorant, and less insipid. From the further disadvantage of Lydia's society she was of course carefully kept, and though Mrs. Wickham frequently invited her to come and stay with her, with the promise of balls and young men, her father would never consent to her going.

Mary was the only daughter who remained at home; and she was necessarily drawn from the pursuit of accomplishments by Mrs. Bennet's being quite unable to sit alone. Mary was obliged to mix more with the world, but she could still moralize over every morning visit; and as she was no longer mortified by comparisons between her sisters' beauty and her own, it was suspected by her father that she submitted to the change without much reluctance.

As for Wickham and Lydia, their characters suffered no revolution from the marriage of her sisters. He bore with philosophy the conviction that Elizabeth must now become acquainted with whatever of his ingratitude and falsehood had before been unknown to her; and in spite of everything, was not wholly without hope that Darcy might yet be prevailed on to make his fortune. The congratulatory letter which Elizabeth received from Lydia on her marriage, explained to her that, by his wife at least, if not by himself, such a hope was cherished. The letter was to this effect:

"MY DEAR LIZZY,

"I wish you joy. If you love Mr. Darcy half as well as I do my dear Wickham, you must be very happy. It is a great comfort to have you so rich, and when you have nothing else to do, I hope you will think of us. I am sure Wickham would like a place at court very much, and I do not think we shall have quite money enough to live upon without some help. Any place would do, of about three or four hundred a year; but however, do not speak to Mr. Darcy about it, if you had rather not.

"Yours, etc."

As it happened that Elizabeth had much rather not, she endeavoured in her answer to put an end to every entreaty and expectation of the kind. Such relief, however, as it was in her power to afford, by the practice of what might be called economy in her own private expenses, she frequently sent them. It had always been evident to her that such an income as theirs, under the direction of two persons so extravagant in their wants, and heedless of the future, must be very insufficient to their support; and whenever they changed their quarters, either Jane or herself were sure of being applied to for some little assistance towards discharging their bills. Their manner of living, even when the restoration of peace dismissed them to a home, was unsettled in the extreme. They were always moving from place to place in quest of a cheap situation, and always spending more than they ought. His affection for her soon sunk into indifference; hers lasted a little longer; and in spite of her youth and her manners, she retained all the claims to reputation which her marriage had given her.

Though Darcy could never receive Wickham at Pemberley, yet, for Elizabeth's sake, he assisted him further in his profession. Lydia was occasionally a visitor there, when Darcy and Rémy were gone to enjoy themselves in London or Bath, though Lydia never stayed long due to Elizabeth's reluctance to hide her relationship with Caroline; and with the Bingleys, Lydia and Wickham both frequently staid so long, that even Bingley's good humour was overcome, and he proceeded so far as to talk of giving them a hint to be gone.

Mrs. Hurst was deeply mortified by Caroline's decision to wed the penniless Rémy, and rightly suspicious of Darcy's marriage to Elizabeth; but as she thought it advisable to regain the right of visiting at Pemberley, she dropt all her attempts at domination of her younger sister and apologised profusely for any past offence; professed more fondness than ever toward Darcy; and paid off every arrear of civility to Elizabeth.

Pemberley was now Georgiana's home; and the affection of his sister for his wife and friends was exactly what Darcy had hoped to see. Georgiana had the highest opinion in the world of both Elizabeth and Caroline; though at first she often listened with an astonishment bordering on alarm at their lively, sportive manner of talking to her brother. He, who had always inspired in herself a respect which almost overcame her affection, she now saw the object of open pleasantry from the other inhabitants of the estate. Rémy treated her with kindness and warmth, and, a tutor in his former life, helped her with her studies. Overall it might be said that Georgiana's mind received forms of knowledge which had never before fallen in her way.

Lady Catherine was extremely indignant on the marriage of her nephew; and as she gave way to all the genuine frankness of her character in her reply to the letter which announced its arrangement, she sent him language so very abusive, especially of Elizabeth, that for some time all intercourse was at an end. But at length, by Elizabeth's persuasion and over Caroline's objections, who had no interest in forgiving the "imperious old dragon," Darcy was prevailed upon to overlook the offence and seek a reconciliation; and, after a little further resistance on the part of his aunt, her resentment gave way, either to her affection for him, or her curiosity to see how his wife conducted herself; and she condescended to wait on them at Pemberley, in spite of that pollution which its woods had received, not merely from the presence of such a mistress, but the prominent presence of Caroline and Rémy and the visits of Elizabeth's relations.

With the Gardiners, the inhabitants of Pemberley were always on the most intimate terms. Darcy and Rémy genuinely enjoyed their company; and Caroline and Elizabeth were both ever sensible of the warmest gratitude towards the persons who, by bringing her into Derbyshire, had been the means of reuniting them.

ABOUT THE AUTHOR

Kate Christie was born and raised in Kalamazoo, Michigan. She first became interested in gay and lesbian history while a student at Smith College in the early 1990s. After graduating with a degree in Women's Studies, she went on eventually to earn a Master's in English at Western Washington University. A long-time Jane Austen fan, she was fascinated and only a little bit nauseated by the release a few years ago of a variation on *P&P* featuring the living dead and ninja warriors. Soon after reading an article on the literary mashup phenomenon surrounding Austen and other classic authors and historic figures, Christie wondered, "If zombies and vampires, why not gays and lesbians?" Not that monsters and queers have anything in common, of course, other than a long history of being denigrated and feared by the general public—a reputation, Christie would argue, more deserved by the former group than the latter.

Currently, Christie lives near Seattle with her wife and daughter and their two dogs. While *Gay Pride & Prejudice* is her first work of literary mashup, she has had three previous novels published by Bella Books: *Solstice*, *Leaving L.A.*, and *Beautiful Game*. For book trailers, first chapters and more, visit www.katejchristie.com.

54267222R00217

Made in the USA
Columbia, SC
28 March 2019